GIRLS WHO PLAY DEAD

Books by Joelle Wellington

THEIR VICIOUS GAMES
THE BLONDE DIES FIRST
GIRLS WHO PLAY DEAD

GIRLS WHO PLAY DEAD

JOELLE WELLINGTON

Harper Fire

First published in the United Kingdom by Harper Fire,
an imprint of HarperCollins *Children's Books*, in 2025
HarperCollins *Children's Books* is a division of HarperCollins*Publishers* Ltd
1 London Bridge Street
London SE1 9GF

www.harpercollins.co.uk

HarperCollins*Publishers*
Macken House, 39/40 Mayor Street Upper
Dublin 1, D01 C9W8, Ireland

1

Text copyright © Joelle Wellington 2025
Cover images copyright © Shutterstock
Cover design copyright © HarperCollins*Publishers* Ltd 2025
All rights reserved

ISBN 978-0-00-879168-1

Joelle Wellington asserts the moral right to be identified as the author of the work.

A CIP catalogue record for this title is available from the British Library.

Printed and bound in the UK using 100% renewable electricity
at CPI Group (UK) Ltd

Conditions of Sale
This book is sold subject to the condition that it shall not, by way of trade or otherwise, be lent, re-sold, hired out or otherwise circulated without the publisher's prior consent in any form, binding or cover other than that in which it is published and without a similar condition including this condition being imposed on the subsequent purchaser. No part of this publication may be reproduced, stored in a retrieval system or transmitted in any form or by any means, electronic, mechanical, photocopying, recording or otherwise, without the prior permission of HarperCollinsPublishers Ltd.

Without limiting the exclusive rights of any author, contributor or the publisher of this publication, any unauthorised use of this publication to train generative artificial intelligence (AI) technologies is expressly prohibited. HarperCollins also exercise their rights under Article 4(3) of the Digital Single Market Directive 2019/790 and expressly reserve this publication from the text and data mining exception.

This book contains FSC™ certified paper and other controlled sources
to ensure responsible forest management.
For more information visit: www.harpercollins.co.uk/green

To my grandpa, whom I miss dearly

CHAPTER ONE

It's a cruel thing, what the Vaughns are asking, but Kyla's father told her that they were allowed a little bit of cruelty, after what someone took from them.

"We don't trust anyone else. We barely trusted the coroner," Mrs. Vaughn said when they came into the funeral home, her voice steadier than her hands. Kyla had watched as the woman fiddled with her ring, loose on her slim finger. "They kept her body for two extra days than they said they would. *Two*. And they wouldn't tell us why. No one would tell us why."

"We want to have the funeral a few days before school starts, so that . . . that Jason can have a chance to mourn. Tell us you can do it by then?" Mr. Vaughn asked gruffly. He kept his eyes trained on the ceiling, in a way that Kyla had seen only twice before. He was trying not to cry.

Kyla wanted to say that was impossible. That they needed more time to put together a half-decent ceremony, let alone the kind of proceedings that someone like Erin *deserved*.

But this was the Vaughns, so it would be done.

Now Kyla stands above her best friend's body. Erin's nails are still chipped from when she and Kyla tried yet another new tumbling pass last Tuesday, but her delicate hands have turned blue. She looks nothing like herself. She looks everything like herself. And Kyla can't believe the Vaughns could bring her here. Could be so, so cruel.

"They're going through something," Dad says.

I've *been going through something,* Kyla thinks. *For six days, three hours, fifty-one minutes.*

She bends closer, close enough that she can see her reflection in Erin's empty, glassy eyes. Kyla knows the cause of death. She's seen the death certificate herself, another rush order made possible by the breadth of the Vaughns' reach.

Manner of death is listed simply—homicide. Kyla mouths the word, rolling it around on her tongue, but can't quite manage to force it out. Cause of death seems to have been far more complicated to discern, but the body never tells a lie, especially not dead ones. Blooming bruises across Erin's back and legs, where she'd collided with the cliff on her way down. Her ankle at a strange angle, like a broken doll. The mark on her head that had ended her pain. The press of ten fingertips forever imprinted on her skin where someone had gripped her tight, shook her, and *shoved*.

"Do they have any idea of who might've—" Kyla starts then stops, struck by the thin line of purple along Erin's temple that disappears into her hair. Kyla used to rap her fingers against Erin's head, a childhood taunt about Erin being a little mindless. Now Erin's had a knock on the head hard enough to make her *truly* mindless. Voiceless. Lifeless.

She lies on the embalming table, so very still, and it's wrong. This is a girl who has always been in motion. Kyla is the still one.

That's no longer true.

Kyla and her father breathe heavily, not sure where to start. Exactly sure where to start.

"Kyla, honey, you don't have to be here," Dad says.

Kyla blinks slowly. Yes, she does. She knows Erin best. She has to be the one to put her back together.

"I'll get my gear." She goes to the locker and pulls her scrubs over her loungewear, already overheating, her oversized T-shirt clinging to slick skin. She doesn't have a wig on, but her hair is braided down, so it's easy to pull the scrub cap over her head.

Her father snaps the respirator around the back of her head and Kyla feels like an alien. Good. An alien belongs to space, to the infinite nothing. An alien does not know Erin Vaughn. An alien does not need to *mourn* Erin Vaughn.

So it's an alien that helps her father through the process of making Erin Vaughn forever sixteen. An alien that freezes Erin's face into a gentle expression, softening her edges into something so different from her usual ferociousness. It's an alien that brushes Erin's hair back from her face, an alien that doesn't flinch when her father makes the small incisions with loving care and pumps the blood from Erin's body, replacing it with formaldehyde.

Kyla Graves peeks through her alien skin and wishes she could steal away Erin's heart and bury it in the wet ground, at the base of their heart tree in the back. But then her father tucks Erin's heart (Kyla's heart) away again where she can't touch it, can't see it, and Kyla is the alien again. This is something that Kyla knows how to do even if she's not quite old enough yet that she should. *It shouldn't make a difference that it's Erin,* she tells herself.

Then Kyla loses time.

She's been doing that a lot in the past six days.

When she comes back, her father is talking and Kyla nods her way through a conversation while she waits for the formaldehyde to fight back rigor mortis.

They must have washed Erin again for the chemical stains. The places that the morgue missed. Because the purple stain at her hairline is gone now and she looks at peace. Alien Kyla can tell herself that Erin is asleep, even though the real Kyla knows Erin always slept wild, twitching and restless. *Maybe it's just a really good sleep, the deep kind after a night out, or a hard dance practice.*

There is one thing left to do and she knows exactly how.

"Let me do her makeup," Kyla says.

"Yeah?" Dad asks quietly.

"Yes. She should look like herself," Kyla decides.

The day they were finally allowed to wear makeup every day came not long after they'd turned thirteen. Mrs. Vaughn promised them she'd take them to work with her to get the basics. It had been a big to-do, Kyla's dad nervous about letting her take off school for something as frivolous as makeup. Mrs. Vaughn had taken his hand and assuredly said, "There is *nothing* more important than a girl's first foundation," and with no other mother to dispute this, Dad had taken her at her word.

Entering Cook Cosmetics, Kyla and Erin had been dressed in their best outfits, ones that they'd painstakingly chosen over the course of a week. Both of them were called "so sophisticated" by the receptionist in the whitewashed lobby, accented by Cook's sea green, and that's how they'd known they were correct in their selections.

When finally lunchtime came around, Mrs. Vaughn had ferried them with smug delight through long hallways lined with large, framed Cook advertisements, each painted and marked with a placard stating the year. They passed years of Cook history, years of one woman climbing to the top, then pulling the women and girls of Prophets Lake along with her, until finally, they came to an unassuming door.

"What is this?" Erin said, voice dripping with disdain. She was already tired, just a few hours in, bored with the monotony of her mother's day-to-day, in sharp contrast to what she'd been expecting—shopping and brand planning. Kyla had been fascinated, even by the number of emails Mrs. Vaughn had been greeted with from the very first moment that she'd opened her swollen inbox. Mrs. Vaughn was a big deal.

"Beauty," Mrs. Vaughn said as she shoved the door open, revealing the most magical place in the entire world—the Cook Cosmetics' product closet.

Each shelf was lined with sea-green matte foundation bottles, slim eye-shadow palettes, pans of bronzer and highlight, tubes of lipstick, and fluffy brushes. Kyla's stomach dropped between her legs, her want so strong, but she shoved her hands behind her back, even as Erin lunged forward, hungry.

"Only three things, girls," Mrs. Vaughn said, nodding at the intern in all black, tucked into the corner. The intern dutifully went to assist Erin.

Kyla had to be brought forward by Mrs. Vaughn.

"You won't ever have to look far for your shade with Cook, Kyla," Mrs. Vaughn reassured her, handing her the soft matte bottle, the sea-green bulb at the top waiting to be twisted open to reveal the thick formula that would melt perfectly into Kyla's skin.

That day, Kyla came away with a lip gloss, a foundation, and a mascara. Mrs. Vaughn spent the evening teaching them how to apply it perfectly.

Not two days later, Kyla returned, eager for another lesson, but instead she watched as Mrs. Vaughn discovered Erin's gluttony, the horde of product that she'd shoved into her pockets and her bag, some of the eye-shadow palettes now crushed to fine powder at the bottom. It was a shouting match, not unusual. "Why can't you ever *listen*, Erin? Kyla listens! You never understand the consequences of your actions," Mrs. Vaughn shouted. The intern that assisted Erin had been dismissed for crimes she hadn't committed.

Kyla doesn't know if Mrs. Vaughn ever told anyone what had really happened, if that intern was ever exonerated.

It doesn't matter now, anyway. Erin's finally faced the consequences of her own actions. She's paid a much higher price.

The thought forces her back to the present. Kyla reaches for Erin's curated assortment of Cook Cosmetics products, delivered by the Vaughns and stained around the edges from use. She is careful as she paints Erin almost back to life. A flawless base with a satiny finish. Feathery eyebrows, no shadow underneath. Erin had no patience for that. Not for precision, either. She liked her liner messy. Mrs. Vaughn would prefer something neater, but Kyla smears kohl around Erin's eyes anyway. Clumps on the mascara, too. She looks like she's going to a party. She looks like Eleanor Rigby.

She looks like the night she died.

"Is that right?" Dad asks, hesitant.

Kyla finishes her off with setting spray. "It's perfect," she says lovingly. "She looks like herself."

"Okay. Good," Dad says. "Good. Kyla . . ."

She doesn't listen. She grips Erin's hand tight in hers.

Erin doesn't squeeze back like she always did.

Kyla can squeeze as hard as she wants, squeeze so hard that all Erin's death-stiffened fingers snap, and the girl wouldn't make a sound. Erin wouldn't scream. She wouldn't laugh. She wouldn't smile and she wouldn't rage. There's nothing but a body that looks like Erin but isn't. There never will be an Erin Vaughn again.

Kyla cradles Erin's hand, thumbing lightly over her knuckles as she comes to terms with the idea that she'll never feel the warmth of Erin's palm again. She comes to terms with the fact—because the alien *needs* facts—that it's all her fault. She commits this thought to her heart.

And then she drops her best friend's hand.

CHAPTER TWO

Mikky drives back to Prophets Lake with only an obituary, his phone, and a weekender bag on his passenger seat. He doesn't even have a full suit. Never needed one. His mother said he'd be fine with a nice black button-down and dress pants, but even those she'd had to take him to buy. Because his idea of too-tight and Prophets Lake's idea of too-tight are very different.

He keeps the windows down despite the heat, breathing in the smell of pine. He loves the city, but even after getting used to Boston's aroma of stale urine and body heat, he's missed this smell. He feels good.

Or as good as he can, knowing that Erin Vaughn is dead.

The Erin in his mind is still thirteen, just growing into herself. A feisty, blond slip of a girl with an ego you'd say was the size of the moon if she didn't have talent the size of a planet to back it up. But even with that ego and talent, she refused to let Kyla relegate herself to the role of sidekick. No, they were the dynamic duo. Equals. Inseparable. It was the only reason Mikky had felt sort of okay leaving Kyla nearly three years ago.

But now Erin's gone. And Kyla is . . . alone.

Mikky shakes the desolate thought away. He's almost there. He's going to see her and he's going to hold her hand and he won't let her feel alone in that big house that smells like formaldehyde and his father's famous chicken chili.

When he pulls off the freeway toward Prophets Lake, he is one of three cars to do so while the rest rush on, passing by the exit. Unsurprising. The namesake lake is pretty but there are prettier ones nearby, with much kinder histories.

He turns onto the main road and then slowly pulls over onto the shoulder and sits there, looking up at the city limits sign.

WELCOME TO PROPHETS LAKE (POP. 6,063.5)

It hasn't changed. That doesn't bode well for Mikky's time here. When Mikky tells people where he's from, he always thinks of this sign. It flashes across his memory in faded sepia glory, the bright blue of the painted lake burnt out by the sun. The shapeless trees that sit on the edge made of sloppy, haphazard brushstrokes. There is no apostrophe. The lake does not belong to the prophets. And no, ".5" isn't a typo either, though Mikky has never been sure what it means.

It's something his dad would know, and he's probably told Mikky enough times, but Mikky always found it hard to retain information passed along to him in long sessions huddled over corpses. Dad's a self-described town historian. His family, like so many other families here, has roots going back three generations. People don't leave Prophets Lake. Those that do tend to become ghost stories.

What kind of haunting has Mikky left behind?

He climbs out of the car, feeling the suspension rock dangerously. He should've done what his mother told him to—get the car serviced before taking the long drive—but Mikky knew *something* was wrong with it and didn't have time for them to figure it out and fix it. He walks evenly on the ground, his platforms crunching over gravel and dirt on the cracked paved road. Slowly, he settles himself on the hood of the car and memorizes the sign again, savoring this last moment of peace before he crosses into town.

He doesn't have to wait long for the peace to break. He hears the Jeep before he sees it, and when he finally does, it's a hulking monstrosity of chrome and black with custom hunter-green rims. The Wrangler makes Mikky's little used sedan look like a toy car, one of those Hot Wheels he used to line up on his headboard before he went to sleep.

Jason Vaughn jumps down from the Jeep, dressed for the funeral already.

"Mikky Graves, welcome home," Jason says, holding his arms wide open.

Mikky slides off the hood and throws his arms around Jason, clapping his back, all manly-like and whatever. They pull apart and Mikky grabs Jason's shoulder, shaking him once.

"Hey, man. I'm so sorry," he says earnestly.

Jason looks up at the sky as if he's willing back tears from his glossy eyes. Then he slips back and shutters his gaze, folding his arms over his chest, carefully evading any more emotions that might erupt from Mikky's sincere condolences.

"Thank you for coming," Jason says. "I didn't think you would."

Mikky gets it. He doesn't hold it against him. Mikky's not the most reliable when he promises to come back, and even when he does . . . he's not always the most sociable. He sighs as he looks back at the sign. "What are you doing out here?"

"I needed to take a drive," Jason says. "I can't . . . go there yet. See her like that. I don't know."

"How are your parents?" Mikky asks, because he doesn't want to ask the question really on his mind: *How did she die?*

Jason plays ball. "Dad is doing as best as he can, considering the circumstances. Mom is . . . struggling," Jason says. His mouth pinches with a strained emotion that Mikky can't read. "She keeps trying to go back to work."

"Sometimes keeping occupied helps," Mikky says. These aren't his words but they come out smoothly anyway. He knows all the slogans of grief because of his father. It's the family trade. "There's no right way to deal with this sort of thing. Your sister was so . . ."

There is no right way to describe Erin Vaughn. Especially not in the past tense.

Jason knows this. "When Mom doesn't try to go to work, she keeps calling the police station. I'm trying to get her to stop. Hamish is getting tired of telling us they have no leads yet," Jason says, pinching the bridge of his nose. The lack of news is taking a toll on him, too.

Suddenly Mikky feels bad for asking even though it's the right thing to do. He knows Jason won't fault him, though. They've been friends too long, anyway, and Jason's already been a little more than generous to him. Mikky left without saying goodbye, after the first semester of their freshman year, and Jason has never held it against him. Not even when Mikky went through a phase of pretending everyone from Prophets Lake but Kyla and his dad didn't exist. Mikky is more self-aware now. He doesn't have to do that anymore.

"This is so fucked," Mikky mumbles.

"Yeah, it is," Jason agrees as he pats himself, searching for something.

Mikky reaches into his own pocket and offers a hit from his vape. Jason looks at him, grateful, and Mikky suddenly remembers thinking Jason was the most beautiful boy in the world, with his golden-brown hair and ears a little too big and scabby knees and skin stretched too thin over bones that outpaced the rest of him. He's grown into those ears and bones now, but Mikky doesn't feel those melting-butter emotions anymore. It's the last thing either of them needs anyway.

Jason looks more grounded on his exhale. "It's barely been a week since they found her out there on the beach. Like, not even half a camp session. I don't miss her yet. I don't know how to," Jason explains. But just as quickly as the admission comes, he sneers at his own vulnerability and passes the vape back roughly. Then he pushes off the car.

Before he can leave, Mikky finally asks the other question he's been holding back: "How's Kyla?"

"You haven't called her?" Jason asks.

Mikky *has* called Kyla, thank you very much. Every single day since he got the news. Not from her. His father had called his mother first; that's how Mikky knew something was wrong. His parents *never* spoke. After his mother had quietly broken the news, Mikky called Kyla ten times in the hour. Then every day until he finally got the funeral details from Dad. She never picked up. Kyla always picks up, because calling indicates an emergency.

The last time Mikky visited for Christmas, he'd broken down on the highway, and Kyla had picked up his call on the second ring. Nothing feels more like an emergency than Erin Vaughn's death, and yet—

"She never answered. Anyway, we shouldn't be late," Mikky says.

"Is that what you're going to wear?" Jason asks.

Mikky laughs. "Do you not like it?" he asks, gesturing down at his slippery black vinyl pants, zippers like gaped mouths around the brown skin on his knees and shins, and his tattered denim jacket, so frayed, the sleeves hang like fringe.

"I don't think my mother will appreciate it, but I think you look sick, dude," Jason says, raising his hands placatingly.

"Don't worry, I've got dress pants. I'll change in the car," Mikky sighs.

Jason nods. "Good man," he says. "See you at the cemetery."

Mikky looks down at his chipped cherry-black nails, and doesn't move until he hears the Wrangler start up again, uproarious and gas guzzling and everything wrong with consumerism and masculinity. He wishes he'd thought to repaint his nails before he came. Or that he'd thought to bring a bottle of polish for a touch-up. Mikky wonders if this is still Kyla's favorite nail color too. Most of all, he wonders if she'd even tell him.

CHAPTER THREE

Mikky promised his mother that he'd quit vaping. As he lingers by his car after the funeral, he can practically hear her voice, spouting off statistics: "Forty-six point seven percent of students use e-cigarettes, and thirty-six point eight percent of high school students who vape also use other tobacco products. It's really just as bad as smoking. That's the facts. You don't want to be a statistic, do you, Mikky?"

And then he takes another hit.

"Sorry about being a statistic," he murmurs to his mom, off in Boston, probably missing him. He squints up at the community center. It's been renovated since the last time he was here. Everything all shiny and new. He wonders if this is the inaugural event—a repast. Christ.

Mikky watches his father approach from the corner of his eye, and doesn't bother to hide his vape. After all, he's not the only one that's part of a statistic. There are three people hovering near the community center doors—two girls and a hawkish boy—all sucking at slim black vapes. But unlike him, they're peering owlishly into a single phone from behind the expensive sheen of their flawless powder, recording themselves. It's grotesque.

Mikky nearly interrupts them, but his father sidles up to him, redirecting Mikky's attention.

"It was a nice service, Dad. Good job," Mikky says.

"Thanks, kiddo," his father says as he wraps an arm around Mikky's shoulders and squeezes. It's an awkward stretch; Mikky is slightly taller than his father now. He slumps to make it a little easier but accidentally smothers his father with his curls instead. Dad goes on, undeterred. "I didn't realize that you were here until I saw you walking out at the end there. Did your sister see you?"

She hadn't, but Mikky had seen her,. It was an outdoor funeral, right in the cemetery, and Kyla was at the very front, at the end of the first row, next to Jason. Too close for Mikky to join her without drawing attention.

The Vaughns hadn't been able to keep their composure. Mikky can still hear the cracked weeping from Mr. Vaughn's shredded throat and see Jason taking swipes at his eyes again and again, banishing any tears that might have shown themselves. But Kyla had been stock-still, staring straight forward. Not crying. Almost expressionless. Only when they had to walk past the casket for one last glance had she leaned in and whispered something. One last secret between two best friends—sisters, almost.

When Mikky went up, he'd looked at Erin and refused to flinch either. The body was perfect. As perfect as it could be after death. Her makeup was impeccable and he knew instantly it had been Kyla—she'd done well. A normal person would think how messed up that is, for Kyla to have worked on Erin's body. But he knows his sister. He can't imagine it being anyone else, and he bets neither could she.

"I met up with Jason before the service," Mikky says, shaking out of the memory.

"Yeah. He's been . . . holding them together. Really stepped up," his dad says gruffly.

Mikky squirms. He needs to step up too. Find his sister. But he looks again at the people taking selfies at a fucking repast, blocking the way.

Dad realizes. "Oh . . . Kyla said those are Erin's internet friends. Some kind of influencers. Like she was."

Mikky vaguely knows that Erin was an influencer. He was one of the precious few that she followed back on Instagram, and the algorithm relentlessly threw her posts at him on the few occasions that he deigned to go on the app. He only ever goes on to check on Kyla.

Kyla, whom he *needs* to see. He pulls away from his dad, tugs at his wrinkled button-down, and opens his arms wide. "How do I look?" he asks, stalling. It's a little narcissistic of him, to be worried about how he looks when he's entering a repast—like the very same influencers that he'd sneered at—but his intent is far more pure than theirs. He doesn't want to draw more attention than he already knows he will.

"You look sharp, Mik," Dad says.

"Thanks," Mikky mutters, and then he turns to go inside. After haphazardly holding the door for his dad, he follows the ambient classical music.

The second he walks into the event space, sure enough, Mikky catches some eyes. Even out of his normal clothes, he's hard to miss—tall, a lot of hair, traces of the black lipstick he tried to scrape off his top lip still caught in the grooves. (He hadn't bothered to wipe away the eyeliner. That was too much work, and he pays too much for waterproof.) Some of them place him immediately—Mikky Graves, the prodigal son, returns.

Mikky forces himself not to think about it and finally catches sight of Kyla by the buffet table, tucked in the farthest corner where his father always places it.

She's staring down at the wilting lettuce in the salad like it holds all the secrets of the world. Jason stands next to her, speaking in hushed tones, but she doesn't answer back. The long, soft curls of her wig skim her elbows, her hands are balled into small fists at her sides. Mikky approaches her slowly, like one might a skittish animal.

Knowing there is nothing that can be said, Mikky reaches down and takes her balled fist, fingers smoothing over her rings. Kyla's expression doesn't change but her fingers unravel.

"Hold my hand," she says, her voice surprisingly steely. "Don't let go."

Mikky takes her command to heart. He holds her hand and their rings click, his silver and hers gold. He doesn't know when Kyla started wearing rings on nearly every dark-cherry-tipped finger like him. She's weighed down with metal around her neck, too, her nameplate most prominent, but has only one piercing in each ear, unlike Mikky, who has taken to body modification like a fish to water.

Kyla has never taken to the extreme, not in emotion or action, always so deliberate and moderated. Mikky'd been *jealous* of her for a long time for that, until he moved to Boston and started therapy and learned to stop comparing himself to other people, the way the citizens of Prophets Lake love to do.

Mikky waits for Kyla to say something else. Anything else. She doesn't. Mikky looks over at Jason, helplessness pulling the corners of his lips down.

Jason rushes to fill the silence. "I thought you were right behind me, man."

"I was," Mikky says.

"You didn't come up to the front," Jason insists.

"I thought it would be rude to interrupt," he explains. He looks over at Kyla, waiting for one of her dry remarks. He gets a listless stare. Not even a frown. Not good. "Did you eat, Kyla? You must be hungry."

Kyla doesn't even offer him a shrug. Her hold on his hand is so tight, his own fingers tingle as the circulation starts to get cut off.

"Deviled eggs," Jason blurts out.

Kyla and Mikky both jerk their heads around to look at him. Jason scratches at the back of his neck.

"Deviled eggs are the best part of a repast," he says.

"Have you been to many repasts?" Mikky asks, surprised.

Jason gives him a strange look. "No. It's . . . that's something you used to say."

Mikky digs deep through the memories of Prophets Lake, all of them blurry now, like the welcome sign. He pulls up a hazy memory of being nine, hiding underneath the food table at their first-grade teacher's repast, convincing Jason to try deviled eggs for the first time.

Mikky leans forward and pops one into his mouth. Around the mouthful, he says, "And I was right. Still the best part."

Jason manages a smile that doesn't reach his eyes. But a smile is a smile, even when forced.

Kyla squints at the grain of the wooden table, tugging at a loose string on the runner with her free hand instead of answering. It unravels and the edge begins to fray. Jason settles his fingers over her knuckles, gently tugging her hand away.

Then he turns to make her a plate, and Mikky tries to stop himself from hating Jason for taking care of Kyla before he can.

It's inconsiderate and Mikky's therapist would say so.

"Mikky? Mikky Graves?"

Mikky doesn't recognize the voice that interrupts these uncharitable thoughts, nor can he place the balding man immediately. Then it comes to him—tasteful oak casket, violet satin lining—their old plumber's eldest son. His father had died in a tragic battle with a septic tank, and he'd talked in the eulogy about carrying on his legacy, despite earlier aspirations of opening a chowder shop. In Prophets Lake, practicality is king. But still, he can't figure out why this man is coming up to him here. Now.

"Uh, hi, how are you?" Mikky asks.

The plumber's son gives a weak smile, tugging at the gaping collar around his neck. "Good. Well, not good," the man amends immediately. He takes a beat. "But . . . just surprised to see you. Had a call down to the funeral home a few days ago because one of your dad's clients clogged up the toilet with tissue from crying. He mentioned you were doing well for yourself out in Boston. He's real proud." Then he turns to Jason and Kyla with a moroseness that looks painted on and says as an afterthought, "My condolences," before he helps himself to some of the wings and goes off to gossip with the others.

Mikky winces. "Sorry about . . . whatever that was."

It's so quintessentially Prophets Lake. The practiced incision into a space where one doesn't belong, all in order to stare at someone else without remorse, assess them and appraise them.

Everything, every decision, every emotion, belongs to the town. Mikky's reminded again of why he left.

Jason doesn't see it that way. "No, I like it," he says as he looks down at Kyla, eyes soft as he passes her the plate of food he's made for her. "We'll use Mikky as a shield so losers don't come up to us and give 'condolences' or ask questions about Erin. That cool?"

Kyla nods. Mikky has to swallow the knot of worry in his throat to get words of agreement out.

They put their plan in action, moving as a trio, with Mikky serving as the distraction for people's curiosity. Well, some of them. The crowd divides into two easy categories. There are the older adults, the ones that remember Mikky from when he was a little kid and get stuck on him. Like his old piano teacher, Mrs. Krause, who tells him, "You look very . . . different," like it's a bad thing, or Mr. Kovacic, owner of one of the two barber shops in the entire town, who tells him, "I like the look. But if you ever want a haircut . . ." But then there are the others who are less delicate about their curiosity, and push past Mikky undeterred. They're the ones that actually knew Erin—Peter, her kinda boyfriend, Jason explains—or those that think they did, like Stevie, a girl from Erin's geometry class last year, and Mr. Briseis, teacher of said geometry class. They think their platitudes are welcome, necessary even, so they go right to Jason and Kyla.

And hanging between these groups like a specter are the tall, ghoulish "internet friends." Everyone else steers around them, hesitating to cross into their orbit and be caught in the beady, bug-like lenses of their phone cameras. They creep closer, eager to approach but more eager not to look it, and as they do, Mikky catches whispers from the surrounding groups: "They're influencers," "What kind of influencers?" "Beauty influencers. Like her," "Erin was getting up there in numbers," "I didn't expect them to come."

All the while, Kyla is still silent, and Mikky feels like an imposter. Or maybe she's the imposter. Kyla is introspective and taciturn at times, but she's always quick with a sarcastic quip and a biting smile. But now she can't even muster up a word. Mikky stands next to her and he knows she'd prefer someone else, would prefer Erin dig herself out of her grave and assume her rightful place.

Kyla sets her plate down on the table. She gives no indication that she's heard anything, but she points vaguely toward the door and steps away.

"Bathroom?" Jason stammers out, and Kyla nods once. For a moment Mikky isn't sure if he's supposed to let go, until Kyla tugs her hand free.

Almost immediately one of the influencers from the parking lot reaches out to her, but Kyla neatly sidesteps the touch, and then disappears. Mikky watches the girl's face contort, her concealer creasing around her eyebrows. But her expression smooths as she turns to Jason and Mikky. Leading her friends toward them, she swaggers with a forced air of casualness. She looks Mikky in the eye, dismisses him, and then turns to Jason.

"I'm *so* sorry about your sister," she simpers, voice dripping with a sticky condolence, half spoiled and insincere.

Jason blinks. Once. Twice. "Thank you?" Clearly, he has no idea who she is.

The girl's perfume is acidic and overpowering, but lurking underneath there's the familiar fresh and powdery scent of Cook Cosmetics.

"How did she, you know, die?" the boy asks.

The other girl scowls. "You can't just ask that," she admonishes, even though she sounds eager to know too. Looking at them is like looking in fun-house mirrors.

They shouldn't need to ask the question, though. Erin's death got coverage, at least in Prophets Lake. Mikky had only needed to go to the town newspaper's decrepit website to see that the police ruled Erin's death a homicide and get a few of the gory details of her discovery at the base of the cliffs on the lakeshore by a rich white woman taking her dog on its morning walk.

"This *sucks*," the first girl says. "Her following was just starting to blow up. She was going to be someone." She says it like it should mean something.

Jason's lips part and he inhales shakily.

Mikky swallows back the knot in his throat and forces out, "Erin already was someone. She doesn't *stop* being someone because someone murdered her."

It's the first time Mikky's said the word. From his reaction, it seems it's the first time that Jason has heard it too. He's ashen under his tan. Mikky expects the girl to feel a sense of shame, but she bristles and then stalks off, her insular clique scurrying after her.

"Are you okay?" Mikky asks.

Jason squints. "I'm . . . glad Kyla didn't have to hear that."

Mikky's lips press into a thin line. "Me too. What's going on with her? She's not . . . speaking."

"I haven't seen her since . . . since we first asked your dad to handle the funeral. And she didn't speak then, either. She didn't even look at us. Mom tried to ask her opinion on things and Kyla, it was weird. She acted as if she hadn't even heard her," Jason says. "Mom . . . she cried in the car after. You know Mom basically sees her as a daughter."

That shouldn't rub Mikky the wrong way, but it does. *Kyla already has a mom,* he wants to say, but he holds his tongue yet again.

"Yeah, of course," he says, and hopes that it doesn't sound as thin as it feels. "I'm sure she's still in shock. Like all of you."

Jason looks over at a cluster of men. One or two of them are Cook Cosmetics executives like Mrs. Vaughn, but some of the others are real estate developers, really another word for landlords—scum of the Earth, that they are—that Mr. Vaughn has surely sold more than a few properties to. Always the odd man out and never minding it, Dad is with him, hand fluttering over Mr. Vaughn's elbow to catch him if he falters.

Their two families couldn't be more different, but Mikky can't remember a time anymore when they weren't entwined. They've all been inseparable ever since Kyla and Erin met at the same daycare center Mikky drove past when he entered town. Even the green playground is the same, now bleached to the color of sea glass by sun and age.

But now, *everything* is different.

Erin is dead. Erin's been *murdered*, and no one knows what to do with it.

Mikky nearly walks up to Mr. Vaughn—he's not sure why that suddenly feels so important—when his line of sight is swallowed up by a swollen bouquet of white roses, lush and woven together with sea-green ribbons. It's huge, bigger than decency allows, cradled between two deliverymen. They seem startled by what they've walked into, crossing through the sea of black with sheepish expressions.

Jason cuts through and Mikky dogs his footsteps, refusing to leave him alone or be left alone. His father seems to have similar thoughts, pulling away from Mr. Vaughn to deal with it.

Neither of them gets there first. Mrs. Vaughn does.

All marks of grief—swollen undereyes and dried tear tracks—have been disguised, hidden by the same expert hand that taught Erin and Kyla how to do their makeup, how to cover up any residual redness or moments of weakness with a perfection that errs on the right side of airbrushed. It's uncanny; Mikky wouldn't think the woman was in mourning at all, except for the way her hands shake.

"What's this?" she asks, her voice creaking.

"A delivery for . . . the Vaughns," the deliveryman on the left says. "Is that you, ma'am?"

"They're a bit late," she says. She looks over at Mikky's father, uncertainly, and he rushes forward to grab the flowers, then stumbles under their unexpected weight. His face disappears behind the swell of roses, and the deliveryman on the right offers a thick white envelope to Mrs. Vaughn, tied up with gold ribbon. She tugs the ribbon loose and loops it around her wrist, before opening the card. Mikky glimpses sea-green ink before Mrs. Vaughn shuts it, and a wretched sound tears free from her throat.

"Well," she chokes out. "Well, then."

Everyone's watching her, like a car crash on the side of a highway.

Except Mikky. He closes his eyes as the pressure on his chest increases. It's an all-too-familiar feeling, the mounting panic that he's mostly learned to manage. Mikky tries to breathe through it, deep inhales to settle his turning stomach and whistling exhales through his nose. Fingers brush against his elbow, and he expects maybe Jason, but when he opens his eyes at the grounding touch, Jason is still by his mother's side. The fingers belong to Kyla.

Immediately he reverses things and pushes all his attention toward his sister. At last, her expression shifts, into one of agony, her face distorting with a sadness so deep that it's like her insides have been carved and hollowed out to make room for it. The gauntness to her face has nothing to do with losing weight but with losing light.

Mikky and Kyla have never heavily resembled each other, but in this very moment Mikky is looking into a mirror three years back.

This goes beyond sadness. Beyond grief.

Kyla closes her eyes tight, her fingers clamping on to Mikky's elbow, as Mrs. Vaughn sucks in a wet sob so hard that Mikky's own throat stings. She drops the note and Kyla darts forward, snatching it up.

She opens the card and Mikky squints, confused.

```
To the Vaughns,
Our dearest sympathies.
From, Cook Cosmetics
```

It's terribly impersonal, a bare-minimum show of condolences for their director of global marketing about her daughter, who was an ambassador for their brand. And still Mrs. Vaughn's mascara doesn't budge. Five-star review. Even now, she's a walking-talking advertisement of the company, and that's all they could give her. Mikky had always thought Cook was soulless and they only continue to prove him right.

But Kyla clutches the note to her chest like a lifeline.

"We put her in the ground," Kyla whispers. He can barely hear her over Mrs. Vaughn's tears. "She must be so lonely."

"Kyla," Mikky starts. He's waited all day for her to speak, and finally, when she does, he doesn't know what to say.

Kyla shakes her head like she can't hear him. "I wanted to climb into the casket with her. I belong there."

Mikky's heart skips a beat, painfully, and his breathing ratchets up. The stirring horrid feeling is back even worse than before, and this time he has to count in his head. *In, two, three, four, five. Out, two, three, four, five.* And again.

"Kyla, what . . . ?" he asks between wheezes. He knows what his therapist would call it, but he can't form the words in his own head, can't believe her comment is *ideation*. Except . . . how else can he take it?

He looks around, wondering if anyone else has heard what Kyla said.

But his father is still sinking under the weight of flowers even as his employees flurry forward to assist. Jason is with Mr. and Mrs. Vaughn, attempting to manage his mother's grief. No one is here with Kyla.

No one except Mikky, and Erin's ghost.

The stench of mourning lingers after a repast. Like old cooking oil and cloying perfume, it fills the space. But it's better than people. Mikky helps his dad out as best as he can, packing the leftovers that Jason rejected as his father attempted to curb his mother's nervous breakdown in the car.

Mikky cradles the foil pans, frowning. He's helped out at repasts before, but it's been a long time and usually his sister is with him. Kyla is all about lists and planning, and they would've been done at least twenty minutes before if she was helping. But Kyla is sitting in the car and Mikky can't stop thinking about what she said about Erin's loneliness in the grave. About how she wants to join her.

"It was a good funeral, wasn't it?" Dad asks. "I wanted to do right by her. She's always done right by Kyla and it's . . . she was *so, so* young."

Usually, Dad is good about sounding impersonal about someone's death, especially with how small the town is, but this has hit too close to home. Mikky's fingers dig into the aluminum. They can't do anything else for Erin, but Kyla . . .

Dad, Kyla's not okay. It should be easy to say, because it's true, and Mikky's always preferred the truth to lies. But he can't seem to make his tongue form the words because saying them out loud makes it more than truth. It becomes fact, and the fact is that Mikky already feels like he's failed her. He hasn't been here. Hasn't done *enough*.

And what will Dad do about it? Dad, who's so kind and loving but never knew how to handle the hard shit. Mikky's shit. Not without Mom's help, and Kyla *definitely* won't let Mom help.

That's when it comes to him. The only solution to an impossible problem.

"Hey, Dad," Mikky calls softly. His dad's fingers hover over the light switch. "I know I'm supposed to go back to Mom's in a few days, but . . . what do you think about me sticking around longer?"

Dad softens. "You know I could never say no to that. But when does school start?"

Mikky grits his teeth. He loves Boston. He loves his friends. His school. His therapist. But . . . He gathers his courage. To the sticking place and all that shit. "I meant, like, a lot longer. Because Kyla doesn't look okay, and I . . . I want to help her be okay."

Dad shakes his head. "Kiddo, she's going through something—"

"Dad, it's not just something. Her best friend was murdered," Mikky says. He takes in his dad's flinch, but pushes on: "Erin was *murdered*. She's not going to be un-murdered. And I know you could handle it, of course, because you're our dad, but I wanna be there for her too."

I want to solve this for her, somehow, he thinks.

"So, like, you asked when does school start. When *does* Prophets Lake High start?"

CHAPTER FOUR

I don't want you to spiral like you did when you were fourteen. One semester at that school was enough," Mikky's mother says. He can picture her pacing about the apartment, searching for her keys, grabbing her laptop and sliding it into her bag. He checks the time; she's going to be late to work.

"I think I have better coping mechanisms now. Dr. Grosse thinks it's fine. I think it's fine. And I . . . Kyla really needs me right now," Mikky says, spinning his rings on his left hand as he waits for her to speak.

She stops shuffling and he can hear only her heavy breathing. "How has she been?"

Not well, he wants to say. It's been a week since the funeral and every day has been different. Sometimes Kyla is up before him, downstairs in the living room, listlessly flicking through channels, eyes unfocused. When he joins her, she won't say much, but she won't tell him to go away. She lets him babble, and one thing about Mikky: he can babble, and well. Mikky goes on and on about nonsense—the new witch show on Netflix that he knows she might be into, the possibility that they take a drive together so that Mikky can refamiliarize himself with Prophets Lake properly. He even asks her if she wants him to buy her the vinyl rerelease of one of her favorite old-school R&B artists. Nothing breaks through.

Sometimes she's in her bedroom all day and Dad has to drag her out to join them for a meal. Through it all, she's entirely barefaced with harsh shadows under her eyes. He could tell their mother this and maybe she'd understand why he has to stay, but it would feel like a betrayal. Kyla wouldn't want her to know.

"I'm glad I'm here," Mikky finally says.

"I talked to her, you know," Mom whispers.

Mikky fumbles his phone. "You *did*? When?"

"The day Erin's body was found. Your dad called me and put her on the phone. I asked her if she wanted me to come to the funeral and she said no. I respected her wishes," his mother recites, like this is something she has had to convince herself was true. Mikky pushes down thoughts like, *You can't pick and choose when to do the hard things, you try with me because I am so much easier than Kyla, I could be less easy if you'd like—* He clears his throat.

"Well, Kyla needs someone. So I'm gonna stay for a bit," Mikky says decisively.

Mom sighs. "You'll still have your weekly calls with Dr. Grosse?" she asks.

"She wouldn't let me stop even if I tried," Mikky says. His therapist is insistent that way.

"Okay," Mom says. "Have a good first day, Mikky."

They say their goodbyes and Mikky leans over his bare dresser to finish his eyeliner. He understands his mom's apprehension. Mikky still remembers the end of his one and only semester at Prophets Lake High. He tried everything to make it work. Went to class, but he struggled to speak up when he'd never been afraid to before. Tried to be unassuming, but he constantly drew stares as his growth spurt got attention for him. Experimented with his look—he liked the nail polish the most but managed to peel it off by third period after the third comment about how nice they looked. It had ended in Mikky breaking down on the kitchen floor, fingers digging hard enough into his scalp to draw blood while he spiraled about how he couldn't get it *right*. Nothing felt *right* anymore and Mikky wanted to disappear, even as his dad got on his knees with him and held him.

Next thing Mikky knew, Dad was on the phone with Mom, and then she was back in Prophets Lake with three therapists' numbers in hand. None of them had clicked with Mikky, but what mattered was that she knew immediately that he needed to be in therapy. So she pivoted to the next option, saying that he needed to be withdrawn from Prophets Lake High School and move in with her. It had been an easy fix from her perspective, because in a lot of ways Mikky was like Mom. Prophets Lake didn't fit her and she didn't fit in it and the roles laid out for her—namely, mother. The small town lines shrank in on her as the depression inside grew bigger and bigger until she nearly cut herself open to free it. Mom didn't want the same to happen to Mikky. So a few weeks later his father and Kyla were packing up his room to send after him.

Now everything's happening in the reverse. After his decision, the first thing his mom started packing were his clothes. She'd fought him about it all the way to the FedEx but knew she couldn't change his mind. The rest of his things are scheduled to get there by the end of the week—his laptop, his books, and his guitar. Most of his jewelry, and his leather duster for when it gets cooler. Plus, his extensive nail polish collection. All the things that make him feel grounded, that make him feel and look like the self he sees in his brain.

Mikky slides his rings on and then hooks his fingers into the back of his Demonias. When he leaves his room, Kyla's door is still closed. He slips by it and goes downstairs, his clothing rattling enough that Dad doesn't even need to look up to know it's him. "Good morning, Mikky."

"Morning," Mikky says, dropping his shoes by the kitchen table. "Oh, you cooked."

"Yeah, I do that," Dad teases.

Mikky rolls his eyes. "You know what I meant. You, like . . . cooked a lot. You didn't have to."

"It's my kids' first day of school. *Your* first day of senior year. Course I had to cook," Dad says, waving Mikky to sit down and bringing the finished platter of potatoes and peppers over to go with the waffles and kielbasa. He finishes it off with Vermont maple syrup, the one from the farmers market one town over. The good stuff. The Christmas Day stuff.

"Thank you, Dad," Mikky says, probably a touch too emotional for what it is. They were close when Mikky was growing up, but when he moved in with his mom, a distance developed, of course. Mikky hasn't missed Prophets Lake, but he's missed his *dad*.

"And you're really sure about this, right, kiddo?" Dad asks. "You know Kyla . . . Kyla will be okay either way."

Mikky's lips thin into a line. His parents are more alike than they care to admit, both so quick to affirm things will be "okay" if *they* will it so, as if becoming "okay" doesn't require an active participant. "I'm very sure about this. Look, I've got this. School won't be an issue. And I'm a well-adjusted, all-grown-up boy. I can manage even if I have a rough start."

"But . . . your friends at home . . . more than friends . . . ?"

Mikky rolls his eyes. "If this is your way of asking if I have a boyfriend, the answer is no. Also, I have friends here, too."

Well, he has Jason. Kyla—eventually. And it's not like he's losing his friends back in Boston. Mikky had a way of collecting older sibling friends, so they understood when he explained the circumstances of his sudden transfer back to his hometown. Besides, Mikky knows how to make friends now. And if he doesn't, he's okay with that. There's a difference between being alone and being lonely, and Mikky doesn't really feel lonely as much anymore.

"I was just *asking*. You never talk about boys in our calls," Dad says with half a laugh.

"Because it's *awkward*," Mikky groans as he starts to serve himself breakfast. The conversation is so easy, so normal. It's nice to feel this warmth is an everyday thing, and not something that Dad saves for holidays. That he really *doesn't* feel any resentment for Mikky leaving two and a half years ago.

It's not like it is with Kyla and Mom, a wasteland of emotional space between them.

"Maybe you'll find someone at school?" Dad says, waggling his eyebrows.

Mikky shakes his head in denial. "It's not practical getting a boyfriend my senior year. I'd have to break up with him at the end of the year. Messy. No, thank you," he says.

Dad sighs. "Now, who said you would have to break up with him?"

"Common sense." Mikky takes after his mother in this way. He's not much of a romantic. Dad is, though, to a fault. It's a funny thing—to be a romantic undertaker. Someone should make a movie about it.

"I don't want you to . . . have a hard time," Dad finishes lamely. He's never as straightforward about Mikky's mental health as his mother is.

Mikky stands suddenly and Dad tracks him toward the cabinet on the left of the fridge. He opens it and spins the lazy Susan a half turn until he sees the fluorescent orange bottle. He picks it up and shakes it at his father with a tiny smile.

"Ten milligrams of Lexapro and a weekly Zoom session with Dr. Grosse has me feeling pretty confident I won't," Mikky says, and he marches back to his breakfast. He pops a pill under his tongue and washes it down with his orange juice. When he looks up, he squirms under the light of his dad's big smile. "Don't be gross."

"What do you mean? I'm not being gross." Dad is still smiling.

"You don't have to be proud of me or whatever," Mikky grumbles.

"I'm always proud of you, Mik," Dad says.

Mikky doesn't know what to say so he starts eating and scrolling through his phone.

"Is she not going to eat breakfast?" Mikky asks finally, looking up at the ceiling.

Dad frowns. "She . . . should . . ."

"I'll go get her," Mikky decides, scraping his chair back against the linoleum. He marches out of the kitchen and up the stairs. He makes sure he's loud enough for Kyla to hear him coming. When he gets to her door, the first one off the stairs, he raises a hand to knock.

The door swings open before he can.

He expects a Kyla with tacky drool dried to her cheek, still in rumpled pajamas and her scarf wrapped around her head. He expects her to beg off school. He would. He can't imagine dragging himself through the day. *This* day.

He gets nothing of the sort. Her curls are in glossy flat twists, accessorized with gold cuffs that lead up to the massive puff atop her head. She has little golden stars at the corners of her eyes like she's ready for a pep rally, and a fresh dark-cherry manicure. Her book bag is slung over her shoulder.

Mikky looks over it, getting his first glimpse into Kyla's inner sanctum. A bookshelf full of not books but vinyl dominates the back wall and—Kyla steps closer, throws the door shut, giving him a warning look.

"I'm ready. Are you?" she asks. It's the most words she's spoken to Mikky in a row since the funeral.

"Y-yeah. Let me put my shoes on, and then . . . can you drive me?" he asks. "I'm not registered for a parking spot yet. Apparently there's an application process for that, which is so stupid."

"Of course," Kyla says.

And that's how Mikky finds himself sitting in the passenger seat of an old hearse, shoving his feet into his shoes because Kyla didn't give him time to put them on at home. She didn't stop to eat breakfast either. She had only enough patience to wish their father goodbye before she booked it to the car and beeped the horn.

"You sure you don't want to stop for coffee?" Mikky asks.

"Give yourself a moment before . . . everything?" She's taken so much time to appear impeccable after barely getting dressed the past few days, it's unsettling. She hasn't referenced what she said at the repast to him again, and she's pretended that she never said it at all when he's tried to ask her about it. Her ability to pull herself together for today should be a good sign, but it only makes Mikky's stomach knot up with even more worry.

"No," Kyla says, voice cold. "Someone will have breakfast for me. I asked in the group chat."

The way she says it, Mikky doesn't think that Kyla *asked* anyone. Or if she did, it wasn't particularly polite. It's eerily Erin-like.

"Okay," Mikky says quietly. Kyla doesn't move to put music on so Mikky doesn't either, but he has to fill the silence with something. He tries to figure out how to push his seat back to allow himself the required legroom. He has a feeling he knows exactly who this seat was adjusted for, and she was half a foot shorter than him. "So . . . you drive the hearse?"

"I drive the old hearse. Dad got a new one," Kyla says. "A Cadillac from that old Polish guy a few towns over. He retired, sold it for dirt cheap."

"Retired? You mean Mr. Nowak? He's not retirement age, is he?" Mikky asks. Last time he saw the man, he was maybe fifty, and it wasn't *that* long ago.

"Crematorium opened in his town. They're taking a lot of business," Kyla says too casually.

Dad hasn't mentioned that and Mikky wonders why. A crematorium is direct competition to the funeral home. A much cheaper option than a full-service funeral. That can't be good.

But Mikky doesn't want to give Kyla another thing to stress

about, so instead of asking any more questions, he inspects her vehicle of choice. The interior is definitely old, but it's glossy, like Kyla takes special care of it. He wonders if anyone looks sideways at her for it. He hopes not because—

"I'm gonna be so real with you. This is sick." Mikky grins.

Kyla's lips twitch into the tiniest smirk. The first show of a nonnegative emotion. Sorta. "Right?" she says. "Dad thought it was, like . . . tacky. He wanted to get me a cute, used sedan like yours."

"It's a piece of shit, Kyla. I'm not unaware," Mikky says.

Kyla doesn't laugh, but her grin widens and that feels like a win. More progress. "I wanted something with character. Besides, Erin thought it would be funny to make each of the frosh dancers lie in the back like they were . . ."

It might've been funny at the time, but not anymore, because Erin is the one who ended up dead in the back of their dad's brand-new Cadillac hearse.

Kyla comes to the same conclusion as Mikky as they arrive at the stop sign. Her smile slips away, and for the briefest of moments her stare grows a thousand yards. But in the next breath she slips back into focus, so sharp, Mikky thinks he might cut himself on her gaze.

He'd finally broken through. Somewhat. But Mikky is suddenly more sure than ever—Kyla isn't okay. And while she might seem to not want Mikky's help, she sure as hell is going to get it.

CHAPTER FIVE

This first day is like any other, Mikky tells himself as he lingers outside the school. It hasn't changed all that much, but *he's* changed. In a good way. The best way. So he shouldn't be bothered. But still, it's . . . hard. He can't help his hesitation.

Kyla doesn't hesitate at all. She storms inside, like there isn't someone missing at her side. It's that insistence that makes Mikky buck the *fuck* up, and walk in.

Everything's slightly different, an uncanny valley that throws Mikky off kilter. He finds the front office easily enough, and finagles his schedule from the secretary, Ms. Armstrong. She recognizes him on sight too, and welcomes him back with a curious once-over that's becoming familiar, like she can't quite compute the newest version of him.

Mikky's schedule is comparable to his old one back in Boston, with the only difference being that his first class of the day, chemistry, is now an AP course instead of an honors course. With AP German, he'll have two APs as a senior, which isn't ideal, but he'll make it work.

He orients himself and finds the science hallway. Everyone's moving so fast around him, with too much single-minded focus for the first day of school. He recognizes some faces, but most of them, he doesn't, and that makes it . . . almost better. Mostly better. Mikky has always been the type to associate faces with bad memories more than places. Who witnessed his worst, not where it took place. Three quarters of those people have graduated now, he reminds himself.

Mikky is the last one to get to the AP Chemistry classroom. He slips in as the teacher sets down his attendance sheet.

"Michael Graves?" the teacher asks quietly. "I'm Mr. Reynolds."

Mikky's nose wrinkles. "It's Mikky. I don't think I've been called 'Michael' a day in my life."

The teacher nods with a wide smile, and Mikky gets the impression that he's one of those "cool" teachers. "Got it. Mikky," he confirms, then turns to the class and claps his hands. It doesn't work, of course. "Yo, listen up! Class, we have a new student. This is—"

"We know who Mikky Graves is," a member of Jason's soccer team says. He doesn't say it rudely, even though he's looking Mikky up and down like he, too, can't square the Mikky he remembers with the one standing here. "He's *Kyla Graves's* brother."

He says Kyla's name with a hushed emphasis, like he's afraid of being overheard. Or maybe summoning her.

"Oh?" The teacher looks frazzled by the lack of interest in his new student. Mikky takes pity on the nonlocal.

"Yeah, that's my little sister. I'm Prophets Lake, born and raised, left for a while and recently returned due to . . . extenuating circumstances," he says. No one says it out loud, but Mikky knows what everyone's thinking. He heard it whispered in the hallways from people who know *of* him, but don't *know* him, the whole walk here: "Erin's murder, he came back because Erin is dead." Mikky shuffles down the narrow aisle, his bag jostling against his hip until he nears one girl sitting at her lab table all alone, playing with the rusting knob on the burner. He thinks he recognizes her as one of the dance team girls from Kyla's pictures. "This seat taken?"

She looks up, blinking. "Oh! No, sit!" she says.

Mikky slides onto the stool, trying to get comfortable for what will surely be a mind-numbing fifty minutes.

"I'm Alicia," the girl whispers as Mr. Reynolds starts the class. Or at least, tries to whisper. It's loud enough to earn a sharp look from the boy sitting one table away.

"Mikky," he says unnecessarily.

Alicia looks like she appreciates the introduction anyway. She fidgets with her hair, then her fingers flit over her jaw, grazing the skin. She's wearing a full face of makeup, expertly applied. Sure enough, he can smell the familiar scent of Cook Cosmetics.

"I'm on the dance team with Kyla." Alicia confirms his guess, leaning against her palm to look at Mikky like he's an intriguing zoo animal.

"That's cool," Mikky says. He tries to think back to whether or not an Alicia was mentioned in any of Kyla's texts. They're not really phone-calling people; Mikky used to keep up with Kyla through long blocks of text messaging or voice memos, like mini podcasts. But he can't remember an Alicia.

In all Kyla's stories, Erin was always her most frequent costar. Everyone else was supporting.

"I think I saw you at the funeral. We were, like, so surprised to see you," Alicia says. "It's really good of you to come back for that . . . but I mean, I guess it makes sense since you're coming *here* for your senior year."

Mikky would think that she was fishing for more information if she didn't come across as so peculiarly earnest.

"Jason and I grew up together, and Kyla and Erin are—were—close. I wanted to be here for them," Mikky explains. Alicia's upbeat smile strains at the mention of "Erin," but she manages to keep it in place.

"Yeah, it's so messed up. The vibes at school are so off without her, and Kyla is so . . . *never mind*," Alicia sighs, cradling her cheek in her palm as she looks up at Mikky through her lashes. "So, how's your first day going?"

Mikky hasn't been asked this yet. By anyone. It's actually nice.

"It's barely started but, okay. Everything looks a little different. I did a semester here my freshman year before I transferred and it used to be a little run down—" Mikky says. He cuts himself off when he sees something from the corner of his eye, a little tiny balled piece of paper that teeters on the edge of their desk.

Alicia nods. "Oh, *yeah*," she says enthusiastically and, again, a touch too loud. Someone across the aisle shushes them, and Alicia giggles, lowering her head but not her voice. "They did a ton of renovations. Florence Cook made a donation that was *supposed* to be anonymous, but my mom is in the PTA and is friends with the secretary and she told her. They fixed up the gym and the entire science block. And then there was a little left over to fix the floors."

That explains everything. Cook Cosmetics'—and its founder, Florence's—influence reigns all over town. Florence was a child of Prophets Lake as much as Mikky is, and the community adores her, despite her never actually deigning to be part of it. But when she was growing up, Prophets Lake had been kept running not on the strength of a cosmetics empire but of Florence's family's tobacco farms. Everyone worked for Cook Farms, just like everyone works for Cook Cosmetics now.

Mikky would resent it like he resents most rich people, but—

"That's actually kinda cool," Mikky admits begrudgingly. "I mean, it's what she should be doing, redistributing her wealth, but putting it into the high school, specifically, is cool."

Alicia blinks at him slowly. "Redistributing her wealth?"

Mikky nods. "Yeah. She's a millionaire, which is inherently unethical, because the hoarding of wealth is unethical. She *should* be giving some of it away, I'm just glad that she chose a school," Mikky says, then he thinks of that corporate bouquet. "She still sucks, though."

Alicia is looking at Mikky like she's never seen anyone like him. He's not used to the pointed stares anymore, but at least it's about something he's said and not his hair or his jewelry or his makeup or his—

Another piece of paper appears on their desk, a little farther in, landing right between Mikky's hands. He ignores it.

"Earlier you started to say something about how Kyla is doing and then . . . changed your mind," Mikky hedges. "What did you mean?"

Alicia purses her lips. "I . . . don't know. She's always been the quieter out of her and Erin, but, like . . . she wasn't responding to anything in our group chat until this morning when she told us to get her breakfast and I saw her in homeroom and asked her if we were canceling dance practice because some of our parents are being a little weird about us being out after school and she—"

"Hi, sorry, are you planning to shut up anytime soon?" the boy across the aisle asks.

Mikky's eyes narrow. "Depends. Do you plan to stop throwing little pieces of paper at me anytime soon?"

"Sure. When you shut up and actually pay attention to the teacher," the boy retorts. Mikky leans forward to get a better look at him. He's shorter than Mikky, but his legs still have to fold up a little to accommodate him on the rickety stool, so not by much. He's got one hoodie string wrapped tight enough around his finger to cut off circulation and a half-chewed pen tucked between two fingers like a cigarette. Mikky is also not blind so he very quickly categorizes this boy with his bronzed skin, thick eyebrows, and wire-framed glasses as hot.

"Sorry. We're shutting up," Mikky says, raising his hands in surrender. "I'm Mikky."

The boy purses his lips. "I know who you are. Everyone knows who you are. You're hard to miss." Mikky takes that like a badge of honor this time. He knows he's a good-looking guy. He puts effort into it.

"Glad to be noticed," Mikky says.

The boy snorts. "Pretty sure it was the hearse you arrived in that caught my attention."

"If that's what you want to tell yourself."

The boy's chest puffs up, annoyed, and his friend mutters, "Truly not worth it, my dude," but the boy is intent on ignoring this. He points at Mikky with all the threatening aura of a kindergarten teacher.

"Look, just because we're sitting at the back doesn't mean that we're not trying to learn. It means we don't want Mr. Reynolds's spit on us when he gets fast and loose with his lips. *We* are here to learn," the boy says.

"And I'm not? Who's making assumptions now?" Mikky asks.

The boy sputters, eyes widening behind those glasses in a way that Mikky can't help but find fascinating. "*Look*," he says with all the venom he can muster.

Before he can spit out another insult, Mr. Reynolds waves his hand awkwardly. "Hey, uh, are we having a problem back there?"

Alicia chirps, "Not at all, Mr. Reynolds."

The chemistry teacher doesn't look like he believes her, and his expression twists into something sly. "That's great. Then can one of you tell me what the first unit will be?" he asks.

Mikky doesn't look down at the syllabus—to look at the syllabus would be to admit that he, in fact, *was* involved in a problem and *wasn't* paying attention. It would be admitting defeat, and Mikky isn't going to do that. He stares over at the boy, waiting for him to contribute, since he's so adamant about being there to learn. The boy purposely rolls his eyes before looking back at Mr. Reynolds, bored.

"It's atomic structure and properties. The second one is molecular and ionic compound structures. The third is intermolecular forces and properties," he recites, like he's been anticipating it for months now. "If we want to get into specifics, I imagine the first lesson will be on moles and molar mass?"

Mr. Reynolds's expression sours. "No, it'll be lab safety. Thank you very much, Mr. Talebi. Now, as I was saying . . ." The chemistry teacher returns to his long diatribe, and Mikky sends Alicia a contrite smile, miming a finger to his lips in a hush, like they're united against their annoyingly smug classmate.

At the end of class, Mr. Reynolds assigns the first chapter in their textbook to familiarize themselves with the tools they'll be using in future experiments, and before he's even done, Mikky's classmates are on the move. Mikky barely scrawls the assignment down in his planner before the bell rings, and he realizes that he has about five minutes to get across the school to his math class.

"I'm sure Kyla already offered," Alicia says with a smile as he packs up quickly, "but if you ever need somewhere to sit during lunch, I would *love* to have you there." She says it like it's a formal invitation, something that doesn't happen often. It disorients Mikky, reminding him of the mean girls in teen movies, except Alicia doesn't seem particularly mean.

It does make him realize Kyla *hasn't* offered, though.

"You think Kyla would be . . . okay with that?" Mikky asks. "I don't want to spring my presence on her."

There's a derisive snort, loud and pointed enough that Mikky looks over again. The boy is still painstakingly writing down the assignment in a heavily color-coded planner that looks like he means *business*, pretending like he isn't eavesdropping *again*. "Hey, uh, look—" Mikky starts.

But the boy instantly packs up his planner like he hasn't heard Mikky at all. His lab partner looks between Mikky and the boy uncertainly.

Mikky presses his lips into a thin line, unable to help his swelling amusement. "Are you . . . are you actually ignoring me?"

The boy *continues* to ignore him, which gives Mikky his answer.

"Well, look, I'm sorry about before—" Mikky tries again, but the boy tosses his navy backpack over his shoulder, turns on his heel, and marches toward the door. His lab partner has to practically jog to keep up.

"Don't worry about him," Alicia tries, but now Mikky squirms. He's used to people not liking him, so he's not sure why *this* one particular person not liking him puts him on edge. Maybe it's the way he snorted like he *knew* something about Kyla that Mikky didn't.

Mikky grabs his bag and uses his God-given long legs to catch up and swing in front of him. "Wait, wait, look, man. I'm really sorry about being loud and distracting you during class and almost getting you in trouble—"

The irritated boy pauses, and finally looks Mikky up and down. Deliberately. "Don't call me 'man.' I'm Nasim," he says, and then he's gone, marching down the hall. But, hey, they're on a first-name basis.

Mikky can't wait to tell Dad that he made a friend.

CHAPTER SIX

The social microcosm of Prophets Lake High School is a never-ending curiosity to Mikky. There's something delightful about how absolutely mundane it is. The jocks and the dance team sit at the center of the cafeteria, farthest from the trash cans. They're the nucleus and everyone else reverberates outward in varying degrees of popularity. The band members and the theater kids. The gifted kids—"nerds" isn't right, because anyone can be a nerd about something—the ones with *school* as their defining personality trait. There's even the emos, in aesthetic only, considering they're all playing XXXTentacion from their phones. It's the picture of a bad teen film, the kind from the early aughts that Erin and Kyla used to watch religiously. Their bible made flesh.

Except it's all fake. All these carefully drawn lines. Having been so far removed from Prophets Lake and then dropped right back down in the middle, Mikky sees how eager his classmates are to be different. So eager that they all actually read the same. It's . . . reassuring. To know that it wasn't only him who didn't feel at home in his own skin once.

If this was a movie from 2004, Mikky would be relegated to the bathroom as the new kid. But in this new world order, Mikky has somewhere to sit.

"Then that's Lynn, Imani, and Fay," Alicia says cheerfully, the end of a dizzying list of names that Mikky knows he'll be hopeless at remembering. "Now, girls, say hi to Kyla's brother, Mikky."

They're all gawking. More and more, Mikky gets the feeling that he's being stared at *not* because of how he presents himself but by virtue of being Kyla's older brother. They chant out a unified hello before looking up, right behind Mikky, as he senses someone hovering over him.

"Don't forget Sabrina," Kyla says. She's as close to Mikky as she can be without touching him, and Mikky tilts his head back to look at her. She's scanning the table, a tray in her hand, her lips pursed. "Make room."

In a uniform fashion, everyone to the right of Mikky, including Alicia, slides down, shuffling their trays. On the opposite side they do the same, creating another empty seat. Kyla sits next to Mikky, just as a petite freckly redhead takes the seat opposite. The tension fractures. The girls start chattering loudly amongst themselves, but none of them dares to address Kyla, outside of quick glances from the corner of their eyes.

"Mikky Graves," the redhead he assumes is Sabrina says in a lofty English accent. "Kyla's elusive elder brother. It's nice to put a face to a name. You don't look how I imagined you would."

Mikky doesn't take the bait. "I'm glad I could shock and awe."

"Worm, man," Sabrina says with a put-on American accent and a wink. It's clearly an inside joke, because Alicia cackles. Kyla doesn't. "So, Ky, Leesh, what is the 7-1-1?"

Mikky winces. Kyla hates most nicknames. He waits for her to respond, but she doesn't, just cradles her cheek in her palm, stares out of the corner of her eye. Sabrina masks her disappointment well.

"My skin is so *bad*," Alicia complains, dragging her fingers over her uneven jaw.

Sabrina leans in, frowning. "Is it still that bad? Have you tried stripping back your routine?"

"Yeah, but it's getting a little cystic. Ugh, I don't want to stop wearing foundation," Alicia complains. Sabrina makes a sympathetic sound, patting the back of Alicia's hand. Of her own accord, Alicia tries to perk up, shaking it off, and she leans forward. "Um, Kyla, we didn't have a chance to finish that, uh, conversation in homeroom," Alicia starts. She's twirling the end of her hair around one finger, poking at the burgeoning signs of a pimple on her jawline, agitating it into being.

"Yes, we did. We have dance practice later. End of discussion," Kyla says, breaking her self-imposed silence.

Alicia nods, even though Kyla isn't looking at her. Uncertain, she looks over at Sabrina, who jerkily shrugs and then looks farther down the table toward the younger members of the squad. They're all looking down at the trays, worried. Clearly, Alicia is advocating for some of the other members, like she'd mentioned to Mikky.

"Yeah, but sometimes our practices run so late, and . . . I mean, I know *my* mom is feeling kinda weird about us being out so late because of what happened to . . . Erin," Alicia says, her voice petering out as Kyla's head jerks up. With Kyla's full attention on her, Alicia launches into double time. "Remember last year? There was that big blizzard and Erin wanted to still have practice because she couldn't decide on what she wanted the routine to be for regionals and she wanted to see both options, and *you* told her that was irresponsible, and we got to go home, and thank God we did because like half the town had a blackout and—"

"It's the first practice of the year," Kyla says coldly.

"I know, but last year—"

"Last year is not this year. And *Erin* isn't here," Kyla snarls, voice dipping into something guttural. She leans over the table, lips pulling back over her teeth. "She may have died but that doesn't make *you* captain. It makes *me* captain. So I say, we have *fucking* practice."

Mikky inhales sharply, lightly touching his fingertips to Kyla's shoulder. "Hey—"

Kyla shrugs off his hand violently and Mikky drops it back to the table. As if she doesn't feel the heavy silence her outburst has caused, Kyla starts to pick at her fries again, dipping one first in the ketchup, then in her honey mustard. It's how she's always eaten fries, ever since they were kids. Some things are the same.

But everything *else* about her is so, so different, and not in a good way.

Kyla's dance practice is a grand finale to a weird day. Mikky floats through his afternoon classes, his mind swirling with the tense expression on Kyla's face at the end of lunch and the implication that he isn't the only one to find her behavior odd.

But then again, everyone's behavior is odd. Even the brand-new library that Mikky had spent the past hour in, organizing his planner for the year, seemed dreary in sharp contrast to its shiny new contents. Everyone is a bit more subdued on this first day, a specter of grief hanging over them.

Grief takes a physical form in Erin's memorial, set up in the glass trophy case outside the gym. Amidst two years of regional dance team championship trophies and a state prize from last year is the dance team photo, showing Erin and Kyla hoisting said trophies over their heads, smirking into the lens. But at the center of the display, it's Erin Vaughn. Not even old enough for graduation photos, it's her sophomore portrait that's framed.

Her hair's white blond with streaks of pink. She has a face of perfect makeup: highlighter, bronzer, blush. Immaculately arched eyebrows. The longer Mikky stares at her, the more he can't make a human out of her. She looks like a painting.

Mikky can see why she was so popular online. Her unattainability is half the charm. Her nearly fifty thousand adoring followers were all dedicated to idealizing her small town life through photos of the lakeshore, of her friends, of Kyla. The dance routine videos. And, of course, the get-ready-with-me's. In each one, she wears a perfect face of Cook Cosmetics makeup. And everyone ate it *up*. Until something ate her up.

Mikky blinks hard and tells himself that he's not running away as he shoves his way into the gym. The dance squad is standing in formation in the center, their coach holding an iPad against her hip. Kyla stands at the front, gaze caught on Mikky as he hovers in the doorway. He waves a hand and Kyla snaps her attention back straight ahead, locking on to the bleachers.

"Five, six, seven, eight," she barks out.

Mikky shuffles to the bleachers and sits, watching as Kyla attempts to pull absolute excellence out of her teammates even though it's only day one. She's barely breaking a sweat, hitting every mark full out. There's no music, just counting and the squeak of white sneakers against the freshly waxed gymnasium floor. Alicia is at her right but slightly too far back in the formation. There's a notable gap.

As Mikky drops his bag to his feet and starts to get comfortable, the dance team backs up, clapping, leaving Kyla toward the center. She breaks through the hard-hitting solo choreography and Mikky can see every microexpression that Erin used to make as a kid on Kyla's face.

"They were working on this all summer," a voice says. Mikky leans back on the bleachers and looks over.

Jason is freshly showered after soccer practice and his book bag and duffel are dangling off his body. He's trailed by someone Mikky struggles to place. Jason introduces his hanger-on with, "This is Peter."

Peter, Erin's kinda boyfriend. Mikky doesn't look too hard at Peter but can't help one sweep of his eyes. Athletic, broad-shouldered, square-jawed. He looks like someone who would go with Erin. He looks appropriately devastated too. It makes Mikky's teeth hurt, so he looks over at Kyla's precise movements and intense grin.

"Oh?" he asks. "I didn't realize Kyla is the choreographer. Thought it was Coach Jen." He gestures lazily at the tall, unsmiling woman who paces in front of them, holding up an iPad to video so the team can review their performance after.

"You think Erin would let anyone else make the routines for her team with a chance at nationals on the line?" Jason asks in disbelief. "She basically psychologically tortured last year's captain into handing over the reins through passive aggression and bribery. Oh, and Cook samples. Then she and Kyla ran that team like the Navy."

"My sister went along with all that?"

"Kyla was always telling her to take it down a notch before someone snitched to a teacher, but, well, you know how Erin is..."

Mikky doesn't remember Erin as well as he wishes he did. He doesn't remember how Erin would react to the possibility of not being in control. But he can almost picture it. It's like Erin is there, hitting every mark, doing an aerial and slamming down hard in unison with his sister.

"Was. She *was* always good at that. Getting people to do what she wanted," Peter says. He sounds almost fond of her penchant for manipulation. His head briefly sags into his hands, until he forces it back up. The way his stare then seems to linger a beat too long on the dancers' toned, exposed thighs makes Mikky frown. Thankfully, Jason doesn't notice.

"How long did you date Erin?" Mikky asks slowly.

Peter sighs. "We'd been talking since last year. My friends were so pissed that *I* was the one she said 'yes' to when I asked her out, but I mean, she was captain of the dance team. I'm captain of the basketball team. We were like... the dream, man."

Mikky purses his lips. "A strange way to describe the girl you had feelings for."

Peter blinks. "I mean, she was my *dream* girl," he says.

Mikky snorts before he very deliberately turns to Jason. "Kyla's a lot better than she used to be. Remember that summer when they practiced cartwheels in your backyard every single day?"

Jason snorts. "Yeah. Dude, they were *so* annoying. They'd start so early in the morning and Erin was so bossy, I couldn't have friends over to the pool to chill because she'd say they needed the *whole* backyard," he says. Slowly, his smile grows more strained and his shoulders curl in on themselves. "That was the summer Erin sprained her . . . she sprained her wrist."

Mikky remembers how Kyla recounted over dinner with total admiration that Erin didn't cry, not *once*, even though it clearly hurt.

But Jason doesn't look like he's reminiscing anymore. Instead, he's concentrating a little too hard on Kyla. She's fallen back into unison with the other girls, but one of them, maybe Lynn, has drifted too far off her mark. She steps on the back of Kyla's heel and Kyla dips forward.

Lynn rights herself almost immediately, but it's enough to bring the routine to a screeching halt. The dance coach slowly lowers the iPad, sensing the shifting atmosphere. Lynn can't be older than a freshman and she's shaking like a leaf, stammering wildly.

"Oh, sorry, I didn't mean . . . I wasn't watching—"

Kyla circles Lynn slowly, prowling like a predator in search of her next meal. From behind Lynn, she lunges forward and Lynn jumps. Kyla doesn't quite smile, but there's a smug satisfaction on her face at making her teammate flinch without saying a single word. She's not done, though. She circles to the front again, and then grabs the girl by the shoulders, turning her sharply.

"Do you see there?" Kyla asks.

"See . . . see where?" Lynn rasps. Her mouth sounds dry, like there's cotton stuffed in it.

"Right . . . there," Kyla says, lifting her hand, pointing at something nonexistent. "*That's* your mark. Keep your eyes on it. Stay on it."

Kyla claps her hands together and she backs away, staying in Lynn's line of sight. "Now . . . do the last sixteen count that you fucked up for us."

Lynn loses her breath again. "What?"

Kyla's grin is a shark's grin.

It's *Erin's* grin.

"Do the sixteen count for us. So I know you can stay in your spot," Kyla says. She waits, looking at her nails like she has all the time in the world.

Something uncomfortable worms its way into the pit of Mikky's belly. Mikky looks over at Jason. There's something . . . expectant about his stare.

Lynn looks over at their coach, but she's not paying attention, her focus is on the iPad. She isn't the master of this gym, Mikky realizes.

Kyla is.

Kyla snaps. "Look. At. *Me*."

Lynn snaps to attention, rapt. "I'm sorry," she gasps again. But it's too late.

"I'll count you in. Five, six, seven, eight . . ."

And then the girl begins. In. Out. Hip, up. Down. But Lynn is drifting, like she's trying to escape the line of Kyla's sight. Sure enough, the second she's a millimeter out of place, Kyla claps once, stopping her.

"You stepped out of your box. Again," Kyla says.

Lynn starts over. She barely makes it three seconds in, though, before Kyla snarls, "You hit that late. *Again!*"

This is how it goes for the next six minutes. Mikky keeps an eye on the clock as Kyla wrings this girl out. Even from far away, he can hear the ragged sobs of mounting frustration that catch in her throat as Kyla makes her start the combination again. And again. And *again*.

Each time Lynn stumbles, Mikky wants to look away, but he can't. Kyla makes a show of the humiliation, and her team are an eager audience, staring wide-eyed and compliant, practically on the verge of applause. None of it is right. None of it is *Kyla*, and still, she's the one who demands, "Again!"

In the end, the freshman never does get it right. Kyla just gets bored.

"Take a break." Kyla yawns, looking at her nails.

Lynn collapses, strings cut, and she falls to her knees, sweat pouring down her forehead. She looks greasy under the harsh gymnasium lights. Her tinted moisturizer is separating on her forehead and her lip gloss is smeared in her Cupid's bow. Meanwhile, Kyla still looks *perfect*.

"I'm . . . no, I can . . . I can do it," the girl wheezes.

"No, you can't. You're done for the day," Kyla decides. "But you will. Next time, right?"

"*Yes,*" Lynn insists, and that's when Mikky realizes she was set up to fail. He sees it now. Lynn will go home, the humiliation still stinging. She'll shower. Her bones will ache. Her joints will screech. And she will still spend the next ten hours hitting every move until it's perfect so that Kyla never has to spare another glance at her.

Kyla offers a hand and pulls Lynn to her feet. Then pulls her in close.

"And *never ever* step on the back of my heel again," Kyla hisses. "Are we clear?"

"Crystal."

Kyla turns back to her squad. "Are we ready?" she asks.

Alicia clears her throat. "Ready, Captain."

Kyla rolls back her shoulders and Coach Jen looks up from the iPad. Kyla nods once then looks straight ahead. At Mikky.

She doesn't look away. "Five. Six. Five, six, seven, eight . . ."

Finally, they use music, and it's so loud, Mikky feels the bass line in his molars.

This time, not a single person is out of place. Not a hair. They are one unit, a mutated beast of rhythmic motion. And the entire time, Kyla stares at Mikky as if to say, *Look at me, see me*. Mikky sees his little sister now, sees the facets of her he's missed these past three years, and he finds each one equally terrifying.

"So . . . that's what Alicia meant," Mikky says finally.

Jason hums. "Who?" he asks.

"She said that Kyla was acting weird. Has she always been this . . . this *mean*?" Mikky asks. The word seems childish to describe what Kyla is doing, but it's what he's seeing.

"Well, I mean . . . you know how Erin was," Peter says with a shrug.

Mikky frowns. "Okay, but has *Kyla* always been so—" he starts, but before he can finish his line of questioning, the doors of the gymnasium slowly screech open, heavy and resistant.

It's not another student. Or even a teacher.

Two uniformed officers step in and look around. Mikky's elbows land on his knees and he leans forward. The officers attempt to look official, instead of like bumbling small town idiots, which Mikky knows is hard for Prophets Lake cops to do. He watches as the woman—slight and jittery—stalks to the dance team coach and grabs on to her elbow. The coach jumps, nearly dropping the iPad.

"Can I help you?" he thinks she mouths beneath the blasting music.

The officer speaks and it comes out loud as the music suddenly cuts. "—Officer Castellanos. We're looking for a student."

Kyla skids to a stop, frowning. "Coach Jen?" she asks.

For a moment Mikky thinks that student is going to be Kyla. He shakes the worrying thought away but can't help tugging on his ring, fingers darting around.

Coach tilts her head, her mouth hanging open. "What's this about?" she asks. She tries to sound unbothered, but Mikky can hear the soft tremble there. She squints at the male officer.

"Erin Vaughn," the male officer says clumsily.

Officer Castellanos glowers at him and makes a frantic hushing move. But it's too late.

Mikky looks up at Jason. He is *ashen*.

"Erin didn't die at a dance practice. I really don't know how anyone on my team can help any further," Coach Jen says protectively.

"Not your team. We were told that he was heading toward the gym. Is there a Peter Moore around here?" the male officer asks gruffly, alert and watching.

Jason turns in a creaking motion to look at Peter. Peter's hands flex on his knees, shoulders curling in, like that will hide his dimpled chin from the officers. Kyla looks at the bleachers but holds her tongue. Alicia doesn't.

"Peter's . . . isn't that Peter there?" she asks.

Kyla's nostrils flare.

The two officers twist around, finally noticing Peter. The second Officer Castellanos takes a step forward, Peter jerks up and hustles down the stairs, like he can simply brush past them. But the male officer grabs him by the shoulder roughly.

"Don't make a scene," he warns.

Peter gapes, making a cowed sound as he shakes his head. "I have somewhere to be. My dad's, like—"

"Your dad can meet us down at the station. Come on, son," the male officer says.

For a moment Mikky thinks Peter's going to resist. Throw a fit. He looks like the type, somehow. There's an air of . . . entitlement that he can't seem to shake.

He doesn't, though. He looks over at Kyla. Like she can do something. But she just stares back at him, arms folded over her chest, hip cocked, questioning. Almost like she's *daring* him to say . . . something.

"I didn't do anything wrong." Peter balks when he finally breaks eye contact.

Mikky sighs—that's what every guilty person says.

CHAPTER SEVEN

Kyla isn't supposed to work the first week of school, especially the first *day* of school. That's Dad's rule. It's her time to get acclimated to her "new normal," because Dad believes each grade brings a shift from the last. For the first time, Kyla feels there's some truth to that.

Kyla's "new normal" makes her feel like a gaping wound.

There is a hole in her side and Dad may want her to fill it with her brother or her dance team or her homework, but Kyla wants nothing more than to do something with her hands.

This morning, when Kyla drove her brother to school, he sat in the passenger seat, pretending like he belonged there, when really he was sitting in Erin's seat. Kyla pretended too, because if she didn't, he would think something is more wrong than he already does. *Everyone* would think something is wrong, and she can't allow that. So every moment of the day, Kyla told herself that she was fine. She went to class. She sat in the middle of the cafeteria, feeling the weight of every single eye on her, waiting for her to crack so that they could feast on her grief. She gave none of them the satisfaction. Erin was dead—"subdural hematoma, it was quick"—but Kyla was *normal*. Kyla was *fine*.

And then Peter Moore decided to get arrested.

Now Kyla grasps for the "old normal." So Kyla is *going* to

work, no matter what Dad says. She abandons her book bag in her room, briefly glancing at the notification on her lock screen from the dance team group chat: Do they really think Peter had something to do with Erin's death? Isn't that insane? She ignores it.

The Graves Funeral Home is six blocks over and one block up from their house, out on the main street. Kyla used to bike that path when she couldn't drive, and even though now she can, today she prefers to walk. Halfway to the funeral home, the sidewalk disappears so Kyla walks carefully along the curb, one foot in front of the other.

She's outside the door when she remembers she's left Mikky behind at home, alone.

Kyla looks down at her phone and checks to see if he's texted her. He hasn't. What a first day to come back to. Well, she's not his keeper, and he's not *hers*, even if he seems to think so. She'll see him after work.

The funeral home appears on the horizon like a beacon. It's an unassuming building, a white-boarded Georgian-style, with navy-blue shutters. Kyla's grandfather once lived there, in the upstairs portion, with her grandmother, father, and her aunt. Now the Graves Funeral Home is a two-story operation, not a house, but to Kyla it still feels like home. She shoves the dark blue door open and walks past the bright parlor that doubles as the receiving room, into the showroom, where all the caskets lie open, waiting to be purchased.

The employees have gone home for the day, but it's only five thirty, so she knows she'll find who she's actually looking for easily.

Kyla climbs the stairs to the old master bedroom, now her father's office. She hip checks the door open.

"Good afternoon," Kyla deadpans with a finger waggle. "I'm clocking in for my shift, old man." She sidles into the office, rounding the desk to lean against his side. She looks down at his evening coffee and grabs it even as he tries to flick her hand away. Her nose wrinkles—it smells too sweet, sugar crusted on the sides. Just the way Dad likes, and just the way Kyla *hates* it.

Dad shuts his laptop, then sits back against the peeling leather of his weathered chair to just look at her. He looks sad for her. There's no need for it. It doesn't help. It's impractical.

"Don't you have homework to be doing?" he asks gently, shuffling through the papers on his desk. He probably thinks that he's being sly, but she catches him trying to tuck one away from sight. Kyla plucks it from underneath his Funko Pop! of the Grim Reaper and says, "No one gives homework on the first day. What's this?"

She makes out only the bank's letterhead before Dad takes it from her.

"Mind your business," Dad says in one breath, and in the next doesn't mind his. "You know you don't work the first week. Especially not this week. Why are you here?"

Kyla frowns but refuses to be distracted. "Is it the mortgage again?" she asks.

"What did I just say, little girl?" Dad asks back. There's too much kindness in his eyes to be properly intimidating. Too many laugh lines. He reminds her of Mikky in that way. But Kyla is good at being intimidating. She learned from the best. Erin knew how to get what she wanted with honey or a fist.

"Are we behind on it?" Kyla asks firmly, hopping up to sit on the edge of his desk. "Or at a deficit? What is it?"

"Kyla . . . ," Dad groans, dragging his hand down his face.

If they just don't have enough for the month, it's at least fixable. She's put in a lot of work into fixing it, making sure that they're in a financially stable enough place to continue functioning. Sometimes at the expense of Erin.

Kyla is *fine*. She has to be if she has to start everything up again so soon.

"This is all because of that *crematorium*—"

"We're fine," Dad blurts out. "For now. I tried to give a discount but . . . the Vaughns insisted on paying for the works. So, we're fine this month."

"That's good," Kyla says robotically, but her mind is still on the last two words.

"This month," he says. Nothing about next month. Okay. It gives her a little time.

Dad sits up and he looks at her with the sharpest stare that he can, and for once it's so incisive that she feels like she's being flayed wide open like a body on the table.

"Go home, Kyla," he commands.

"Why?" Kyla spits.

"Your best friend . . . Erin is *dead*."

Dad doesn't shy away from the facts around death. It's impossible in the family business. At school, the one thing that no one can seem to do is look Kyla in the eye and say Erin's name. Kyla can say it. She says it every night before she goes to sleep, to make sure that *she* can't forget what it sounds like. "You're on bereavement leave," Dad insists.

Kyla doesn't need bereavement leave. She is bereaved, but that's what she needs leave from, not her job. "I need to work."

Dad looks at her with the air of someone who pities her, or . . . sees her as a child. And Kyla *hates* being seen as a child, even if she technically still is, even by her own father. "You really don't, sweetheart. Go home. Listen to some music. Call Alicia. Talk to your brother," Dad suggests.

Kyla's nose wrinkles at this list of things that would be mostly a waste of her time. She looks away from him, hands balled into fists. She doesn't want to go home. She doesn't want to listen to music. She doesn't want to call *Alicia*.

And Mikky. She can't stand to see the look on Mikky's face, the one he pretends that he hasn't got on his face when she catches him staring. It's like Mikky's forgotten what their father taught them about grief—not everything *means* something. Maybe Kyla said that Erin is lonely. Maybe she said she wanted to be in the ground with her. It doesn't mean she needs him to stop her.

"He's doing homework," Kyla says weakly.

"No, he's not. You just told me that no one assigns homework on the first day, and he just texted me asking where you were. Now go hang out with your brother," Dad commands. "That's not a hardship, is it?"

Kyla glowers at her father but jumps off the desk and stomps to the door. Dad calls after her, "I love you. I'll be home for dinner soon."

For a moment Kyla thinks of saying nothing at all. Then she thinks of a night barely two weeks ago. She looks over her shoulder and says, "I love you too."

Dad's right cheek dimples and Kyla is *fine*.

• • •

"Come in the kitchen! I don't know if Dad told you, but I'm making dinner!"

Kyla's startled by her brother's sudden call as she walks back in. *Did Dad text him?* What else has her father told Mikky about her?

Slowly, she toes off her shoes by the door, making sure they're in the corner so that Dad doesn't trip over them when he gets back home. Kyla considers going up to her room and putting on a record. And then decides against it. She's been avoiding her brother, she can admit that, at least to herself. But doing it tonight doesn't signal that she's fine, and she needs him to think she's fine, especially after dance practice.

The sound of sizzling is tonight's soundtrack in the kitchen. "Oh, shit," Mikky mumbles as he semisuccessfully dumps ground beef into a pan of onions and seasoning while trying to put angel hair pasta in a massive pot of briny water at the same time.

Kyla rolls her eyes. "Do you know how reductive it is that you can't cook?" she asks as she joins him at the stove. "Move. You finish the sauce, I'll put in the pasta. Can you turn on the oven? We have garlic bread in the freezer."

Mikky does as he's told, grinning down at her. He's still in his school clothes but his curls are pineappled atop his head. "Thanks," Mikky says easily as he focuses on the meat with a single-mindedness that . . . doesn't save it from sticking. "Isn't this pan supposed to be nonstick?"

"That's not the problem," Kyla says. She lifts the spoon with a warning, pointing it at Mikky. "*You* have the fire too high and you need a little oil in the pan."

"Heard," Mikky says with a salute, turning down the fire and pouring a little more olive oil in. A soft plume of smoke goes up right into his face, and Mikky turns to cough into his sleeve. It's all comical enough that Kyla cracks a smile without forcing herself to. Mikky catches her before she can hide it away.

"Oh, so she *can* smile?" Mikky taunts.

"Who is 'she'?" Kyla asks.

"Sure, sure," Mikky says easily. He keeps his gaze down on the meat when he says, "I didn't think you'd be working on weekdays."

It feels pointed, like he disapproves. *You think I'd just leave Dad to run the funeral home by himself? Like you did? You think it's bad that I can do my job* and *mourn my best friend? You think that I feel too bad? Then you think that I don't feel bad enough? Am I not performing my grief well enough for you?* Kyla bites back every nasty thing she wants to ask.

"I work at the funeral home whenever Dad needs me to," Kyla says instead as she stirs the pasta into the water with precision.

Mikky gnaws at his bottom lip. "And you get paid?"

Kyla looks up sharply, ignoring the smell of burning butter. "Of *course* Dad pays me. You think he believes in free child labor?" It would probably be beneficial for him to *stop* paying her, but it's fine. She slips that money right back in with the other payments he has no idea she makes.

"I'm making sure that Dad hasn't turned you into a cog in the capitalist machine so early," he sighs with a joking smile.

"I was born into the machine just like the rest of us," Kyla retorts, and Mikky's smile widens.

"Damn right. And we fight against it, yeah?" Mikky pushes.

It's something that he taught her, growing up. He wants it to be something else, another moment to connect, but it tastes bad, like an old memory on her tongue.

"Bleed the rich and don't feel bad about it," she says anyway, because Kyla is fine and fine Kyla *would* say it to him.

Mikky nods. "Exactly. You get it. Okay, I think time for the sauce." He pops open the jar, pouring in what Kyla knows that *he* knows is her favorite sauce and their dad's least favorite. He doesn't look away as he starts, "Kyla . . . ," with an awkward tenderness that grates somehow. Like she needs to be handled with kid gloves.

Kyla grits her teeth, braces for impact. "What?"

"Dance practice was something else. That guy, Peter—"

Kyla isn't expecting *that*. "What about Peter?" she demands.

"He told me he dated Erin. And the cops think he hurt her. I mean . . . they always think it's the boyfriend, but you must've known him too. I wanted to ask if you were okay?"

Kyla does *know* Peter. She hopes that's all Mikky assumes about their relationship. God, the last thing she needs is another person in her business. She nods slowly.

"The cops will do what they do. They'll figure out if it's him or they won't. It won't change what happened, though," Kyla says, looking at the clock over the oven. "I think the oven's been preheating long enough."

Mikky jumps into action. "Let me get the bread."

"I can do it. Pay attention to the sauce," Kyla insists.

But Mikky is already putting down the spoon, splattering the stovetop with red sauce. He doesn't even notice the carnage he's leaving behind. "No, it's fine, I got it—"

"I can get the fucking garlic bread. My best friend is dead, not me."

Mikky doesn't gasp like Dad would, but Kyla wishes he did, to give her something to focus on besides her stomach turning at her own callousness. The self-revulsion bubbles up like vomit and she closes her eyes as she shudders once and her eyes sting. She sticks her head in the freezer as her body temperature rises, then takes a deep breath, fighting against it.

Erin is dead. Kyla is *not*.

Mikky is here. Erin is *not*.

This is the "new normal." It's all turned around. It's all *opposite*. But Kyla is *fine*. She has to be if she's going to pull this lie off.

CHAPTER EIGHT

If the rumor mill is bubbling by the end of homeroom on the second day of school, it's overflowing by lunch. Everywhere Mikky turns, he overhears a new piece of speculation. In the classrooms, the hallways, even the bathrooms. No one is immune, not even Frau Fischer, Mikky's new AP German teacher, who walks alongside an older woman in a smock splattered with drying clay.

"Well, we can't have him back in the school if he's dangerous." Frau Fischer tuts. She hauls her workbag closer to her chest as if Peter might jump out at her from around the next corner and steal it from her.

The other teacher hums her agreement. "Erin was such a lively young girl. It's a shame."

"Did you ever have her as a student?"

"Oh, no. Never even met the poor thing, but you can just *tell*," the art teacher says. "I bet she'd have had an eye for art, you know. Such a little creative."

Mikky doesn't manage to muffle his snort in time.

Frau Fischer's face creases as she glances over her shoulder. Mikky looks up at the ceiling, humming under his breath, but he knows that he's not fooling anyone.

"Junger Herr Graves, ich hoffe, dass du dein Teil der Übersetzung bereit hast," Frau Fischer rattles off in her Boston-accented

German. "Ich glaube, du wurdest die ersten zwei Seiten zugewiesen?"

Mikky clenches his jaw. *Fuck*. He was assigned two pages of translation and of course he hasn't done them. Fuck, fuck, fuck.

"Uh, yes, Frau Fischer, I'm ready," Mikky says, already backing away from the conversation.

"Auf Deutsch, Herr Graves," Frau Fischer commands severely, clearly not forgiving him for eavesdropping.

Over his shoulder, Mikky tosses, "Uh, ja!"

"Shit," Mikky mutters as he tears off from the crowd heading to the lunchroom and starts toward the library instead. With everything that happened and Kyla's insistent refrain to Dad over dinner that "No one gives homework on the first day," Mikky had basically gaslit himself into believing it. Now he has a translation to rush through.

He nearly spirals—it's just like last time. All his painstaking organization, his plans, will be for nothing and he won't do well and he won't find any friends and Kyla will blow up at him again—and then he breathes through it, managing his expectations. Mikky counts as he inhales, then exhales as he rationalizes with himself.

Next time, Mikky won't forget his German homework until right before the period it's due, because next time, he's going to *actually* consult his planner. As his heart rate comes down, Mikky reminds himself that it's one day—just one lunch that he's missing. And he'll see Kyla after school. At home. Then he reasons with himself that if neither teacher wanted him to eavesdrop, they shouldn't have been gossiping just as loud as the rest of the students.

Despite his breathing exercises, Mikky's a little out of breath when he reaches the third floor, and he takes a moment to let his chest stop burning before he enters the library.

Mikky expects absolute silence but instead finds the dull roar of whispers coalescing into a lively atmosphere, different from the tomb-like silence of the very first day. All the life sounds push away the dull ache that sits heavy in his belly. But as he stands by the librarian's desk, he notes every table is occupied and he's not feeling friendly.

"Library's a popular place," the librarian says apologetically.

Mikky frowns, folding his arms over his chest, and then he stops when he spots a familiar-ish face. "No, it's fine," he says distractedly. "I see someone."

Mikky beelines between the crowded tables, jumping over one black backpack tossed carelessly in the middle of a walkway. He wheels to a stop at the edge of a table. No one else has dared to sit here with Nasim because it would mean asking him to clear away all his books. Each is opened to a random page, giving the illusion that he's looking at them all, but on closer inspection, Mikky sees that each is on a different subject. It's a clever way to keep people away. It's just too bad for Nasim that Mikky is well versed in ignoring unspoken social cues when he wants to.

"Hey," Mikky says. He takes a beat, pretending to snap to remember. "Uh, Nasim, right?"

Nasim looks up at him, almost offended. Mikky has to bite the inside of his cheek to keep from smiling. Nasim leans back in his seat, arms folded over his chest.

"Do you need something?" he asks, loftily.

"You mind if I sit? It's weirdly crowded in here," Mikky says, gesturing wildly at the library. It's in a part of the school Mikky can't remember all that well. Mikky never joined any clubs or sports when he was here. No extracurriculars, even though his parents had encouraged him to find *something*, like maybe band, since he played guitar. All his middle-school friends had found their niche with what seemed like ease. But Mikky's brain had simply given up, repeating endlessly that his friends from middle school would leave him behind, that he'd have no one, he'd be no one. The only thing that had made everything go quiet was to go smoke behind the bleachers like a cliché and peel the nail polish from his fingernails and then move on to his cuticles like the nervous wreck he was well on his way to becoming.

Nasim looks like he wants to say that he does mind. But he doesn't do that. Instead, he warns, "I'm taking a practice quiz so you have to be quiet."

"You have homework too? Someone told me no one gives homework on the first day but . . . ," Mikky says, already unzipping his bag and setting it on the table next to him. He flips open his planner and, yup, there it is. The assignment.

Nasim is looking pointedly at his practice quiz, so Mikky goes to work examining the short story. Luckily, Mikky realizes he doesn't necessarily need to write everything down. He can probably translate from sight reading, there are just a few vocabulary words that he's not so sure of. He squints down at the words, preparing to prove himself more than capable. Then—

"German? You take *German*?"

Mikky looks up with a raised eyebrow. "*AP* German, actually. Thoughts?"

"Why would I have thoughts?" Nasim asks. He's staring way

too hard at his precalc textbook, which makes Mikky curious enough to abandon his homework for the moment.

"I don't know," Mikky says. He sets down his pen and leans forward, propping his chin up on a fist. "Is the German surprising?"

"There are like five people in that class. Yeah, it's surprising," Nasim snaps.

"Well, what language do *you* take?" Mikky asks.

Nasim shuts his textbook, giving up the pretense that he's studying at all. He leans forward in his seat and his glasses slip down the slope of his nose. He doesn't make a move to adjust them and instead stares at Mikky severely over the rims, giving him such a teacher look, Mikky has to smother another laugh.

"I take Spanish. A practical language," Nasim says.

"How do you know German isn't practical for *my* plans in the future?" Mikky asks. For once, Nasim considers his words seriously.

"Well, is it?"

Mikky's always had an interest in linguistics, the roots of languages, all of that. He *could* explain that, but it's not nearly as fun as saying—

"No. But my favorite metal band is from Germany. They have a Black front man. It's *super* cool," Mikky explains, leaning back.

Nasim squints. "So, this isn't . . . pretend?" he asks, waving his hand at Mikky's ensemble.

Personally, Mikky thinks he looks good. He's on day three hair—best day. He skipped the lipstick today and just went with eyeliner and he's got his favorite nose stud in, the one that looks like a squiggle on his nostril. He's foregone his lip ring, though, because he has gym sixth period, and nothing hurts worse than a Wiffle ball to the lip ring.

"You think I'd invest time and money in body modification for a bit?" Mikky asks.

Nasim shrugs. "I don't know you. I don't know how far you'd go for a bit."

"Not *that* far," Mikky says.

Nasim rubs his chin, properly curious now. "Which one was first?"

Mikky bites down on his tongue, worrying his piercing with his teeth. He sees Nasim's gaze flicker down curiously at it and Mikky grins. "You're not at the level yet to unlock that kind of lore."

Nasim looks put out.

It's kinda cute.

Before he can get properly up in arms about it, though, they're—unfortunately—interrupted.

"Dude, we've been looking everywhere . . . for . . . you . . ." Nasim's lab partner, a short plaid-clad kid with sandy brown curls, trails off as he takes Mikky in.

Mikky wiggles his fingers in greeting. "Hello there, fellow classmate."

"Uh . . . 'sup, dude," the other kid with the lab partner says, looking uncertainly back over at Nasim.

"Sit, sit, I thought Nasim was all alone and was keeping him company, but I see he was just waiting. Join us," Mikky says, making it very clear that he doesn't plan to go anywhere.

"You're late," Nasim says derisively.

"Sorry, sorry, we know," the lab partner says, with an air of having heard Nasim's complaints time and again. "We were hungry. Went to grab something from the caf. Chicken nuggets?" He pulls a Styrofoam container from his bag and shakes it at Nasim.

"Thanks, no thanks," Nasim says. "I've been eating cereal bars all day. I've got too much to do."

The lab partner shrugs. "More for me," he says. Then he folds onto his chair in an exceptionally uncomfortable way and nods at Mikky. "I'm Gregory, he/him. I didn't get a chance to introduce myself yesterday. And this is Rowan, they/them."

Rowan doesn't bother to speak. Or take off their sunglasses. Or even really look at Mikky, now that Mikky thinks about it. Rowan just sits down in their oversized clothing, jaw clenched and sharp. They'll get jaw tension that way but that's not Mikky's problem.

"Mikky, he/him," he introduces himself. "I'm working on my German homework."

Rowan looks up sharply. "You're in German 301 too? We're not in the same section, I don't think."

"No, we're not. I'm in the AP course." Mikky raises an eyebrow at Nasim. "You made it seem like no one was taking German," he accuses. Nasim shrugs and Gregory already looks tired of discussing schoolwork. He leans forward, looking Mikky up and down. *Here we go again*, Mikky thinks.

Before Gregory can ask Mikky whatever strange insensitive thing he wants to ask, Rowan leans toward Nasim and says, "Vibes in the cafeteria were so off."

Gregory's stare snaps away, properly distracted, and his head bobbles. "Oh, yeah, man, just so, so *dark*. Everyone was talking about Peter getting arrested yesterday. Erin's, like, gone, man. And for it to be her boyfriend?"

Mikky is careful not to divulge what he knows, looking down at his work again, adding another translation in the margin for when he has to read aloud.

"Yeah, well," Nasim says. He's almost clinical in his dismissal of the entire situation, like he could not care less about Peter and even *less* about Erin, if that were possible.

"They said it happened in front of the dance team," Rowan says anyway, trying to sound unaffected, but they don't quite pull it off. "As in, Kyla saw it happen."

There's a break in the conversation, an awkward one, and Mikky finally looks up. The three are all staring at him, as if just realizing that talking about Kyla Graves in front of Kyla Graves's brother might be a little weird.

"She did," Mikky allows. He doesn't add, *I did too*. Gregory opens his mouth. Closes it again. Sighing, Mikky prompts, "What about it?"

"So . . . what's it like to be Kyla Graves's big brother?" Gregory blurts out.

Well. Mikky *wasn't* expecting that. He can admit when he's wrong.

"Dude . . . what?" Mikky asks.

Nasim groans, pinching the bridge of his nose.

"What . . . is . . . it . . . *like* to be Kyla Graves's brother?" Gregory asks, like Mikky is stupid, which he certainly isn't.

"Uh . . . normal? She's just Kyla." Or she was. Now he's not so sure.

"But what's that *like*?" Gregory insists.

Mikky's nose wrinkles as he actually considers the odd question.

"She's my little sister. We get along. Really well, usually." Mikky shrugs. "Contrary to the common consensus of American television, we're not the siblings that fight and get into physical altercations. We've never been like that. She's Kyla. She's baby."

"My baby," his parents say he called her when she was an infant and he was barely a toddler. He'd hobble over on chunky little legs asking for his *baby*.

But it's different, being her brother in person versus over the phone. In person, Kyla is far more prickly than he remembers. Kyla from before wasn't softer, but she wasn't cold. Sometimes, when he looks at her now, he's surprised that there's not frost in her eyes.

Gregory looks disappointed by the answer. "Oh . . . I never imagined Kyla as, like, a baby. She seems like she'd have come out fully formed."

"Gregory, you're insipid," Nasim sighs.

"Okay, SAT words," Gregory retorts.

Nasim ignores this and looks over at Mikky, like he's weighing his options, before saying, "Gregory is fascinated by your sister. That's why he's asking."

"Fascinated?" Mikky asks sharply. "She's not a zoo animal."

Gregory sputters. "She's gorgeous—"

"Maybe, but she sure is feral," Rowan mutters under their breath.

Mikky sits up immediately. "What did you say about my sister?" he asks coldly.

Rowan's cool exterior cracks. They go ashen. "No, I didn't mean—"

"No. Explain yourself. What do you mean by calling her 'feral'?" Mikky demands.

Gregory holds up his hands in mock surrender. "I think they mean that your sister is intense. No harm, no foul."

"She's passionate," Mikky defends, tone flat.

"Sure," Rowan says. "That's a nice way to put it."

"And the not-nice way?" Mikky pushes. "Besides 'feral.'"

"They were mean. Erin and Kyla. They were *mean*," Rowan says with relish, like they know from firsthand experience.

Mikky's emotions war between irritation and curiosity. Erin being mean isn't surprising. *Kyla* being lumped in still is to him. A defense sits ready at the tip of Mikky's tongue, and then he regains control to wait it out. He's wanted answers since the dance practice. And there's something about the way they talk about her, on the edge of loathing and terror.

"*Erin* was the mean one. She . . . she just had to have her way, and if she didn't, if *you* were the obstacle, she'd obliterate you," Gregory insists. "It was never Kyla. She just—"

"Did nothing to stop it," Nasim interjects. "She was indifferent. She'd watch while Erin would just *destroy* someone for fun."

Gregory gnaws on his lip. "Doesn't mean Kyla's the problem, though."

Rowan's mouth puckers like they don't quite agree, and they add, "She might become a bigger problem than Erin, though."

Mikky's racing mind reframes everything as he waits, but they don't elaborate.

He sinks into his chair, and cuts a look at Rowan. "Interesting. Doesn't mean you get to call her 'feral,' though. She's not an *animal*."

Rowan shrinks into their chair like they want to disappear.

"I'm sorry," they say.

Mikky doesn't *accept* the apology. But he doesn't leave, either.

Because their perspective on Kyla—and by extension, Erin—just made things a whole lot more interesting. Clearly, Erin isn't as missed as Mikky thought she was, nor was she quite as loved. Mikky knows Erin's death wasn't an accident, but now her behavior—and Kyla's acceptance of it—gives a lot more weight to the idea that maybe the person responsible is closer to home.

CHAPTER NINE

Kyla doesn't remember the day of Erin's funeral except in short bursts. She remembers bits of the pastor's sermon, all about lives cut short and being given unto the Lord for safekeeping. She remembers the procession, when they all marched around the casket and she kissed Erin's cold cheek. She remembers how she hadn't been able to find Erin's scent—roses and cedar all layered like the garden of Eden. And she remembers getting the notification that the vultures, those fine-boned gawkers Erin was mutuals with, were going live from outside the community center. Mostly, she remembers Mikky.

Everything she doesn't remember in between, Alicia remembers for her. Kyla used to affectionately call her a wind-up doll in private. Erin was more blunt about it. She found Alicia, first and foremost, annoying. She would call Alicia her cracker-eating bitch. Alicia could theoretically do something as innocuous as eat a cracker and Erin would find it rage-inducing. But Erin put up with it because Alicia was of use to her.

Kyla needs Alicia's memory now. It's the only reason she's trying not to imagine sewing Alicia's lips shut to stop all her yapping. She doesn't call her out on it—Kyla knows that she wasn't the kindest about her dance practice objections on the first day. As an apology of sorts, Kyla lets Alicia's words fade into a strange monotone drone that accompanies her all the way to her locker, where she switches out her trig textbook for the novel they're reading in their English elective—her mother's old favorite. Kyla reconsidered her class choice when she saw *Frankenstein* was at the top of the curriculum for Science, Fiction, and the Beyond. Then she'd resigned herself; she's already read it anyway. More times than she can count.

Kyla shuts her locker and turns to walk to English, her second class of the day. Alicia still going on and on.

"—I thought that I had seen that sweater before, and Kyla, I *swear* Thomas Gatlin is cheating on his girlfriend with Penny Dreyfuss," Alicia concludes as they get to the door. She sucks in a long, wet breath, having expelled every bit of air in her monologue, and Kyla jumps in before she can continue talking about people that Kyla doesn't care about.

God, it used to be so easy for Kyla to at least pretend to care. She can't even manage that anymore.

"We're here," Kyla announces to her English teacher, Ms. Blosser.

"Just on time," the woman says in her singsong voice.

Kyla walks to the back of the classroom, joining Sabrina. Sabrina and Kyla have never been super close necessarily, but she likes her. Unlike Alicia, Kyla, and practically everyone else, Sabrina didn't grow up in Prophets Lake. She moved last year, when her dad got transferred to the Cook Cosmetics headquarters from the London office. She was a hot commodity when she transferred. The boys had eaten her up. Erin hadn't liked that. Hadn't liked *her*.

But since Kyla did, Erin had to put up with her, and Kyla

likes her even more now. She serves as a good buffer for when Alicia is talking too much for Kyla to ignore. She brightens as she sees them, her rosy, freckled cheeks growing bigger with her smile.

"Ky, did you do the trig homework?" she asks with that sweet, crisp tone. She's the only person who has ever gotten away with shortening Kyla's name. Not even Erin could do that—not that she'd ever want to—and it's only because Sabrina shortens everyone's name but her own. Kyla feels differently about it now.

Kyla purses her lips. "Yes, but I'm certainly not passing it along to you," she says. "And it's *Kyla*."

"Since when?" Sabrina pouts and slumps in her chair.

"Since I was born," Kyla retorts snippily.

"First I forget my trig homework; now you won't let me call you 'Ky,'" Sabrina sighs. "*Ugh*, and our teacher hates me. She'll give me a demerit, I swear."

Kyla gives her that. Their trig teacher is one of *those* teachers. The kind who loves to joke around with the boys, call them her favorites, and sneer at any girl that might dare to have a question. Kyla can sniff out a loser who peaked in high school a mile away.

"Well, I *might* consider helping you during my free period."

"Thank you," Sabrina says in earnest, bouncing at the quiet promise.

"For a price," Kyla finishes.

Sabrina narrows her eyes. "I'll buy you lunch. It's Chicken Caesar Salad day. I'll even give you my extra garlic bread."

"Deal. But I want a Diet Coke with it," Kyla says.

"Worm, man. I'll get you a Diet Coke." Sabrina sniffs like the idea of anything else is ridiculous. Alicia shakes back and forth in her seat, itching to hear the sound of her own voice again. Sabrina notices and far more patiently than Kyla ever could, she says, "Have something to share, Leesh?"

"Peter was released Tuesday night. They couldn't hold him for long," Alicia says, a little quieter than before. "He should be back in school today. His parents let him take a chill day yesterday because of the excitement, but . . . yeah. He'll be here."

Kyla freezes. Slowly, she goes back through everything Alicia has told her since they met in the parking lot. Something-something about a teen drama on Netflix. Something-something about someone cheating on someone else. Nothing about Peter.

"You really buried the lede," Kyla accuses.

Alicia shrugs. "I was waiting until it was the three of us. Everyone's been staring at us all morning."

Kyla didn't notice that, either. It's not unusual that they're stared at. Erin said it was good to be stared at—it meant that they were beautiful, popular, undeniable. Now when she notices it, though, she feels like she's under a microscope. Kyla can't tell if they're searching her for clues or just signs of grief.

"So, they think it's him? Since he's the boyfriend?" Sabrina asks.

"Boyfriend's a stretch," Alicia titters.

Erin had never told Kyla that she started dating Peter. Kyla had just found out. One day, tired of waiting to drive Erin home after school since Erin had failed her driver's test *again*, she had walked in on them making out by the locker rooms.

In the car ride on the way home, Kyla had said, "This is beneath you."

"He *is* beneath me," Erin had leered. "Or he will be."

Kyla's disgust had nearly physically manifested itself on her dashboard. "Since when have you been interested in Peter *Moore*?" she demanded. "What do you even have to talk about? His head is literally empty. He's barely qualified to be our errand boy."

That's what he'd been at the time. He knew where to get the good shit.

But Erin had just picked at her cuticles before saying, "It's not about what *he* has to say. It's about what everyone *else* will say. And who will hear it. Plus, he's Superman. He'll look good on my feed. Everyone's gonna be *so* jealous, and Mom actually admitted that I *am* boosting sales. She sounded so pissed when she told me." Erin sounds *gleeful* about her mother's misery.

"Desperate," Kyla had said, softening the word just enough for it to be almost a joke. And then she'd taken Erin's hand and kissed her knuckles before she'd driven them to Dunkin', because Erin's success called for celebratory donuts and an iced coffee.

Sabrina shakes her head. "I'm just saying, it's always the boyfriend, label or no label. You know how Peter was. So *needy*. She couldn't stand it. Maybe she finally told him and he, like . . . cracked."

Alicia winces, dramatically rubbing at the goose pimples on her arms. "God, that's so creepy," she moans. "They were asking about where he was the night of . . . you know. Erin's . . ."

"Murder?" Sabrina says. *Finally.* Someone names it what it is. She'd be relieved if the first part didn't make her blood run cold.

"Anyway, you're just, like . . . what's it called in those cop shows? Speculating, or whatever. Plus, he got released. We don't even know what the cops had on him or if they *did* have something on him. I wish we knew someone at the station. Do we?"

Alicia sounds irate at being denied information. As if this is just more petty gossip for her to feast upon.

"Why would we need to know?" Sabrina asks.

"Because, like, what if he says something about the . . . you know—"

"Be quiet," Kyla says sharply. Alicia falls silent for once.

Kyla doesn't want to think about that night or Peter or Erin at all, because when she does, her lungs tighten and she can't *breathe*—

Kyla pinches the visible skin on her thigh, digging her fake nails in until the skin flushes red. No one will notice the bruise. Kyla is usually covered in them, from failed tumbles or bumping into sharp edges practicing in her room.

". . . Kyla? Kyla, are you okay?"

Kyla looks up sharply, meeting Alicia's eyes. Her enthusiasm has dampened into worry and Kyla feels her skin itch worse at *that* than the forming bruise.

"I'm fab," Kyla says.

Alicia nods slowly, not quite accepting Kyla's words. She hates that. If Erin had said it, Alicia would have taken it as gospel. Erin was *Jesus* to this girl. But without Erin here, Alicia thinks she can question Kyla, or worse, become her equal. Kyla doesn't need that. She doesn't need someone who asks her if she's *okay*. She doesn't need someone to tell her to *chill*. She doesn't need someone to dull the sharpness of her so that she's easier for the rest of the world to handle. Kyla doesn't need a carbon copy of who she used to be.

Kyla needs a cracker-eating bitch.

"We don't know anyone at the station," Kyla announces,

looking at both of them. "But there are other ways to get information. I'll figure all of this out." She turns back to face the front, feigning interest in the English lesson Ms. Blosser is picking her way through.

Alicia leans in, eager to hear Kyla's plans. But Kyla keeps them close to her chest, and Alicia and Sabrina wait for her command. It's a heady thing, their trust. *Powerful*, strong enough to curb any sense of anxiety around Peter Moore. For now.

The bell rings and Kyla grabs her bag. She takes her time packing up, shifts her eyes to the prize. This other girl—Kyla's prey—doesn't even notice that she's being watched, despite *stinking* of the desperation to be looked at.

"I'll see you both at lunch," Kyla says dismissively when Alicia pauses like she's going to wait for her.

Alicia hates being dismissed, and she takes a beat longer than she would have with Erin, but eventually she scurries off to her next class with Sabrina. Then Kyla follows the girl who'll give her all the information she needs out of the room, a few paces behind. They're the last out of the classroom, which is perfect.

"Indigo," Kyla calls. Summons. She watches the class president's shoulders tense. Kyla knows she's fixing her expression into something less eager.

Indigo Glass has too large of a chip on her shoulder for how accomplished she is. Student UN champion, AP connoisseur, class president, and not a bad face to match. In some circles, Indigo would even be considered pretty, which is good because pretty people tend to do better in life. This isn't something Kyla believes to be right, of course, but it's a fact of life. One of the many Mrs. Vaughn had been good enough to teach Kyla as well as Erin since

Kyla's mom hadn't bothered to be around to do it. "Pretty privilege is a real thing, girls," she'd said, "and the more you have, the higher you'll climb, that's what makeup is for. Power." Indigo has a moderate amount, but every day she practices her eyeliner and her blush placement, she gains more. She owes that to Kyla and Kyla looks forward to reminding her of that.

Indigo turns on her heel to face her and brushes away her wispy braids, attempting to affect a casualness that doesn't suit her. Kyla catalogs her. She's wearing the Cook Cosmetics Bright-Eyed and Bare Tinted Moisturizer. It's the new formulation, Kyla can tell by how it's sitting on Indigo's dry patches where she skimped on her primer. Her brows are full and fluffy, just touching her bangs, which are . . . a choice, but maybe she's going through something. Let Kyla not be the one to throw the first stone, at least not this time; she can't say that she hasn't considered bangs these past few weeks. She's already cut some onto her favorite dance wig.

"Kyla," Indigo says, dragging out her name with a false sympathy. "I haven't had a chance to speak with you. I'm so sorry—"

"Let's not do this," Kyla interrupts. She takes a step closer and is thrilled when Indigo mirrors her, tilting her head forward. "I want to talk to you about something."

"Me?" Indigo asks, immediately smug.

She's getting off on this. Really, she should fix her attitude and be *thankful* that Kyla injects some excitement into her little try-hard life.

"I'm sure you've heard about Peter Moore's arrest," Kyla says plainly. "What do you know?"

Indigo seems thrown by the question. Kyla is usually the smooth talker. The one who talks in circles before getting to the real business. But she's tired of honey now and goes straight for the jugular.

Indigo frowns. "Why would I know anything about that?"

"Because you're always in literally everyone's business, Indigo," Kyla says impatiently, and Indigo actually has the nerve to be offended, like Erin didn't catch her with a Notes app full of everyone's weaselly secrets.

"I would think *you* would know, considering . . . Your house not in order?" Indigo asks.

Kyla thinks about making her regret that. She thinks about what Erin would say.

"Obviously I'm trying to reestablish said order. Anyway, even if you don't know, I figure your brother might, he's down at the police station often enough—" she says.

"Fuck you," Indigo growls out.

Kyla pauses. "It wasn't meant to be an insult, it's just a fact," she says. A fact that makes him useful. Indigo's brother is considered mostly harmless, usually in trouble just for disturbing the peace, but that's because the police are too stupid to ask enough questions to find out the other things that he occasionally gets up to. "Now, walk with me."

Indigo swallows hard, eyes wandering. "Whatever. What does my brother have to do with this?" She dutifully follows Kyla to her locker. It's like she doesn't even notice how easily she does as she's told.

"I want to know if he's heard anything about why the police think that Peter had something to do with Erin's death," Kyla explains.

Indigo looks at Kyla's ear as she says, "Maybe he did. He's her boyfriend."

If only Indigo knew.

"It's always—" *The boyfriend,* she braces to hear yet again.

In most cases, Kyla would agree. But she knows what Peter Moore is made of. Spineless. Gutless. He doesn't have it in him. It's what made him perfect as Erin's boy toy. A living Ken doll to pose next to for the photos then discard to do what she really wanted. Who she really wanted without anyone saying shit. Whatever. It's also what makes him dangerous now, but not to Erin. To her.

"I don't care what *you* think. I want to know what the *cops* think," Kyla says.

Indigo frowns. "I haven't seen him yet today. Anyway, why should I ask him? What are you gonna do for me?"

Kyla sighs. "You seem to misunderstand what's being asked of you."

"How so?" Indigo asks. "You want a favor? Quid pro quo, Kyla."

If she were Erin, Indigo would have folded by now. Most people did when on the end of one of Erin's frigid stares. Kyla can pretend all she likes, but she *isn't* Erin. Not yet.

"You know what . . . never mind. Go on your way, Indigo Glass," Kyla says dismissively. She doesn't bother smiling, because it's a waste of her energy, just like this girl.

Kyla turns back to her locker and makes a show of unlocking it, even though all her books are in her bag already.

In her hindbrain, she hears Erin like she's standing there, right behind her shoulder, hissing poison into her ear: *Indigo Glass doesn't just want your attention. She wants to be* worthy *of it. Let her feel unworthy and she is putty. She's pudding. Then feast, Duck.*

Kyla doesn't have to wait long. She barely has her locker open when Indigo clears her throat, shifting awkwardly behind her. Kyla glances over her shoulder with a look that she hopes says, *Oh, you're still here?*

"Fine, I'll do it, but, um, Kyla . . . when are you hosting again?" Indigo asks seriously. She's trying not to touch her chin—the dry patch—self-consciously, but every time her hand flutters up and she forces it down, it brings attention to it.

"Don't worry about it," Kyla says.

Indigo hesitates but then blurts out, "I just feel like I'm not getting what I'm literally paying for. You said more of the good stuff was coming. Like, I get that you're fucked up after what happened, but Test Kitchen—"

The words are a trigger. Kyla reaches out, grabbing Indigo by the arm and jerking her close until they're in each other's faces. Indigo's eyes go wide behind her purple frames.

"Get *off* me," she sputters, and Kyla presses one finger to her lip-gloss-sticky lips.

"Not until you shut up," Kyla says carefully. She doesn't raise her voice. She doesn't whisper. She just speaks as if everything is normal. "Don't talk about that shit here."

"Then when?" Indigo mumbles.

"I don't know, but you know not to talk about our shit here," Kyla says. She releases Indigo and ignores the angry red on the girl's arm. It's irritated, like Kyla, but it wasn't hard enough to bruise. "That's the rule."

"Kyla, but if Erin's—"

"It's *my* rule, and *I'm* in charge now," Kyla snarls. "When I make a rule, it's law. You get me?"

Indigo nods slowly.

Kyla takes a step back. "Give your degenerate brother a call and find out what the police know and how they know it and I'll give you something good. You understand me?"

Indigo nods. "By homeroom tomorrow," she says like she got the last word.

Kyla allows her the luxury of thinking that for now and lets her walk off to wherever the Indigo Glasses of the world go. Kyla turns on her heel, determined to rush to class, and hopefully avoid anyone who might wonder what she had to say to Indigo. She only makes it two steps, though, before someone cuts directly into her path. Kyla drags her stare up from the ground, lips already curling back from her teeth.

She takes in tanned, scabbed legs, the ragged hem of cargo shorts, a Manchester United shirt. She gets all the way to his broad shoulders before she recognizes who it is and then she's quick to meet his sometimes-hazel, mostly green eyes. Kyla has always been equally thrilled and disgusted by the way Jason Vaughn can see right through her. She tips more toward disgusted now that Erin isn't here to buffer it. She folds her arms over her chest, immediately cutting herself off from his all-knowing gaze.

"You're friends with Indigo Glass?" Jason asks.

Damn it.

"You can't be serious."

Jason raises an eyebrow. "What? I just saw you talking to her, and I have literally never seen you guys interact."

"No, I'm not friends with *Indigo Glass*," Kyla bites out. She can already hear Jason gearing up to ask what they were talking about then, and she racks her brain, searching until— "We're in

English together and I wanted to know which character she was picking for her analysis of the text this week."

Jason accepts Kyla's words easily. He has no reason to doubt her.

"Okay," Jason says, his smile toward her widening.

"What?" Kyla asks brusquely.

"What are you doing for lunch?"

She raises an eyebrow. "Getting lunch with my squad like always. Why?"

"You wanna sit with me, instead?"

"With you and your table of boorish soccer players? I'll pass. But you can sit with *me* if you miss my company so much," Kyla says. She can hear the teasing in his voice, can feel herself leaning closer, and if she closes her eyes, can imagine Erin standing there, making fake gagging noises.

The flirtation isn't new. Kyla has always found Jason attractive. For her it was *there* and obvious but insurmountable, because there was always Erin, and Kyla was loyal. Kyla knew that you weren't supposed to go after your best friend's brother. At least, that's what Google had told her when she'd had a moment of weakness in eighth grade and suddenly Jason was growing into his shoulders and there were rumors that he was skipping JV soccer and going straight to varsity as a freshman. Which he had.

In fact, it's all so normal for them that it makes Kyla sick. Nothing will ever be normal again. She wishes that she could take those words back, swallow them up, and shit them out, so that they would disappear into the sewer.

"Sit with you and your vapid dance team? I'm good," Jason ribs.

"Then we're at an impasse. Goodbye—"

"I meant just us," Jason says.

Kyla wants to say yes. She wants to sit with Jason at an empty table and talk about nothing or maybe sit in silence. She wants to stew in the grief she knows he shares, or maybe, ignore it together too. But she can't. There are more pressing things to take care of. Motives to uncover. Secrets to bury.

Very carefully, she says, "I don't want to sit in the middle of the lunchroom with you and have a broken kumbaya over our loss for everyone else to see and dissect like vultures." She doesn't say it to be mean. But that's what everyone would do. Even Alicia. Even Sabrina. Still, he looks hurt by it. Almost childishly, Kyla pokes him in the cheek and tries to give him what she thinks could be, should be, a smile that looks like her old one. "Goodbye, Jason."

CHAPTER TEN

Peter Moore is back in school by AP Euro, Kyla's last class before lunch, and he doesn't have the energy of a boy who's just been questioned for murder. He's way too relaxed, ignoring their teacher's lecture on the Protestant Reformation and everyone giving him a wide berth, casting doubtful, suspicious looks his way. All of it rolls off Peter's back. Kyla understands why. His father is one of the partners at the only law firm in town. His mother works for the legal team at Cook Cosmetics. He's captain of the basketball team, and until as recently as three weeks ago, he was dating the most popular girl in school. In short, he's used to sitting pretty and shitting gold.

"Okay, everyone. I want you to break out into pairs so that you can discuss Martin Luther's theological concerns that prompted his challenging of the Catholic Church for the next five minutes. Go on. You need to be prepared to share your conclusions at the end of that discussion."

Kyla is out of her seat before she thinks better of it, cutting across to the other side of the classroom while Peter peers around, searching for his little basketball buddy. Said basketball buddy is looking everywhere *but* at Peter. Kyla moves quickly, so fast that she accidentally kicks another student's backpack over.

"Hey!" the owner of said backpack snarks.

Kyla looks over her shoulder, flatly tossing, "Sorry," before she stops in front of Peter, arms folded over her chest. "We should work together."

Kyla has never said those words to Peter in her entire life. Knowing that, she allows him the thirty seconds it takes him to process her not-suggestion.

"Uh, sure," he croaks, rolling with this, too. Erin liked that about him. She thought he was a bit like Play-Doh. She could squish him into the shape that she liked and make him talk and dance. Her puppet.

Kyla doesn't think Peter ever knew that. She doubts it, but she also doubts it was all that much more real for him, despite his overwrought reaction. Kyla doesn't buy it. She slips into the seat next to Peter's and tilts her head.

"You should be thanking me right now," Kyla says.

Peter jerks, looking at the tip of her nose. "Why?"

"Because the only thing saving you from social death is that I've deigned to talk to you," she says. She doesn't have to look around to know it's true. Everyone will still regard Peter with caution, especially with every cliché working against him, but Kyla's presence grants him a slight reprieve.

"You *know* I didn't do it."

"You didn't?" Kyla pushes, leaning over into Peter's personal space. He seems uncomfortable, but he's a *boy*. He's a tough guy. He refuses to let it show, except for how he can't meet her eyes. "I don't know, you seem a little guilty."

"I'm not," he says shortly.

"And you were able to convince the police of that?"

"I was," Peter says, his breathing coming slower.

"And how were you able to do that?" Kyla says, drumming her fingers against the edge of Peter's desk. She lowers her voice to barely above a whisper, dragging her nails over where someone has carved their name into the desk. The desks are brand-new, paid for with Cook money, and someone's ruined one already. "When they asked you where you were that night, did you tell them? When they asked you why Erin was at the lake, did you say why? When they asked you if . . . Erin had any enemies, did you say who?"

Peter finally, *finally*, meets her eyes. They're blue. Now Kyla knows why Erin called him "Superman."

"Kyla, I didn't say shit, because I didn't *do* shit," Peter snaps. "I didn't see Erin that night. I was in a friend's backyard with the entire varsity basketball team, hazing this year's JV squad wannabes. The last time I even saw Erin was the week before. We went on a lame date to get ice cream. She told me she would be busy that week, she didn't want me at . . . you know, the thing, which I didn't mention by the way, because you guys had enough *stuff* from last time, so I had no reason to even *be* by the lake. Is that what you want to hear? Did I pass the test?"

Kyla smiles. "A-plus. Good job, Peter. For extra credit, keep quiet about Erin."

She prepares to get up, to walk away without even talking about the Protestant Reformation, but Peter reaches out to grab her wrist.

"What?" Kyla asks.

"The cops got my name from *someone*," Peter says, and for the first time he sounds shaken. "Someone thinks I hurt Erin."

"They always suspect the boyfriend. Don't take it personal," Kyla says.

Peter shakes his head. "This *was* personal. Someone at the school reported me. Hamish let it slip when my dad came and threatened to tear the police department a new one for questioning me without him, because I'm a minor. I want to know who," Peter says.

Kyla shakes her head. "Peter, I'm already ahead of you." She hopes, anyway.

This time she doesn't let him stop her as she goes to evict whatever poor soul thought to sit in her seat. Peter isn't nearly as stupid as she thought he was. He didn't say anything Kyla didn't want him to.

Maybe Erin was right about him. Erin liked to say that she was always right. She and Kyla would argue about it, trade their rights and wrongs back and forth.

But she had to have been wrong about something. Otherwise, she wouldn't have ended up dead.

Kyla regrets not agreeing to lunch with Jason when Sabrina and Alicia show up without even a sliver of new information. They each try to offer morsels of gossip. Some freshman nervously vomited all over the girl's locker room. Two sophomores were caught hooking up in one of the science classrooms and singed their sweaters when they accidentally turned on a Bunsen burner. None of the information is relevant to who reported Peter or why.

Kyla slowly chews her salad, purposely not masking how unimpressed she is. The anxiety rolls off Alicia and instills a deep weariness in Kyla. She's actually excited when she sees Indigo standing by the vending machines, until she realizes the girl is not even bothering to pretend that she's not staring *directly* at Kyla. Kyla holds out her hand to Sabrina.

"My Diet Coke money, please," she says. And then she adds, "My trig homework is in my bag, you can copy it, but make a mistake or two."

"You are a *gem*, Kyla Graves," Sabrina crows as she slaps a five-dollar bill in Kyla's hand.

Kyla makes her way to the drink vending machine, staring directly at it, refusing to acknowledge Indigo standing at the snack vending machine right next to her. Kyla smooths the bill against the side, the back of her neck prickling.

"You aren't very good at being subtle," she says, as she pretends to waffle between her Diet Coke and a Sprite. "I thought we were meeting in homeroom tomorrow. You couldn't send a text?"

"I don't have your phone number," Indigo retorts.

"Don't be obtuse. You know there are other ways to reach me," Kyla reminds her.

"Do you *not* want to know what I've learned?" she asks.

Kyla presses her lips into a thin line. "You work fast."

"I'm nothing if not efficient," Indigo retorts. "I gave my brother a call from the bathroom. He said there were so many tips coming in that the officers were complaining about it the entire time that he was being held. A lot of them were prank calls from students and some of Erin's followers. They're really upset."

"Of course," Kyla says dryly. Everyone thought they knew Erin, from what she posted. They thought they knew Kyla, too, especially the ones so obsessed with Erin that they started to follow her friends. But they didn't know anything. "Is that all?"

"Would I be talking to you in public if it was?" Indigo asks. Little pretender, like she isn't vibrating with excitement at the idea of sharing oxygen with Kyla in public.

"I'm raising your social capital by the second. Now, I don't have all *fucking* day."

Indigo tugs at the end of her long hair, ragged and in need of a trim. If Kyla liked her, she'd do that for her, like she does for the freshmen on her squad, especially the Black girls with their curly natural hair that they're just starting to learn how to do. Finally, Indigo says, "My brother was discharged before he could get anything about Peter specifically, but one of his friends works for the department."

A police officer and a delinquent as friends. It's like an elephant and a mouse.

"Who?" Kyla asks, inserting the bill.

Indigo shakes her head. "I can't say."

"Fine. What did the friend say?"

"They said that they were outside taking a smoke break and they saw this white kid walk in. Soft brown curls, big eyes, medium height, lean build. Baggy clothes. They drove an old Hyundai. They had, like, a bag with them and when they went in, they went *right* into Chief Hamish's office for about ten minutes, and then the cops left for the school in a police car and picked Peter up."

It's such a nondescript image. It could be almost anyone in town, given the population is 83 percent white. But Kyla knows. She knows *exactly* who fits it and drives an ugly-ass beige mom sedan.

"Fantastic, thank you for your service, Indigo," she says, as she presses 4A and watches the machine slowly creak into motion to drop her Diet Coke.

"Anytime," Indigo says, taking a step back, swanning from the praise. "Anything else?"

"Yes, actually. I'll need your brother's number. When . . . yes, *when* I start everything up again, let him know I'll be in touch. I think it's high time to renegotiate pricing," Kyla says.

Indigo nods. "Yeah, I can give it to you. But don't forget what you promised me. Tomorrow morning. Homeroom. Something someone else doesn't have, preferably."

"Don't make me repeat myself. Begone," Kyla says. She waits for Indigo to leave first, before she snatches up her drink and rushes back to her lunch table, sliding into her seat.

"Indigo Glass?" Alicia asks immediately, nose crinkling. "What did she want?"

"Peter has an alibi. It wasn't him. But it wasn't routine. Someone reported him. Rowan Villareal," Kyla offers instead. "They tried to sic the police on Peter."

"What do *they* know?" Sabrina demands. "And *why*?"

Kyla has more than a few ideas.

She purses her lips instead of sharing. "Don't worry about it. Just know that they really need to shut the fuck *up*." No one knows how to keep a goddamn secret anymore.

"Rowan Villareal is punching above their weight," Sabrina growls out, so much venom for a body so tiny.

"Well, they're about to learn why you don't do that," Kyla says, scanning the cafeteria.

Kyla finds Rowan easily. They're staring morosely down into their lunch tray, picking at limp arugula leaves and tearing off the crust from their grilled cheese. They look sad. It makes Kyla sneer. They don't get to be sad. Not about this. Not about *Erin*.

It's easy for Kyla to ignore the questioning look from Mikky, who is annoyingly sitting with Rowan for some reason. Her brother doesn't remember the pettiness of small town life. He doesn't remember how *delicious* it is. Or maybe he left too early to find his appetite for it. He's too big city. But Kyla? Her palate was formed by the women who raised her, and the Vaughn women *relished* pettiness. The only way that Kyla can handle this—*fix* this—is if she uses the tools that made Erin so powerful.

Kyla looks at Rowan's little friends, too. All two of them, excluding her brother. She rolls her neck, refusing to look away. *Look at me,* she thinks with all the force she can muster. *Look at me, I dare you.*

"Let's end them," Alicia says, affecting a familiar tone. She's trying to sound like Erin.

Kyla doesn't *need* fake Erin. She needs Erin's *cracker-eating bitch*.

Kyla shoves aside her lunch tray with a screech, one loud enough to draw everyone's attention. Not Rowan's, though. Oh. So they're *purposely* not looking at her. Kyla presses her hands flat to the cafeteria table, assisting her as she slowly stands. This isn't about defending Peter, she reasons with herself. No, this is about consequences. Erin always made sure people faced the *fucking* consequences. Putting the cops onto Peter opens a door that has to stay closed. So to make sure it does, Kyla will have to make them face the consequences too.

"More than that. Let's make them suffer," Kyla says.

After all, traitors should *always* suffer.

CHAPTER ELEVEN

Mikky feels her staring at Rowan at lunch. He's careful not to raise anyone's suspicion as he meets her eyes and raises an eyebrow in question. Kyla's nose wrinkles and then she looks away just long enough for Mikky to be drawn back into conversation. But as he laughs at Gregory's bad joke about their terribly ranked basketball team, he can feel the staring start up again.

Nasim doesn't notice. Gregory doesn't notice. But Mikky knows that Rowan does. They sit stiffly like they can feel the weight of her judgment.

Nothing happens until the end of lunch, when Lynn, a dance-team freshman, approaches Rowan with a note, discreet. Nasim doesn't see this, either, too preoccupied with helping Gregory study for the possibility of a chemistry pop quiz, since he's—somehow—already familiar with the material. Rowan takes the note and opens it.

Immediately, they pale and look back at the dance-team table. But Kyla doesn't look their way again.

After lunch Mikky catches Kyla alone by her locker, right before the bell rings for next period. She is so *rarely* alone at this school, and in any other circumstances, that would make Mikky happy, but in this one, it only makes him nervous.

"Are you good?" he asks her.

"Why wouldn't I be?" Kyla asks blandly.

Mikky could write an essay on the reasons that Kyla wouldn't be good.

"I mean, Peter is back and everyone, *including* the police, think he had something to do with Erin's death," Mikky points out. "And you were looking at me weird." He's careful not to bring up Rowan first, trying to wait her out.

Kyla looks at him, knowingly, as she says, "Who says I was looking at you?"

"Kyla, it's okay if *you're* not okay. The Peter thing is heavy," Mikky tries to gentle her.

Kyla slams her locker shut without even exchanging her books, like it's slipped her mind altogether. Her thunderous expression is at war with how tense she holds her shoulders, bottom lip nearly jutting out in a pout. Working her jaw, Kyla says, "Mikky, I'm going to be nice, because you haven't been here. You don't know how this . . . how *I* work. But I'm warning you now, stay out of my shit. You don't have the stomach for it."

And then she storms down the hallway without a backward glance, an utter dismissal that hits Mikky in the gut.

Mikky thinks back to a time in elementary school. Kyla and Erin had been in fourth grade. Jason and Mikky had been in fifth. It was May and the air smelled green.

It was just after Kyla and Erin's joint birthday party and that day, at recess, everyone was talking about the *epic* time they had. Everyone except one girl. Mikky remembered her getting an invitation, but she hadn't been at the party. Everyone thought it was because she didn't like Erin. But that day the girl had confronted

Erin, tried to fight her at recess. She'd been given an invitation, sure. A special one with the wrong address. She'd shown up an hour's drive away at a Dave & Buster's and no one was there.

Erin had simply *laughed*. She'd laughed and laughed, so hard that she cried. That girl cried too. Kyla had watched. Didn't laugh. But didn't apologize. And she certainly didn't tell Erin to stop, either. Instead, she'd grabbed Erin's hand. At the time he thought she was trying to pull her back, but on reflection, it seemed more like a *keep going*.

Later, Mikky will realize that this is how it started.

On Monday, when Mikky overhears Rowan telling Nasim that they misplaced their pencil case and failed a pop quiz because they had nothing to write with and it was too late to ask for a pen, with how strict their teacher was about silence during testing, Mikky chalks it up to coincidence. He's forgotten his pens and notebooks at home before. It happens. They're all human.

When the next day Rowan comes to the library and says that someone broke into their locker and stole everything, leaving only a treasure map to find all their shit, that's when Mikky recognizes that there's a problem. A very Kyla-shaped problem, even if none of it can be definitively traced back to her.

At lunch, Rowan and Gregory partner on one half of the map, fetching Rowan's textbooks from different rooms in the arts hallway while Nasim and Mikky pair up on the other to fetch Rowan's jacket from the soccer field. It's brisk and a sharp wind carries them across the green.

"I don't think you were right," Mikky blurts out into the silence.

"Weird, because I usually am," Nasim says. "What am I wrong about?"

"You called Kyla indifferent. This doesn't feel very indifferent. This feels *extremely* personal," Mikky says. "So, it begs the question . . . why. Like, sorry, but why does Kyla even know who Rowan is?"

"Who cares about why?" Nasim's dark eyes harden until they're opaque like colored glass. Mikky can't read them at all. "I know she's your sister, but usually when one mean girl goes, there's *always* someone to take her place. Looks like that's Kyla," Nasim says, voice chilly.

"I'm going to talk to her. Get her to lay off," Mikky decides.

"She'll deny it. You won't be able to prove it's her doing this."

Mikky knows that. Everything that's happened to Rowan so far has been . . . distant. It's petty and cruel, which is very Erin. But the subtlety and deniability is all Kyla. It's also been childish, though, which is neither of them. It lacks a specific finesse. Mikky wouldn't be surprised if Kyla simply said, *Make their life hell,* and her little minions concocted bullshit schemes in the hopes of appeasing their leader.

Mikky can't stop thinking of Rowan's word. "Feral."

"Look, I know Erin was . . . a lot, *excitable* and brash and yeah, sometimes mean, but she took care of Kyla. And now she's *gone*, plus the guy who might have done it is back in school, so if Kyla's orchestrating this, maybe Rowan . . . I don't know, knows something?" Mikky rasps. He reaches out to grab Nasim by the wrist, but then thinks better of it, reminding himself some people don't like to be touched. "Remember her best friend was killed—"

Nasim whips around. "That's a reason. Not an excuse. You

don't see Jason Vaughn going around taunting people just because his sister died," Nasim says.

He marches to the flagpole, looking up with a sigh. When Mikky looks up too, instead of the Massachusetts state flag, a very nice Carhartt jacket flaps in the wind.

Nasim sucks his teeth then grabs the rope and tugs to slowly lower the Carhartt.

"Like, what would Rowan even know?" Nasim demands. "That doesn't make sense."

It's a good question, one that strengthens Mikky's resolve to stick closer and find out.

There's a brief reprieve on Wednesday, where Mikky hopes that Kyla has stopped.

His hopes are dashed the next day, at lunchtime, when Mikky, Rowan, Gregory, and Nasim run into Kyla and some of her squad directly. Mikky and Kyla nod at each other as they pass through the halls—Mikky and his friends on the way to the library and Kyla and her friends to the cafeteria—but that's where the courtesy ends.

Alicia bumps shoulders with Rowan like she doesn't see them. She doesn't apologize. Sabrina, just behind her, does the same, except she's far shorter than Rowan, so she only manages to elbow them in the side. Rowan flinches both times.

"Say excuse me," Nasim snarls.

Alicia blinks widely. "I'm sorry?" she asks, voice sugar sweet. "Did I bump into someone?"

"I don't think so," Sabrina says. "I didn't see anyone."

Kyla doesn't smile. She doesn't laugh like Mikky thinks the

girls want her to. Instead, she stares right at Rowan. Wait, that's not accurate. She stares *through* them, like they're not there at all, gaze unwavering but slightly out of focus.

"Oh, you and your coven are a piece of work," Nasim hisses at her.

Rowan grabs Nasim's elbow, squeezing. "Come on, Nasim. It's not worth it. I'm fine."

"It's *not* fine, Rowan," Nasim says, shaking off their hold. He takes a step forward, glaring at Kyla, and says, "You're a bully."

"Okay," Kyla says, not agreeing or disagreeing. Just accepting. "Are you going to do something about it?"

Nasim balks. "I—"

"So . . . a Poindexter, a burnout, and a bald-faced liar. Quite the collection of friends for my brother," Kyla continues dismissively, then juts her chin at Rowan. Rowan stills, freezing up. "Yeah, you didn't think I'd say anything out loud, did you, Rowan?"

"I didn't . . . ," Rowan says, their voice trembling. Something about it is . . . off.

"You did," Kyla interrupts. Soft and cutting. "You reported Peter, didn't you? What other lies did you tell the cops?"

Mikky jerks, taken aback. He looks over at Nasim, who's not good at hiding his reaction either, eyes wide and round.

"I *didn't* lie to anyone about anything," Rowan says. Mikky catches it again, the way their plea almost whines. Like they're forcing it.

"Then who else could it have been at the police station that day matching your exact description going to talk to the police chief? Care to share with the class?" Kyla asks, waving at Mikky,

Nasim, and Gregory. Mikky watches Rowan's face, waiting for them to break, but they keep that guileless look in their eyes.

"I was there but not for that," Rowan says.

"Sorry, I don't believe you. You're not exactly known for your honesty, *remember*?" Kyla asks loftily.

She sounds so sure about Peter, and it makes Mikky realize now that Peter was never a question for her, not like it is for everyone else. To Kyla, *Rowan* reporting him is the problem. Rowan *knows* something.

"Neither are you. You and Peter and your friends tell a lot of lies too. And you keep *secrets*," Rowan says. They take a step closer, and the gloves come off. "Secrets like the Test Kitchen." They drop the words like they're supposed to mean something.

Kyla's expression doesn't twitch. She doesn't break either. It's Alicia that gives it away. She gasps, clapping her hand to her mouth, and then looks horrified that she's done so. Kyla takes a step closer, looking up into Rowan's face.

"I've let you get away with a lot of shit before," Kyla warns, "but I'm telling you now, once and for all, you don't wanna play games with me, Rowan Villareal."

Rowan squares their shoulders. "I don't play games, period."

Kyla steps back and smiles, unnervingly. "I know for a fact that you do. But unlike you, I play to win."

That afternoon the last bell rings, and Mikky leaves his AP German class with a distracted "Guten Abend, Frau Fischer." He makes his way to his locker to grab his car keys and his jacket. Mikky wants to shed his skin, it itches so much as he thinks about the cool smile that twisted Kyla's face.

Mikky only stops thinking of it when he sees a flash of a bright yellow sweatshirt and latches on to it, the one familiar thing in the hall in a sea of faces he's relearning.

"Nasim, what's up?" Mikky asks, stuttering to a stop as he watches the other boy tap his foot, leaning against a locker that is not his own. Mikky would've noticed a cute boy at a nearby locker the first day.

Nasim looks up blankly. "Oh. Mikky, hey," he says, distracted. "I can't find Rowan. And they're not answering their phone. We have plans today."

Mikky purses his lips. "Uh . . . what kind of plans?"

"Gregory says going home right after school is for losers. So we usually go to the lake to hang out until we get bored." Nasim shakes his head before he looks over at Mikky with a tired smile on his face. "What was your last class?"

"Uh, AP German," Mikky says.

"Right, the impractical practical language," Nasim teases.

They talk about small shit as the hallways clear out, shit that doesn't matter, shit that Mikky would rather not be talking about when the problem of Kyla stretches between them, gummy and suffocating. All the while, Nasim remains stubbornly by Rowan's locker, looking up and down the halls. The hallway is nearly clear by the time they start hearing the banging.

Just as they do, Gregory turns down the hall, waving his hands. "Hey, I've been looking for them everywhere and I for real can't . . . what is that?"

"Oh, what the *fuck*," Nasim mutters under his breath as he stalks closer to the sound. It's coming from a nondescript door, one without a window. It has the kind of knob that locks from the outside and immediately Mikky knows.

When Nasim unlocks and wrenches open the door, Rowan is there, sitting in the middle of the janitor's closet, unimpressed. One arm is folded over their chest, the other holds a broom that they've clearly been knocking against the door. They squint, readjusting to the light, then unfurl and stand. They lift their phone, shaking it at Nasim.

"Tried to call, but my phone is dead," they say as they walk out, nonchalant about having been locked in the janitor's closet of all places. "Are you ready to go?"

"I'm assuming you didn't accidentally wander in there," Gregory says weakly.

Rowan snorts. "Obviously not."

"I'm going to fight her. I'm not afraid to fight a girl," Nasim snarls, eyes wide.

Rowan shakes their head. "You'd probably lose. And also, it wasn't her. At least not directly. It was these freshmen boys. I think they're JV basketball, so . . . we know who that was." Peter has obviously heard about Kyla's accusations and didn't take too kindly to being "lied" about.

They're nonchalant about their humiliation in a way that sits wrong in Mikky's stomach, next to something that burns hot. Something that's been burning hotter and hotter as Mikky's mind spirals. Kyla could've hurt Rowan. Or at least gotten them *hurt*, and Mikky doesn't know *why*. It's that thought that makes Mikky break out into a run. Platforms be damned, he flies down the hallway and skids around the corner until he's behind the last dregs of students rushing out the doors to their cars or buses.

Absently, Mikky can hear Gregory and Nasim calling after

him, but he's focused in, tunnel-visioned as he rushes through the parking lot. It's easy to spot the hearse as it begins to pull out, and he skids to a stop right in front of it, forcing Kyla to brake so hard, Alicia nearly cracks her head on the dashboard.

"You!" Mikky shouts, voice booming through the parking lot as he stands in front of the hood.

Kyla purses her lips, leaning over the steering wheel, staring him down. She inches the car forward, once. Mikky doesn't move. She revs the engine, as if he's someone to play chicken with. As if Mikky is someone to be fucked with.

"Run me over. I dare you. I'll haunt you, Kyla. Remember, I know where you *live*!" Mikky roars. He points into the car, slamming his fist on the hood as he leans over it, glowering at his little sister. "Pull that shit again and—"

"And what?" Kyla asks through her open window. "Do you *think* I want to be wasting time on Rowan Villareal?"

"Then don't! Just stop!"

"I don't take kindly to people lying about my friends, *especially* about Erin's murder. Tell them to take back whatever they said to the cops and it's done," Kyla says, like she's being the reasonable one. It makes Mikky feel like he's crazy, and he knows he's not being the crazy one. "Now, get out of my way. You're holding up traffic."

Mikky finally steps to the side, still glaring at Kyla, but she smiles at him as she speeds out of the parking lot, cutting off some poor Honda. Like she's won. This isn't over, though. There's no way she's getting away from him tonight.

Mikky lingers in the middle of the lot until Nasim finally catches up, panting. Rowan and Gregory arrive just a few seconds behind.

"I swear to God, she is so . . . ," Mikky drawls. He shakes his head, looking over at Rowan. "Sorry about her."

Rowan nods slowly. "Thanks for that. It really was more . . . annoying than, like, traumatizing."

Gregory blinks in awe. "That was so cool? I know . . . *some* of us weren't sure of you, but I am. Come with us to the lake. You're officially *in*." He's bouncing up and down like a kid on a sugar high.

Nasim looks at Mikky like he's seeing him in a new light; something about it makes Mikky stand taller, lifting his chin, like he's under inspection.

"I guess you did *attempt* to stand up to your evil grief-stricken little sister for us," Nasim says, tilting his head. "And you helped us find Rowan."

Mikky winces. "I mean 'grief-stricken' for sure, but 'evil'? Strong words."

"At the moment it's very much feeling like the right one," Nasim retorts, in a tone that means he's not ready to debate it. At least not yet. Then after a long look at Mikky, he relaxes and says, "Come with us. Gregory is right. Going home immediately after school *is* for losers."

And that's how Mikky finds himself driving all of them to the lake. He thanks a God he doesn't believe in that he got a car wash over the weekend and someone vacuumed all the chip crumbs out from the drink wells, because that would've been embarrassing. Gregory and Rowan are in the backseat, but Mikky isn't nearly as hyperaware of them as he is of Nasim sitting next to him in the front. It's exactly what he *didn't* want, these feelings that are starting to creep up, but Mikky can't help the fact that he finds Nasim attractive. That's just brain chemistry, he tells himself.

"Okay, so, why does Kyla Graves think you had anything to do with reporting Peter to the police?" Gregory demands.

Nasim looks into the backseat, eyes narrowing. "Yeah, and *why* did she call you a liar?"

"I'm not in her head. I have no idea. I was at the police station, but I *wasn't* reporting anything about Peter," Rowan says defensively. Mikky looks in his rearview mirror and sees Rowan wrapping their arms around themselves.

"Well, *why* were you at the police station?" Nasim pushes. Rowan tries to play off like they don't hear this, but Nasim isn't one to be ignored. "Rowan, what's going on? You have to tell us."

The tension in Mikky's car is thick enough to suffocate them.

"I was just giving Lydia's sister back some of her stuff, because she refuses to see me."

Nasim and Gregory let out a slow chorus of, *"Ooooh."*

"Lydia?" Mikky repeats innocently.

Rowan purses their lips, looking out the window. "My ex-girlfriend. Her sister's a police officer."

Gregory brings a quick hand over his neck, nixing all further questioning on what's clearly a touchy topic. Briefly, Mikky thinks about pushing anyway. Something niggles at the edge of his brain—the very last part of the conversation when Rowan had brought up something called the Test Kitchen—but he holds back when Nasim gives him a severe look that doubles down on Gregory's gesture.

With the interrogation out of the way, Mikky learns that Gregory's the chatty one, but he doesn't mind a fellow yapper. Mikky used to think that he was quiet and observant, until he learned that was his anxiety tricking him into thinking that no one wanted to hear what he had to say.

The yapping is all very convenient for Rowan, though, Mikky thinks, uncharitably. Having someone to change the topic and fill the silence, on top of having an excuse tied up with a touchy subject so they'll just stop asking more questions.

"Dude, dude, so, like, what's different so far in town, what have you noticed?" Gregory asks, leaning forward between Mikky and Nasim as much as the seat belt allows.

Mikky looks at Main Street and takes it in, tries to see two versions of it at the same time—the here and now and the way it looks in his memory, all sepia toned. This isn't his first time back, but when he's here for the holidays, he doesn't go *out*. He stays at home with Dad and Kyla.

"Okay, so there are like three more Dunkin's since I moved away. It's an infestation," Mikky says. He surveys the area as he stops at the red light. "I'm pretty sure this red light is new too."

"Oh, it *is*," Gregory says like he's impressed by Mikky's realization. "Okay, okay, what else?"

Mikky makes other casual observations. The community center, obviously, with its shiny new upgrades. The thrift store that used to be right off the main street is shut down, but the taffy spot is still there, which is nice, even though Mikky isn't the biggest fan of the stuff.

"I want to do a drive around. Go down to the Tobacco Fields too," Mikky says. The Tobacco Fields no longer serve the purpose of their name, but no one in Prophets Lake has taken to calling the land anything else. Mikky remembers it being a place that a lot of the older kids would throw parties, if they could get away with it. For Mikky, it was one of the places that he found solace in his first semester at Prophets Lake High School, blasting music through the tinny speakers of his iPhone while he did his history readings.

"You can't get to the Tobacco Fields anymore," Nasim says.

"Wait. Why?" Mikky blurts out.

Nasim cuts him a sideways look. "Cook Cosmetics is annexing it into what they *want* to be a campus. They built another lab there because they're expanding into skin care. It's going to be this whole new launch because they're trying to open up another physical location soon too. In Boston. They're supposed to announce it in a few days."

"How do you *know* that?" Mikky asks.

Nasim shrugs. "My mom is a cosmetic chemist for them."

"Your mom works for Cook?" Mikky asks, even though his question is so clearly redundant.

"Doesn't everyone's?" Nasim asks. "Greg's dad is their night security."

"My parents don't work for them," Rowan volunteers. "They work at the hospital in the next town over."

On the rest of the short ride to the lakeside, Gregory points out a few more businesses that have closed or reopened, places that Mikky remembers from childhood that have had to grow or downsize. He trusts as they arrive at it that the lake at least has stayed the same. Mikky pulls into a parking spot right up against the fence near the cliff, and when he gets out of the car he stretches.

"Come on!" Gregory says, overly excited, grabbing Rowan's and Nasim's hands and dragging them down toward the shore.

Mikky prefers to take his time descending the wooden steps that are built into the side of the cliff and as he does, he gets his first view of the lake in such a long time.

Prophets Lake isn't the most impressive man-made lake in the state. Not by a long shot. The water isn't clear. The shore is a little too rocky for bare feet, and there are a few seagulls eyeing them rather evilly from their perch atop the DON'T FEED THE SEAGULLS sign, which is rusted and fading. But Mikky can't help but be mesmerized by the familiar beauty and its gravitas all the same.

They don't see *that* many tourists, not even during the height of the summer, but that's part of why Mikky likes it. The few bigger tourist groups they do get tend to come for a reason that has nothing to do with the lake—Cook Cosmetics, its enigmatic founder, Florence, and the only brick-and-mortar location in the entire country, situated right near its headquarters.

Mikky looks back up at the cliffs some twelve or thirteen feet up and the lake houses that sit atop them, kept in place by massive beams of wood that look almost like they're growing out of the face of the rock.

"So, this is where you hang out?" Mikky asks as he gets to the bottom, where Nasim waits for him.

Nasim hums and nods. "This is where we hang out," he says, then smiles slyly. "I *guess* that makes you part of the club or whatever."

"Do I get a membership card? Do I have to pay dues?" Mikky teases.

Nasim nods again, very solemnly. "You'll be sent your membership card in the mail and should receive it in about ten business days. Dues are paid bimonthly. Printing is very expensive, so they're very high; we hope you can afford it."

"I can scrounge up the pennies, I think."

Warmly, Nasim says, "Good." He doesn't toe off his shoes and brave the pebbled shores like Gregory, but he walks dangerously close to the water, letting it lick at the toes of his Converses as he stands there, hands on his hips, head tilted back like he's even judging the lake.

"So . . . that's just your face," Mikky realizes.

Nasim jerks, looking up at him with a slowly forming frown. "What's . . . is there something wrong with my face?"

"No, it's actually very nice to look at," Mikky says easily, and delights when Nasim's cheeks slowly flush, capillaries opening up so they bloom pink. "I thought you were always judging me, but I think you just have resting judgment face."

"I *am* always judging you," Nasim sniffs. Then he relaxes. "But after today, you're all right."

"Thanks," Mikky says, rubbing at the back of his neck. Even thinking about it makes his skin tingle. "Just making sure because people love to make, you know, assumptions. About me. Because of who I kiss. The music I listen to. How I look. How I choose to present myself."

"You think you have the monopoly on that?" Nasim retorts. "I'm Iranian, dude."

"Fair," Mikky acquiesces.

Prophets Lake is liberal for a small town, which is to say, not very liberal at all. Everyone may preach those values, but they all come with their own strange biases, and Mikky has no doubt that Nasim has faced a slur or two.

"So . . . ," Nasim says, dragging out the word, "who comes to a new school in their senior year?"

"It's not a new school," Mikky says. "This is more of a homecoming than anything else. I went here for half a semester as a freshman."

"Oh, I thought you said something like that on the first day." Nasim looks like he regrets sharing with the class almost immediately.

Mikky considers not teasing him. He really does. And then he decides he can't: "So, you were paying attention, huh? My presence was such a disruption that you just *had* to know my tragic backstory?"

"You were at the front of the class, announcing it to everyone. I wasn't . . . *ugh*," Nasim says, then pivots easily. "Why did you leave?"

Mikky doesn't deflate as he decides exactly how to word this. He's used to disclosing what happened his freshman year. Trying out six different therapists before settling on Dr. Grosse, and then having to explain *again* to his psychiatrist, and to all his friends at his old school, has made this old hat. "I had a mental breakdown my freshman year. I was struggling with the transition to high school, the social aspect and the schoolwork and all this shit. All my friends from middle school found what they wanted to do and were discovering who they wanted to be, and it was just . . . easier for them. I thought I'd never fit in because I'm Black, I'm gay, and I like shit that makes you weird in Prophets Lake. And all of that's true, but mostly it was that I have an anxiety disorder and a smidge of depression. Extensive therapy, Lexapro, and a change of scenery have really done wonders for managing it."

Nasim watches him with begrudging admiration.

"You're very open," he says.

Mikky shrugs. "You asked and I don't really think it's something to hide? It is what it is."

"That's really cool," Nasim admits.

Mikky laughs. "I like to think so," he says with a shrug. "But, uh, now I'm back. Because of . . . Erin Vaughn." *Because of Kyla,* he doesn't say.

Nasim bites his bottom lip. "Death will do that to you. Make you consider . . . where you are, and stuff like that," he says, staring down at the ground hard, kicking up the rocky shore.

"Yeah? You sound like you have personal experience," Mikky says gently.

Nasim doesn't take to bold word-vomit honesty like Mikky. It takes him a moment to find his, and Mikky lets him, patient.

"My grandma died last year. She lived with me and my parents. We were super close. I was going to go away over the summer to this program in New York and get college credits and graduate earlier, but losing her made me realize . . . I was rushing. I need to take my time more. There's no shame in taking my time." Nasim says those last words like they're a mantra, something someone else has told him time and again. Mikky wonders if it was his grandmother.

"You're right," Mikky agrees.

Nasim shakes his head. "This is so heavy. I'm not trying to be a downer."

"No, I know," Mikky says. "Okay, so you know about me. What I like. What about you? Who are you, Nasim Talebi?"

Nasim Talebi is, according to Nasim Talebi, not complicated. He wants to be a chemist, like his mom, and he enjoys math and sciences over English. He doesn't do well with subjectivity. He tells people that his favorite food is sambuseh, but he'd live on jelly donuts if he could, even though he hates fruit fillings in cake. Mikky feeds on each tidbit of information greedily, stowing it away for later, before he remembers he shouldn't be.

By the time Gregory and Rowan shout at them that they're craving a snack, Nasim is pink in the face. "I feel like I've been dominating the conversation and it's already late," he says.

"No. I like hearing you talk," Mikky insists with a smile as they start to ascend the wooden steps again, following after Rowan and Gregory.

Some of the other cars in the lot have disappeared, but there's still a few left over, mostly with teenagers sitting on the hoods, chatting. But only one car—Mikky's car—has a police officer circling it.

"Hey, can I help you?" Mikky calls.

Nasim winces. "Please, *shh*," he insists, tugging on Mikky's arm.

Mikky shrugs him off and takes a step closer, arms folded over his chest as the police officer takes two large steps away from his car. "Officer, can I help you?" He can't help the utter disdain that drips off him and the officer seems to read it immediately.

"Nope. Just keeping an eye on things," the officer says, waltzing back to his cruiser. He slides in, rejoining his partner, and Mikky waits for them to leave.

They don't. They sit and wait.

"Come on. I can take you guys home?" Mikky suggests finally.

"Actually, they're coming to my house for the evening," Rowan answers.

Mikky doesn't hear an invitation in that but he shrugs it off. "Cool. Give me your address," he says. He sighs, glaring over at the cops, who still haven't moved. "Man, I hate the fucking cops. What are they even doing here?"

"Maybe they're here because . . . you know," Gregory says.

"I know, what?" Mikky asks forcefully.

Rowan stares blankly at the lake. "Erin's body was found around here." They can't meet anyone's eye, and they even shy away from the cops' line of sight, like they don't want to be noticed. Like they actually do have something to hide.

Slowly, Mikky gets into his car and turns on the engine.

He can't stop thinking about Kyla's insistence that Rowan is a liar. And Rowan pushing about *Kyla's* secrets. Now more than ever, Mikky is convinced that they do know something about Kyla, and even more alarmingly—something about Erin's death.

CHAPTER TWELVE

The strangest part is that Kyla knows she's dreaming. She understands by the way the sky looks like it's made of opaque bubbles, and the vivid green of the grass beneath her feet, even though otherwise it's all the same. It's real and not real and it actually doesn't matter at all. That's what Kyla decides.

She's in her own backyard. She knows it because of the tire swing tied to the big oak, though it's not there anymore in the real world. The rope wore away so much after years of use that it snapped right before Mikky's freshman year, after one last summer challenge to see who could spin as many times as they could without throwing up. (Kyla won.)

But, here, in the dream, the tire swing is still there.

And so is someone else.

Erin is sitting in it, cross-legged, somehow, her ass hanging through the hole in the middle. She holds the rope and without moving her lips, she calls in a watery voice, *Duck, come push me.*

Erin has always called Kyla "Duck," ever since preschool, when Erin didn't quite understand how duck, duck, goose worked and that she couldn't always be goose and Kyla couldn't be the only duck. Kyla slowly approaches Erin and pushes the tire swing, kick-starting the swinging motion. With each swoop through the air, the wind picks up, but only Erin's hair, the ends tinged with aqua, whips around.

The space around Kyla is utterly still. She trains her gaze between Erin's shoulder blades as Erin says, *Duck, I'm dead.*

"I know, Erin," Kyla whispers.

No, I've been dying for a long time.

"How?" Kyla asks.

Slowly. And then all at once. That's the way poison works. It was all poison.

"How do I know this isn't one of your games?"

I'd never play dead with you.

Kyla wakes up.

Kyla has had plenty of nightmares but never a lucid one, and she feels off kilter, like her bed is a rickety ship rocking beneath her. She grunts, swallowing down the bile, trying to catch her breath like she just won a marathon while drowning. Then she drags herself to the edge of her bed to feel the solid ground beneath her bare feet. That helps more than the breathing. The reminder that there is old wood beneath her feet. She reaches back to grab the soft sateen sheets, rolling them between her fingers. Also real. Good.

The yawning grief that fills every bit of her is real too. It almost feels like something that she's always had but has only made itself known since Erin died. This thing that's inextricably chained to her, that she can't get rid of, not even when she tries to shake it loose.

I get it, Kyla can imagine Erin saying. *You've always been a haunted person.*

She was always so matter of fact when saying the most outlandish things. No one outright describes another person as "haunted" to their face. She didn't care if it made her sound odd, though.

Kyla used to talk to Erin about her hauntings. Sometimes, she would feel so hollow, she could practically hear a whistling in her chest. Other times, the heaviness would threaten to flatten her. And then, sometimes, Kyla felt normal. Mundane. No matter what, she had nightmares. When she would have one, she would call Erin after and they would both sneak out and meet at the graveyard. Kyla has always felt at home there. It's like the funeral home, but bigger. Now Erin is always at home in that very graveyard too and there is no one to call.

Still, she reaches for her phone on the nightstand. She squints against the sudden brightness, bringing it all the way down before she opens Instagram. It loads the last profile she was looking at. Erin's. She has more followers than ever, now that she's dead. The last photo—Kyla can't look at it. It makes her sick, seeing her own face reflected back at her.

Kyla reads the comments instead:

> We love you, Erin! We miss you!

> Why hasn't Cook said anything? Erin was one of their best. Not even a mention on their page?

> Erin, you were like a big sis, this is crazy.

> You're all vultures. She's dead, she can't read your posts.

> Blond bitch deserved what she got.

> Performative grief, all of y'all make me sick.

> Where is Cook in all of this? Their fastest-growing girl was killed and what? Nothing. DisGOSTING.

Kyla shuts her phone, plunging her world into darkness again. All these people that didn't know Erin, talking to her ghost, are part of the poison. It's not fair that they can still post toxic shit and Kyla can't even manage to look at her best friend's page head-on without her eyes blurring.

Kyla gracefully steps over the pile of dirty clothes in the middle of her bedroom and goes up to the window. She stares out, attempting to parse through the heavy glaze of fog. The chill of midnight reaches into the house and rubs at Kyla's nose. She covers it with her hand, as if the cold is a physical touch, as her eyes find the graveyard.

There's so much Kyla wants to tell her. So much Kyla wants to ask. *Why are you gone? Why is everything falling apart? What do I do? About Peter? About Rowan? About the secrets I kept for you? The secrets are so big, I feel like they're going to spill out of me or I'll choke to death on them or—*

Kyla turns and grabs a pair of sweatpants off the floor. She shoves her legs into them, then goes to the closet to grab her favorite rugby sweater, and pulls that over her head. A compulsion draws her to her vanity. She looks down at the organized mess of it, the sea green of Cook Cosmetics the most dominant. Of course. She grabs a lip balm—Cook Cosmetics' new Hydrating Lip Peptide Treatment or whatever. It's still sealed. She plucks at the tape over the top. Then she hears Erin's voice, as if she's back in the dream: *No, not that one, Duck, not yet. That one's for someone else to try first.*

Kyla tucks it out of sight and lets out a shaky breath. She sees her own reflection and can't quite recognize herself in the dark.

For some reason, she does her eyebrows. She doesn't realize that she's fluffing them with the Cook Cosmetics Dandelion Brow Wand in Chocolate until she's done with one eyebrow. Slowly, she sets the wand down and backs away. She refuses to acknowledge the lopsidedness of her face. It doesn't matter. It's dark outside.

And it's only Erin. Erin wouldn't say anything about her eyebrows. Not unless they had a meet.

Or a Test Kitchen.

Kyla grabs her sneakers and creeps toward her bedroom door. She grips the knob and takes a deep breath, then tears the door open. Immediately, she comes to a stop.

Mikky's awake.

Her heart begins to thud hard as she stares at his half-open door, a sliver of light from a bedside table dimly illuminating the space between their rooms. She knows he's heard her, because suddenly she hears bedsprings shifting and then he pads forward and pulls the door open entirely. He has wired headphones wrapped around his neck, still connected to the phone he clutches tight in his grip like someone's going to steal it.

Mikky looks so much softer without all his piercings in. He still has studs in the second holes in his ears, but otherwise, he's not wearing a speck of body jewelry. Not even his septum. His curls are pineappled atop his head, a navy-blue scarf holding them up.

She saw him after their showdown in the parking lot, when he arrived home just in time for dinner. The meal was a standoff. Kyla knows her brother isn't a narc, so he didn't say anything in front of Dad, but he looked at her like he'd never seen her before. It felt a little vindicating, to see that bewildered look on his face over the chicken skewers and rice. Mikky *doesn't* know her as well as he thinks he does. He doesn't know what she *needs* like he thinks he does. Kyla doesn't need to be taken care of, and she doesn't need comforting. He's starting to realize that now.

But in the dampened moonlight, he seems to have started to forget again. He's awake, staring at her with concern. She doesn't want his concern. She wants his anger. God, Kyla wishes someone would get angry. She wishes someone would be as *angry* as she is.

"Kyla," Mikky says, and Kyla *hates* it. He never spoke to her like that before. Her name was an afterthought because he never *had* to call her name. His voice memos always started as if they were midconversation, in the same room, and not hundreds of miles apart. Now that they are in the same room, he calls to her like he's summoning her from far away.

"I thought I heard something," Kyla says.

Mikky looks down at her clothing and Kyla glowers at him, daring him to address it. If it was Before—Before Erin's Murder, like a measure of time—he wouldn't. He would let it go. Now he handles her with kid gloves.

Mikky purses his lips, and she can tell he's caught between confronting her and asking her if she's okay. If he asks her that, Kyla might actually scream.

"*O*-kay. It was just me. I can't sleep." Mikky demurs. "Are you going somewhere?"

"Is that normal?" Kyla asks, ignoring his question. She hopes it's not. She's got too much shit to do when the moon is high.

"Only sometimes, if I don't time my Lexapro right. I didn't today." Mikky is so casual about discussing his medication. He thinks that she doesn't see what he's doing, the gentle implication that she needs to *talk* to someone. It's like when he dropped an unnecessary mention of his therapist over dinner, making a show of excusing himself from the table for a makeup session with Dr. Grosse.

"Oh," Kyla whispers. She frowns, looking out at the window on the back wall. She wants to make the walk to the cemetery. It's not far. She can even see the top of the oak tree.

"Kyla, do you want to come in?" Mikky asks, breaking the strange silence between them. There he goes—saying her name *again*.

"Why?" she asks. He'll want to talk about Rowan. She's never wanted to talk about anyone less.

"When I get insomnia, I usually listen to music. If Dead Kennedys isn't your vibe, I'm also not opposed to like . . . SZA."

Kyla *does* like SZA. She likes Dead Kennedys too. She doesn't say that, though. She shakes her head and doesn't bother forcing an awkward smile. After all, he's not Dad.

"I'm going to go back to bed. Now that I know it's you. So . . . yeah. Good night," she says decisively, and then she backs into her room, keeping Mikky in her line of sight until she shuts the door with a soft click. She presses her head against the wood and listens.

Mikky doesn't move for a moment and then she hears him shuffling into his room and his door shutting too. *Why couldn't he have shut it before?* Kyla shoves her sweatpants down over her hips and leaves them in the middle of the floor. She smooths out the sleep shorts she'd had bunched under her pants and crawls into bed. She's glad she didn't bother taking off her scarf. That at least *kinda* gives her plausible deniability if Mikky thinks to mention it over breakfast.

But now she can't go see Erin.

Kyla turns over to face the wall and pretends that she's not looking down at her phone through her lashes when she presses call, like someone else is doing it.

It rings three times before a muddled, "Hello," is grunted from the other end.

Kyla inhales sharply and bites down hard on her lower lip, hard enough that it splits. "Ow," she hisses to herself, and then hates that she spoke at all.

"Kyla?" Jason asks. He still doesn't sound any more awake. This doesn't surprise her. When she had sleepovers with Erin, Jason would always stumble downstairs, rubbing sleep out of his eyes, past noon. He was also prone to naps, especially before games. "Are you hurt?"

"I bit my lip," she says finally.

Jason hums sympathetically. "Sucks."

"I know. It hurts," she admits. She wouldn't usually ever admit that. Not even to Erin. Instead, she would've smiled through it, so sure she was on her own until Erin would've grabbed her hand and squeezed tight. No words would've needed to be exchanged. Erin and Kyla shared everything, even their pain.

Erin isn't there to share the pain anymore. It all belongs to Kyla.

I've been going through something, she thinks once again.

She's been going through something, but there's no one that will get it, not even Jason. And Kyla doesn't know how to make them. She just wants someone to sit up with her now that she can't go sit with Erin.

"Did you want to . . . talk?" Jason asks.

Kyla snorts. "No," she says.

"Okay. We can just . . . be on the phone, I guess," Jason suggests carefully, like he really wants to get it right, even though he can't.

Still, Kyla shifts to lie on her back, phone on her pillow next to her. "Okay."

He's not even silent for a minute before he acknowledges the impossibility of it. "I'm sorry I'm not her."

Kyla closes her eyes. "Me too."

CHAPTER THIRTEEN

Mikky's entire head is tucked in his locker as he tries to decide if he's truly misplaced his textbook or simply left it at home, when he hears someone rattle a pattern against his locker door. Mikky knows without question who it is, and sure enough when he ejects himself from his locker, he's looking right into Jason's grinning face.

"Good morning to you too, Jason."

"What's up? I'm just checking on you. Now that you're back and all," Jason says.

Mikky rolls his eyes. "I can manage, man."

"I know, I *know*, but I haven't been seeing you. Too cool to hang out with me?" Jason asks. He doesn't sound like he's hurt by it, but there's a kernel of truth there. Guilt sits like a lump in Mikky's throat. In his quest to be a good brother, despite how much Kyla fights him, he hasn't been the greatest friend.

"Too cool to hang out with your meathead friends, yeah," Mikky says with a small smile as he slides in next to Jason, walking with him as they try to navigate the crowded hall.

"Right, right. You'd rather be hanging out with Nasim Talebi and that group, huh? The weird nerds," Jason says. He's grinning good-naturedly as he says it.

"Nerds? Yeah. Weird? Debatable," Mikky says.

"That wasn't an insult," Jason insists, and Mikky knows that's true. Jason has always been like that. Part of the in-crowd, but kind to those that aren't. "I'm glad you've found your people. I know it's been hard before. So . . . they're being good to you?" His earnestness hits like a punch to the face. Jason remembers Mikky's troubles from freshmen year too, and it makes Mikky feel worse.

"Yeah, they're a good bunch. Had a rocky start with Nasim because he's a stickler for rules but . . . uh, I think we're good now," Mikky says. He rubs his chin, trying to assess how much he wants to admit. Well, in for a penny, in for a pound, or whatever. "He's, like, extremely hot, so I'd like to stay on his good side."

Jason guffaws, stopping right in his tracks in the middle of the hallway, waggling his eyebrows. "Oh-*ho*, so you're trying to get it in with Nasim, huh?"

Mikky snorts. "You're being so gross and heterosexual about this."

"I'm trying to be a good friend, dude," Jason says, shoving him back and laughing. Even though he's going through the same thing, he gives his laughter so much more freely than Kyla does. God, Mikky wishes he could drag a laugh out of his grim-faced little sister. Instead, all his efforts seem to encourage the rage spiral to grow, not abate.

"No, but really. I'm glad you have someone to sit with at lunch, since I heard that you and Kyla had a bit of a fight yesterday?" Jason pushes. He is staring at Mikky with bright green eyes, strangely and politely insistent about it.

"I think that if I tried to sit with Kyla after very publicly taking the side of her current target, she'd castrate me."

"Fair," Jason agrees with a strange laugh. He firms up his face with courage and asks, "Is . . . is Kyla okay?"

Mikky squints at him for a long moment and then drawls out, "I think that might be relative," because he doesn't know how to say, *No, she's not okay, her best friend—your sister—is dead. Probably murdered and they let their only suspect go free,* in a polite way.

"Right, right," Jason murmurs like he hears every bit of subtext. But he can't have because he follows up with, "But is she? Okay, I mean?"

"Why? Did she say something to you?" Mikky asks. Suspicion coils in his stomach, against his will.

Jason shakes his head. "No. Nothing like that. I was just . . . nothing, man."

"No come on, man. She's been on one and I can't get her to back off. What do you know?" Mikky asks.

"It's no big deal," Jason says, waving away Mikky's concern. "I thought I . . . I was wrong. I'm just tired."

He does look tired. There's a limpness to his golden-brown curls. His summer tan has disappeared, and he looks pale, dark circles around his eyes. Mikky would lose sleep too if he went through what Jason's going through.

So he says, "Me too, dude. Insomnia."

Jason's shoulders relax and he nods, switching to carry his book bag in his hand as they approach his locker. "I usually go to bed pretty early. You know I like to sleep, but I've been having like . . . really weird dreams lately. It's been getting worse the closer it gets to the season opener," he says. He doesn't even open his locker. He leans against it, looking harried. "I'm usually excited for the first game but . . . I don't know. I'm not feeling it tonight."

Mikky knows why but refuses to show the pang he feels at this; after all, he's not in mourning. Well, he is, but not like the Vaughns or Kyla. A memorial before the season opener feels strange and inappropriate, but also like something Erin might've approved of. She will be the star, a specter looming over long after the final whistle. And even if not everyone is crushed by her absence (the more Mikky gets to know who Erin had become, the more he feels that some people might actually be relieved she's gone), there is a sense of emptiness in the halls her personality would have filled. The school has to acknowledge what happened somehow.

"How are you feeling about the memorial?" Mikky asks.

Jason huffs, shaking his head. "It's weird, man. It's so weird. So many people are going to talk about Erin like they knew her, but they didn't know her. Not like us." He says "us" so easily like Mikky didn't disappear for two and a half years. Like he still knew Erin intimately. Maybe he did because childhood is forever, somehow, even when you grow out of it.

Mikky's realizing that more and more, the longer that he stays in Prophets Lake.

"It's weird," he agrees.

It's even weirder that Jason's going to have to play a game after, dedicated to his sister's memory. Kyla will have to smile and dance like she didn't just spend a second day hearing eulogies about her best friend. It's grotesque, in a way.

"Would it make me a bad brother if I say that I'm thinking more about the game than the memorial?" Jason asks suddenly.

"I don't think so," Mikky says almost immediately. His dad has always told him that people experience grief in different ways. Mikky is in no position to judge how Jason deals with his.

"The night she died . . . it was still preseason, but we took a bus to play this really good travel team. We wanted to test ourselves, see how we were looking this year. We won in a penalty shoot-out. I feel like I have to win again because it's the opening game, but I don't know how because I'll . . . *know* this time. That she's not there, that she won't be again," Jason groans. "And, like, how am I supposed to focus when my parents are . . . Christ, my mom is liable to have a breakdown. *Again.*"

"Does she . . . have those often?" Mikky asks. Jason doesn't answer, lost in his own thoughts, so Mikky pushes forward. "I know my dad gave y'all pamphlets for grief counselors but—"

"My mom isn't going to see a shrink. She's going to sob herself to sleep, then go work a twelve-hour day at Cook Cosmetics, and then have a glass of wine or three until she does it over again. Her regular MO," Jason interrupts, voice flat. He shakes his head, flexing his fingers as he tries to force the nerves out of himself. It doesn't work. Mikky can see right through him; he still has the same tells. "But it'll be fine. I'm fine."

"It's okay not to be fine," Mikky tries again.

Jason's smile is grim, almost mocking. "Well, one of us has to be. I'll see you after the game."

The air vibrates with a nervous energy as the start time to the memorial gets closer and closer. Mikky and the others killed time at the last local café in the town that hasn't fallen to the mighty Dunkin' empire, and then circled back to the school.

As they fight to keep up with the crush of students spilling out to the edges of the soccer field, Mikky has to keep his fingers wrapped around Nasim's wrist so as not to lose him like they've already lost Gregory and Rowan. Mikky wishes he had the moxie to lace his fingers through Nasim's, but he hears Jason's good-natured laughing in his ear and refrains.

"Did you know that Jason thinks that I'm hanging out with you just to avoid the natural call of popularity?" Mikky asks.

It's the first thing he can think of to say and Nasim sounds distracted as he demands, "Well, are you?"

"I'm not sure I know how to be popular," Mikky says honestly.

"It's easy. Be hot and smart and funny. You've got two of those down."

Mikky stops in the middle of the crowd and drops Nasim's wrist, drawing irritated glowers as people have to cut around him. Nasim makes it two steps before he looks over his shoulder and rolls his eyes.

"You are so dramatic. You don't even know which two I'm talking about," he insists, even as his cheeks turn pink.

"You think I'm *hot*," Mikky drawls with a slowly dawning grin.

Nasim gives him the middle finger and grabs his wrist this time, tugging him along as he says, "Come on."

They get stuck in the midst of a pack of sophomores, though, and Nasim has to adjust his glasses twice as he's jostled by a pair of rowdy boys.

"Chill," Mikky barks the third time, as they nearly elbow Nasim's glasses off his face.

One of them—dark-haired with a swell of freckles across his forehead—turns around to say something vicious before he sees Mikky and is properly cowed. Mikky can't lie, sometimes he enjoys being intimidating.

Nasim smirks as they push a little farther into the crowd, closer to the makeshift stage, a platform that will be removed swiftly when the neighboring team files in forty-five minutes from now. Mikky searches and sees the dance team up by the very front, purposefully separated from the rest of the crowd, almost elevated to a place of honor. Mikky looks for familiar curls, but his vision is quickly obscured by a surge of people, all fighting to see too.

He crowds closer to his friend, making sure not to lose him, and Nasim leans back against him. Mikky holds his breath—an accident or on purpose? He weighs the options and decides that Nasim did it on purpose, wanted to be in his space, even if he would never, ever admit it.

Well, Mikky hopes he likes awkwardly vulnerable boys on SSRIs.

"Your sister just got up there," Nasim says.

Mikky drags his eyes away from the side of Nasim's head to the stage, and sure enough, there she is. Kyla is in her dance team uniform, a metallic take on the school colors of maroon and white. The maroon on her sleeves is the color of oxidizing blood. She's wearing beautifully applied dance makeup too, her face sculpted to perfection. The only thing that makes her look off is the lack of lipstick. For a moment Mikky thinks she might've forgotten. But it's not like her. Even now, Kyla is meticulous. Based on how she acts in practice, he suspects she would go rabid on another girl for dancing without lipstick.

Then he sees her biting her lip. No, she didn't forget. She had the foresight to know that she'd be biting her lip to keep from crying. She used to do that as a kid, too. Better forgo it altogether than get lipstick on her teeth.

She looks so lonely standing up there, almost ghostly, and Mikky is nauseous as the crowd gets impatient. He considers pushing through the crowd to get to the stage when the Vaughns appear. Mr. and Mrs. Vaughn walk from the long path between the bleachers with Jason right in between them, led by the solemn procession of soccer players. Neither of Jason's parents are in black, though their mourning is still long from over. They're draped in soft shades of yellow. *Erin's favorite color?* Mikky wonders.

Mrs. Vaughn looks as fragile as a bird, and even from so far away, Mikky can track her trembling as she grips Jason's arm so tight, his skin lightens from blood loss. Jason bears it with a set jaw and lips pressed tight into a thin line.

The crowd finally shows some semblance of respect, parting to make it easier for the Vaughns to get on the stage. The students aren't the only ones who've turned out tonight. Most of the town has shown up. And a local news van is set up at the very fringe, the dark eye of a camera pointed up at the platform.

"There's Rowan and Gregory," Nasim murmurs. "I don't think we can get over to them, though. It's pretty packed." He doesn't make an effort to move.

Rowan has sunglasses and a baseball cap on, brown hair long and curling out from under it at the base of their neck. Both are a lame attempt to go unseen. It definitely draws more attention from the other students than Rowan would probably prefer.

"—think they know something?"

"Who knows what?"

"That that kid Rowan might know something?"

"Rowan? Rowan Villareal?"

"Yeah, them."

"They reported Peter to the cops. But Kyla says they're lying . . ."

"Ha. Clout chaser, then?"

Mikky hears snatches of the same words shaped and reshaped again, an infectious rumor that spreads through the crowd. Mikky's not an idiot, he knows who patient zero is. He watches her as she's folded into the Vaughns' small circle, Jason's arm around her shoulders cleaving her tight to his side.

"Do you hear everyone?" Nasim hisses, whipping around to glower up at Mikky. "Everyone thinks that Rowan reported Peter. They just accept that as fact because your sister said so. Rowan said they had nothing to do with this, and now everyone thinks they're an attention-seeking *liar*."

A pit begins to develop in Mikky's stomach—no, that pit's been there for a while now, and he has a name for it. Dread.

"Nasim . . . ," he says helplessly.

"Do you know how heinous you have to be—" Nasim snarls.

Mikky snaps at this. "Erin is dead, Nasim, that's what's heinous. Kyla helped to prepare her best friend's *body*. Her best friend who was *murdered*."

It's the ugliest word Mikky can think of in the moment, but it does the trick. "Dead" is too abstract for what happened to Erin. A girl like Erin Vaughn doesn't simply die. She seemed immortal, someone who would live forever through the sheer force of her own will. It wasn't normal circumstances that put an end to that. Someone did that to her.

"I just . . . ," Nasim starts.

But thankfully they are interrupted. Nasim looks to the stage as the principal steps up to the microphones and says, "Testing . . . testing . . ." He's clearly not testing anything, just searching for something to say. "Thank you all for gathering here before our season-opening soccer game against the Eastview Charter Stallions. We are here today to pay tribute to a lost member of our community, Erin Vaughn."

A knot forms in Mikky's throat as he looks at Kyla. She has that thousand-yard stare that she had at the funeral, fully dissociated, in contrast to the Vaughns, who are frighteningly present. Mr. Vaughn's shoulders jump with each swallowed sob.

Nasim tugs impatiently on Mikky's sleeve.

"What?" Mikky hisses softly.

Nasim's stare has turned pleading, almost against his will. "I'm sorry. I'm not being empathetic. I'm *sorry*." On the second sorry, his hand slips from Mikky's sleeve to his hand, lacing their fingers together. Nasim's hand isn't nearly as soft as Mikky's and yet, it's so *warm*.

Mikky keeps his hands moisturized, just has calluses on his fingertips from guitar strings, but the sorry state of Nasim's is one of the first things Mikky ever noticed about him. They're large, which Mikky likes, but his knuckles are a mess of scars, like he's spent time picking at the skin.

"Mikky?" Nasim whispers, voice even smaller.

Finally, Mikky grips Nasim's hand tighter, anchoring himself to the ground, and looks into his face.

Thirty seconds later there's a stirring in the crowd, enough to finally kill the staring contest that they've been locked in. Mikky looks up at the makeshift stage and watches as the principal stutters to a stop and steps back, blinking while the crowd shifts and pulses around the person making their way to the front.

Mikky sees the ochre of her hair first. Perfectly coiffed atop her head, not a single glossy strand out of place. The woman isn't especially tall, but she *feels* tall as she walks up the stairs. Her long neck is birdlike, and Mikky isn't far so he can see the thin skin at her throat, the only thing that betrays her age besides the gentle, graceful lines framing her painted mouth. Mikky has seen photos of this woman in the local newspaper his entire life. He *knows* who Florence Cook is.

And so does everyone else.

Florence is swathed in black like she's just come from the funeral that she didn't actually attend. She walks up to the principal and murmurs something that the microphone, unfortunately, doesn't catch. Then she approaches the Vaughns.

Mrs. Vaughn throws herself into Florence's arms without prompting. There's something cold about Florence, and Mikky expects her to shove the woman away. He's surprised when she wraps her arms tightly around Mrs. Vaughn, one hand pressed to the back of her head like she's cradling a baby.

Mrs. Vaughn is the one who pulls away first. Her cheeks are pink, embarrassed, but Florence shakes her head and presses a kiss to Mrs. Vaughn's cheek. Her lipstick—almost certainly of her own brand—doesn't transfer.

Then Florence takes a step away, toward the microphone. She raises a delicate hand and makes as if she's going to remove the large blue sunglasses from her face, but she doesn't, instead just brushes a nonexistent stray hair flat back into her chignon. Then she leans forward and in the breathiest whisper says, "Good evening, Prophets Lake High School."

She pauses as if this is an assembly and we're meant to rumble back in greeting. Nothing of the sort happens. Instead, it feels like everyone's holding their breath, waiting for her next words.

"I am Florence Cook," she introduces herself, unnecessarily. "I am a woman who values privacy over nearly everything else. A woman who chooses to let what she creates speak in place of herself. I am also not a woman of much emotion. But when the news that my dear friend and colleague's daughter had died in such a vicious way came to me, I was beside myself. Utterly so." Her face crumples, but her makeup never creases.

"And while I could not make it to the funeral, I knew I had to be here. At this memorial. A celebration of the life that was lost far too early. Erin Vaughn, oh, the ways I could describe you," Florence says, twirling her fingers in the air as if Erin is in front of her, a sprite on the wind, that deliciously cruel giggle. "Strong-willed, strong-minded, and fiercely loyal. Funny, compassionate, and ambitious. A young woman growing into her power until it was taken from her."

There's a severely long beat and Mikky closes his eyes, stomach turning anxiously as he hears the distant echo of Mrs. Vaughn's whimper. When he opens his eyes again, Mikky looks around at his classmates. They're captivated. Even Nasim is staring, attention rapt. But Mikky is distracted by the sea of phones, each a blinking screen recording Florence Cook's face. Like this is a concert, not a memorial.

"I worked closely with Erin too, you see. As many of you know, she was a teen ambassador for Cook Cosmetics on social media. A point of aspiration for many young women. One would think that I approached Erin, seeing the young woman that she was growing into, but it was quite the opposite. I remember it well, the day she came up to me, as a freshman, demanding that she be a Cook Girl. That's what she called it. Not me. She created the name a 'Cook Girl.' She told me that I needed her. That I may be the restauranteur, but that she was the *chef*. That all the girls that wore my product were the chefs. In many ways, Erin was emblematic of the very young woman that I wanted to inspire when I started this company.

"Once, the name 'Cook' was associated not just with Prophets Lake but with poison and cancer. And so in the creation of Cook Cosmetics, my mission was to create something beautiful from the ashes of my father's sins by using the wealth that he built up from tobacco farming to expand on the definition of what it means to be beautiful. By creating a clean, vegan, cruelty-free beauty company, primarily employing residents of Prophets Lake, I wanted to inject the local economy and, on a national level, use my brand to change industry standards and the conversation around beauty, empowering young women like Erin. Yet I cannot help but think that in some way, I, on a personal level, and we, as a community, failed her," Florence says. She shifts ever so slightly until she's staring down the barrel of the local news channel camera. That's when Mikky realizes this isn't just for them. She's broadcasting out her enduring message.

"Gendered violence is all too common in this world, and to be clear, that is what happened here. Someone thought to snuff out the bright light that was Erin Vaughn *because* she was a teenage girl. It is on all of us to remember her as she was: talented, lovely, tenacious, with a bright future. And to ruminate on what was lost. We must do better. We must protect teenage girls in the world that so desperately needs their relentless passion and genius."

There are nods throughout the crowd, but Mikky's skin crawls. There's something so strange about it all. Something disconnected.

And yet, Mikky can't help but think maybe Florence Cook knows what she's talking about. She's *convincing*. But Kyla's grimacing, her face twisting with distaste and disbelief, before it's overridden by that vacant expression again.

When he goes to look back at Florence, his gaze catches on Peter Moore's clenched jaw in profile. His teammates are giving him the side-eye, some of them even sidling away, like despite the rumors about Rowan, the stench of presumed guilt is wafting off of him.

Florence Cook closes out with, "This night is dedicated to Erin Julie Vaughn. But so too must our efforts be after this night. To find who committed this heinous crime and ensure it does not happen to any other young women in our community."

Mrs. Vaughn warbles, "To Erin."

And Mikky joins in as the rest of them chorus, "To Erin." Even Nasim can't refrain from doing so, and there's a strange grimness that doesn't lend itself to a high school soccer game, one that Mikky can't imagine someone breaking. Except someone does.

A voice crows out, "Let's go, Knights!" and it earns some cheers. It's enough for everyone to begin to shake off Erin's death like old hand-me-downs. Despite the immediate dismissal, Florence Cook doesn't look dissatisfied with her speech. There's a tiredness to her face now that she's not performing, like she really *isn't* used to emoting so much. She steps back, gives two feathery kisses that don't connect to both of Mrs. Vaughn's cheeks, shakes Mr. Vaughn's hand, then offers a tepid smile to Jason before she turns to leave. Clearly, she's not staying for the homecoming game.

As Florence walks down the stairs, Mikky's eyes catch on Kyla, and she's glaring at the CEO with the fury of a thousand suns. She grabs the hem of her skirt like she has to physically stop herself from moving. Her eyes burn like she's willing Florence, *Look at me, dammit.*

And Florence Cook does. She looks directly at her, tilting her head like Kyla is a fascinating specimen. The precise line of her painted mouth doesn't change. She nods, and then she's gone.

Mikky can feel the knot in his throat growing and he slowly looks over at Nasim, who is texting furiously in the group chat that Mikky *has* been invited to, which is . . . nice. But also not important. At least not right now. Mikky tugs on Nasim's sleeve.

"What?" Nasim says without looking Mikky's way. Mikky tugs the sleeve harder. "What is it?"

Mikky swallows hard and he leans down to whisper, "I think . . . I think Kyla knows something."

This grabs Nasim's attention. "What," he says for the third time, this time not a question at all. Mikky takes Nasim's chin and redirects his attention back to Kyla. She *still* hasn't looked away from Florence Cook's back, even as the Vaughns—Jason included—swarm her, hugging her tight. Mikky thinks too about the grimace on Kyla's face when Florence shifted just slightly to turn her face toward the camera, speaking to the dark lens. Something doesn't add up.

"I think she might know more about Erin's death than she's said."

CHAPTER FOURTEEN

Even after the game starts, it's hard for Mikky to wrap his head around what he's said. For once, Nasim gives him the time to think it through instead of attempting to pull every single thought out of Mikky's head while it's still half formed. It's not a hardship this time, because he's distracted, more invested in the soccer game being played than either team. Nasim doesn't look the type, but Mikky should know better than anyone to not judge someone by their appearance.

"Yes!" Nasim shouts, pumping his fist as a focused Jason drives the ball down the field.

Mikky's not sure if Jason's good enough to go pro, but he knows Jason's *good*. He dribbles it out of the reach of one of the opposing players, ducking and weaving with the ball as he approaches the goal, then kicks it straight into the top right corner of the net, no hesitation. He celebrates with his hands in the air, and the crowd roars its delight. The triumph of a brokenhearted brother, playing his heart out in memory of his sister. It really is a nice narrative.

But Mikky can't help but remember Jason's words from earlier that day, his face as he thought grimly of the memorial that he didn't even want to attend and the pressure on him to perform now. Mikky searches for the Vaughn parentals, but he can find only Mr. Vaughn, surrounded by other dads of the team as they try to show their support with as much masculinity as they possibly can.

Nasim turns to the girl next to him, and they celebrate, slapping each other on the back.

"Do you know her?" Mikky asks.

Nasim gives him a stink eye. "No, dude, we scored. Pay attention to the game. The other team has possession now."

Mikky isn't really sure what that has to do with anything, but he does as he's instructed, turning to look back at the game. The players in maroon—Prophets Lake—careen around Jason like little planets to his sun. They fall into some kind of loose defensive formation, if Mikky had to guess, but it's not enough. They're better on offense—or at least Jason is. The other team blows by him, their small forward spinning and moving with a skill that goes beyond high school. Mikky wouldn't be surprised if there was a scout or two here.

He doesn't think the other team is good enough to *win*, but this player is good enough to keep them in it, carrying them on his back.

The Prophets Lake goalie seems confused and practically dives out of the way of the soccer ball, like he's afraid of getting hit. The home side boos as the goal goes in. Now it's tied up.

"Come *on*," Nasim groans, like it's a personal slight to mess up a block. "My maman-joon could guard better than that, what the fuck?"

"If I didn't know any better, I'd say you were drunk," Mikky says, trying to break through Nasim's concentration.

He gets Nasim's partial attention. "No, I'm just very passionate about sports. You should see how I get about men's figure skating during the Olympics. I'm a terror," Nasim says casually. Then he's watching the soccer game again, tracking the ball as it goes from team to team. "Vaughn's playing really well tonight."

Mikky nods, glad that he has confirmation that Jason is *actually* good by someone who is apparently into sports.

Jason scores again, and the dance team jumps up, cheering. They're all smiling, functioning perfectly as a hype squad, with Kyla front and center, the fiercest and most precise of them all. Jason backpedals, pointing right at her and Kyla points back, like they're having their own private conversation. He throws back his head with a laugh Mikky can't hear, the sound swallowed by the crowd, and Kyla is folded back into her squad.

Mikky's thoughts from earlier begin to click more. "Remember what I was saying before?" he asks.

"You say a lot of things. Can you be more specific?" Nasim asks. He almost turns to look at Mikky, but instead he hisses between his teeth. "That big blond kid. He's gonna be a problem. Someone needs to cover him better."

Mikky can't even find it annoying. There's something endearing about learning more about his new friend. About a . . . potential more-than-friend, if the earlier hand-holding is any indication.

"What I said about Kyla. And how I think she might know more than she's been saying," Mikky explains, leaning closer to Nasim so he's not overheard.

"Right. I'm still waiting for you to share what gave you that impression," Nasim whispers back.

Mikky scoffs. "Did you not *see* the scathing hatred that she directed at Florence Cook with her eyes alone?" he asks.

"I don't really know her all that well. I thought that was just her face," Nasim explains, being almost diplomatic for once.

And . . . Mikky gets that, actually. Kyla's always been an opaque person. She's not easily readable. From the way she moves through school, he can tell she prefers it when people can't see beneath the surface. But, unfortunately for Kyla, Mikky can still see her down to her core. He's watched her assemble her masks and he knows that's all they are. He can't stop thinking about the way her latest one faltered, ever so slightly, as she realized—just as he had—that Florence Cook was addressing her speech to the camera, directly. Where Mikky had read it as sincerity, clearly, Kyla hadn't felt the same. She'd looked *enraged* from the second Florence met her eyes.

Mikky almost goes to explain this to Nasim, but then he stops. Nasim isn't paying attention right now. And like he said— he doesn't know Kyla like Mikky does. To Nasim, Kyla is the girl who's terrorizing his friend, not someone to be given the benefit of the doubt.

He'll go right to the source. If she knows something more than she said, something that would make her that angry, there must be a reason.

"You can come hang with us. We're going to the lakeside again, but with the jazz band and some of the theater kids," Nasim offers, even as Rowan impatiently honks the horn of their car. "They're cool. One of Gregory's exes is a theater kid, and they're still friends too."

Mikky has to stop himself from grinning. "So, what you're

saying is that you *really* don't want to stop hanging out with me."

Nasim rolls his eyes. "I'm offering you the chance to continue basking in my presence," he retorts, and Mikky barks out a laugh. Nasim smiles despite himself but jumps when Rowan holds their car horn a little longer this time, drawing attention to them.

A group of kids crossing in front of the car watch Rowan like they're a circus attraction, and they sink deeper into the driver's seat.

"Shit," Nasim mumbles to himself. "We gotta head out. So . . . are you coming?"

Mikky wants to say yes. He *really*, really wants to say yes. He can imagine it so easily. Huddled around a bonfire built by clumsy hands, singing and laughing, with Nasim's elbow tucked up against his. It's the kind of thing that he used to *dream* of having when he was a freshman here. And then he looks across the parking lot, and he sees her.

Kyla is walking to the hearse, her dance duffel thrown over her shoulder, chin tucked against her chest. She hasn't even bothered to change out of her uniform. Mikky came back for her, first and foremost. To make sure that she wasn't alone. She looks pretty alone right now.

"I can't. I gotta . . ." Mikky jerks his head over toward his sister.

Nasim's face screws up and Mikky knows him enough now to know that he's holding back every spiteful thing he might even be right to say. "Yeah, you gotta," he manages to get out, his tone scathing despite his restraint. "See you next week."

Mikky backs away, watching him until Nasim slides into the backseat of Rowan's car. And then Mikky's sprinting across the parking lot, in the opposite direction of his car. He manages to get to the hearse as Kyla turns the key in the ignition. She doesn't look surprised.

Mikky must be losing his touch.

"Hey, can I get a ride home?" he asks.

"Have you forgotten how to drive?" Kyla retorts.

Mikky counts his lucky stars that she didn't just roll up the window and hit him with her bumper. "No, but I'm kinda tired and I don't want to fall asleep at the wheel."

"It's eight p.m., Mikky."

Mikky lets out a long dramatic sigh. "*Look*, I am offering a truce because I think you've had a very trying day, and I know you think I'm annoying for checking in on you and whatever, but maybe you want to take a day off for once? I think Dad is getting suspicious. He thinks we're fighting." A little white lie never hurt anyone.

Kyla squints at him, looking him up and down. She tucks her tongue into her cheek, eyes shifting back and forth over her dashboard. Finally, she says, "Get in, then."

Mikky pumps his fist and Kyla rolls her eyes so hard that he's surprised they don't fall out of her head and into her lap. When he slips into the passenger seat, she doesn't even give him a chance to buckle the seat belt before she peels out. It's hard to cut through the crowd and their raucous display of excitement, but Kyla is liberal with the horn, and people recognize the hearse and *move*.

"Going pretty hard tonight. I guess it *is* the season opener," Mikky says as Kyla tries to navigate out of the overcrowded field parking lot.

"Do you expect me to drive you back here tomorrow?" Kyla deadpans.

Mikky groans. It's like a forty-minute walk back to the school, especially with the hills, and he left his ugly and only pair of sneakers back in his gym locker. "Shit, I mean, I don't have to leave the house this weekend . . . ," he says, rubbing at his chin. "I *do* have a Common App essay to write. Can you just drive me to school on Monday?"

Kyla cuts a look over at him, like she's regretting agreeing to drive him home. Pursing her lips, she offers, "If you're up early enough tomorrow, I can drive you and double back to the funeral home for work." It's as much of an agreement to the truce as he's going to get.

"Thanks," Mikky says. "But you're going to work tomorrow? I thought you were going out tonight."

"No," Kyla scoffs. "Why did you think I was?"

Mikky stares at her. Kyla is *popular*. He knows what popular people do after big games. They go out to one of the players' houses and drink and make out and cause general havoc in the name of youth. Mikky would've expected Kyla to go for sure, considering that's almost certainly where the rest of the dance squad will be.

"I mean, are you not a partier?"

"My best friend is dead. Do I look like I'm in the mood to party?"

Every time she says it, Mikky has to stop himself from flinching.

"Fair."

As soon as they hit the street, it's a much smoother ride.

"I thought *you* would've gone out, though. With your . . . friends," Kyla says, her voice curling around her distaste. She worries her bottom lip between her teeth like she has been all night.

"I thought about it," Mikky says, ignoring her tone. "But I wanted to go with you."

Kyla's expression twists into something heavy with disgust. "I don't need a *babysitter*, Mikky. I've been on my own long enough now."

Mikky turns fully in his seat and very seriously says, "No, you haven't. You haven't been alone in your entire life."

Mikky can read the story Kyla has written out for herself. Abandoned by their mother. Abandoned by Mikky. Lonely little Kyla with cadavers for friends, except for Erin, who would never abandon her. But then she was taken from her. Except the story's not true. Kyla has always been surrounded by people—Dad, the Vaughns, her team, Mikky, even if from afar, all of fucking Prophets Lake, even—that loved her when their mother wasn't enough.

Kyla looks into the pitch-blackness of the suburb, but says nothing.

Mikky reaches into his pocket, searching for his vape for courage. "Do you mind?" he asks.

"Roll down the window."

Mikky does and takes a hit. When he exhales, he puts his foot up on the seat before he turns back to look at his little sister. "What did you think of the memorial?"

"Stupid," Kyla mumbles.

Mikky inhales. "You think?"

"Of course."

"Do you know Florence Cook?" Mikky blurts out. No games. He takes another hit from the vape as he waits for Kyla's response.

"I've met her in passing at the Vaughns' New Year's parties," Kyla says finally. "Why?"

As a kid, Erin was always the reactionary one, sugary sweet with her lies at first, but easily caught up in them if you had a little too much information. From the sound of it, she didn't evolve much. But Kyla is quiet and careful about the things that she does, and sure enough her face gives nothing away now, not even to Mikky.

"I don't know . . . when you two looked at each other, I just got the impression that you did. And you didn't seem all that pleased," he explains.

Kyla nods slowly. "I was just surprised that she would come. She wasn't at the funeral. Besides, Florence isn't really known for attending community events, even if her name *is* plastered on literally everything in this damn town."

"It's kinda good, though, right?" he asks to gauge her reaction. Because Kyla hadn't looked simply surprised, she'd been angry.

"How?"

"I mean . . . she's really famous. And there was a news reporter there, and I know you think . . . Rowan reported Peter and it was a lie or whatever—"

"Stop."

"Okay, what *do* you have against Rowan specifically, though? Like this is starting to feel a little personal," he blurts out, unable to help himself. "Like, I know they called you feral—" *And threatened you with telling your secrets in the hallway. Secrets that they're somehow privy to.*

Kyla slams on the brakes so violently that Mikky lurches forward, his seat belt knocking the wind out of him. "Mention Rowan Villareal again in this car and I'll drive you to the outskirts of town and make you walk."

It's absurd enough that Mikky has to swallow the inappropriate urge to laugh. It's not until he says, "Fine," that Kyla eases the car forward again.

Mikky changes tactics. "I *mean*, the whole thing about gendered violence, statistically, it's true, right? Maybe the cops missed something with Peter. Or missed something in general. Maybe after what she said, someone else will come forward. Maybe someone saw something," he says, needling. Kyla's hands tighten on the steering wheel and she leans farther over it, glaring into the dark.

"No one saw anything," Kyla snaps. "You can't see anything that late by the lake."

Mikky frowns. "You don't know that. None of us knows that," he says. Something inside of him whispers, *Unless you do*. "But even still . . . you know I hate rich people, but it's good she's bringing eyes to it, right?"

"Florence came because it's starting to look bad that she didn't. She doesn't care about Erin." Kyla sneers, shaking her head.

She uses her first name with a practiced familiarity. Like that's how she always refers to her. Like she's had a reason to.

"How do you know she doesn't care about Erin? I thought you said you didn't know her," he says. He thinks back to how Florence returned Kyla's look. *Does she know you?*

"I don't," Kyla says immediately. She's lying but Mikky has no real evidence to call bullshit with. Just a feeling. And it's growing.

Kyla's smile looks more like a grimace when she looks up. "But you're right."

"About what, this time?" Mikky asks. He can't quite manage to hide his eagerness, his fingers twitching along his thighs. He balls his hands into fists to calm himself.

"Everyone's gonna be talking about it again."

The way she says it, Kyla thinks that's a *bad* thing. And now Mikky is sure that Kyla does know something. And she wants nothing more than for what she knows to be buried along with Erin.

CHAPTER FIFTEEN

With the memorial fresh in his mind, Mikky takes the weekend to organize his thoughts. By the dim light of his desk lamp, with Knocked Loose blaring into his ears from his headphones, he first tries to write the facts out. The second he writes the words KYLA CONNECTION TO ERIN'S DEATH? he immediately blacks them out and flushes the paper down the toilet.

The one thing he does know is Kyla would never have killed Erin, and he doesn't need anyone to find his paper and get the wrong idea. There are surely other reasons that she'd have something to hide, and *that's* what Mikky needs to focus on.

Mikky starts again, listing what he knows on his phone, in a locked Note. He knows that Erin died at the lakeside by blunt force trauma. He knows it was ruled a homicide. He knows that Erin worked as a Cook Cosmetics influencer, that Erin was close to Florence, and yet, Kyla seems to have a personal intense dislike for the woman. Kyla *knows* that woman but won't admit it.

There are a lot of things he doesn't know, though. He doesn't know what Erin was doing at the lakeside. He doesn't know how Kyla knows Rowan or why she would think they would lie about Peter. He doesn't know why Kyla is going so hard defending Peter.

He doesn't know *why* Kyla won't admit to knowing Florence. None of it connects. He has no clues. Except.

That one thing from the confrontation, that thing Rowan said, niggles at Mikky again.

Mikky doesn't know what the fuck a Test Kitchen is. And he doesn't know why the very mention of it sent Kyla's hackles rising. His instincts rear their heads again. He shouldn't have let it go before, he thinks. Rowan had so deftly gotten their way, gotten their friends to give in too easily.

Too bad Mikky's a pusher.

By the Monday after the game, Kyla still hasn't called off her minions, even though Mikky can sense the shifting tide—Florence Cook's speech resonated with the town's population, and the spotlight that had been waning on Peter Moore is back in full force. People aren't calling Rowan a liar anymore, but that just makes Kyla's rage more palpable. So Mikky's little group draws in even tighter around them. It's not all bad, though, because it means Mikky can volunteer for a turn to walk Rowan from their free period to lunch, when both Gregory and Nasim happen to be in class on the other side of the building. And he'll finally get a chance to question them. If he can find them.

Mikky spends far too long playing scavenger hunt, weaving through the mazelike hallways of Prophets Lake High, before he finally catches up to Rowan, finding them close to the library. He groans. He already checked the library before.

Mikky jogs, finally falling in step with them.

"Rowan, you were supposed to wait for me," Mikky crows. He throws his arm around Rowan's shoulders, feels them tense beneath the weight. Mikky doesn't allow them to get away, though. He guides them with purpose *away* from the library, closer to the swimming pool and the locker room, where they are much less likely to be interrupted.

"Oh, was I?" Rowan mumbles under their breath.

"You know you were," Mikky says. "I've been looking everywhere for you. Have you been *avoiding* me?"

Rowan's mouth moves like they're chewing gum, hands fluttering over their pockets, as they nervously chatter, "Had a few things to do. Went to a teacher's office hours. Went to pee. Now I just gotta return this book to the library, and then I was going to meet you guys for lunch. Nasim was looking forward to that really gross pizza he's super into, and he's gonna notice—"

"Nasim isn't really my top priority at the moment, I'm afraid." Mikky honestly regrets that. He likes the idea of making Nasim a priority, but Kyla is always going to top his list.

"Nasim would say he should always be top priority," Rowan says.

Mikky snorts. "Yeah, he probably would," he agrees, unable to help the affection that warms his voice. For a moment Mikky regrets softening before he realizes that his warmth for Nasim has allowed Rowan to relax. To be off guard. Good. That's exactly what Mikky needs Rowan to be. After Friday night, Mikky knows he can't wait any longer.

"So, what's this Test Kitchen business you mentioned to my sister?" he finally asks.

Rowan's expression tells Mikky everything he needs to know. They pull themselves from under Mikky's arm, eyes darting back and forth, searching for a way out. "I don't know what you're talking about."

"I think you do. Since you threatened her with exposing her 'secrets,' and the Test Kitchen, whatever that is, is apparently one of them. How do you even know my sister's secrets?" Mikky asks.

Rowan folds their arms over their chest, defensively. "I've heard some things."

"What things?"

"Drop it, Mikky."

"I really don't like being treated like an idiot, Rowan," Mikky says cheerfully.

"I'm *not*," Rowan mumbles. "I just don't want to talk about this."

Mikky's smile widens. "Oh, you don't?"

Rowan's brown eyes harden into flint. "You and your sister are kinda the same."

"How so?"

"You both like to bulldoze people when you don't get your way," Rowan says.

"Oh, and you can't be bulldozed, right?" Mikky asks, taking a step closer. Rowan doesn't flinch, not like they did when there were others around. "Not like everyone thinks you can. Don't you get tired of pretending to be spineless?"

Rowan doesn't get a chance to respond.

"What are you doing back here? You two were supposed to meet us in the cafeteria! You're lucky I have your location, Rowan," a familiar voice grumbles.

Mikky has never dreaded Nasim's presence, but he does now. Almost immediately, Rowan's face flushes with relief.

"I wanted to chat with Rowan about a few things. No big deal," Mikky says, trying to dismiss everything before Nasim notices.

Rowan refuses to let that happen. "He was asking me about his evil sister," they say.

Mikky's eyes narrow. "Watch your mouth," he starts, but Rowan's words light a fire under Nasim's ass.

He shoves between Mikky and Rowan, grabbing Rowan's shoulders and rubbing them. "Did she do anything new today?"

"She's ignoring me today, which is good," Rowan says, sounding appropriately pitiful. "I'm just . . . tired of talking about it, mostly."

Mikky's eyes narrow. Rowan is good. But not good enough. The problem with good liars is that they assume that most of the time no one will call them out on their shit. Rowan's unlucky that Mikky doesn't really *give* a fuck. Rowan is unlucky that Mikky still remembers the exact word they used to describe Mikky's *sister*.

"They're lying," he says bluntly.

Nasim lets go of Rowan and turns around, defensive. Rowan is already stiffening back up.

Mikky folds his arms over his chest, lifting his chin.

"Don't assume you know how they feel. If they're tired of talking about it, they're tired," Nasim snaps.

"They're tired of talking about it, because they don't want you and I to ask the right questions. Like why does Kyla even know who the fuck you are?"

And isn't that the million-dollar question? Nasim frowns, opening his mouth like he means to find an answer for that. Then he stops, because it's true. There was no reason for Rowan and

Kyla to ever cross paths before Mikky dropped in. No reason for her to even know they exist. Rowan, Nasim, and the others take pride in being on the fringe. Gregory's crush on Kyla isn't even based on anything real, all of it purely aesthetic. And yet, Kyla focused in on *Rowan*. Specifically.

"This is why it would be better for you to tell me what's going on."

"Nothing's going on!" Nasim squawks, but he doesn't look so sure now.

"Unfortunately, that's not true," Mikky says, apologetic. "So, Rowan, Kyla accused you of reporting Peter to the police and you threw something called the 'Test Kitchen' in her face. What is it and what's going on between you two?"

Rowan grows cagier by the second. Then, quietly, they say, "Look, I really *didn't* report Peter, but . . . I *do* think it's him. I knew Erin. That's why I think he could've . . . hurt her."

Nasim gapes.

Mikky's eyes narrow. "How did you know Erin?"

"Like, I hooked up with her," Rowan snaps.

"You *what*?" Nasim demands.

Rowan pinches the bridge of their nose, shaking their head. "Look, we . . . I don't know. We were hooking up for months. Since last February."

Mikky doesn't even know where Erin would *meet* Rowan. Can't even figure out a circumstance in which they'd start interacting. Maybe a school project turned into more? Maybe Erin got off on it, hooking up with someone who was so below her social stratosphere. That sounds like her. Or at least the version of Erin that everyone seems to have known.

"You were dating Lydia in February," Nasim says slowly.

Rowan can't meet Nasim's eyes, staring up at the ceiling. "Yeah."

"But you still . . ." Nasim trails off, shaking his head, like he can't compute that his "oh-so-very-nice" friend isn't all that nice, at least not to the girl they dated.

"So, how does Peter factor into this?" Mikky asks.

Rowan scoffs, and it's a cruel sound. "She thought he was stupid. She started dating him to make me jealous."

"Did it work?" Mikky challenges, because he can see it. Nasim might not be able to see what Rowan is capable of, but Mikky isn't in the business of underestimating *anyone*.

"Oh my God, *no*," Rowan spits.

Nasim pushes. "But then what's the 'Test Kitchen' thing?"

Rowan shakes their head, rubbing at their knuckles in an odd nervous quirk. "Uh . . . I don't really know, I just wanted her to think I did. It's something Erin would mention her and Kyla working on in passing, but she wouldn't tell me what it was. I know it's supposed to be a secret, though, so I tried to use it to get her off my back."

Mikky focuses all his attention on Rowan, waiting with a pursed mouth for more.

"But there's this Instagram," they blurt out. "Erin's secret Instagram account. *Not* a finsta. Not really. It's called @eleanor.rigby_1. It's got something to do with that." And then they clamp their mouth shut, shaking their head as they take a step back, away from Mikky and Nasim, like they already regret the admission.

Nasim follows them, clucking softly. "Thank you for telling us, Rowan," he says kindly. Then he leans forward, wrapping his arms around Rowan in a tight hug that Rowan returns.

They don't blink as they stare over Nasim's shoulder, right at Mikky. Mikky narrows his eyes and Rowan glowers back.

Caught you, Mikky doesn't say out loud. *I see you for what you are.*

This is the Prophets Lake that Mikky remembers. Things aren't completely the same as before, but the den of vipers is. They all just wear different stripes.

CHAPTER SIXTEEN

"*—tenacious, with a bright future, and to ruminate on what was lost. We must do better. We must protect teenage girls in the world that so desperately needs their relentless passion and genius.*" Florence Cook's voice comes through Mikky's shitty, outdated iPhone with a slightly tinny quality, but her words reverberate in the form of hundreds of thousands of likes. Dumbfounded, Mikky refreshes the page and the likes climb from 836,000 to 842,000. He knows that if he waits another fifteen minutes, they'll climb again, probably clearing a million.

Mikky didn't even know that the speech went viral until a friend back in Boston DM'ed it to him during last period. He doesn't recognize the credit tag, but when he presses it, it takes him to a Prophets Lake freshman's page. Her page is public, and from her posts, she looks like a dance team hopeful, following all of Kyla's squad and regularly posting clips of herself doing layouts and double twists and eight-count combos. But by far, her most liked post is her video of Florence Cook at Erin's memorial.

The comments are filled with well-meaning, mournful strangers.

this is so sad 💔 💔

rip Erin Vaughn

> teenage girls deserve so much more
>
> how can we help?

They're filled with vultures, too.

> Do you own this video? Do you consent to our usage? We work at Fox.
>
> Do you own this video? Do you consent to our usage? We're from CNN.
>
> We're from NBC. Do you consent to our usage?

On and on it goes, news corporations, blogs, Twitter accounts. And under each one, that same dance team hopeful has sent a:

> Yes, of course, spread the word so we can find who did this. #flyhigherin 💔

That hashtag has stuck. It's everywhere, sticky with sentiment, all from people that didn't know Erin Vaughn at all.

"It's gone viral on TikTok, too. My squad was distracted all through practice by it. I had to ban phones halfway through."

Kyla moves so silently that her voice nearly sends Mikky into a panic attack.

Mikky slumps at the kitchen table, fumbling his phone as he tries to turn it off but only succeeds in making it louder so that it blares out, tinny and distorted: *"This night is dedicated to Erin Julie Vaughn."*

Holding his breath, he waits for Kyla to react with the same simmering rage that pooled in her eyes the night of the game.

It doesn't come. Instead, she rolls her eyes and drops into the chair across from Mikky, then leans forward to squint at him.

"Are you . . . okay, Kyla?" Mikky asks when she doesn't say anything right away.

Kyla's nose twitches again, the same way it seems to whenever Mikky says her name.

"I told you. *She* got what she wanted. Everyone's getting what they wanted," Kyla says.

"What?"

"Now people will comment on this instead of her silence under Cook Cosmetics' IG posts," Kyla says simply.

Mikky nods slowly. "Yes, but I think . . . I think it's going to be bigger than just that tomorrow. You need to be careful."

"Careful, why?"

Mikky can see tomorrow morning's headlines so clearly in his head. Florence Cook comes out of her own self-imposed hermitage to speak on gendered violence, reigniting the dying embers of a murder investigation. At the center of which is a beautiful white girl, brimming with potential, now stolen. He can see the vultures descending, all looking for another angle on the story, another quote, and finding Kyla Graves, the living best friend of the deceased.

"Just . . . don't talk to strangers," Mikky warns.

Kyla rolls her eyes. "I learned that lesson when I was five, Mikky." She sits back in her chair, scrolling through her own phone. She looks younger in the nighttime, devoid of makeup. Kyla takes good care of her skin, but there are tiny imperfections beneath the glitz and glam of Cook Cosmetics. The texture on her forehead. The milia at the corner of her eye. The bump along her jaw. All of it makes her look more human.

More vulnerable.

It makes Mikky not want to *believe* that Kyla might know more than what she's been claiming to, even though he can't shake the thought.

He recalls that finsta Rowan mentioned again. Between getting his homework done and dinner, he hasn't had a chance to look. In the quiet, when it's just the two of them, Mikky types in @eleanor.rigby_1.

He takes one last quick look at Kyla, thumb hovering over that name. And then he presses.

The crush of disappointment is hard to keep away, even though he knew it wouldn't be that easy.

The @eleanor.rigby_1 account is private. Whatever's behind the lock is something that Erin guarded closely, if Rowan is to be believed. But there's still enough information to tell Mikky *something* about where to look next.

> @eleanor.rigby_1   11 posts   30 followers   1 following

Instead of a profile description, there's a blank space where something identifying might be. But that one following . . . He goes onto Kyla's Instagram quickly, entering her follower list, thumbing to search. There's a swell of premature relief that bubbles up, spreading through his limbs when he searches and finds not a hint of an Eleanor. Not even an Ellie. He tamps that reassurance down quickly. Kyla is still involved somehow.

When Mikky looks up, Kyla is staring him right in the eye, a pint of ice cream cradled in her hands, spoon tucked on the inside of her cheek. He didn't even notice her get up to get ice cream. She opens her mouth to say something when suddenly she winces and slaps a hand to her head.

Mikky snorts. "Are you good?"

Kyla glowers at him and mumbles something indecipherable around her spoon before it drops from her mouth, clattering on the table. She's trying to school her face, unwilling to show weakness, but can't quite manage it as she winces. Mikky's lips slowly pull into a grin.

"Ooooh," he coos. "Brain freeze."

Kyla can't fight it any longer. *"Ow,"* she whines.

It's so childish that it makes Mikky throw his head back and laugh. "Wo-ow," he sings.

"Shut *up*," Kyla insists, but she's smiling too. It's tiny, but it's there, and Mikky warms again. She looks like herself, before grief took her and twisted her into something that he doesn't recognize. They're nine and ten again and she's showing him the gaping space where her tooth was, lower lip still a little bloody. He gave her ice cream then too, and she got a brain freeze, just like this.

When he looks at her, he thinks she might remember that very moment too.

He sets his phone down on the table and sits in the relief for now that the Kyla he knows is still there. Somewhere. Maybe he's wrong.

Tuesday goes about as well as Mikky predicted. The parking lot is overpacked to the point that it's hard for him to find a spot. Mostly because of the seven news vans scattered around the front, all with their own respective crews relaying the same tragic tale of Erin Vaughn to the rest of the world. The students of Prophets Lake vie to be in the background, eager for a moment in the spotlight, to recount how they knew Erin Vaughn. Eager to point out and identify every single person who knew her a little more.

The stares are different now. Not judgmental but hungry. Mikky is used to being stared at, and so is Kyla. But Jason isn't. Not like this. And he's not as well versed in pretending it's not happening, as demonstrated when he snaps at some sophomores across the hall from him who are pretending not to gossip.

And then there's Peter Moore, who wilts under the attention in one breath, and then lashes out with rage in the next. Not even Kyla's flagging campaign against Rowan can help Peter when he's doing nothing to help his own case. In the grim fluorescent school lighting, his handsomeness almost works against him, making him look exactly like the soulless kind of boy that *could* hurt Erin, if he really wanted to.

Everywhere Mikky goes, he hears the echo of Florence Cook's words, divorced from context, and he's no longer surprised that they're echoing across the country, too. Mikky wanted this to be a good thing—maybe it would push someone to finally speak up. It's what he told Kyla. Only, now he feels a little foolish. This isn't about Erin, not like how it should've been. The virality of his little sister's best friend's murder and how it's been made into a girlboss moment by a rich white woman who knew her in passing would be sickening if it wasn't so expected.

Dead pretty white blond girls are always a story that people pay attention to and follow until the very end. They are always venerated to sainthood, and no one cares about who they really were, in life. Not really. It was about what they *represent*.

Mikky knows this won't die down. Not again. Until this is solved, there's always going to be a news van. There's always going to be a spotlight. There's always going to be someone there, pointing at Kyla and calling her "the dead girl's best friend."

Not unless Mikky ends it, by finding out what happened to Erin once and for all, for her.

"I didn't get a chance to ask you today," Nasim says as they walk through the teeming parking lot. Mikky slows down his steps to keep pace with him and Nasim doesn't even seem to notice, taking it for granted in the most endearing way. Mikky tries to duck and dodge the cameras before they figure out who he is. Luckily, he's saved when they all zero in on Peter exiting, every dark lens pointed at him, as he runs toward his BMW. "Did you look into that Instagram account?"

"Yeah," Mikky admits. "No connections so far. It's locked and pretty unidentifiable. Are we sure—"

"Rowan wouldn't lie," Nasim interrupts.

Unless cheating no longer counts as lying, Mikky doesn't think that's true. When they reach Mikky's car, Nasim looks over at him expectantly, hand on the door handle.

When he meets Nasim's extremely unimpressed expression, his lips pursed into an almost-pout, glasses slipping down his nose, he finally asks, "Am I taking you somewhere?"

Nasim scoffs. "Yeah. Your house."

"*My* house?" Mikky sputters, because he's never really had friends over to either of his houses. It's weird because it's not like no one has ever wanted to come by. Plenty of people wanted to see his mother's state-of-the-art doorman apartment. But Mikky is weird about having people in his space, even people he likes. Dr. Grosse helped him realize that his defensiveness is a result of his bad freshman year.

Yet despite his initial reaction, for some reason he doesn't feel defensive now.

"Yeah. We need to collaborate on a plan to get into the Instagram account, because I don't think you'll do it on your own," Nasim says.

It makes Mikky laugh.

"Yeah, okay, let's go to my house," he agrees, and opens the door. After stowing his things and settling behind the wheel, he puts the car in reverse, beginning the delicate task of navigating his way out of the overcrowded lot.

As he does, Nasim says, "I saw the video. I think I get what you meant now."

"What do *you* mean?" Mikky says as he drives very slowly behind a group of unhurried students searching for their ride.

"Your sister *did* look like she knew Florence Cook. And she looked . . . angry," Nasim says. He turns in his seat, pulling against the seat belt. "I'm guessing you think Rowan had something to do with Erin's death now, but have you ever stopped to think that Kyla might—"

"No. Never," Mikky interrupts.

Because Kyla might know something about Florence Cook. She might know things about Rowan and their relationship with Erin. She might even know what Erin was doing out at the lakeside that night. But she doesn't know what happened to Erin. To even think that she might know implies that she was there when her best friend was killed and hasn't said anything. It's . . . inconceivable. The only thing more inconceivable would be the idea that she might have killed her.

"Look, it's important we consider all options—"

"Not that one, though," Mikky says firmly. He shakes his head as he finally pulls out of the parking lot, and once he's on the road, it's easier to find the words. "You don't get it. Erin and Kyla have known each other since they were in diapers. Their birthdays are *weeks* apart, but they always had a party right on the midpoint so that they wouldn't have to celebrate separately."

"That's a very warm and fuzzy story, but do you know anything about their relationship right before Erin died?" Nasim challenges.

"Do you?" Mikky challenges right back.

Nasim sighs, shaking his head. "Come on, man."

The thing is . . . Mikky *does* know how their relationship was. He may not have witnessed it, but he talked to his sister. Erin and Kyla were getting ready for their second year as cocaptains of the dance team, and Kyla was sure they were going to win regionals in early December and sail right to state in January. Then they'd take nationals in May. They'd even been talking about some back-to-school party, and Erin had been dropping hints the entire time that someone wanted to ask Kyla to the party, but she wouldn't say who. It had *infuriated* Kyla because Kyla hates not knowing, but the entire time she'd recounted the story in her voice memo, Mikky could hear the fondness overtaking the annoyance. The scope of Kyla's love for Erin isn't compatible with the idea that she might have killed her.

But it feels . . . oddly revealing to share that with Nasim in a way that makes Mikky's skin crawl. So, he doesn't. He just sighs and keeps driving.

"Are you serious about going to my house?" Mikky asks.

"Why would I waste my time joking about it? Yeah, we gotta do this, and besides, I wanna see your house."

"It looks like every other house," Mikky says.

Nasim rubs his chin, surprisingly thoughtful. "I know, but like . . . sometimes, I look at you and your sister and I think it might look like the Addams Family on the inside."

Mikky laughs, glad for the subject change. "Do we give off Addams Family to you?"

"Well, she definitely has the Wednesday deadpan down," Nasim insists. "And she drives a hearse. And you're . . . all of that." He vaguely gestures to Mikky's outfit, and Mikky laughs even louder this time.

"We own a funeral home, but I'm the only punk in the household. And Kyla drives a hearse because . . . she thinks it's rad," he says. It always makes him grin, the oxymoron that his sister is. "And she's right. It's really rad."

Mikky pulls into the driveway easily and leaves a wide enough space for Kyla, who tends to park crooked. He jumps out and ignores Nasim, who is taking in the Colonial farmhouse that looks just like everyone else's, except for the big tree in the back that arches up high over the second story. Mikky grabs his book bag and clomps up the slightly overgrown path, over the loose bricks that need to be fixed.

"Kyla's going to be home right after practice, by the way, so we can't be plotting all day," Mikky says as he searches his pocket for his house keys.

"Yeah, our paths crossing sounds like a bad idea," Nasim agrees. He stares at Mikky as he searches, bemused. "You really think your keys are in your pocket?"

"Uh, where else?" Mikky asks.

"I'm just saying, your pants are, like . . . really tight, man," Nasim says.

And he does *not* sound like he hates that fact. Nasim is right, though, so Mikky hides his smirk in his book bag as he searches the front pocket and finds his house keys there. Once they enter, Nasim toes off his sneakers right there at the door, next to the neat row of shoes, including a pair of Mikky's Doc Martens and Kyla's HOKAs.

"Do you want something to drink?" Mikky asks as he sets his keys down in the bowl.

"No, I'm good," Nasim says, wandering distractedly into the kitchen. "Oh, hello?"

Mikky whips around. Nasim is staring into the living room. The television's not on, but the room is indeed occupied.

"You're . . . home," Mikky says.

Dad raises an eyebrow and gestures wildly at the living room. "I do, in fact, live here."

Nasim hums his amusement while Mikky fights every urge telling him to turn around and say they have to leave, especially when Dad looks directly at him, waiting patiently for an introduction.

Mikky postpones it. "Yeah, I know, but the funeral home?"

"No one's died," Dad says.

Nasim smothers a laugh. "Dark humor runs in the family, then?" he asks.

"Mikky and Kyla get it from somewhere," Dad says with a small smile.

He doesn't look worried, but Mikky can tell that there's something that's . . . off. Dad likes to say that someone is always dying. Mostly because it's true. For Dad to be home . . .

"So . . . who's your *friend*, Mik?" Dad asks, putting far too much emphasis on that word.

Jesus.

"Uh—"

Nasim confidently marches up to Dad with his hand out. Dad takes it and shakes.

"I'm Nasim Talebi. We're in AP Chem together." Nasim offers the introduction Mikky withheld.

"I'm Mr. Graves. Good to meet you, Nasim," Dad says. He doesn't look like he's moving anytime soon, with a book folded over in his lap, drumming his fingers against the flimsy back cover. "We are a snack-forward household, so please help yourself. Mikky knows where everything is."

"I'm not hungry, but I'll keep it in mind, thanks," Nasim says. He smiles broadly at Mikky.

"We should do our work," Mikky says. He reaches out, grabbing the back of Nasim's jacket and gently tugging him away. "We're gonna be upstairs in my room. See you in a bit, Dad?"

Dad nods slowly and says nothing until Mikky has one foot on the stairs. Then, "Keep the door open, all right, bud?"

Mikky's boot catches on the step and he nearly tumbles onto his face. Nasim throws his head back and cackles as Mikky rights himself and scurries up the stairs, leading them into his bedroom. He groans, pinching his nose bridge as he looks around.

Mikky hadn't expected anyone over, but at least he keeps reasonably clean. There's makeup all over the top of his dresser, a broken nail polish bottle, and he hasn't made his bed, but there's no dirty laundry on the floor. Mikky throws the covers up quickly then sits at the edge of his bed and starts undoing the laces of his knee-high boots while Nasim takes the liberty of looking around, inspecting each part of the room with a keen eye.

"Guitar, huh?" Nasim tosses over his shoulder. "Okay, stereotype."

"Am I?" Mikky says, keeping his eyes focused on his boots. "I always thought I was singular."

"Alt boy that plays guitar? There are a thousand of you," Nasim says with a sly smile. He drops his bag by Mikky's desk and leans back against it, quirking an eyebrow. "Your dad is a funny guy."

Mikky groans again, shaking his head as he tosses his boots farther from his bed, and pulls open his backpack, searching for the copy of *Das Parfum* he's supposed to read and annotate before the next German class.

"He's ridiculous is what he is," he says.

"So, that's genetic too," Nasim retorts, pushing off from the desk, not even bothering to bring his backpack when he sits on the edge of the bed, next to Mikky. He looks over at the open door and lets out another laugh.

"We can close the door," Mikky says. It would make sense; they'll probably be discussing things that Dad shouldn't overhear, and certainly not Kyla if she decides to end dance practice earlier than usual.

"Your dad said not to," Nasim insists.

"You're not even gay." Mikky knows he's fishing, but whatever.

Nasim lets out a soft laugh as he leans in, tilting his head just so. Suddenly, he's no longer overeager, know-it-all Nasim Talebi. He's not just *casually* hot. Suddenly, there's all this *intention*, and Mikky's breath catches in his throat as Nasim sidles over, sliding his hand over the rumpled sheets, until his fingers are ghosting over

Mikky's thigh. He leans up, lips a few inches away from Mikky's.

"Don't presume my alphabet," he whispers.

"My mistake," Mikky says, unable to speak above a hush.

Nasim leans in even closer and says, "Good. And I'm the B. For bisexual."

And then his smile spreads like molasses, slow until he throws himself back and *cackles* once again.

Mikky's cheeks bloom with heat. "You *fucker*."

"I have game, yeah?" Nasim asks. He's showing all his teeth as he grins, which should be unattractive but isn't, even with his glasses crooked on his nose. "You would've let me kiss you."

"Yeah, *right*," Mikky mumbles.

Nasim shakes his head. "Nah, I'm a *respectful* boy. I wouldn't have done it here."

At "here," Mikky swallows the shy embarrassment and turns fully to look at Nasim. He lifts a hand, hesitant, waiting for Nasim to say no, and when he doesn't, he presses his fingers against the underside of Nasim's chin. It's already stubbly there and Nasim's lips part, probably to say something smart, as Mikky presses his thumb into the jut of his chin.

"Listen, Nasim," Mikky says with borrowed courage, "if I ever do kiss you, it *won't* be to prove a point."

Nasim is the one letting out a shuddering breath now, his smile gone. There's a beat of silence where Mikky worries that he might've gotten it wrong. That he might've fucked this all up before it even became something more.

And then: "Good."

Nasim tugs his face away, his cheeks burning now, and Mikky's hand falls back into his own lap. He clears his throat and smiles as he watches Nasim reorient himself, coughing then clapping his hands together and turning to meet Mikky's eye seriously, facing the potential awkwardness head-on.

It's what Mikky likes most about him, he thinks.

"I know you have homework, but can you do that while we brainstorm about how to get into this Instagram account?" Nasim asks as he finally leans back and turns to grab his backpack.

"So . . . you *really* want to help me get into the account when you know I don't think Kyla did this?" Mikky asks.

Nasim purses his lips. "You think Rowan did, right?"

"Well . . . I have my suspicions," Mikky admits. "But Erin was popular. I suspect nearly everyone."

For a moment Nasim looks like he might argue with him. But he doesn't. Instead, he says, "Well, I *do* suspect everyone."

That's new. "Oh?"

"Everyone's going to be looked at differently now, with all the media attention. The police have got nothing on Peter, so when it gets out that Rowan was sneaking around with Erin—and it *will* get out eventually—I want unequivocal proof that Rowan had nothing to do with this. Not some false narrative that Rowan was jealous."

It's sound. If Rowan's not guilty, that is.

"So . . . breaking into an Instagram account. I'm sure you've already got a few ideas," Mikky says casually. When he looks down at the notebook Nasim has pulled out, he sees it's *full* of notes like the ones on his own phone, all the information they already know and the questions they have.

Nasim flashes his teeth in a wide grin. "I have a few."

CHAPTER SEVENTEEN

Before Mikky left, breakfast was an important affair in the Graves household. It's a tradition that's returned now. This morning Dad is on duty, serving up waffles and fresh fruit. Exactly what Kyla was considering for her next breakfast duty. She'll have to amend her plans—maybe fancy up some oatmeal. Overnight oats it.

Kyla watches her brother as she eats her waffles, and he looks up like he can sense her staring. She sneakily shows him her middle finger, and he chokes on a waffle piece in his laughter. She sits back in satisfaction. Sometimes she doesn't mind a return to tradition. She wouldn't actually mind her brother's presence, if it were only just about breakfast and missing her and Dad. No, unfortunately, Mikky is still convinced Kyla needs *saving*.

"The mailman hadn't come by yesterday when I got home, so I didn't grab the mail. Did either of you?" Dad asks as he starts to wash up the waffle maker before he even sits down to eat. It's one of Kyla's biggest pet peeves—her father's insistence on cleaning up before eating, ensuring that his food is always lukewarm when he finally gets to it.

"No, you know I was . . ." Mikky cuts a sideways look over at Kyla, a touch embarrassed. "I had my friend over so I didn't even think about it."

Kyla snorts at "friend." She doesn't care that her brother seems to have the world's biggest crush on Nasim Talebi. She thinks Mikky can do better, but at least Nasim has a spine, unlike most people in Prophets Lake. The way he looked hard at Kyla as they met at the door when she returned from dance practice and Mikky was leaving to drive him home lives rent-free in Kyla's head. She has to respect that kind of loathing.

"I didn't even think about it," Kyla admits. She'd had to make dance practice grueling. The girls are distracted, of course. More than one was stopped by a reporter asking for a tidbit about Erin. Kyla laid down her law clearly—no one says anything, and if they do, she'll know.

"I'll go grab it, no big deal," she says. She finishes up her waffles in record time and stands, going to slip the plate into the sink. Dad takes the opportunity to press a kiss to her hairline, one that Kyla doesn't dodge for once.

She accepts it and then leaves the kitchen with a tiny smile. She makes her way to the mailbox, absentmindedly scrolling through her Instagram feed. She lingers over one of Alicia's photos that she hasn't liked yet, and then does just that, hoping that Alicia doesn't make a big fucking deal over it. In the most surface-level way, today has the makings of a good day. Her bag is packed, she's done all her homework, it's a rare day off from dance practice after school. Kyla is so *tired* of all the bad days, where she's sinking deeper and deeper into the pit of her life, she just wants this one good day.

And then she remembers—Erin is dead. There are news vans in the parking lot, waiting for her to crack. More and more people are suspecting Peter, and Kyla's dread mounts with each passing moment, because he's weak. He'll crack eventually, and then everything she's done—all the lies and the manipulation and the maneuvering—will be for nothing. She has to make Erin's death mean something, because if it doesn't—

Kyla flips open the mailbox. There's not too much. A pamphlet advertising a touring Broadway show. A catalog addressed to Mikky, which is bizarre, because who gets catalogs anymore? And, finally, a letter from the bank.

It's like second nature now. Kyla tucks her nail underneath the flap and tears it open. She knows Dad will get on her for opening mail that's not addressed to her, again. He'll say that it's a felony, but Kyla is fairly certain her dad isn't going to have her arrested.

Her stomach drops when she scans the letter and gets to the words AMOUNT DUE.

Four thousand one hundred seventy-four dollars.

$4,174.

That's the mortgage payment for September. Just under what Kyla should have in her possession, but doesn't. For a brief moment she slips and says what she's thinking out loud: "Dammit, Erin." Her fingertips burn as she stares down at the damning number.

She knows how much her dad has in the bank for this. She knows how much Erin's funeral was, and knows that after expenses, it's not enough to pay this. They'll be short by half, and Kyla won't be able to contribute the difference like she has been from the stash that she keeps in the vinyl crate marked A–C, because the bills fit nicely in ABBA's *Arrival* 1976 jacket.

The stash that's almost depleted now because Kyla never got her payday from the night Erin died.

She only has six hundred dollars left. It's why they'd been out that night instead of having their regular weekly sleepover. Now the cash that would've helped Kyla over the next month or so is gone, just like Erin. The cops never mentioned finding it and no one else would know where it is, so it might as well have been buried with her.

Her spit sours on the back of her tongue. Kyla hates thinking about that missing money almost as much as she hates thinking about what happened to Erin, because she gets like this. Uncontrolled and lost. She inhales the dew-edged air through her nose, exhaling through her mouth. It's a bit like the warm-up breathing before a dance competition, to center herself and keep her edge. Her edges are not to be dulled.

The only problem is that now that Kyla has begun to think about them both, the money and Erin, she can't stop. Over and over again, she thinks about that night. The way they went back and forth over their product selection, over Erin's sudden hesitation and lack of nerve, over Kyla's hunger. Back and forth, back and forth, each time brushing each other a little more raw, until the tension between them was drum tight. Until the tension had nearly boiled over into screams, and now Kyla wants to *scream*—

The spiral has begun again and nothing can halt the bad day. She can't see the end of the bad days, only knows that it goes round and round, a merry-go-round of vomit-inducing unease. She'll have to start everything up again. Intellectually, Kyla has known this was coming—protecting Peter was the start of clearing the way—but the threat of being found out had still loomed larger than life. Now the threat to the funeral home is larger.

It's a bit like her nightmares, where she is aware of how

horrible and wrong everything is but can't wake up. So it's no wonder that she doesn't think, doesn't even blink, before she pulls out her phone and calls. She puts the phone to her ear, clutching the mail so tight that she crumples Mikky's catalog.

The phone rings twice and then there's the click of someone picking up.

"Hey." Kyla doesn't know what else to say. She hears the heavy breathing of someone still half asleep. In. Out. In. Out. It's so steady that she suspects maybe he picked up in his sleep. It's *early*, and yes, there's school, but Jason likes to roll up *as* the bell rings. She considers hanging up and then—

"Are you okay?" Jason slurs. He sounds like his head is shoved beneath a pillow, muffled and barely audible.

"Um. Not really." It's easier to admit on the phone, when she doesn't have to look him in the eye as she confesses her own weakness.

A beat of silence. And then Kyla hears him lurching up, fumbling with his phone. "What's wrong?" he asks, suddenly shockingly awake for someone who was probably deep in a REM cycle only moments ago.

"I'm sorry for calling."

"Don't say sorry," Jason says firmly. "What's wrong?"

Kyla opens her mouth to explain it all. But. *But.* There's too much to explain. Too much that Jason doesn't know. Because he might know that Erin and Kyla were up to something, but he doesn't know the how or why. He doesn't know about the money. And he can't. Kyla can never tell *anyone*, because if she does, they'll know that she was there that night. And no one else can ever know.

"Sorry. This was a mistake—"

"*Don't* say sorry," Jason says again, voice a little harder. He takes another deep breath, even, like when she suspected that he might be asleep still. "Will you meet me for breakfast?"

Kyla's first instinct is to say no. She doesn't skip class. She's not obsessed with perfect attendance like Indigo, but she hates to make her dad worry when he has too many other things to stress about.

Then she rethinks it. Her good day is ruined the longer she thinks about everything she's up against. The mortgage. The missing money. The vultures hiding behind their cameras. Mikky, who wants to help but can't *help* because she doesn't need fucking help. "Where?"

"Fable Street Pantry. You know where that is?"

"Yeah, of course, I know where it is."

A vague memory of sticky seats and sticky fingers and her mother's empty eyes hits her. Hours of her mother driving in circles around the outskirts of Prophets Lake with Johnny Cash playing on the radio. On and on they drove until Mikky's and Kyla's complaints of hunger got too loud to drown out.

"Okay. Good. I'll see you in fifteen. Promise."

Jason hangs up before she does, and it's a reversal of their usual dynamic. Kyla shoves her phone into her pocket, takes another deep, centering breath, and then forcefully shuts the mailbox like she's going to war.

Inside the house, she makes an equal exchange, putting down the mail, the open mortgage statement on top, and taking her house and car keys.

Kyla will be halfway down the block before Mikky or Dad notices.

• • •

"This is what they call playing hooky, right?" Jason says, because of course he sees her first. Kyla gives a fake smile to the older woman who greeted her at the door and marches down the tight row of empty booths in the direction of his voice.

"Maybe in the eighties," Kyla says as she sits, scooting over the tear in the plastic booth seat. She picks at the fluff peeking out from the seams and looks across the table at Jason. "Thanks for meeting me."

"You called," Jason says like that's all Kyla has ever had to do to summon him to her side. "Thank you for slumming it."

Fable Street Pantry is a tiny, kitschy diner. Each menu item has a fairy-tale description that's meant to read as charming but mostly comes off as gimmicky. A throwback to the Midwestern diners of old, the floors are black-and-white-checkered vinyl. But the harshness of the Route 51 aesthetic is otherwise softened by pastels—soft sea greens and blooming rose and pale blue—that have grown dingy with time.

Kyla picks up the stained menu. It's not as weird being here with him as she thought it would be, in the daylight. Jason's presence is comforting even now.

"You look fresh, Kyla," Jason says.

Kyla stills, thrown off kilter. She raises her fingers to her face—something she never does—and touches bare skin. She hadn't put on her makeup yet when she went to the mailbox. Not even mascara. Kyla can't remember the last time she's gone somewhere without even a tinted moisturizer. She feels naked, stripped back. She shakes her head, haphazardly adjusting her curly fringe, attempting not to show the self-consciousness that has set in.

"You look *good*, I mean," Jason clarifies.

Kyla sits back in her seat, feeling it creak beneath her. She doesn't know what to say. She knows what Jason is doing.

So she decides the best response is none at all. Instead, she asks, "What do you usually get?"

"The Humpty Dumpty Grand Slam is always good. And cheap," Jason says.

Kyla recoils. She pulls apart the words, rooting for a dig at her family's finances. But she comes up empty.

"I don't really like eggs. Maybe . . . the Just-Right Corned Beef Hash?" Kyla asks. She's already eaten a full breakfast.

"That's good too. Family recipe from Meg. She's the owner," Jason says. He sighs to himself, cradling his cheek in his hand, staring at her from underneath his lashes. He looks tired, but also . . . soft. She wants to hide him from the world, but also drag him out, kicking and screaming. Force him to say something mean, like the new jagged edge inside herself demands.

"I think I need coffee, too," Kyla says instead.

She has always been an early morning girl, energized by dawn. She *likes* going to bed early unless she has a Test Kitchen to worry about or a sleepover with Erin.

Not anymore. Maybe not ever again. Her bones weep with exhaustion, and her limbs are sore but not from dance practice. It's not the feel of microtears that build together more to form muscle. It's deeper. Kyla is too young for the weary soul she has. And yet, it's all she can feel, everywhere.

"I'm *exhausted*," Kyla admits like a weakness, and she looks at Jason, hoping that he understands. That he sees.

Erin always said he understood. That he saw. It's why she

trusted him to always drive her home after Test Kitchens, because he wouldn't ask. He'd just get it. She could talk to him too, though. Once, as freshmen, Kyla got offended when Jason brought up another one of the bullshit arguments that Mrs. Vaughn and Erin got into that she hadn't mentioned to Kyla yet.

"It's different," Erin had said. "Me and Jason, and you and me. You're my soul. He's a safe place to land."

Kyla wants somewhere to land where it doesn't have to hurt.

Jason smiles and she sees the same weariness in the dark, sagging skin under his eyes. He isn't so golden anymore. No longer freckled. So nothing can hide the grief that's eating away at him.

Softly, ever so softly, he says, "I'm tired too. I'm exhausted."

It's nice to admit out loud to someone who gets it. Someone who's as tired as her. Someone who *misses* Erin for who she was. Not who the world saw her as.

This doesn't make Kyla feel better. But for now, it's enough.

CHAPTER EIGHTEEN

It takes Mikky a whole day and a half to muster up the courage to put their first plan into action: confront Jason about the secret Instagram account that he most likely knows nothing about. And he only sets out to do it after Nasim gives him a look that bores into his soul at the end of AP Chemistry.

Mikky finds Jason before lunch, right after macroeconomics, because that's when Jason will be in the best mood. Jason is *good* at macroeconomics. He's his father's son or whatever. Jason doesn't see him immediately, too busy ribbing one of his soccer buddies over a failed pop quiz.

"I'll tutor you next time, bro," Jason says with a grin, waving his own quiz, with a bright red 100 at the top, like a flag.

"Fuck off," his teammate says good-naturedly. He notices Mikky first and waves with a tight smile. Mikky vaguely remembers being introduced to him, but he can't remember his name. "Hey, man."

"Mik," Jason says, throwing an arm around Mikky's shoulders as best as he can when he's four inches shorter than him in his platforms. "To what do I owe the pleasure?"

"Maybe I want to escort my childhood bestie to lunch," Mikky suggests.

Jason grins at his teammate. "Hear that, Christian? I'm being *escorted*," he says in the fakest British accent he can muster.

Mikky can't begrudge him that or the smile that it drags out of him. It's only been a few days, but Jason sounds far more upbeat than Mikky thought he would post–viral video. It seems that he's adapting better to the near-constant media presence in the parking lot. Jason's bullheaded optimism has always been the best and worst part of him. It's why asking how he's doing keeps slipping Mikky's mind. Mikky's been a bad friend, and he's about to be an even worse one.

"Unfortunately, this is a date, which means two. You don't mind, do you, Christian?" Mikky asks with a tight smile of his own.

Christian looks like he very much does mind, but Jason doesn't even notice. Dismissively, he says, "I'll see you at lunch. Save two spots for us?"

Mikky doesn't say two isn't necessary because it feels dickish. Christian disappears down the hallway, following the flow of the student body to the cafeteria, and Mikky begins to walk against it, pointedly, in the opposite direction. Jason matches him stride for stride, despite the artificial height difference.

"Are you good, Mikky?" Jason asks.

Mikky groans under his breath. "I should be asking you that, man. I'm sorry I didn't check in about everything with that video—"

Jason shakes his head. Mikky only knows that it actually bothers him because he drops the arm from around his shoulders and folds his hands behind his neck. "It's no big deal," he says.

It's clearly a big deal. Everyone thinks the video is a big deal, including the cops. Peter Moore is out of school again and a few members of the basketball team have been pulled from class and brought to the principal's office, including their manager, who is also Rowan's ex-girlfriend Lydia, according to Alicia's gossip in AP Chem. Peter's lawyer father can't save him now. They're already making a timeline of Peter's movements from that entire week, looking for a single bubble in his airtight alibi.

Even Kyla has had to pull back on Rowan, now that her failed attempt at making them out to be a liar has faltered.

"No, man, I'm a bad friend. I'm sorry for being a bad friend," Mikky says, not making excuses for himself.

Jason stops suddenly. There's a bewildered smile on his face. "You are so . . . dude, the way you just say that like it doesn't bother you to admit it."

"The joys of therapy," Mikky says dryly.

"Maybe I need to get into therapy," Jason says thoughtfully.

"Everyone should be in therapy, even if you didn't suffer a lot of trauma," Mikky says.

Maybe his sister should be in therapy.

"Trauma," Jason says, rolling the word around on his tongue. "Is that what it's called when your sister is murdered and CNN is squatting on your lawn?"

"Are they really?" Mikky winces.

Jason frowns. "Yeah. We called Hamish, though. So now they're on the sidewalk. Whatever." He rubs his chin. "Therapy, huh . . . I don't think my parents would be cool with it."

"You've got to take care of yourself," Mikky insists.

"Nah, I have too much on my plate anyway." Jason sounds resigned. It makes Mikky feel that much worse about the fact that he's going to be a dick in the next 2.5 seconds. But he needs to figure this out, for Kyla, and for Jason, too, by the look of it.

"Jason, I need to ask you about something," he blurts out.

Jason's expression goes serious. "I thought you might."

Mikky's stomach lurches as he searches his friend's face. Jason looks oddly guilty, gnawing at the corner of his mouth. Maybe he does know about it . . .

"Have you ever seen this Instagram account?" Mikky asks, tugging his phone from the back pocket of his overly tight jeans. He already has the profile open and he presents it to Jason, who frowns.

"I have no idea what I'm looking at?" Jason says like a question.

The guilt peels away from Jason's face, only further piquing Mikky's curiosity about what Jason thought he was going to ask.

"You really don't know what this is?"

"Am I supposed to? I mean . . . it's a reference to the Beatles song, right? Erin liked it," Jason mumbles.

Mikky straightens. "Did she really? Did she say anything specific about it? Like, a specific line or something?" he asks, too fast. He knows immediately he's overshot himself.

Jason frowns at him. "Dude . . . no, she didn't. What is this about?"

Mikky tries to put his phone away, but Jason's reflexes are fast—from soccer or maybe just being athletic—and he snatches it away then hops back, squinting down at the screen.

"Hey, give it back—"

"Is this . . . you think this is Erin's finsta? Are you trying to get into her finsta, dude?"

Mikky hesitates. "I don't . . . know *whose* finsta it is, but I have reason to believe that it was Erin's, yeah," he admits. He won't give up Rowan as his source, even if he wants to; Rowan still might have important information.

"Mikky, what are you doing?" Jason asks, his voice hard. He doesn't look angry, per se, but Mikky knows he's played this all wrong.

"I'm just . . . ," he starts lamely.

He can imagine what would come out next: *Your sister was murdered and I think—I hope—that my sister doesn't know who did it, but she might know more about it than she said, and I think it has to do with this finsta your sister's secret hookup showed me, but no, I don't know why, it's all based on conjecture and this glare that my little sister gave Florence Cook at your dead sister's memorial, did you get all that, old bestie?*

Yeah. Right. He knows he'll sound crazy—even though his therapist would tell him how reductive the use of the word "crazy" is—and he knows that's what Jason will think.

"Whatever it is you're doing? Cut it out. Now."

"Jason—"

"I'm being serious, man," he says firmly. "Instead of trying to break into a finsta that's probably full of my little sister's dumb shitposts, you should be worrying about *your* sister."

Mikky's breath stops. He stares at Jason in bewilderment, like he's seeing him for the first time. But Jason doesn't apologize. He *means* it.

"What is *that* supposed to mean?" Mikky bites out.

"Kyla isn't doing well—"

"She's doing just fine," Mikky snaps. It tastes like a lie. They had that moment over ice cream, and Mikky allowed himself to believe that she might be healing, a little bit. But at the same time, yesterday morning she'd left abruptly in the middle of breakfast and wasn't in the school parking lot when Mikky finally arrived. And Mikky thinks about the way sometimes, when no one is looking, she still looks so incandescently angry, he thinks she might be capable of anything. Even the one thing that Mikky insists to Nasim that she couldn't have possibly done.

"No, she's really not, so maybe go save the day over there like you supposedly came here to do so you can go back to your life in Boston or whatever," Jason says cuttingly.

He takes a step back and folds his arms over his chest, like he's considering saying more, but Mikky doesn't give him the chance. "Forget about lunch. I don't think I really want to talk to you right now."

Jason is quick to snap, "Right back at you, man," and then he turns and walks off, all sanctimonious.

Mikky is glad to have the longer stride, because even if Jason got the last word, he at least gets to exit the corridor first.

When they get to Mikky's house, Dad isn't home this time. Neither is Kyla. There's really no reason for Mikky to close his door. But as Nasim flops down at the center of Mikky's bed, he closes it anyway. After staring up at the ceiling for a moment, Nasim sits up, crisscross applesauce.

"So, what have we got?" he asks immediately, all business and no play.

Mikky firms up his jaw, reorganizing the mess that his confrontation with Jason left in his brain. Self-righteous anger slices through his guilt deftly as he sits in his desk chair and drags himself over to Nasim by his heels. He pulls his legs up so that he's practically squatting on top of the rolling chair. "You know . . .

I've never really had anyone over before. Not even when I lived with my mom."

"I'm honored," Nasim replies.

"Good. Keep that in mind when I tell you that I struck out . . . *miserably* with Jason today," Mikky says. He scratches the back of his neck. "He was such an asshole. He accused me of trying to 'save the day' so that I could leave and go back to Boston."

"Aren't you trying to save the day, though? Or exonerate your sister?" Nasim asks.

"Well, she's innocent, so no exoneration necessary," Mikky retorts. "It's more of the . . . leaving part that bothered me."

Nasim is quieter and won't meet his eyes when he asks, "Well, after this is over . . . *are* you going to leave?"

"No," Mikky blurts out, wide-eyed. He's more surprised by his own answer than he has any right to be. In the beginning, he hadn't *missed* Boston exactly. It was more that he'd rather be there than here. Now everything's changed. Then, quieter, he admits, "I . . . don't think I could leave her again. Or my dad. I'm going to see the year out."

"Well, good," Nasim says as he sits back. "But what did Jason say about the finsta?"

"He doesn't know what the Instagram is and then told me that I need to be paying attention to my little sister, not his," Mikky says.

Nasim sits up straighter. "Yikes."

"Look, I'm just saying he's a dead end, so I think we're gonna have to . . . do this in the most tedious way possible and search through everyone at school's Instagrams and see who they're following," Mikky says.

Nasim groans, but he's already pulling out his phone. "Do you have parameters for what constitutes 'everyone'?"

"I was thinking Erin's following list?" Mikky asks.

"I don't follow Erin," Nasim says faux sadly, as if that should exempt him from doing any of the legwork.

"Oh, no, you don't. Erin was a literal influencer. She's on public. Get to searching," Mikky insists.

Nasim sighs long-sufferingly. But, together, they begin.

Strangely enough, Mikky hasn't been on Erin's Instagram since she died. He's followed her for years, of course, but looking at it now feels . . . bad, worse than expected.

> @erinvaughnthegreat
>
> 231 posts   200.2k followers   430 following
>
> @CookCosmeticsOfficial Teen Ambassador
>
> Make me over, makeup lover, express yourself.
> Look at all the lonely people—I'm not one of them.

Her follower count has shot up since Florence's video about her went viral. He reads her caption again and hums to himself.

"What is it?" Nasim asks.

"At least we can definitely confirm that @eleanor.rigby_1 is her finsta," Mikky says.

"Well, Rowan did say it was, but what makes you think so?"

"Her caption. That's a lyric from 'Eleanor Rigby': 'Ah, look at all the lonely people,'" Mikky points out.

While Nasim takes a closer look, Mikky scrolls to the photos. The most recent isn't a solo shot. It's of her and Kyla. A selfie. Mikky isn't sure where they are, but it's beautifully decorated—cream couches and glass walls that show the bright blue sky. Kyla is looking into the camera with a lip-glossed smirk tugging at her lips. Erin is cackling, her head tipped onto Kyla's shoulder. It's captioned "Duck and Goose are up to no good."

It's dated the day before Erin's death. Or, rather . . . the day before Erin was found.

"'Duck and Goose'?" Nasim asks, now staring at the same photo.

"Erin called Kyla 'Duck.' That was her nickname for her," Mikky says. "And she called herself 'Goose.' She came up with that when we were little and it stuck, even though Kyla hates nicknames."

Nasim nods slowly and doesn't comment further, diving into the following list instead, but Mikky is stuck on her profile. "Up to no good." He wants to know what that "no good" was. Out of the first six posts on her grid, four feature Kyla and the lake in some way, even some of the sponsored Cook Cosmetics posts. It's eerie.

"Okay, she follows a respectable amount of people," Nasim says. "We should think about who would have access to her finsta to narrow it down. The dance team?"

Mikky is on it. He scrolls down Erin's robust feed and finds one shot with the entire team from over the summer, during their pre–school year boot camp. All the girls are tagged.

"You take the top row, I'll take the bottom row," Mikky says, flashing the photo at Nasim. Nasim nods while Mikky searches Alicia's page—the page he should've looked at first, anyway. She's following him already. Mikky hesitates, wondering if he should follow her back, and then doesn't. He's not a frequent user of Instagram. It would be suspicious if he did now.

He searches @eleanor.rigby_1 in her following and nothing pops up. Mikky is methodical as he makes his way through the bottom row of girls, skipping over Kyla and Erin. Pragmatism and chaos side by side. That's when he realizes something. If anyone from the dance team follows that account, it'll be from a finsta too.

"Any luck?" Nasim asks. From his tone, Mikky gleans that Nasim has hit a dead end as well.

"Nope," Mikky says, then clears his throat. "Okay, let's think. Who are other prominent people in Erin's life?"

"Peter?" Nasim points out.

"You think he knows about the Test Kitchens?" Mikky asks.

"He was kinda her boyfriend. It's a possibility," Nasim says. He searches Peter's account, but when he flashes the screen at Mikky, all that shows are the words NO RESULTS. "Guess not. Who else would have access to Erin Vaughn? She was really popular, but I never really got the impression that she had that many actual friends, if you know what I mean?"

Mikky doesn't think that Erin really ever thought that she needed any other friends besides Kyla. Privately, he thinks that Rowan and Peter—both of them—were just means to an end. Mikky doesn't know what "end" other than getting off. But with Erin there was always more to it, as proven by this very locked-down finsta.

"This is going to take a while," Nasim sighs.

And it does. They work for the next thirty-five minutes, going back to Erin's page and painstakingly combing through her following list, searching for names that they recognize amongst the sea of brands, low-level celebrities, and other influencers. Mikky notes that she's following Florence Cook's public Instagram. In spite of himself, he checks it. There's only two new posts since Erin's death. One announcing Cook Cosmetics' new "Makeup so good, it's skin care" line—GloMo—and the other, a teaser post with a sea-green SOMETHING'S COMING in a stylized serif font on a cream background. But she's not following the account.

Mikky goes back to his tedious self-set task. He doesn't cross-check with Nasim often as they motor through the list, going through basketball team members and volleyball girls. Once Mikky finishes going through the more athletic, traditionally popular people in the school, he reframes it. Erin wasn't just some regular high schooler. She set her sights on something bigger—being an influencer. It wasn't just about popularity for her, it was about being known. It figures the people on the outside would be the ones who most wanted in—to be known by someone like Erin Vaughn.

So, Mikky is quick to go through the people who are desperate to be *known,* too. It might be petty, going into Rowan's Instagram first, but he can't feel bad about it. He feels even less bad when he notices that Rowan doesn't follow him. Which is . . . fine. Mikky doesn't care except that he actually really does.

He looks at their follow list and doesn't find @eleanor.rigby_1. Not that he really expected to, but it's annoying nonetheless.

Then Mikky goes through the theater kids. Only the leading players, never anyone relegated to the ensemble. It doesn't seem Erin's vibe for whatever she's up to. Nasim sighs and sets his phone face down. He stretches, T-shirt riding up, flashing a strip of bronzed skin that may or may not make Mikky dumb for half a second.

"I have to go to the bathroom. I'll be back," Nasim says, then points warningly at Mikky. "Don't stop looking."

"I'm just as committed to finding evidence as you," Mikky retorts.

Nasim looks at him like he knows something Mikky doesn't. "Sure," he drawls as he pushes himself up from the bed then leaves the room. Mikky can't help staring after him for just a little longer before he returns to his phone, pretending that he didn't notice how nicely Nasim's jeans fit.

Barely a few seconds later, Mikky groans and falls onto his back. He's just finished going through a girl named Sophie's profile and found nothing except the inkling that she might be hooking up with her leading man, if he's reading the undertones to her comments right. He's running out of cliques.

Then it comes to him—student council. Mikky doesn't know much about the student council, but he does know *of* the overeager leader of said group.

He types in her name—Indigo Glass. She's not the flashiest girl, but her profile has a respectable number of posts with overlong and overpersonal life updates that function as captions, interspersed with official school announcements from the student council. Mikky goes into her following list and simply types in "E."

And there it is.

FOLLOWING
@eleanor.rigby_1

"Holy shit. Indigo. *Indigo Glass*." The class fucking president. Mikky slips out of his chair and stumbles over the edge of his carpet in excitement. He looks around and then remembers that Nasim is in the bathroom. Unable to contain himself, he stalks out and crosses the floor, knocking heavily on the bathroom door. "Okay, I know you're probably pissing, but, Nasim, I think I found something."

He waits for Nasim to tell him to fuck off. To be patient. He doesn't. Mikky doesn't hear anything. At least, not anything from the bathroom. He *does* hear something from the room directly across from his. The door is haphazardly open, which is not normal. Kyla is a big door shutter, unlike Mikky *or* Dad.

"No," Mikky murmurs in disbelief.

Kyla has to be home and he didn't hear her come in. But that seems impossible. Dance practice can't be over yet. But if she's not home, that means someone else is in there, and Mikky isn't an idiot. He's *really* not.

Mikky stalks across the landing and throws the ajar door fully open. It's the first time that he's been in Kyla's room since he moved back, and it makes his stomach turn, but greedily, he looks around. The walls are a pale yellow, which he didn't really expect for Kyla. She's got a large vanity, most of it covered with Cook Cosmetics, though he spots a few skin-care items that he uses himself, plus a plethora of curling cream and shampoo. There's a dummy head with her dance competition wig all plucked, lace already cut, knots bleached.

Bluetooth speakers are in each corner of the room and the record player looks *expensive*, like if someone who didn't know what they were doing breathed on it, it would shatter. And judging by her shelves and shelves of vinyl, the one thing he has already seen, it's important to her.

Finally, Mikky looks at the person who's *not* supposed to be in the room, standing by the precious vinyls. He doesn't even bother to look guilty.

"What the *fuck* are you doing in here?" Mikky bites out.

Nasim looks up from whatever he's staring at. "Investigating what you won't."

"My *sister*?" Mikky demands.

"Yeah, your sister."

"My sister didn't kill Erin."

"Yeah, that's what you want to believe, but we have to pay attention to the facts," Nasim says, and he lifts a little black notebook like a trump card. "And this is fact. *This* is cold hard evidence."

Mikky doesn't want to ask what it is. He knows Nasim will wait for him to do so to rub it in his face. So, he doesn't just yet. He stalks around Kyla's bed, careful not to step on her plush carpet, fearful that she'll notice the imprints of their footsteps when she gets back. He jumps over a pair of her beat-up dance sneakers and then he lands right in front of Nasim. He stands as tall as he can, glowering down at him.

"You have no right to be in here. There are lines that shouldn't be crossed and you're crossing them. I invited you into my house, man, and you took that as permission to go through my sister's shit?"

Nasim doesn't cower. Once again Mikky admires how he'll stand on business even if he's *wrong*.

"Look," Nasim says, "I'm investigating Erin's death because I want to clear Rowan's name after your sister put a target on their back. Why are you?"

Because I don't want Kyla to end up the same if she is mixed up in this shit.

"I want the truth, because I think Kyla would benefit from it," Mikky bites out instead.

Nasim's lip curls up over his teeth. "I don't think Kyla cares about the truth, because if she did, then she would've shown you, and the cops, *this*." He taps the book against Mikky's chest.

"What is 'this'?" Mikky demands finally. He goes to snatch it from Nasim's hands, but Nasim rocks back, shaking his head, clutching the book to his chest.

"A notebook that I found tucked between *Yellow Submarine* and *Abbey Road*. Shocker, look at what's on the very first page," he says, opening the book and revealing the lined pages.

It's a simple notebook—a Moleskine. But almost immediately Mikky knows that it's not a journal. The very top is labeled neatly as "TK Dollars," and beneath it is a list of initials, each dated like an attendance record with a dollar amount next to each. At the end of each list is a "TOTAL AMOUNT." The first page alone adds up to fifteen hundred dollars.

"What is this?" Mikky repeats, softer this time.

"'TK Dollars.' Hmm, I wonder what *that* stands for?" Nasim says.

Mikky pauses and stares at Nasim severely. Usually, Mikky finds Nasim's attitude a little funny, but he's not laughing now. "Condescension isn't a good look, Nasim, especially after you crossed a boundary," he says firmly.

Nasim's haughtiness finally falters. He clears his throat, awkward at being called out so directly, and limply offers the ledger. Mikky takes it, flipping through the pages. The first date listed is from last year, a random day in December, two weeks before Christmas. Mikky flips the page. The next isn't until February.

From then on, it becomes more frequent, every two weeks. A few of the initials shift, but the core group stays the same. Mikky would be remiss if he didn't notice the I. G. lingering at the center of almost every list. Then he gets to August 19. The day is familiar.

"August nineteenth," Nasim says out loud. "That's . . ."

"The day before Erin's body was found. And this is a ledger. Whoever these people are, they were paying Kyla and Erin for something," Mikky says. "For the Test Kitchen."

"But what *is* the Test Kitchen? Rowan didn't . . . they didn't mention money or anything," Nasim says, voice weaker. He seems to have realized that with money involved this doesn't just look bad for Kyla. Because Rowan brought up the Test Kitchen to get Kyla off their back, but they didn't tell the police. It makes it seem like they do know what this is. That they might even have a *stake* in whatever this is, despite the fact that their initials don't appear.

Mikky snaps a few quick photos of the pages and then skirts around Nasim, sliding the ledger firmly back between the Beatles albums. He's not letting Nasim take it.

"Mikky," Nasim starts, and then he falters, like he doesn't know what to say.

"I think we're done for the day," Mikky says, not waiting for him to figure it out.

Nasim winces. *"Mikky—"*

"I'm serious," Mikky says, and then he carefully leaves Kyla's room, making sure not to disturb anything. He waits by the door for Nasim to exit past him before he shuts it firmly behind them. Then he folds his arms over his chest and follows Nasim back to his bedroom.

Nasim grabs his backpack and says, "Mikky, we have to be

objective about everything. It was important to look around her room, because I *knew* you wouldn't and . . . and I know the method was wrong, but the result—"

"I really don't want to, like, litigate this with you right now. I don't think I'm in the headspace to do that," Mikky says. They feel like Dr. Grosse's words, not his, but maybe that's what he needs right now, distance so that he can organize his thoughts. His heart is beating fast in his chest, like it sometimes does around Nasim, but it's not for the usual reason. Not exactly. Anxiety is a bitch.

Nasim pulls his backpack to his chest. "Okay," he whispers. "I'll walk home."

"No. I'll still drive you. You live across town," Mikky says, going to grab the easiest shoes he can slide on, a pair of loafers that don't really match. Whatever, they'll be good enough for driving.

Nasim doesn't push back against Mikky's offer. And if Mikky feels a little better as Nasim's chagrin stinks up his car in the tense silence, that's no one else's business.

Except for Dr. Grosse's, because suddenly, Mikky can't ignore how unsure he is about Kyla anymore. He can't pretend that she's not involved or what she knows might be innocent. Because the more and more Mikky thinks about everything objectively—just as Nasim told him to, *fuck*—the more Mikky can see it. Kyla was involved in the Test Kitchens. Money was involved. Peter and Rowan were involved too. What the Test Kitchens are has to be why Kyla is so intent on protecting Peter and condemning Rowan.

There's a link somewhere in the midst of Erin's fog, and Mikky is one step closer to clearing it and finding out what that connection is at the center. He's just not so sure now that he'll like the answer.

CHAPTER NINETEEN

Mikky is very well versed in pretending that he can't hear someone calling his name. It's even easier when he breaks out the headphones. Noise-canceling *and* wired? He's giving off "don't fuck with me" vibes, "and if you do, I really can't hear you" vibes. Even though he does technically hear Nasim call his name while dogging his steps to AP Chemistry.

Mikky looks down at his phone and bumps up the volume on Gatecreeper. It's easy to ignore Nasim and Gregory behind him as he enters the room and goes to sit down at his desk, seemingly just keeping calm before their exam on the first three units of the year. Mikky sits there, pulling out only a pen and a pencil and drums his fingers on the table, pretending that he doesn't feel the weight of Nasim's pleading stare. He only pulls his headphones off when Alicia flounces into the room and into the seat next to him.

"Hey, Alicia," Mikky says to her. "Ready for the exam?"

Alicia's twitchy and overexcited. "I'm not great at tests," she admits as she tries her best not to pick at the three-cluster star of pimple patches around her jaw.

"I get the material, but the *test* . . ." She sighs.

Mikky has done more than enough labs with Alicia at this point to be able to confidently say, "You get what we're doing more than I do, so at least there's that. Here's to us doing well?"

"Yeah?" Alicia asks with a shy smile.

"Yeah, and if we don't, it's fine because at least it's not the actual AP exam."

"So real," Alicia gasps. Already, she seems more relaxed, a far cry from the nervous chatty energy she usually gives off, and Mikky's glad. He's got a threshold for enthusiasm and Alicia often exceeds it, even if she's always been nice to him. Mikky turns back to the front as their teacher finally walks in, clutching a stack of papers to his chest. The groans from the front seem to reverberate.

"TGIF, my dear students! I know, I know, the dastardly first exam of the semester. Daunting, it's true," Mr. Reynolds says good-naturedly. "I want you all to know that if you do well, that's fantastic, I'm super proud of you. But if you don't? Partially, that's on me. It means that there's a disconnect between you guys and the material, and I'll do my best to correct it. So let's take the pressure off, shall we, class?" It's the classic good guy/cool teacher chat, but it works. Just as Mikky's words seemed to penetrate Alicia's anxiety, the class burbles with whispers again, last-minute tips and study mnemonics.

One last time Mikky hears Nasim hiss, "*Michael* Graves—"

This he can't ignore. Mikky's head snaps around. "Are you planning to shut up anytime soon?" he snarls, throwing back the very first words that Nasim spoke to him.

Gregory lets out a hiss of air between his teeth, eyes darting back and forth between them like a tennis match, as Mr. Reynolds shouts, "Okay, take one and pass the rest back."

Nasim looks between the quickly approaching test and Mikky. "We'll talk after," he says. Not a question, nor a suggestion. Nasim prides himself on being good at chemistry—it's one of the things Mikky likes about him—and he won't let something like this mess with his ability to ace a test.

Mikky cares less for the fact that Nasim seems to have simply *decided* that they'll be talking.

He turns back, takes the test paper offered to him, and dives in, trying to throw all his attention into it. The test shouldn't be hard, but he didn't really utilize his study time yesterday. All his thoughts were preoccupied with the picture of the ledger and whether or not Kyla would notice that someone had been in her room.

For all Nasim's faults, overstepping and searching Kyla's room, Mikky can't ignore the results. Proof that his sister was involved in this secret thing that Erin had been running, involved enough that she was the one to keep the ledger. Mikky recognizes her handwriting. But more than that he knows that it's her organization leading to such meticulous bookkeeping.

Mikky shakes his head and focuses on the first question again:

```
All measurements in science
involve a degree of:
```

Mikky has got this one. *Uncertainty.* He knows a bit about that.

After that he focuses for real, goes through the questions with a careful eye and a fine pen, falls into a rhythm. Mikky doesn't rush; he barely registers when some of the other kids finish and go to the front to hand in their tests. By the time he wraps up, he's one of the last people left, but he's reasonably confident that he's pulled at least a high B, if not an A-. Mikky checks his work one more time, then eases out of his seat and grabs his bag.

But the minute he does, Nasim jumps up *right* after him. Shocker. He follows a few inches behind Mikky as they hand in their tests and go to the classroom door so Mikky can't lose him. Nasim clearly expects Mikky to ignore him again until he's out of the room, so Mikky decides to mix things up. He holds open the door and bows mockingly.

"After you," he taunts.

Nasim frowns but he stalks out, clutching his bag to his chest, and Mikky pulls the door shut after them. They linger in front of the doorway, in the empty hall.

"Can we . . . talk?" Nasim asks.

"Now you're asking?" Mikky rolls his eyes and storms down the hallway, forcing Nasim to speed walk to keep up with him. Punishing one's friend for overstepping boundaries is exhausting. Dr. Grosse would probably tell him to cut that shit out (in a far more professional, nicer way).

They turn off from the science hallway and slow by the art classrooms, a place where no one they know is likely to be. Finally, Mikky stops and they stand together in an alcove right next to the pottery studio. He props a leg up against the wall and Nasim drops his bag and leans back against the opposite wall but doesn't speak until Mikky waves him on.

"Mikky, I am . . . *so* sorry," Nasim says finally. He deflates, all false bravado and fake irritation gone. "I was overeager and—"

"Self-righteous and convinced that you're always right," Mikky lists.

Nasim's jaw tightens. "I . . . was thinking last night. After you dropped me off. I really did feel like the ends justified the means.

Then I realized . . . if someone went into my grandma's room and searched through her stuff, I'd be furious. I was wrong. I definitely crossed some boundaries and I'm sorry for breaking your trust that way," Nasim says. He sounds like he actually means it, his words dripping with sincerity. He tugs at the ragged edge of his hoodie sleeve, fighting to meet Mikky's eyes, like apologizing hurts, like *vulnerability* hurts. Even though, to Mikky, that vulnerability makes him look fuzzy at the edges, in the very best way.

Mikky considers drawing this out. He knows that Nasim will fight harder for his forgiveness, will work to prove to Mikky that he really does mean it.

But it sounds so *boring*.

"You owe me, dude," Mikky begins.

Nasim gasps, already nodding, then reaches forward to grab Mikky's hand in his, lacing their fingers together and squeezing. Mikky's hold tightens despite himself.

"Yes, yes. Ice cream?" Nasim blurts out.

Mikky scoffs. "Ice cream?"

"Yeah, at the next soccer game? I'll buy you ice cream. Do you know how much the ice cream costs? It's like six dollars for a scoop because it's from the student council and they're raising money for prom already," Nasim rambles.

Mikky tries not to smile. He pushes off the wall and steps closer to Nasim, who doesn't shrink away. Mikky tips his head down enough that he's looking Nasim right in the eye.

"Not ice cream. Trust. If we're going to be partners, you can't do shit like that. Break my trust," Mikky says.

This close, in this kind of quiet, Mikky can hear the soft crack that catches in Nasim's throat.

"Partners, huh? That's what we are?" Nasim asks. If Mikky didn't know better, he'd say Nasim was flirting, but the only time he's seen Nasim flirt was on Tuesday and that was to prove a point. This isn't that. This is . . . something else. Something more concrete.

"Yeah, maybe," Mikky hedges.

Nasim reaches out with his free hand, tugging at the curl that falls over Mikky's ear, the one that's escaped from Mikky's low puff. "I like the sound of that."

Mikky can't even pretend anymore. He knows what he wants from Nasim. It's all real, the chemical reactions and the amorphous thing that sits in his chest and heats up whenever they're together. But he also knows that this isn't the time for it. Not yet. Not until he's accomplished his first and most important goal—helping Kyla.

"You know what I don't like the sound of? You calling me by my government name," Mikky says. He hopes—*prays*, even—for Nasim to take the bait, to let it go and not make a big deal out of it.

And because Nasim is getting better at meeting Mikky where he is, or at least trying to, he does.

"I'm sorry," he says good-naturedly, "but you weren't listening."

"I *was* listening. I was ignoring you," Mikky says.

Nasim gives a false gasp and his hand flies up to his mouth. "You jerk."

Mikky says, "I was definitely not the jerk in this entire situation, Nasim."

"Fair," Nasim admits sourly.

The bell rings. Doors creak open and the sound of students spilling into the hallway shatters any kind of atmosphere that they may or may not have had going on. Mikky is equally relieved and frustrated. He swallows a sigh and steps back from Nasim, letting go of his hand. He immediately misses the scarred warmth of it.

The first half of the exiting pottery class passes by without noticing them, but they're still standing close together and they don't quite escape the observation of a few stragglers that follow. When they catch sight of Nasim and Mikky, they immediately start giggling, whispering behind hands. Mikky cracks his neck, refusing to show that he's heard them or that he cares, even as his brain screams, *What are you saying? Have you heard anything about us? Do you think we're cute together? What do you think happened? Should anything have happened?*

But then a girl from the biology class darts forward, giggling as she throws herself into a *Bachelorette* run-and-jump at one of the art students. His hands smear paint on her thighs and suddenly the attention is on them.

"Hey, you two! No running in the hallways," another girl commands as she emerges from the classroom. Her face is elfin, all sharp and thin, with a smattering of freckles across the bridge of her nose and mirrored across her forehead. Her thin hair is pulled back in two wispy, no-nonsense braids, and while Prophets Lake High School doesn't have a uniform, you wouldn't know it looking at the girl in her green plaid skirt and her sensible oxford button-down and loafers.

Indigo Glass.

"Also, PDA isn't allowed," she continues like a shaming hall monitor.

The girl rolls her eyes and does nothing to dismount the boy. Instead, she makes a bigger show of showering his face with her satin lipstick kisses. Indigo folds her arms over her chest and storms away, self-righteous. She rushes right past Mikky and Nasim's alcove, not deeming them worthy of her ire, presumably heading toward her next class instead.

"Indigo Glass," Mikky says, remembering the revelation that was immediately overtaken by Nasim's scheming.

"What about her?" Nasim asks.

"She follows the finsta. She's got to know something," Mikky insists. It's not a slipup, that Indigo follows the finsta from her main account. Just looking at her, Mikky can tell that she's too straightlaced to make a burner account, and he doubts even Kyla would worry that anyone else was looking through her following list, searching for an anonymous, faceless account that could be anyone.

Nasim checks his phone. "I have a class with her later today. Should I ask her about the . . . you know?" He grabs Mikky by his wrist and pulls him from the alcove. They follow Indigo but keep at least six heads behind her in the crowd.

Mikky considers it before shaking his head. "No. It's too secretive for it to be okay for her to answer in the open. And you're not close. I doubt she'd answer even if you were alone. It would only serve to put her on guard."

"Then what?" Nasim asks.

"We need to get her phone," Mikky says.

Nasim nearly stumbles to a stop, but Mikky pulls him along, keeping up with the flow of hallway traffic. He tosses an arm around Nasim's shoulders to keep him close and Nasim tenses.

Mikky thinks better of it, prepares to apologize. But then Nasim melts into Mikky's side, walking in step with him.

Now they don't look like they're plotting. They look no different from every other couple clinging to each other in a public space. Mikky tries not to give that too much thought or energy.

"How do you propose we get her phone?" Nasim asks as they turn out of the subject hallways into the general locker area. Indigo is already at her locker, which is not far from Kyla's.

She opens it up and moves a box of paints into her locker. She reaches up, and Mikky watches as her face is dimly lit by the glow of her phone that she then . . . places right back into her locker. It's so odd that it takes Mikky aback. It's school policy that all phones are to be kept out of sight. The handbook says they're supposed to be in lockers, but nobody follows those rules and almost nobody enforces them. But Indigo Glass is clearly nothing if not a rule follower.

Before Mikky can propose his plan to Nasim, though, his view of Indigo Glass is disrupted as her locker slams shut on her shoulder and she cries out loudly.

"What are you doing?" she squawks, but no one answers her as a crowd begins to form, smelling violence in the air.

"You think I'm stupid?!"

Mikky doesn't recognize the voice, but Nasim seems to. He perks up and his face twists with apprehension as the shouter continues, with more bass in his voice. "You didn't think I'd find out?"

Mikky pulls away and shoves through the crowd. Nasim follows close on his heels and they break through two sophomores with their phones held up, recording, to finally survey the scene.

Mikky pauses a moment. Peter is facing off against Rowan. And Mikky has a front-row seat.

It's hard to reconcile what he knows now. Erin and Peter. Erin and Rowan.

Peter is the exact kind of boy that Erin would've been seeing. Bullish, wide and tall. An All-American quarterback who plays basketball because despite its vast number of clubs and teams, Prophets Lake High School does *not* have a football team. Mr. Friday Night Lights is a weight class above his opponent.

"I don't know what you're talking about," Rowan mumbles, eyes darting around, searching for a way out. They find Nasim and Mikky, and they make a move toward the pair, as if *Mikky* is going to get between them and Peter. But Peter grabs them by the backpack and whips them around.

"You were *fucking* her!" Peter seethes.

There is no mistaking who the "her" is. Or, rather, was.

Rowan flushes, humiliated. "I wasn't!" they manage. They nearly sound convincing, but there are too many eyes, too many people thirsty for the drama to be true.

"Is that why you lied to the cops about me?" Peter accuses. He stalks closer, looming as much as he can when Rowan can meet his eyes. "Jealous that she was too embarrassed to be seen with you? Maybe *you're* the one that hurt her—"

Nasim neatly slides halfway in front of Rowan. "Hey, this seems like a private conversation, don't you think?" he demands.

Peter blinks. He can't put together who Nasim is. But he's too hot and high on his own anger to care. He takes another lumbering step forward and Mikky resigns himself to the fact that he's about to stomp out the wannabe Gigachad.

Before it can escalate further, though, a teacher finally arrives to break it up. The entire situation deflates like a balloon, and the crowd boos as the fight is finished before it could begin. The damage is done, though. The accusatory words sit heavy in the atmosphere, sure to be disseminated through the school. "You were fucking her. Maybe you're the one that hurt her."

Soon everyone will know Rowan Villareal was hooking up with Erin Vaughn behind Peter Moore's back. Everyone will believe that *Rowan* is suspect number one.

Nasim darts forward and approaches the teacher, quick to rat on Peter in the name of protecting his friend. Mikky really needs to talk to Nasim about snitching. He even thinks about interrupting, making a joke about it, when he sees *them*.

At the end of the hallway, Kyla and Jason are watching. Peter backs up into them and Jason claps him on the shoulder, almost like he's consoling him. Peter says something that Mikky can't catch in the noise of the hallway, but Kyla nods, the same kind of nod of approval she'd give one of her dance team members for hitting their routine just right.

Mikky meets Kyla's eyes first, finds her expression impenetrable. When he goes to read his friend's expression, though, Jason is already gone.

CHAPTER TWENTY

After a hard dance practice, the brisk fall Massachusetts air penetrates to the bone. Kyla shivers, pulling her scarf tighter around her neck and pressing her hands into her deep pockets. She stares across the well-lit field from the bleachers, unnoticed by the team as they finish their practice with a cooldown.

Their coach claps his hands together and calls, "Strong work, boys. Looks like you're in good shape for the game tomorrow. I expect to see you ten o'clock. Sharp."

Kyla hates away games on Fridays, but Saturday away games are rare and coveted. If there's a game on Saturday, her squad doesn't have to pile into a musky school bus to go two hours away when there are much better ways to spend the weekend.

She watches as the sweaty boys jog off the field to their near identical black bags on the sidelines. She can't tell them apart from the angle she sits at, but she knows the soft-sea-green water bottle that gets left behind, because she has the exact same one tucked into the back of one of the kitchen cupboards—Cook Cosmetics swag. Kyla abandons her bag and rushes down to snatch it, and then hustles back to her seat, setting it sideways on her lap.

Then there's nothing to do but wait. Fifteen minutes later she sees the golden-brown head of hair she's looking for emerge again from the tunnel that leads away from the locker rooms. He jogs to where he picked up his bag, and Kyla's mouth twitches as he spins in a circle like his water bottle is capable of hiding from him.

"Looking for something?" she calls. She doesn't bother moving from her slouch on the bleachers. She's finally in a comfortable position, legs stretched out, back resting along the edge of the bleacher riser right above, bundled up in a coat and scarf. The cold doesn't bite at the fragile skin of her neck this way.

Jason turns and grins up at her, still in his soccer practice uniform, his puffer open over his jersey. He abandons his book bag, ignores the stairs, and bounds up the risers, soccer duffel bouncing against his hip where it's slung across one shoulder. He comes to a stop just below Kyla, like he enjoys looking up at her. She hates it.

Hates it enough that she does a leg raise, and nods at the seat next to her, now unoccupied. Jason takes the hint and slides in to it, then Kyla lowers her legs back onto his lap. She can feel the adrenaline-fueled heat rolling off his body as she passes his water bottle to him.

Jason dumps half the water down his throat while Kyla pretends not to notice the way his Adam's apple bobs beneath the stubbled layer of skin. She looks over at the blinding lights that haunt the field instead.

"Why are you still here? Practice ended for you like twenty minutes ago, right?" Jason asks finally.

"Yeah, but I . . . don't feel like going home yet, you know?" For her, home means Dad and Mikky and more of their same pity-not-pity. The worried looks and the strange pouting, all because Kyla is grieving in ways they can't understand. At any moment Kyla knows she's under threat of Mikky confronting her about skipping out on class Wednesday morning. Now she has to worry about him questioning her about Peter, too. It's just all too much, when she could be focusing on more important things, like the funeral home.

She doesn't expect it when Jason says, "Yeah, I know what you mean." He leans back on his elbows and looks at Kyla like he knows more than what she means, like he knows *her*. Kyla squirms under his stare. Jason and Erin don't even really look alike. They're both blondish, but Jason is more golden brown, while Erin's hair is so blond it's nearly white. Jason is predisposed to tanning and freckles, and Erin's skin has never been like that. They don't even have the same eyes—Jason's are green. Erin's are brown. Were brown.

"Today was eventful," Jason says.

An understatement.

"Yeah," Kyla croaks out.

Jason raises a thick eyebrow—Erin was always jealous of how thick his eyebrows are—and laughs at her. "I've been trying to tell Peter to leave it alone. I thought it would die down on its own."

"It wouldn't, and it hasn't. So I told him we had to take care of it," Kyla says.

Jason stills. "Kyla . . ." He trails off.

"I had to," Kyla says firmly, because he doesn't get it. It'd all gone wrong. All of it. Peter's first escape from the scrutiny of the public eye had been temporary, facilitated by the fact that his father's a partner at the town's only law firm, and his own social cachet. She knows she'd been close to getting Rowan to retract their statements and putting it all to bed for good, without betraying Erin's secrets. But after the memorial, that became impossible. Everyone decided Peter's guilt, shaped by the narrative Florence put forward for some strange reason.

With Peter firmly back in the cops' sights, Kyla could feel her hard work unraveling like loose thread. She had no other choice than to play this card. Erin would've handled this better. She was so adept at handling Peter's and Rowan's whims like it was her job. Kyla can only pray that Peter's timeline checks out, that his alibis are airtight. That he doesn't need to use the Test Kitchens as a scapegoat or a bargaining chip. If anyone finds out about them—about the money—it would be bad. For *all* of them.

Jason shakes his head in dismay. "So Mikky was right? You've been trying to psychologically torment that kid into silence?"

"Mikky talked about me to you?" Kyla asks.

Jason purses his lips. "Well, we're not really talking at all anymore. But even if we were, I don't want to talk about you with him," he says. "You and me, we're separate from me and Mikky."

Erin and Kyla were never separate from Jason and Kyla. "Erin and Kyla" had been the reason there could never *be* a "Jason and Kyla."

"Why did you tell Peter?" he asks finally.

"Because. He wanted to know why Rowan would target him. All I told him was that they hooked up," Kyla says simply. If Peter had drawn his own conclusions about jealousy and motives, well, that was on him and the rabid audience he'd drawn with his outburst.

Let the public do Kyla's job now. She has larger concerns. Test Kitchens to plan. Money to make. Funeral homes to save.

"God . . . so how long did you know about them?" Jason asks. "Erin and Rowan?"

Erin and Kyla didn't keep secrets, or at least Kyla had thought they didn't. At first, though, all she knew was that Rowan and Erin were paired for a math project last semester. It had cut into dance team practice. Sometimes Kyla even had to set up for Test Kitchens alone, blowing up Erin's phone, waiting for her response that always came too late. Erin would moan about being "forced" to ditch, gaining the sympathy of the rest of the team for being forced to be in the company of someone as whiny as Rowan.

God, she'd complain to Kyla during sleepovers, snipe that "today Rowan thinks they're so much smarter than me. I can do the work too." Or she'd storm into the hearse earlier than Kyla'd expected, and sneer, "Rowan can't take a fucking joke. All I said was that their little girlfriend needs a bit of help in the blush department. You know Lydia, right? She looks like a *ghost* with the pancake makeup. And they told me that my makeup makes me look like a drag queen."

But Kyla always knew when Erin liked someone. She got *extra* intense, white blood cells defending against the infection of her crush. Kyla waited, but weeks passed and Erin didn't tell her. So Kyla forced the issue. She looked for them until she caught them, in the back of the library, tucked against the stacks, Rowan's fingers up Erin's skirt, Erin's fingers curled into the dark hair at the nape of Rowan's neck, pulling so hard that they'd hissed in pain. When Erin had finally emerged to join Kyla in her hearse, sliding into the passenger seat, she hadn't apologized for hiding it or had the grace to look embarrassed. She only grinned and said, "I hope you enjoyed the show."

Suddenly, every Test Kitchen ended with Kyla's hearse pulling out of Florence Cook's driveway and Rowan's ugly sedan pulling in. They didn't know about what Erin and Kyla were up to, and they didn't care as long as they got to hook up with Erin.

"I sort of did," Kyla says, because there's no good way to sum all of that up.

"Why didn't she break it off with Peter and . . . date them? Why was she sneaking around?" Jason asks.

"It wasn't ever going to work."

Rowan wasn't an all-American athlete. Rowan didn't have the square jaw. Rowan wasn't *Superman*—they didn't fit into the life that Erin had constructed for herself online. And that life was everything Erin dreamed of. She wanted to be a monument. Besides, Rowan was as ashamed of Erin as she was of them. Kyla could see it so obviously, the way they shied away from Erin if she passed them at school. In the way they looked at Erin like she was a strange science experiment, with equal parts disgust and fascination.

"You don't like them, do you?" Jason asks.

Kyla weighs the words on her tongue. Carefully, she says, "They don't like me."

"A lot of people don't like you, Kyla. Come on, be serious," Jason says.

Kyla barks a laugh. No one has ever said that to her. It's refreshing.

"You know, Peter had it all wrong today. She was with him, not only for the likes, but because she wanted to make *Rowan* jealous, not the other way around. She liked them so much. Too much. She didn't want to be public, but she wanted to be chased. She wanted them to be *obsessed*. But Rowan's not like that. I don't even think they liked her. This one time, when they thought they were alone, I overheard them call her a 'vapid, cruel cheerleader, but a good fuck.' All because she made a dumb joke about their friend Gregory having a crush on me. *That's* why I don't like them. They thought they were too good for her, but it didn't stop them from wanting her," Kyla bites out, sneering.

She remembers the rest of that night, packing up after a Test Kitchen, hearing the sneering condescension dripping from those words. Then the door slam. When Kyla had crept into the living room, Erin had been standing there, smiling at nothing with glossy eyes. She'd sniffed, and simply said, "Well." And then she'd finished a bottle of the wine in one go. "Just like Mom," she said.

"They don't like me because I see right through that act. They can hide behind that soft-spoken bullshit, but I see past it. I know who they really are." Kyla finishes venomously.

"God, they sound like an asshole," Jason says, shaking his head with a darkening expression. "Erin *would* be into that."

Kyla lets out a sharp huff, approximating a laugh. "Yeah, and then they had the nerve to call me *feral*. Fucking asshole. *I'm* a mean bitch," Kyla says, and Jason flinches at that word like that's the problem. "But Erin was meaner and bitchier, and they would've *never* called the blond girl 'feral.' It's gross."

Jason's smile drips away like her words are sitting heavy in his stomach. "Oh, fuck."

"Yeah, *oh*." Kyla nods. "But you know, the thing about people like Rowan is that they can only feel big if they make you feel small. They did that to Erin. But they can't do that to me. They'd never say that shit to *my* face because I can't be made small." She forces herself to believe it. Kyla used to think of herself as part of a unit. Sometimes, in her darkest moments, she'd consider herself a shadow, indivisible from Erin. She can't be a shadow anymore. Shadows can't get shit done on their own, and Kyla's on her own now.

"There you are," Jason says softly, reaching for her. The blunt edges of his nails brush against her jawline. "I nearly forgot what you looked like—colder-than-a-corpse Kyla Graves."

Kyla wrangles her mouth into a smile. "Aren't I always?"

"Not lately. Lately it seems like you're burning."

"Aren't you?" Kyla asks.

Jason sighs. "Kyla, to be honest, I don't think I could put how I feel into words."

Jason seems content with sitting in their shared silence after this, but something about it makes Kyla nervous. Interrupting it seems much worse, though. To shatter the atmosphere would make Jason leave, and she doesn't really want him to leave just yet.

Minutes pass, and still Kyla can't relax.

"It's late," she says finally. "Are you going to get in trouble?"

Jason shakes his head. "Yeah, right. I'll blame it on the walk and a hard practice."

"Walk?" Kyla asks.

"Yeah, I have to walk home. My mom's borrowing the Wrangler again today. Dad needed his car to drive into Boston for a meeting and the Mercedes has been in the shop since summer, waiting for a part to come in. This is what happens when you get custom specs that you don't need," Jason says, sounding pretty bitter for something so trivial.

Kyla nudges her shoulder against his. "Kinda hypocritical, Mr. Custom Rims. Now come on, I'll drive you home," she says.

"You really don't have to," Jason insists.

"I am *not* going to let you walk home. It's freezing, Jason."

Jason waffles only a second longer. "Then let me pay for your gas. Or, wait, let's do Fable Street tomorrow morning? Before you go to work and I have to get to my game?" he suggests.

"Deal," Kyla says. She stands up and offers him a hand. Jason takes it immediately, requiring no further convincing. He doesn't let go as they walk down from the bleachers, and, to her own internal confusion, Kyla doesn't tug away.

Jason's hand in hers is a weakness, just like every other moment that she's shared with him over the past few weeks. But she'll let herself have it. Just this once. The guilt will have to make room.

When they get into the hearse, Jason makes himself at home. He immediately flips on her radio and lowers it so that it fills the car but doesn't destroy the ambiance for their nice cruising ride to the Vaughns' place.

When they arrive, Kyla looks over at Jason, expectantly. But he's staring down at his lap.

"I kinda don't want to go in," he says.

Kyla unbuckles her seat belt and turns toward him, propping her knee up on the center console. "Why not?"

Jason takes his time answering. "What's even in there?"

"Your parents," Kyla says. *Not Erin.*

"Ah, yes, emotionally absent father and a drunk for a mother. Two *wonderfully refreshing* inhabitants." Jason laughs, but it comes out callous and angry. She hasn't seen him angry, not even at the funeral. It's refreshing to see someone angry like her. Someone who might also have stuffing coming out of them at the seams.

"My dad always says people experience grief in different ways," Kyla says as charitably as she can. She's not great at the emotional parts of the family trade, but she knows the right things to say.

"Kyla... why do you think it started with the grief?"

Kyla's always known that the woman that Mrs. Vaughn is to her, is different from how she was to Erin. She knows because of Erin's constant sly comments, sometimes bordering on open disdain. But Kyla never really thought it could compare to what she had been dealt with her own mother. Complicated and ruinous and only sometimes rational. At least Mrs. Vaughn was *there*.

But it changes things, hearing that Jason, too, has a differing picture of the woman Kyla viewed as a surrogate mother for so long. Kyla's stomach turns because Erin and Kyla didn't keep secrets, yet this feels like another one.

"Jason... you don't have to go in, if you don't want to," Kyla finally says.

He laughs like she's said something funny. "Sometimes, we do things because we *have* to, not because we want to." Kyla sits there, staring straight ahead at the passenger door as Jason leans over and brushes his nose against her cheek. She expects the warmth of his mouth and hates her disappointment when it doesn't happen. Instead, he whispers, "Good night, Kyla Graves."

Then the car door swings open and he heads into the house without looking back.

Kyla stares up at the second home that she's always been welcomed into, now with a ghost haunting the upstairs bedroom behind the third door to the left, absolutely gutted by the revelation that ghosts can still keep secrets, long after they're gone.

CHAPTER TWENTY-ONE

I know this isn't something any of you will *want* to attend, but after last week's . . . events, and with the current climate *outside* of the school, it's been decided that this will be a good way to address the grieving within our community," Mikky's homeroom teacher, Mr. Cross, says.

Mr. Cross is doing a good job of pretending not to hear the mass of moaning about Monday's impending assembly, which is replacing fifth period, right after lunch, but Mikky's not taking part. This assembly stinks of *opportunity*. Mikky pulls out his phone and he has to hide a smile when he sees the preview of Nasim's text.

So . . . who's in the mood for a heist during assembly?

Once more Mikky is reminded of how well matched they are.

"Peter and Rowan were the ones fighting about Erin. Why do *we* need to be punished?" one girl complains. There's a grumbling of agreement from some of the others.

Mr. Cross's stare is flaccid; he's already over the idea of arguing with them when nothing will change.

"This isn't about punishment. It's about healing, coming together as a community to process something that's been difficult for us." He raises his head and declares, "Instead of talking to the news, let's consider the idea that we speak a bit more to *each other*."

Before anyone else can get brave enough to complain, the bell rings. Mr. Cross sags with relief and then he calls out, "Remember, fifth period, report to the gym."

Mikky is already halfway to the door, bag thrown over his shoulder. He makes a beeline toward Nasim's homeroom two halls away, and meets him halfway. Nasim reaches out and grabs his wrist immediately.

"I had to literally *run* from Rowan. Come this way," Nasim says, dragging him down the hallway in the direction of Indigo Glass's locker. The minute they make it there, it's already packed with people rushing to their first class of the day. "We need to do a bit of recon."

"Recon, how?" Mikky asks.

Nasim crowds so close that Mikky could slip his hands beneath Nasim's sweater and no one would notice. Well, Nasim would notice, but that would probably be the point.

"Well, we need to get her locker combo, of course. Look alive, Mikky, here she comes," Nasim says, staring down the hallway at their target. Mikky doesn't turn around, only turns his head so he can catch a glimpse of her from the corner of his eye. There goes Indigo Glass, gunning right for her locker, phone in hand.

Nasim pulls out his phone and backs away, lifting it up.

"What are you doing?" Mikky croaks, unintentionally grabbing Indigo's attention.

She sees Nasim's phone, and her lips pull back into a sneer, but Nasim throws a charming smile at Mikky that doesn't look like his real smile at *all*.

"I'm filming you, Mikky. Now do something funny," Nasim says.

Mikky rolls his eyes. "I'm not your entertainment—"

"*Mikky*," Nasim insists, eyes wide.

Mikky stills and throws another glance over his shoulder. Indigo has turned back to her locker and she's reaching for the lock. Mikky looks down at the phone that's not quite trained on him and exhales softly, nodding. He slowly shifts to the right and forces a smile onto his face. Then he starts to dance.

"You're lucky you're cute, you hear me, Talebi?" Mikky says through his teeth as he half remembers the Electric Slide. "Doing line dances in the hallway like an asshole."

"Oh, you think I'm cute," Nasim drawls, staring intently, ostensibly at Mikky's shoulder but actually at Indigo.

"This is very embarrassing."

"For you? Sure. For me? It's hilarious." Nasim leans in and Mikky can imagine him zooming in his camera to focus right on Indigo's fingers. Mikky hears the locker open, and Nasim lets out a breath before he stops recording and tucks his phone in his back pocket. "Thank you. In exchange for you humoring me, I'll escort you to class."

"A gentleman," Mikky says with a laugh, taking Nasim's offered arm.

Nasim's grin is far more genuine when he says, "My mother raised one, it's true."

The recon is done and the plans are set. Now it's all up to the execution.

By the time fifth period rolls around, Mikky twitches with anticipation. He can't stop fidgeting, picking at the loose thread on the frayed hem of his denim vest. It's unraveling, faster and faster, and while it adds to Mikky's messy punk aesthetic, he actually *likes* this vest, dammit. It took a long time to find the exact pins and patches for it to fit exactly how he wanted it to look. Still, he can't help it.

Mikky is trapped in the sea of freshmen dragging their feet, but he can easily see over their heads since most of them have yet to hit their growth spurts. Eventually, he recognizes the backs of Nasim's and Rowan's heads. He can see Nasim trying to squirm away, but Rowan sticks close, searching for security in the thick of a crowd that's now casting them side-eyes the way it used to do with Peter. Mikky goes to push through and stand by them when a voice booms, "Sit by homerooms! We're sitting by homerooms."

Well, there goes that plan. Plan B will have to be made on the fly, then. Mikky sighs, turning and searching for one of the people from his homeroom. Fingers brush against his wrist. Mikky doesn't jump, though. He'll always recognize the presence of his sister. Still, he looks down at her in surprise that they've ended up together in the crowd, slowly shuffling into the gym that's sure to be sweltering, stinking of teenage BO.

"This is so stupid," Kyla says, her body held tight, like she wants to backflip her way out of the situation. Everyone's looking at her, of course, which means everyone is looking at him, too. Not ideal.

"Making Erin's business everyone's business is so . . ." Mikky trails off, shaking his head.

"She would like it, though. She liked being the center of attention." From anyone else, that would be a dig, but Kyla says it with a bone-deep fondness.

"How much you want to bet they won't even say her name?"

Mikky asks. He knows how this goes. His old school used to talk about mental health too. It was one of the things that drew his mother to enroll him there. But the school administration never *really* addressed it, only the vague idea that it mattered.

"I'm not taking that bet," Kyla says.

Mikky *needs* everyone to be at the assembly, especially Kyla. He needs the hallways empty to give him the chance to commit literal theft. And yet, against his better judgment, he says, "I bet if you asked, you could get excused."

He doesn't get a reply, though, because he's shoved into her as two boys playfight. Kyla stumbles, and when she rights herself, she snaps, "What are you doing?"

The cut of her voice stops the two boys in their tracks and they pale. One of them stutters, "Kyla, I-I'm sor—"

"Save your sorry for someone who cares. Maybe try to act like you weren't raised in a barn?" she hisses out, then holds up a hand when the other tries to answer her. "It was rhetorical. Shut up and walk."

Mikky feels his skin crawl. Authority has never been his cup of tea, but Kyla has it in spades. He can't help but wonder if she ever spoke to Erin that way. He can't imagine it. Every time Kyla mentions Erin, her voice softens, back more toward the sister he remembers. But it's a reminder that there are versions of her—some harder and colder—and Mikky doesn't necessarily know what those versions are capable of.

"I have to go. It'll be worse if I don't," Kyla says without looking at Mikky again, and then she slips into a gap between two other students, disappearing from view.

Eventually, Mikky gets inside and the echoing din gives him

an instant headache. The gym is overpacked; even the chill from outside doesn't ease the sweltering heat that comes with putting too many bodies into a space. Mikky sees his homeroom classmates, halfway up the bleachers, and he joins them, sitting on the very end of a sweaty bench. His homeroom teacher checks him off on his clipboard very dramatically.

Indigo Glass sits in the middle of the gym, tucked between her VP and the secretary of the student council, atop a slightly raised dais that they've rolled out from some dusty closet. The principal is posed in front of a microphone with his arms folded over his chest, but not in a closed-off way. He's puffing his chest out authoritatively, showing off for . . . someone.

"What is that?" Mikky hisses, identifying the "someone" as the film crew lined up at the wall.

"I believe that's the evening news," the homeroom teacher says, lips pursed. "Been a small bit of . . . discussion among the teachers. Don't pay it any mind, Mikky. Just sit tight."

Mikky squirms, distracted by the all-seeing eye of the camera lens as it sweeps over the student body. He cringes away from the demanding weight of its gaze and searches for Kyla in the crowd. But there are too many students, and his eyes skip over her again and again until the camera and a photographer shift forward and he realizes they're trained right on her.

He knows that Kyla sees them; there's no way she couldn't. But she refuses to look, instead staring down at her phone. Her own homeroom teacher—Mikky's AP German teacher, Frau Fischer, incidentally—is watching her with a mix of disapproval and pity. The latter clearly wins out.

Kyla shouldn't be here. It's not fair for her to have to be at the center of this, and Mikky is sure someone would've excused her. Her continued presence only functions as a means of punishment, and for the first time, Mikky wonders at that. Whether Kyla is punishing herself somehow. And why.

"This is so fucked," Mikky mutters under his breath as he stares at his knees, counting down the seconds until the assembly starts.

Soon Principal Morton clears his throat into the microphone, causing a feedback shriek that makes Mikky wince. "Hello, settle down, everyone," he begins. His prompting has the opposite effect, and the students don't quiet until a number of teachers hush them aggressively, threatening detentions with single looks. When it's finally quiet *enough*, Principal Morton continues, "Thank you for taking the time out of your day so we can come together as a school during a very trying and troubling time."

He delivers those words with the air of someone who's rehearsed them, but not enough for them to sound natural. He shifts back and forth, awkwardly shooting sideway glances at the news cameras.

"As many of you know, we lost a towering figure in our community, and from the past few weeks it's clear we don't yet have the skills to cope with that," he says. Then he holds a hand out to someone Mikky can't quite see yet. "This is Dr. Julian London, a grief counselor from Boston, who has so graciously given his time today as a favor to our generous benefactor, Florence Cook."

There's that name again. Florence Cook. Dr. London jumps up onto the dais to a round of lukewarm applause that Mikky half-heartedly joins in on.

"Thank you for welcoming me into your space," Dr. London

says, hands clasped over his chest, shaking them like he's won a prize. "Thank you for letting me see your grief."

Mikky isn't really sure what the good doctor is *seeing* other than the faces of weary teenagers that want to be anywhere other than in this gymnasium.

"I'm Dr. Julian London. I received my masters in psychology from Harvard University, and my PhD from Columbia University. Ivy through and through," he says with a wink, like they should be impressed by that. It clearly works on some people, but not on Mikky. "I'm also the bestselling author of a number of books, most popularly *I Don't Know and Other Little Lies We Tell Ourselves*."

Red flag. Red *fucking* flag. Still, he hopes the man is as long winded as he already seems to be—it'll give Mikky long enough to actually do what he needs to do.

"Grief is real. It comes from a very real place. But I want all of us to move past this grief into something more productive," Dr. London says immediately. He holds up his hands and commands, "Now, everyone stand with me."

There's a brief moment of uncertainty, where everyone shifts in their seats. Everyone but Indigo Glass, who jumps up immediately, yanking her council members to their feet by their sleeves. Dr. London notices and says, "Thank you for trusting in me. Everyone, join your class president."

Mikky doesn't. He feels the disapproving side-eye from Mr. Cross but refuses to engage. He looks past the so-called grief counselor at Kyla and sees that she *is* standing, but her eyes are like daggers.

"Now, I would like everyone to scream," Dr. London says pleasantly.

Principal Morton barely covers his ears before an unholy blast of sound bleats throughout the room. Mikky's shoulders rise involuntarily as he cringes away from it, and his ears are ringing by the time Dr. London cuts them all off.

"Good. Very good. How did that feel?" he asks, his smile never shifting. "Great, I'm sure. But unproductive, huh? Everyone sit. I want to tell you all about how to transform that excess energy and emotion of our grief into something more conducive to learning."

And that's when Mikky knows for sure that quite literally nothing helpful will be happening here except for keeping the entire school distracted while Mikky and Nasim take their thievery from theoretical to practical.

"Can I go to the bathroom?" Mikky whispers.

Mr. Cross frowns disapprovingly down at him. "Mikky . . . the counselor is speaking."

"I really have to go to the bathroom," Mikky insists. Mr. Cross sighs, and for a second Mikky thinks that he won't get his way. That he'll have to abort the plan. So he goes for the jugular: "Erin was my little sister's best friend. We grew up together. I just . . . I think I'm gonna be sick."

It's a slimy thing to do, but it works. His homeroom teacher nods and Mikky tiptoes easily down the bleachers, pleased that he's curbed his need to express himself with clunky platform boots today. No one is watching him. Half the students are either vying for or shying from the camera lens. The other half are staring at his sister or Jason like they're zoo animals.

As soon as the doors swing closed behind Mikky, the counselor's voice noticeably muffles. The air out of the crowded gym feels icier than before, like the air-conditioning is still on despite the quickly dropping temperatures outside.

The quietness is awful, so oppressive that every breath and squeak of Mikky's shoes feels like it will call someone to bust him for misdeeds he hasn't yet committed. The hallways seem to stretch longer the quicker he walks, and Mikky's mind triggers hall monitors at each sharp turn. But he *knows* where everyone is. Everyone is in the gym, and the people that aren't are probably smoking by the dumpsters at the opposite side of the school, outside the cafeteria. There's no reason for him to stress, except Mikky has never stolen anything in his life besides a pack of gum when he was seven, and that was by accident.

When he arrives at Indigo Glass's locker, his heart sinks into his stomach. Nasim isn't here yet. They'd agreed that whoever got there first would start right away, though, which means Mikky will have to go it alone.

Indigo's locker doesn't look any different from anyone else's. But inside, Mikky knows that it'll have at least some of the answers that he's been searching for since he came back to Prophets Lake. He doesn't have time for any more hesitation. He already knows what Nasim would say anyway—feeling bad about what they have to do isn't constructive or helpful right now. They need *evidence* and that need is paramount.

He tugs his phone out of his back pocket and looks down at the video that he didn't have the courage to watch before in his text thread with Nasim. There are three messages he's missed below it: Can't get out yet. Rowan is in my homeroom and they're like moping next to me. Gonna fake sick in a bit. Mikky presses play without thinking and nearly jumps when the surge of morning noise hits him, a little tinnier. His voice comes through, "What are you doing?" and Mikky gags.

He sounds more than flirty. He sounds *lovesick*. How embarrassing. More embarrassing than the dancing even.

Mikky shakes it away and mutes his phone entirely before he plays the video again. This time, he ignores himself, looking to the left—that's the bread and butter.

They're angled in such a way that Nasim easily captured Indigo entering her combination. Mikky presses close to the locker, lifting a knee up against the metal so that he can balance his phone and grasp the combination lock with two hands. He follows along in real time, twisting it to the right first, just after Indigo does. Twenty-nine. Quickly a full turn to the left, stopping at thirteen. Mikky squints back down at his screen.

"Fuck," he hisses as Indigo crowds closer to it. He watches her hand twist back to the right—not very far, but he can't see the *number*. "Nasim, a cinematographer, you are *not*."

Mikky tries to push down the panic that immediately starts to well in his belly. It's not helpful. Panic rarely is, but he's only human, and a human with anxiety disorder, to be more specific. Mikky's mouth goes dry, tongue swollen like the corpses in his father's morgue, shortly before they shit out their remains and Dad has to go in and pump them with formaldehyde. The cold sweat on the back of his neck stings, frizzing up the nape of his neck, where the curls have escaped his puff.

Mikky closes his eyes and *breathes*, the way Dr. Grosse taught him to do. Inhale. Exhale. Inhale. Exhale.

When he opens his eyes again, he has a firmer grasp of himself. Despite the fraying edges, he won't let them unravel. Not until he's really failed. In his attempt to calm himself, Mikky's phone has gone dark. He reawakens it and shoves his face closer to the screen, running the video back the tiniest bit, watching carefully. Okay. So, he does see a little bit of the lock turning before she shifts in front of it.

It goes past zero counterclockwise, but not before thirty, he's pretty sure. Thirty to zero. A range.

Mikky tries thirty first and yanks at the lock. He jumps at the echo of metal on metal. Nope.

"Okay, then. I'll just try it until it works," he tells himself, shoving his phone back into his pocket. Saying it out loud solidifies the plan, and pushes his anxiety even further away than before.

29-13-31.

No.

29-13-32.

Also no. Mikky will try something a little farther up.

29-13-38.

Damn. Maybe he should wait for Nasim—

No. There's no time to wait. It's got to happen now.

Mikky takes another centering breath. Closer to the thirty again this time.

29-13-34.

Mikky tugs on the lock and . . . feels it give. He hisses out a relieved exhale through his teeth. Gently, as if he's doing surgery even, he pulls the door open and looks into the depths of Indigo Glass's locker. It is so painfully organized that the very idea of disturbing it nearly sends Mikky into a panic.

She has her lunch hanging on one hook and her coat hanging on the other. Her class schedule, color coded of course, is on the inside of the locker door, laminated and held up by a gold star magnet at each corner. On the top shelf, each subject book is organized alphabetically. Then her planner. And finally, nestled on top of a hat, her *phone*.

Mikky grabs it and shuts the locker quickly, locking it back up before he slides the phone into his other back pocket, exchanging it for his own.

Meet me in the bathroom closest to the gym, he fires off to Nasim.

Mikky gets there first, despite being farther away. As soon as he enters the bathroom, Mikky slams each stall open, looking inside. When he finds no one, he leans back against the middle sink, tapping his foot. Indigo's phone feels heavy in his pocket and he tilts his head, cracking his neck and sighing to himself, frustrated when he checks his phone again and sees thirty seconds have passed since he's entered the bathroom.

He strains, trying to hear any movement outside, but there's nothing except that weird alien silence again that makes his breath sound even louder in his ears. He hates that silence. He begins to move, pacing back and forth, the soundtrack of his own footsteps much better than waiting in quiet.

When the door slams open, Mikky freezes, wide-eyed.

"You look like you've seen a ghost," Nasim says.

Mikky immediately relaxes, and covers with an eye roll. "Dude, I just stole something. Forgive me for being a little jumpy."

Nasim softens. "You're right. And while I know you're doing this for mostly your sister, I appreciate this," he says earnestly.

Mikky presents his find to Nasim, who stares down at the phone in wonder.

"I really can't believe you got it," he murmurs.

"Dude, your filming skills need work. I couldn't see the third number so I had to guess a bunch."

Nasim looks up from the phone, offended. "I was forming a plan on the fly, okay? I work well under pressure but not even I can control all the variables."

"Even though you'd certainly try," Mikky mumbles under his breath. Nasim ignores this and flicks his thumb over the screen.

Mikky's heart plummets when he sees it: "ENTER PASS-CODE."

"Oh, *fuck* me," Nasim whispers. "I knew I forgot something."

Before Mikky can respond, the bathroom door swings open, and they both twist to look at the doorway.

"You two, out of the bathroom," Mikky's homeroom teacher says, a distinct lack of pity in his voice now.

Nasim neatly puts his hands behind his back, shoving the phone into a back pocket as he files out in front of Mikky, shifty and nervous in the face of getting caught doing something wrong. Mikky keeps close, refusing to meet Mr. Cross's eyes, unable to muster up the shame that he knows the man wants him to feel. He leans back against the wall, sullen.

"I thought you were feeling ill, Mikky," Mr. Cross says.

"I was. Nasim saw me leave and was worried, so he came to check on me," Mikky says.

"If you were feeling so ill that you've been gone for . . ." The man pauses to dramatically check his watch. Who even wears watches in this day and age? "Fifteen minutes," he continues, "why didn't you go to the nurse?"

"It wasn't bad enough to go to the nurse," Mikky says.

All plausibly true, but his teacher isn't convinced yet.

"So . . . you. Nasim, was it?" Mr. Cross asks. "What grade are you in?"

"Um, I'm a junior," Nasim says. In the face of an authority figure, he's more cowed than Mikky has ever seen him, meek in a way that doesn't suit him. He's wearing a sweater today, instead of a hoodie, and he pulls on a piece of yarn at the wrist.

"You saw Mikky leave and you were worried?"

"Yes. We're . . . friends . . ." Nasim trails off, looking over at Mikky, who smiles, hoping that he looks at least a little reassuring.

"Friends," Mr. Cross says, like he sees something else in the smile. "Right."

"We are," Nasim insists.

"Huh. And you knew which bathroom he was in?"

"He texted me," Nasim says.

Fuck.

Mikky's lips press into a thin line as his homeroom teacher straightens, eyes brighter.

"I'd like to remind you that cell phone use during school hours is strictly prohibited except for during your lunch periods," Mr. Cross says. "In any other circumstances, I would give you a warning, but this assembly is very serious." Code for: *My bosses are taking this too seriously, and you, Mikky, are far too close to this to be out and about when you should be looking sad for the fucking news cameras.*

"Okay, so what are you doing in *this* circumstance?" Nasim asks.

"Sorry, boys, I think it'll be detention today."

Mikky's never gotten detention in his entire life, and from

Nasim's expression, neither has he. But Mikky's also learned to think on the bright side of things. Downside: his sister is involved in some shady shit that might have to do with Erin's death. Bright side: he's now a step closer to clearing her of murder. Downside: his closeness to Erin is what's getting him in trouble. Bright side: it's also what got him out of assembly in order to steal Indigo's phone. Downside: Mikky got caught outside of assembly doing something that he wasn't supposed to be doing, and now he has detention.

Bright side: detention is more than enough time to break into a phone.

CHAPTER TWENTY-TWO

Kyla is over it. She's so *fucking* over it. The tears and the platitudes and the way that everyone wants their moment in front of the lens. She can feel the weight of the camera pointed at her and she already knows what chyron they'll add under her face: ERIN VAUGHN'S BEST FRIEND. Everyone will be dissecting her expressions, reading her reactions as something they're not, judging her for not grieving loud enough, or grieving *too* much, or not grieving the right way. Forget Dad and Mikky staring at her, watching for her to crack. It'll be all of America. Fuck them, fuck everyone, fuck this *shit*.

When Principal Morton finally dismisses everyone with, "All right, make sure to get to your next class in an orderly fashion," he has a magnanimous smile on his face like he *did* something.

He didn't do shit. Mikky was right, no one even said Erin's name.

Her throat burns the way it does when a cold is coming on, and her vision goes fuzzy around the edges. For a moment she's terrified that it's tears, that gut-wrenching sobs are going to rip their way from her body and possess her in a way that she has been so diligent about restraining.

She takes one breath to preempt it. Then another. She doesn't deserve the release. It's not helpful, anyway.

And that's when she realizes—she's not *sad*. She's *enraged*. And that's an emotion she can channel into something useful.

"Move," Kyla commands, and her classmate slides out of the way so she can storm down the bleacher steps. She keeps her eyes trained single-mindedly on the door, refusing to acknowledge the cameras *still* being pointed at her.

She feels a hand on her wrist, dainty jewelry paired with calluses. Kyla twitches and looks into Alicia's pouting mouth, furrowed brows, and a face full of *pity*.

"Kyla, are you okay?" Alicia asks. "Because that was *not* okay."

Kyla draws closer, nostrils flaring involuntarily. It's like she can smell the coppery blood in the water already and she wouldn't mind spilling more.

"'Are you okay?'" Kyla asks. "What kind of question is that?"

Alicia shrinks in on herself. Kyla hates it. Erin would *never* shrink herself, and here is this girl who is so desperate to fill in the empty spot next to Kyla yet can't stop herself from getting smaller. Kyla wants to grab her by her limbs and stretch and stretch her until she takes up so much space that Kyla can't breathe. Maybe *then* Alicia will be worthy of replacing Erin Vaughn as Kyla's best friend. Maybe.

"I just wanted to check in . . . ," Alicia says, cowed.

"I don't want *you* to check in with me, Alicia," Kyla grunts out. "Now leave me *alone*."

Alicia hangs back immediately. At least that's one thing about her. Kyla doesn't have to repeat herself like she has to with the other girls.

She isn't sure how she escapes the gym, whether she shoves her way out or everyone parts for her like the Red Sea, but finally she gets free. She doesn't feel free, though. She feels like she's being chased, like the ghost of Erin is nipping closer and closer at her heels with a jackal's laugh. It sets her heart pounding.

Kyla has English for last period. She can't even remember what book she's reading in that class, let alone anything interesting to say about it. For a second, she thinks about going and sitting there blankly. Her teacher won't mind. But it's more effort than it's worth and Kyla is a practical person. She has better shit to do with her time.

It's that thought that makes her turn on her heel and walk in the opposite direction of her classroom, fighting against the rolling wave of students to get to her locker. She grabs her books, stuffs them in her bag, then throws her coat around her shoulders and keeps her head down as she goes through the lobby and out the doors to the parking lot.

She sits in her hearse and doesn't move. The car parked in front of hers is owned by Melissa Fitzgerald, one of the only sophomores with a car because her daddy owns the dealership in town. She always smiles across the way at Kyla, waiting for her to smile back, as if she thinks that one day Kyla will wave and ask her to join her at her lunch table and suddenly she'll be on the path to popularity.

Kyla would rather stick her eye out with a fork. Erin was always so much better at situations like that. She would've found a way to make Melissa useful, facilitating her way into the in crowd for a price, and if she proved to be *un*useful, Erin would've disposed of her just as quickly. Kyla can't muster up the energy—she'd always been down for the ride with Erin's schemes, quick to smooth out the execution for the least amount of damage to themselves, but she'd never been one to start it all off. It's *exhausting*, Kyla's realized in the past couple of weeks.

She lets her head fall against the wheel, and the dull feeling of petty irritation grounds her. Then Kyla lays out the facts of her problems: her expression will be all over the five p.m. local news tonight for everyone to dissect, her father can't make their mortgage on the funeral home this month, people are on the verge of talking about the Test Kitchens, and Erin is dead. All of them are strangely connected in a way that makes Kyla's life feel like an evidence board snaked by red string. She guffaws to herself—if only Erin could see her now.

At least Kyla can address one of those problems, her most prominent. She might as well stop putting it off and do it now.

Kyla pulls up the Notes app on her phone and scrolls down halfway. There's one note that's password protected, and even though it's been a while, it's still second nature to type in "duckduckgoose3." There's only one phone number at the top. Kyla presses it and puts her phone on speaker, waiting for it to ring. It does for fifteen seconds, and then there's the click of someone picking up.

"Hello, Erin gave me this number in case of an emergency," Kyla says by way of greeting.

Someone's breath hitches and then an upbeat voice says, "Hello, thank you for calling Cook Cosmetics, how can I help you? Tilly from Influencer speaking."

"Tilly, I'm Kyla Graves. I'm Erin Vaughn's best friend. I was featured in some of her posts," Kyla says. A lot of her posts. Erin would always split those payments with Kyla, because she knew Kyla needed the money. She'd done it even after they started up the Test Kitchens, when Kyla's need was a little less dire.

Now it's dire again.

Tilly makes a sweet awed sound. "Oh, yes, I do remember you, Kyla! Your post together about the Power Play Palette had such high engagement, we talked about it a lot in the office." Kyla remembers that shoot, the video of Kyla and Erin doing each other's makeup in a Reel. They'd gone viral, just talking about how they knew each other, how long they'd known each other. All the comments had been sweet enough to give both of them a cavity.

"Yes, that was us. I know that Erin was *technically* the brand ambassador, but since she's . . . no longer around, I was wondering if you'd consider me to fill her slot," Kyla pushes out.

There's a beat of silence. Then a slow, drawled-out, "Oh." Tilly's voice loses its enthusiasm.

"Florence came to Erin's memorial and what she said about teenage girls and how we're the future and how we're not as protected as we should be went viral, and I think that I would have an excellent platform to showcase that message and Cook Cosmetics products. Especially the new skin-care makeup line, GloMo," Kyla pitches. She sounds confident, more than she feels, but she knows it's a good plan. She knows it and Tilly knows it.

Erin, blond and beautiful, was aspirational.

But Kyla could be aspirational too. She's Black, driven, and accomplished. It'll be a new direction for Cook. A much-needed introduction to a new customer base. They've been stupid not to ask Kyla sooner, frankly, and Kyla needs this. She needs this job and she needs that ad money, and most of all she needs product for the *Test Kitchens*.

"I'm not sure I'm the best person to assist you, Kyla," Tilly says.

Kyla glares into Melissa Fitzgerald's headlights. "But you're the number that Erin was given."

"I know but that was Erin . . . I'm just not sure that I can help *you*. Let me pass this message along to my boss and you'll receive a callback, okay?" Tilly asks. There's an edge to her perkiness now, and Kyla can shut her eyes and picture the sharpness of her smile, the gleaming white of her dentist-bleached teeth.

"Sure," Kyla spits out, knowing damn well that no one's going to call her back. After all, Kyla isn't the daughter of the director of global marketing. She's always suspected that's why she hasn't ever been invited to the influencer program too, despite the so-called high engagement. She was already doing posts with her friend for free. There'd been no incentive for them. Tilly hangs up.

Kyla watches the screen until it turns black and then fights the urge to scream and hurl her phone across the parking lot. It would be so satisfying to hear it crack on the pavement, to run her fingers along a shattered screen and feel every ridge. But she knows how much a replacement would cost and it's not worth it.

It always comes back to that—*money*. Kyla bites her own tongue, refusing to give in to her rage-fueled urges. Time to pivot.

She methodically forms a to-do list in her head.

First: cancel dance practice.

That's handled with a simple, swift text message to the group chat. The squad doesn't complain—of course, they don't. They think she needs time and flood her with well wishes to feel better. For once, she doesn't fight the idea of presumed weakness, even though she knows for a fact that Erin would've made it work. She lets the sense of failure wash over her as motivation.

Next, she needs to make another call, though Kyla hates

talking to people on the phone. She hates that everything happens in the moment. A phone call leaves more room for mistakes. Kyla resents that room. She's a voice-memo girl, like the countless ones saved on her text thread between her and Mikky. Kyla looks at their messages, stalling. They haven't texted much since he came back to Prophets Lake, which makes sense. He lives in the room across the landing. But at the same time . . . Kyla hasn't really *talked* to him all that much either.

Things would be easier if he were still far away. She might be likelier to tell him more. Now he's too close. Closer than a phone call. Kyla could make mistakes if she talked to him.

She shudders the thought away and presses CALL ANTHONY GLASS.

The phone rings only once before he picks up. Jesus.

"Kyla Graves, to what do I owe the pleasure?" Anthony asks in his slimy, loose voice. It always sends a gross feeling down her spine, the way Ant talks, walks. The way Ant looks at girls that are too young for him. "I don't ever get treated to your sweet, sweet voice. I usually have to deal with Peter's ugly mug."

"Peter is indisposed, and . . . we're doing budget cuts. I'm cutting out the middleman. I need wine," Kyla says, shaking it off.

"Heard. Usual amount?" Anthony asks.

It's not a Friday, and Kyla and Erin usually gave a few days' notice before a Test Kitchen, but if Indigo was so eager for another Test Kitchen, she's *sure* that everyone else will drop everything to come.

"Yes." Kyla folds her arms over her chest. "Bring it when you drop off your sister."

"Have my money," Anthony says.

"See you in forty."

Kyla has to go home first.

Kyla keeps the spare keys to Florence Cook's lakeside home tucked behind a Johnny Cash album. It's in a vinyl crate that she barely goes into: J–L. Her favorites that would go in that crate are always tucked beneath her record player in a neat line: Janet Jackson, Kendrick Lamar, and Kaytranada. She pulls the keys out and secures them to a belt loop with a carabiner. Kyla doesn't want to lose these; she's not sure where Erin hid her own set and she doesn't know if she has the strength to go into that house and look for them.

Between Mrs. Vaughn being her right-hand woman and Erin becoming a brand ambassador, Florence had trusted Erin more and more, sending her to pick up the mail, to check in to make sure the housekeepers did a good job (aka, didn't steal anything). Florence had to stay in New York a lot, and when she came back to Prophets Lake, she allegedly had a suite at Cook headquarters, preferring the place that she had built to her family home, for one reason or another. At least, that's what Erin said when she gave Kyla the duplicate set of keys.

Once, too wine-drunk to drive home after a Test Kitchen, before Rowan and Peter entered the picture, they'd played a game, one-upping each other with ridiculous theory after ridiculous theory. A rough relationship with her father. Bodies in the foundations. A generational family feud. Pod people. Aliens. Traveling circus clowns.

There's no one to play such games with Kyla now. Kyla goes to another crate. Behind *Yellow Submarine* but before *Abbey*

Road is her ledger. Erin always let her handle accounting. Except for that one night. That's when Kyla should've known something was up.

Then from under her bed she retrieves the very last of their supplies for the Test Kitchens. There's the usual heavy hitters—the expensive eyeshadow palettes and lipsticks and bronzers everyone reaches for—but more importantly, Kyla knows, there's the last of Cook Cosmetics' not-yet-released combo skin-care and makeup line, GloMo. The flatbed crate is heavy, filled with a wide range of shades for each product. Each one promising to make the health of your skin better even as you paint it so much that it can't be seen. She begins to fill the numerous tote bags she has littering her room, making quick work of it.

Kyla knows she should be glad that Tilly didn't ask after any leftover supplies from Erin's last request for product. They probably think all of it is collecting dust at the back of her closet, and that assumption is well suited to Kyla's purposes.

Erin had been the one to pick out the girls—and rare boys—who made up the inner circle that is their Test Kitchen. Each teenager, a varying amount of desperate and flush with cash, would pay for entry. Then pay for bona fide, unreleased Cook Cosmetics product, right underneath Cook's nose, in Florence's grand home, in exchange for the *tiniest* rule that there was to be no posting. And Kyla was *strict* about the rule. It was why they rarely invited newbies, and never without good reason. Peter had been good for supplying the alcohol. He had a regular thing going with Indigo's brother, and he didn't ask for much—proud to hook up with Erin and satisfied with two hundred dollars, a measly portion of the earnings. Erin said it would be easy. Erin said it wouldn't be a *problem*. As long as they kept it quiet, kept it secret. So Kyla doesn't know how it went so, so wrong.

School is just finishing up by the time Kyla parks in the driveway of the massive lake house. She can practically hear the bell, shrill and abrupt, and her English teacher reminding them to pick up where they left off the night before because *nothing* is worse than being behind in your reading.

Kyla can think of a lot worse things—her family funeral home foreclosing, her father losing his job, all the other funeral workers losing their jobs.

But, no, it won't happen. Not if Kyla has anything to say about it.

She swings out of the car and opens the rear door. She hooks two bags in the crux of each elbow and then waddles to the door, standing on her toes so that she doesn't have to unhook the carabiner from her jeans to unlock it. And suddenly Kyla stands in the foyer, in a place she hasn't been since the night Erin died—a place that seemingly no one has been in since she died—and it's almost like she can still smell Erin's perfume. She sinks into it and walks to the wide windows to look out at the lake.

There's a sliver of rocky beach and then the flat darkness of the lake. She could launch herself off the deck, hit the rocky cliffs, crash into the water, and no one would find her until the morning. Maybe even longer. She could sink into the silt and dig into the dark sand and choke on it.

Or maybe Kyla would turn into a mermaid. She would grow gills and stay in the dark murky waters, and she wouldn't have to come up to rediscover the tragedy. She could forget for good.

An alien, a mermaid, Frankenstein's creature, there is no difference. Kyla craves it all, because those things are not human. They wouldn't *feel* this yawning thing in her chest she tries so hard not to think about.

And then she does think about it. She forces herself to think about it. Because Kyla can't forget Erin. She doesn't care if it's an act of self-harm, if it means that someone doesn't forget.

Kyla can't forget her. She keeps thinking of Erin as she forces herself to set up, taking in the wide living room with its tall ceilings and expensive furniture.

Florence Cook's home awed Kyla the very first time she entered it freshman year. There was a holiday party that the Vaughns had been invited to and Erin had *begged* her mother to let Kyla come along.

"I'll be so bored, Mom. I don't even care about Cook," she'd said, lying through her teeth. She clung to Kyla's side, refusing to let her go, as if Kyla leaving Mrs. Vaughn's sight line would mean an automatic no.

Mrs. Vaughn had pretended to give it a think, hemming and hawing, her mouth twitching with what Kyla now sees as her refusal to smile. When she finally said yes, Mrs. Vaughn gathered Kyla into her arms, petting her hair and promising that she'd let her borrow the sparkly designer heels that Kyla secretly coveted, the ones that Erin had borrowed for the winter formal last year.

When Kyla entered the Christmas party, in the shadow of the Vaughns, she expected a modern monstrosity on the inside, despite the gorgeous white wood cladding and green roof tiles outside, each one shaped like the little shells at the bottom of the lake. Instead, everything was beautiful and classic, white walls with crown molding and actual oil paintings in heavy gold frames. There were updated touches, of course, that spoke to wealth, but Kyla understood this to be older than old money. This money had literally *created* Prophets Lake. This money now kept it alive. And this money could kill Prophets Lake the second it stopped showing up.

Kyla had kept to the walls at first, gossiping with Erin, who pointed out everyone who was anyone. The man to the right was on the board of Cook Cosmetics. The woman next to Mrs. Vaughn was the head of a rival brand. The woman next to her was her mistress and her VP of finance, and the man across the way by the bar, slightly teetering to the side, was her husband.

When Kyla had asked, "How do you know all of this?" Erin grinned and said, "My mom and Florence talk about literally everything, not just work. She's like . . . Florence's favorite person. Come on, you should meet her."

Erin was always good at peeling Kyla off the wall, forcing her into the middle of everything. "You're so beautiful, Duck, and so talented. You gotta get out of your own way, and then you're going to *shine*," she liked to tell Kyla, because she knew Kyla could thrive if she just tried. It was how she'd convinced Kyla to try out with her for the varsity dance team as freshmen. She'd been right that time too. Erin was so often right, it was easy for Kyla to be caught in her wave of schemes.

Erin marched right through the crowd, as if she belonged, and being tall, blond, and beautiful, with her perfectly done face, she did. Kyla could never so easily fit into that mold, and that was one thing Erin never quite got.

"Excuse me," Erin interrupted, releasing Kyla so that she

could part two adults in Florence Cook's circle like they were nothing but Barbie dolls. Kyla expected some offense, but if anything, they were all fascinated by Erin's confidence.

Mrs. Vaughn, though, was annoyed. "Erin, the adults are speaking," she said through clenched teeth. "If you'll excuse her—"

"That's what I said, Mom," Erin said, rolling her eyes. "Excuse me."

Mrs. Vaughn was always good at holding a tight rein to her rage. She was the one who taught Kyla to hold her contempt back with a painted smile. *Don't show them how bothered you are,* she'd say. Kyla had only been able to tell because she knew her better than her own mother, and it was only when Mrs. Vaughn saw the amusement of everyone around her that she relented, for the time being.

"Duckie," Erin said, holding her hand out. When Kyla took it, Erin pulled her forward toward the most elegant woman alive. "Florence, this is my very best friend, Kyla Graves."

"Duckie?" Florence Cook asked instead of introducing herself.

"Erin has called me that since we were kids," Kyla explained, breathless. It was like Florence Cook's presence sucked all the air out of the room. There was so much pressure, and she wondered if this was what power *felt* like.

"I only see a swan. Odile, in the flesh," Florence had said with a fine smile. She had reached forward, the ends of her French manicure nearly touching Kyla's jaw, but not quite. Even still, Kyla lifted her head, as if the woman had guided it up so that she could look at her better. "You are *lovely*."

No one had ever called Kyla "lovely" before. It sounded

different coming from a self-possessed woman like Florence Cook. Nurturing, like she wanted Kyla to believe it.

"Thank you," Kyla gasped.

Erin beamed, bright as a comet, and giddily she said, "The prettiest girl in the world, right?"

"That's you, Erin," Kyla jeered lightly, rolling her eyes.

Erin shook her head and Florence Cook looked between the two of them, something settling in her expression. She hummed.

"You two are the kind of girls I want to change the world for."

She had not explained herself, but she didn't need to. Kyla, even then, had known all that Cook Cosmetics was supposed to stand for, and those words connecting her to it had carried her through the night, and every night since.

Florence Cook had kept them at her side all night, introducing them to everyone at the party, like they were *her* girls. At first Kyla clung to Erin's hand, slightly unsure. And slowly, with each new face, she'd let her grip get looser, until she was standing tucked between Erin and Florence on her own two feet with her back straight. Soon, she was introducing herself. Florence noticed, the corner of her mouth twisting up with what seemed like pride. Erin's had too, and she was *beaming*, bright eyed. Kyla, champagne loose and hungry, had never wanted the party to end.

She has remembered that night like a tattoo over the years. Felt it beating over and over again in her heart. A night she can't forget.

And one that she regrets more than *anything* in her life.

Because what she hadn't known then was it was the start of the end of her world.

CHAPTER TWENTY-THREE

The detention monitor is an overworked teacher's assistant far more interested in her cell phone than in watching the six students who have found themselves in detention. So it's easy for Mikky and Nasim to abscond to a back corner of the classroom and huddle around Indigo's stolen phone.

"She keeps this thing in *pristine* condition. Not even a scuff and this is an older model," Mikky says with a hint of admiration. He's gotten into trouble with his mother more than once for not being as careful as he should be with his. His mom had especially not appreciated the random call from a stranger's phone because his got busted in the mosh pit of his first metal concert.

"I'm not surprised. Indigo Glass is supremely organized. She's probably freaking out by now," Nasim says. Nervously, he looks up at the detention monitor, but she's got her feet propped up on the desk and she's still scrolling. He looks back down at Indigo's phone with a frown, cradling his cheek in his palm. "Now . . . the password. I know that we should've considered it, but I . . ."

"Didn't," Mikky says. Before Nasim can get defensive, Mikky rushes on to say, "I mean one hurdle at a time. I didn't think about it either. I was more preoccupied with managing to get it out of her locker."

It doesn't seem to soothe Nasim, who still looks down at the phone with frustration, grumbling under his breath. Mikky is almost surprised how well he knows Nasim now, after just a few weeks. He knows Nasim will spiral in his frustration and refuse to move forward, because *he's* the one who's failed.

"You have class with her, right? Anything that stands out in terms of what passcode she would use?" Mikky asks, redirecting him.

"It'll be almost impossible to guess. I change mine twice a year. Different birthdays. I'm on my youngest cousin's on my dad's side now," Nasim says.

Mikky laughs. "How do you remember it?"

"I don't know. I just do," Nasim says stiffly. When Mikky can't smother his giggles, Nasim protests, "Don't laugh at me."

"I can't help it. I've never heard that before. People tend to use the same password across stuff. You're not supposed to but, like, it's a lot of passcodes to remember," Mikky says. When he looks at Nasim, he knows that the other boy is on the same train of thought as he is. "Okay, so she definitely uses the same password across her stuff. Numbers, numbers."

"Her birthday's April third," Nasim says.

Mikky raises an eyebrow. "You're close enough with Indigo to know her birthday?"

"She made a really big show of it in elementary school. I'd call it weird, but, like, everyone makes a big deal out of their birthday in elementary school."

Mikky nods and puts in "040308." Access denied.

"Okay, so not her birthday," Mikky mumbles. "What's another set of numbers that would be important to her? Does she have any siblings?"

"Yeah, an older brother, but I don't know when that guy was born," Nasim says dismissively. He drums his fingers against the edge of the table.

"What about . . . this?" Mikky asks as he types in "258709." It doesn't work either.

Nasim raises an eyebrow. "What was that supposed to be?"

"It's an arrow pointing down. Then you swipe up." Mikky sighs at the look Nasim gives him. "Look, I'm a visual person."

"Okay, obvious one," Nasim tosses out, "her locker combination."

"Doesn't that come with the lock?" Mikky asks.

Nasim shakes his head. "*A* combination comes with the lock, but you can reset it. How much you want to bet that she did?"

Mikky swipes up again on Indigo's phone, looking down at the six empty spaces. Then he carefully taps in "291334."

"Yes," Nasim hisses as the phone opens up to a screenshot of Indigo's class schedule as the background. There are no free-floating apps here. Like her locker, everything is neatly organized into folders, to the point of compulsion. But it makes it easier to find Instagram without scrolling through endless pages of apps.

"Go to her profile," Nasim says, but Mikky is already two steps ahead of him, pulling up Indigo's following list. He searches @eleanor.rigby_1 and presses it before he's ready.

"This is definitely Erin's account," Nasim says.

Mikky isn't sure what he expected, but it's not this. Her grid is made up of eerie selfies taken from odd angles, catching the shimmer of her highlight or the dark kohl around her eyes, but never her full face. Under each caption is a song lyric. Interspersed throughout are random isolated shots of body parts. Her hands.

An ear. Her tongue. Her knee. All decorated with color swatches of what seems to be makeup.

"What the fuck *is* this?" Nasim whispers, shaking his head.

"There," Mikky says, pointing at the very latest post. It's a black square with white typewriter font spelled out, HELLO, CHEFS. TEST KITCHEN TONIGHT. THIS POST WILL SELF-DESTRUCT. Apparently it never had.

"Still doesn't tell us what the Test Kitchen *is*," Nasim mumbles. "I mean, they could be cooking meth."

"This isn't *Breaking Bad*," Mikky retorts.

Nasim frowns. "What's *Breaking Bad*?"

Mikky stills. "Do you not watch television?"

"I prefer *Better Call Saul*." Nasim smirks at Mikky's gullibility.

"Check her following," Mikky insists, forcing them back on task.

"It's one account," Nasim narrates. "@katy2too. Who do you think that is?"

A memory hits Mikky, hazy around the corners. He and Kyla are young, still in booster seats. They're in the back of their mother's car and she's slouched in the seat in silence. He asks if she's okay and she turns around and smiles.

"I'm fine," she says, and he believes her because he doesn't know better yet. "Wanna listen to music?"

Then she turns on the radio and Johnny Cash's crooning voice fills the car.

"I still think about Katy too."

Now all these years later, dread sits low in his stomach. He doesn't answer Nasim's question, instead watches as he presses on the account without delay. Sure enough, Indigo follows

@katy2too. Unlike Erin's page, there's nothing identifiable at first glance. It's mostly glamor shots of new Cook Cosmetics products and captions describing them. It's almost a review page, except there's a price listed at the bottom with the words, BIDDING STARTS AT. Mikky thinks of the ledger. Nasim presses on a photo that Indigo has already liked, the latest, the first post in months. It's an entire range of skin care, all in that signature sea-green packaging. "GLOMO," it's captioned as. The price is horrendously high—$130, and that's the starting bid price. He swipes to the next photo on the grid, and it's a line of lip glosses, the swatches on the back of a brown hand.

Mikky tells himself it can be any girl.

"Is that your sister?" Nasim asks, forcing the point.

Mikky is about to say no. He's going to say that not every Black girl with Kyla's skin tone is Kyla.

But then he sees the nails. Perfectly shaped into ovals, the way she likes. And the nail polish—it's the dark-cherry nail polish that she always wears. The same shade as Mikky's. The nail polish she still had on her fingernails at Erin's funeral.

"Yeah, it's her," Mikky murmurs. There's nothing inherently wrong about her posting products, so he doesn't know why it feels dangerous to admit it, but he can't help but think of her caginess. Her aggressive response when the Test Kitchen was brought up. Kyla has secrets, and with each one he confronts, he can see the picture of Kyla that exists in his head crumbling away more. He wants to reach for it, to pull the pieces back together, but he can't seem to manage it this time, because Kyla has lied and manipulated an entire school to mask this. Whatever the Test Kitchens are for, they're *dangerous*.

"Oh my God, she posted a story," Nasim says, and he presses on it. It's from only forty-five minutes or so ago, a little after Nasim and Mikky started detention.

It's a shot of the lake from one of the best vantage points that Mikky has ever seen it from, through a glass wall. Overlaid in black bold letters it reads: CHEFS, REPORT TO THE TEST KITCHEN AT 7:30 P.M. SHARP. ENTRY IS DOUBLE FOR ACCESS TO THE MOST EXCLUSIVE GOODIES. Nasim taps but there's nothing else.

"Mikky," Nasim murmurs, voice strangely gentle. "It's . . . look, we knew she was involved."

Mikky grasps at straws. "I mean, we still don't even really know what she's involved in."

Nasim scratches at the back of his neck. "Um . . . I can give you a hypothesis if you need it."

"Maybe I do."

Nasim leans in and presses his hand to Mikky's wrist, rubbing away the tension that sits there. He's being delicate with Mikky's feelings, like he wants him to know he hasn't forgotten about the mistakes he made before. "I think that they're selling Cook products. Shit that isn't in the stores yet, because why would they be selling stuff that anyone could get? I think they host the sales by the lake. And I think that Erin *died* after one. That's why she was found there and that's why Kyla was so defensive after Rowan brought it up."

"*Why* would she accuse Rowan of reporting Peter then?" Mikky insists.

"Peter . . . maybe, he's involved too? That would explain why she wouldn't want him considered a suspect," Nasim says, voice still soft.

Mikky screws his eyes shut, shaking his head. "And . . . and starting it up again? After what happened to Erin?"

When Nasim doesn't speak right away, Mikky looks back at him, waiting for an answer. Nasim always has an answer, but this time . . .

"You know her better than me," Nasim says.

Except that can't be true. Mikky doesn't know Kyla at all, because he's never known a Kyla capable of a web of lies like this.

Until now.

"The Vaughns don't have lakeshore property," Mikky says. He looks down at the finsta account, looking at the soft matte sea-green packaging that appears in every listing. And then he remembers the thing he hasn't pieced together yet. The way Kyla looked at Florence like she *knew* her and the way Florence looked back. "Does Florence Cook own property on the lakeshore?"

"Of course she does," Nasim says grimly.

"Do you know which house?"

Nasim nods solemnly. "Yeah. My mom went to a Christmas party there last year. I dropped her off and picked her up with my dad. You think that's where your sister is hosting this?"

Somehow, Mikky feels like he knows less the more he finds out. All the puzzle pieces are spread out in front of him, but he's not sure how they go together, and he doesn't have the box in front of him as a guide. Yet something tells him that that picture has to be coming from Florence Cook's home. That Florence Cook has something to do with all of this. Somehow.

"Yeah, I do. After detention, I think it's time for a stakeout," Mikky decides. "What do you say, Watson?"

"I say that *I'm* the Holmes of the operation."

"Oh, fuck off, Watson."

CHAPTER TWENTY-FOUR

When detention wraps up, Mikky and Nasim are the first out of the classroom. After school hours, Mikky feels less pressure as he goes down the hallway with the stolen cell phone. The corridor where Indigo's locker is, is deserted, and Mikky unlocks it quickly, ready to place the phone back.

"Ugh, it's so messy," Nasim says, surprised when he looks into Indigo's locker.

"It wasn't before." It's a far cry from the order that it had been in when Mikky first swiped the phone. There are papers at the bottom of the locker, books spilled haphazardly like she tore them out and then threw them back in, only to rush away before she could properly set everything right. "I think someone was looking for her phone. Which means she'll notice if we put it in. Maybe we should drop it in the lost and found on our way out." It's right inside the front office. They won't even have to tell the secretary.

"Good thinking," Nasim agrees as Mikky shuts the locker, careful not to disturb the mess. They start toward the office before Nasim screeches to a stop. "Wait. Screenshot the photos and send them to yourself."

Mikky shakes his head. "No way. What if she has her text messages go to the cloud? I could delete it here and it wouldn't delete on her laptop or anything else she has connected to her messages," he says. Then he pauses. "But you're right. We need to preserve the evidence. We'll take pictures of her screen."

When he's satisfied that he's got as clear a shot of Kyla's fingers as he's going to get, they start walking again. Then it's as easy as half slipping inside the office and dropping the phone into the wooden box before continuing out to Mikky's car.

Nasim is staring down at his phone for half the drive over to the lake before Mikky asks what's got his attention.

"Rowan and Gregory were asking earlier about how we got detention. They wanted to wait for us but I told them no," Nasim says.

"Good," Mikky says. "We don't want them involved."

"Yet," Nasim adds.

Mikky frowns as he pulls into the parking lot by the lake and starts searching for a good space for their stakeout. "How are you so sure that Rowan isn't involved in all of this? They knew about it."

Nasim purses his lips. "I never said they *weren't* involved."

"You're one of their best friends and they've hidden shit from you again and again. They're just as likely to be a villain in this as you want to believe Kyla is," Mikky points out.

"Kyla is the one with a secret Instagram," Nasim retorts obstinately.

"Rowan is the one who was secretly *fucking* the girl who is *dead*," Mikky spits. "Kyla was her best friend. Which is more likely to be a murderer?"

There's a beat of silence while Nasim seems to wrestle with it all laid out in the open.

"Rowan and I have been friends for a long time," he starts

slowly. "And they haven't had it easy, so I guess I do feel protective of them. When they came out, most people were cool about it, but the people who weren't . . . really weren't. Some people said that they were doing it for attention. That they were trying to get people to trust them so they could do . . . whatever."

Mikky knows how that goes. He knows that some small town people, some Prophets Lake people specifically, come with small-minded thinking. "Your overprotectiveness is fair," he acknowledges. "But was *Kyla* one of the people that wasn't cool with Rowan?"

Nasim doesn't meet his eyes and for a second Mikky's heart stops.

But then Nasim admits, "No. She . . . stuck up for them. Not nicely, mind you. Mostly she told people to shut the fuck up and mind their business. She, uh, once told that British girl—Sabrina, I think—that misgendering Rowan was lazy and transphobic and that she needed to get a bit more creative about her insults. And then Kyla told Rowan that they had their whole life to dress like a try-hard, artsy asshole and that they should take a day off for once. It made Erin laugh. That's why I was so surprised when they said . . ."

Nasim cringes, letting his forehead fall against the glass, and Mikky is kind enough not to push. Instead, he turns on the radio and they wait until the silence between them slowly eases back into something a little more comfortable.

The public lot gives them a good vantage point of what Nasim points out is Florence Cook's lake house, meaning they'll be able to see who at least some of the Test Kitchen attendees are. It's easy to tell the difference. Most people come up the wooden stairs from the lakeshore, but others cut through the strange brush that's supposed to deter people from private property.

They sit in the car for hours, watching as the lakeshore visitors empty out the closer it gets to sunset.

The first person doesn't return to the parking lot through the brush until the sun has long set, and Mikky is already yawning into the crease of his arm. Nasim is slumped in his seat, rubbing exhaustion from his eyes, but perks up when he sees her.

"Look who it is," he murmurs.

Mikky recognizes a frazzled, anxious-looking Indigo Glass heading toward a beat-up Beamer from the nineties that spits and puffs its way into the parking lot. Indigo looks behind her like she's being hunted, and she's so distracted, her gaze thankfully glazes over Mikky's car as she gets into the Beamer.

"How do you think she knew there was a Test Kitchen?" Mikky murmurs.

Nasim purses his lips. "That's her brother, Ant, in the driver's seat. Well-known ne'er-do-well. Buys the alcohol for the sports teams' parties. Odds are he's supplying some, maybe even *choice* drugs too for these little parties."

Mikky shakes his head. "If he is, Kyla's not taking them. But wine? I could see that. I mean, they're in a lake mansion. They'll want to class it up a bit," he says. He can't help the older brotherly disapproval he feels at the implication of her facilitating if not partaking in possible drinking and driving.

"Maybe she called Ant for supply and told him to bring it with his sister," Nasim says. He's practically leaning over the dashboard, eyes trained on the path—too obvious.

Mikky grabs him by the jacket and gently tugs him back. "Relax. You don't want them to see you," he insists, his fingers playing with the soft hairs at the nape of Nasim's neck. It's more of a nervous thing for him than to calm Nasim, and Nasim seems to realize that. He doesn't shove Mikky's hand away.

Next, two people walk out together—a boy and a girl that Mikky doesn't recognize—and slide into a Lexus. Then Alicia and Sabrina, of course, giggling to each other, arm in arm. There are no other dance team members, at least as far as Mikky can tell, but the next girl does seem to get a reaction out of Nasim.

"Is that *Lydia*?" he blurts out.

Maybe. Lydia is tall with a head of frizzy blond hair tamed back haphazardly into a ponytail that it's fighting to escape. She adjusts her slipping overalls strap as she trudges toward her very shiny, big pickup truck.

"Who is Lydia, again?" Mikky asks, feeling like he's missed a chapter.

"Uh, the basketball team manager and Rowan's ex," Nasim says. "I can't *believe* she would be here. She *hated* Erin."

"Do you think she knew?" Mikky asks. "About Erin and Rowan?"

Nasim frowns. "I want to believe that Rowan told her when they broke up, but I don't think they did."

"Why did they break up again?" Mikky asks.

"I thought they were happy. Like, really happy. Rowan liked her so much that they were going to basketball games. Our basketball team *sucks*, man, and Rowan would go and actually talk to the guys, because Lydia's really good friends with all of them. They kinda look at her like she's a little sister," Nasim says. "And then . . . all of a sudden, Rowan was complaining about her being clingy? That she kept asking them about, like . . . the future. College. And Rowan was really busy with . . . a school project so they asked for some space, and she didn't handle it well. They broke up."

Well. At least that's what Rowan *told* Nasim. Mikky isn't so sure if that's all true now that he knows what, or rather whom, Rowan was really doing. From Nasim's expression, Mikky can tell he's having his own doubts too.

But still, if Lydia hated Erin, why would she be here?

Mikky remembers elementary school again, the fake invitation.

"I bet Erin invited Lydia because she found it funny," Mikky says, "and Rowan couldn't tell her not to go without coming clean about cheating on her." He gets great pleasure in seeing Nasim have to compute that Rowan is even less the harmless little bean that they portray themselves to be. Rowan is as capable of being terrible to their girlfriend as the next person.

"God, Rowan, look at what you got yourself into," Nasim mutters.

Another group passes by, bags clutched to their chests. More people across other cliques. The girl who stars in all the plays. A boy on the debate team whose mother is the head of cardio at the neighboring hospital. Nasim rattles off their names, far more familiar to him than Mikky, and Mikky is glad to have him on his side. On it goes, until twenty people have gone. Mikky sits there with Nasim's words echoing in his ears still.

"Rowan, look at what you got yourself into."

"Do you think she's by herself now?" Nasim asks.

Kyla, look at what you got yourself into.

"If you call her, do you think she'd pick up? Would she admit where she is? Should we try to catch her in a lie or . . ." Nasim trails off. Or maybe he's still talking. Mikky isn't sure because everything that has preoccupied Mikky's thoughts since this mess started is racing through his head. He sees Erin looming, larger than life, snakelike, and then she's cut down, and Kyla takes her place, springing up like another head of Hydra.

Hydra ended up slain at the end of that story. He won't let that shit happen to *his* sister like it happened to Erin, and Mikky's not letting anyone get in his way anymore, not even Kyla herself.

He's out of the car before he can even finish the thought. He might hear Nasim running after him, but if he does, he doesn't care. Mikky doesn't even bother to lock his car—let someone steal his fucked-up, beat-up sedan. That'll be Kyla's fault too.

"Do you even know where you're going? Mikky! Are you listening to me?" Nasim cries out, but Mikky moves with a single-minded focus.

It doesn't take rocket science to know to follow the road that has a sign staked by the side of it that says PRIVATE PROPERTY/NO TRESPASSING. He hustles through the brush and down the long, winding dirt road until it turns into brick and mortar and he spies the big white lake house that he's only ever seen from the back. Most of the windows are dark except for one downstairs and a single porch lamp.

Even in his anger Mikky has some decorum. He rings the doorbell. He waits.

When Kyla opens the door, she doesn't even give him the satisfaction of looking surprised. She doesn't say anything at all.

So Mikky does. "Kyla, what the *fuck* have you gotten yourself into?"

CHAPTER TWENTY-FIVE

They know not to come back, even if they've forgotten something. And Kyla made sure that they all picked up after themselves. Each wineglass is washed, dried, and back in its place in the state-of-the-art kitchen. There are no crumbs and even if there were, a cleaner comes to the house an excessive twice a week to clear out all the dust. Still, when someone rings the bell, Kyla is prepared to bitch them out.

She's not prepared for her brother.

She is careful to keep her expression under her control like Mrs. Vaughn taught her as she looks up into the familiar planes of his face.

"Kyla, what the *fuck* have you gotten yourself into?" he demands. Like he's their dad. Like she's a child. Like she's not trying to do the best that she can.

"I'm not doing this on the porch. I was raised right," Kyla says. She means it as a dig, and she's glad when it lands right where she wants it to, between Mikky's ribs.

Through gritted teeth, Mikky forces out, "We have the same parents. We were raised the exact same, girl."

Kyla smiles, razor sharp. He *really* believes that. "Were we?"

Mikky shoves his way inside and Kyla is about to close the door when she sees who lurks in his shadow. As always lately,

Nasim Talebi is right at her brother's side. Kyla would like nothing more than to shut the door in his smug face, and Nasim knows it. It's why he pointedly swans in and shuts the door for her behind himself.

"Kyla!"

Mikky's saying her name again but it doesn't have that pity-not-pity tone. It's *angry*.

Finally. Fucking *finally*.

Her personal feeling of satisfaction wars with the tension that holds her ramrod straight. She is careful to keep her back positioned away from him, so Mikky and his self-righteous shadow don't see the bulge of money there.

He has yet to throw any accusations at her, which tells her that he knows very little. And she cut Peter out tonight, so it couldn't have been him who snitched. It's someone else, and Kyla will find out. "Can I help you?"

"I asked you a question, Kyla. What are you doing?" Mikky asks.

Kyla tilts her head. "What do you *think* I've been doing?"

Mikky opens his mouth and closes it again, like he can't believe that she's answered his question with a question.

"Test Kitchens," Mikky says.

"Sure," Kyla allows.

Try harder, Mikky.

"You're a bit of a criminal, huh, Kyla? Just *begging* for a lawsuit? Selling proprietary product without owner permissions, breaking and entering, what else can we add to the list?" Nasim asks. At least he stops short of calling her a murderer.

Kyla watches as her brother looks at Nasim with shock that

he remembers to veil too late. So clearly, he didn't expect Nasim to come in so hot. Kyla looks between them, wondering where she can wedge more conflict between them, break it up before they can get closer to the full picture.

Nasim steps out of her brother's shadow. "I know brand ambassadors get to try all the new stuff months in advance. Your bestie wouldn't think to give away the exclusive shit that makes her cool, though. That doesn't sound like her. But you . . . you're the brains behind it, right? Selling the goods she got for free without Cook knowing. Getting paid. Splitting it. Maybe splitting all that money didn't sound fun anymore. Didn't sound *fair*. So, Kyla . . . what did you do with the money the night she died?"

Kyla doesn't say anything. She can't. This isn't just her secret. It's Erin's, too.

"Is that . . . is that what this is about?" Mikky asks, his words dripping with disgust. "It's about *money*?" His nose screws up, *judging* her. Like he doesn't know everything's about money. It's *always* about money.

"Did you and Erin ever argue about who got the money?" Nasim asks.

And that's it. He says her name like it's the thing meant to push her over the edge, catch her out. Like she's supposed to be afraid.

"Mind your business, Talebi," she warns.

"You made this my business when you involved my friend," Nasim insists.

And there it is. Back to *Rowan*. Nasim and Mikky are so stupid, especially when they think they're the smartest people in the room. Kyla isn't thinking about Rowan, not anymore, not now that she's dented their credibility and made her power over their life if they don't stay quiet very clear to them.

"Don't make me laugh. Rowan shouldn't have reported Peter. They got themself into this shit so they could have the public nice-enough girlfriend their judgy friends would respect *and* the blond baddie getting them off too. They got to feel good by making the most popular girl in school feel like an embarrassing secret. And then they didn't even have the decency to dump their girlfriend in person. They dumped her over a goddamn text message while they were on *top* of my best friend. They're not a saint. Grow up."

"For the last time, Rowan didn't report—" Nasim snaps.

Mikky steps between them, towering over her. Other people might be intimidated, but she's never been. There's nothing about Mikky that's scary except the way he sometimes *looks* at her, like he's trying to see into her brain. Like maybe he can. It's how he's looking at her now, and it's these moments when she wishes she could *hate* her brother.

"Don't talk to him like that, Kyla," Mikky scolds. "Don't deflect."

"Oh, you can fuck off too, Mikky. You don't know *shit* about why I'm doing this," Kyla insists, shoving past him. She doesn't want him looking too long.

"Because you won't tell me!"

Kyla laughs, mean and hard. "Why would I? You weren't *here*."

Mikky's jaw goes slack and Kyla takes her chance to grab her tote bags from the foyer and shove past him and Nasim's outstretched hand.

She runs to her car, her keys bouncing against her hip, and

throws herself into the driver's seat, turning on the hearse just as Mikky barrels out of the house. Kyla doesn't waste any time before shifting into reverse and backing down the driveway. She's probably going too fast and the way she swings out onto the road is dangerous, but no one else is around.

She's not sure where she's going until she's on the same block as the house. Kyla's phone won't stop blowing up with phone calls from Mikky, each of which she ignores. He takes the time to leave a voicemail to most of them, and Kyla can already predict what will be in them. More yelling. More questions. More demanding answers. He believes the worst of her now. But if he ever looked somewhere that wasn't *her* or Nasim, if he actually paid any attention, maybe he'd understand why she has secrets to keep.

All it would take to know why she's doing this is a cursory look at the mail. Maybe then Mikky would see the old bank letters stuffed underneath the bowl that they all drop their keys in.

Kyla looks at her phone one more time. He's calling again. She thinks about picking up. Explaining everything to him. Asking for help. But Kyla never asks for help. Erin, her partner in crime, knew how to help without being asked. And she's gone now. Erin's *gone*. It's just Kyla. She doesn't want or *deserve* anyone else's help. She is on her own.

Except. Except maybe not.

She turns her phone off and sets it face down on the passenger seat before leveraging herself out of her car and approaching the door. She has a set of keys. A short month ago she would've used them to let herself in. Now she doesn't. She rings the bell.

A beat passes and Kyla looks at the driveway. The Wrangler is there. So one person is probably home at least.

When the door swings open, Kyla is prepared to see Jason. She knows what she might say to him. She is not prepared for Mrs. Vaughn or the aching want to fall into the woman's arms. Mrs. Vaughn, who once would fold her into her chest and brush her hair back, and swaddle Kyla in the scent of jasmine and sandalwood.

Except this is not the version of Mrs. Vaughn that opens the door. Mrs. Vaughn has always been the picture of elegance to Kyla. She is far from it now. She's draped in one of her favored cashmere lounge sets, but it's disheveled and hangs looser around her shoulders now, exposing bony clavicles. Her Pilates-toned muscles have shrunk so she is all skin and bone. Even her fingers are so skinny that her wedding ring sits loose. She clutches at a glass of white wine that's filled a little too high, a peach lipstick mark on the rim.

"Kyla, darling, I haven't seen you around in some time," Mrs. Vaughn says. Her words slur just the tiniest bit around "darling," but she's holding herself well enough that Kyla wouldn't suspect that she's wasted if not for the glass and what Jason said the other night.

"Hi, Mrs. Vaughn, I hope I'm not disturbing you," she says evenly.

She waits for Mrs. Vaughn to follow the script. *You're like my own daughter, you could never disturb us. You should've just used your key. Come in, Erin's upstairs. Erin's in the backyard. Erin's in the kitchen. Erin's in the ground—*

"Well, it is rather late," Mrs. Vaughn says instead.

Kyla's breath catches in her throat. "Oh," she whispers. She isn't sure what to do with that. Mrs. Vaughn has *never* said that to her.

"Shouldn't you be on your way home?" Mrs. Vaughn acts as if she didn't hear Kyla's moment of hesitation. She takes a sip of her wine and then shakes the long sleeve back on her free hand to scratch at her wrist.

"I was . . . wondering if I could sleep over," Kyla blurts out. "I don't want to go home."

"It's a school night. Your father will be looking for you. Everyone will be looking for you," Mrs. Vaughn says, and she no longer looks . . . there. She's somewhere else. Her once second mother takes a step back, like she's changing her mind and letting Kyla in, but the yawning maw of the house behind her looks darker than Kyla remembers, and her next words are just as dark. "As they should. Haven't you learned that it's not safe at night for pretty girls like you?"

Mrs. Vaughn says this in the same way she used to give instructions to Erin and Kyla on how to contour a jaw out of their child-round faces. Precise and pointed, like it was something that they needed to correct. As if the night not being safe is all Kyla's fault. Like that night and all its horrors were Kyla's fault too and she still hasn't corrected it.

"Exactly, so I really don't want to go back out alone, Mrs. Vaughn," Kyla pleads, shoving her unease aside. In her brain, she chants over and over again, *everyone grieves differently*. This version of Mrs. Vaughn is temporary. The idea of losing the woman who practically raised her is . . .

Mrs. Vaughn looks over her shoulder at the stairway. "Jason can drive you home then. Jason!"

A few seconds later Jason barrels down the stairs like there's a fire, eyes wild. "What is it, Mom? You all good? Everything's good. You're *good*," he insists, like saying it will make it true. When he gets a good look at Kyla, he doesn't ask what she's doing here. Instead, he asks, "What's wrong?"

"I don't want to go home," she confesses. Her voice cracks under the truth, and she hates feeling weak, especially in front of the woman who taught her to be strong, but her limbs are soft and her joints ache and she just wants to curl up under a blanket and never wake up.

"Then don't," Jason says. "Come in, it's cold."

Mrs. Vaughn drains the glass that was full when Kyla arrived. She seesaws from side to side down the hall, and Kyla sees the wine bottle on the receiving table. She pours the rest into her glass, right to the rim, and takes a deep slurp before she says, "No, you should drive her home. Like you *always* drove Erin home, even when it was late."

She squints at Jason, and Jason is better than Kyla. He doesn't flinch from his mother's judgment. *His fault too,* Mrs. Vaughn seems to say.

"Didn't you hear her?" Jason demands. "She doesn't want to go home."

Kyla looks down at her feet, but Jason's fingers wrap around her elbow, properly pulling her inside. He shuts the door behind them and locks it before he looks back over at Mrs. Vaughn.

"Besides, I can't take her," Jason says. "Someone needs to stay with *you*, so you don't try to take my car keys again when it's so . . . late."

He's too kind to say, *When you're too drunk.*

"I wouldn't have to drive your car if mine was out of the auto shop," Mrs. Vaughn says nastily. She mumbles something else unkind about "lazy workers" under her breath, jarring Kyla again.

"Well, you're in luck," Jason retorts. "Your car is ready, so we'll go get the Mercedes out of the shop tomorrow when you're feeling better."

"I feel just *fine*," Mrs. Vaughn spits, even as she sloshes wine over her hands, soaking the cuff of her sweater.

"Come upstairs, Kyla," Jason says, taking her hand properly and leading her up, refusing to look back at his mother even as she stares up at them with glossy eyes. When they get on the second floor, Jason speaks: "I'm sorry about her."

"Don't be . . . don't be sorry," Kyla whispers. "I remember what you said about how she's been."

"Yeah," Jason mumbles grimly as he leads her to the guest bedroom, behind the first door on the right. "You can stay here. I can get you some of my pajamas? Or if you want to take anything from—"

Kyla turns to Erin's door. It's shut, and she imagines it has been for a long time. Slowly, she pulls away from Jason and walks toward it, like there's a string hooked behind her navel, pulling her forward. The string is so strong that when she pushes the door open, she practically falls rather than steps in.

Kyla stands in the center of a room that is frozen still in a state of half chaos. No one else knew where to find a thing in this room, not even Kyla. But Erin knew exactly where her favorite sneakers lived, where her single church dress was hung up, where her summer perfumes were stored. Only she knew.

She can feel the weight of Jason's eyes on her as she drags her fingers over the dresser, stirring up the lightest layer of dust that has settled there. There's an unopened box of green hair dye on it.

Kyla didn't know that Erin was going to put a green streak in her hair. Maybe she didn't know a lot of things.

"Kyla," Jason says.

She turns and looks over at him. He leans against the doorframe, uncertain, watching her like he wants to stay with her and like he wants to get away from Erin. She wants to test which he wants more.

Kyla kneels on the edge of Erin's queen-sized bed. She'd gotten it when they were just turning ten, and Kyla had been *so* jealous until Erin said, "It'll be perfect for sleepovers!" She kicks off her shoes, letting them fall to the ground, before she crawls into the middle of the bed and looks at Jason.

"Sit with me, please?"

Kyla feels like an animal, showing off its underbelly, offering her wet innards. But it's different with Jason. He isn't a witness to her grief, like Mikky, like everyone else. He's sitting in it with her.

Jason frowns. "Kyla, come on," he says. "I'll sit with you in my room."

"Are you scared of ghosts, Jason?" Kyla asks softly.

"Don't do this," he warns. He says that but he steps into the room and gently turns the knob so that it doesn't click when he pulls the door shut behind him.

Kyla waits as Jason takes his time, but soon he sits gingerly on the edge of the bed, looking at her like she might eat him. He picks at a thread in the duvet as he says, "It's my first time in here since Erin died."

"Me too," Kyla says.

It makes Jason smile, even though she didn't mean it to, but she's glad.

"She wasn't always my favorite person but . . . we got each other," Jason says.

"She found you annoying. She used to say that everything came so *easy* for you. You barely had to try, and she was always trying. Trying with your mom, because she liked you better. Trying with her makeup and dance and being in charge of basically everything. Even the whole influencer thing was just her *trying*. But I know she loved you a lot," Kyla says, and she doesn't feel like she's placating him or using one of Dad's grief-isms. It's true.

Jason laughs. "I know she found me annoying. She would tell me all the time. In the bathroom too long? 'You're so annoying.' Didn't want to take her to the outlet mall, like, forty-five minutes away? 'You're so annoying.' Looked at her wrong too early in the morning? 'You are being so annoying right now,'" Jason says. He matches her cadence perfectly even if he can't quite find the pitch. He collapses on his back, his head next to Kyla's thigh, legs hanging off the edge of the bed. "I found her just as annoying but, God, I miss being annoyed by her so, so much."

Kyla doesn't say anything as she rolls onto her back too and closes her eyes. Like this, she almost feels like she's floating. There's nothing to tether her here. No Mikky, no Dad, no bills. No funeral. No worries. No Erin.

"Kyla, are you okay?" Jason sounds like he's trying to speak underwater.

Kyla is *exhausted* again. She doesn't understand how Erin played herself, day in and day out. Kyla's tired of being double-cast, playing the part. It's time to take a bow. But she's not a shadow anymore either. "Why is it that Erin had to *die* for me to realize I've never been my own person?"

It's an awful question. It's an awful thing to *say*. But Kyla can feel the truth of it. There's no one else to heave through her emotions with. She never once conceived of a future where she'd have to solve all of her problems by herself. It wasn't a future she ever *wanted*. She was content being part of a team of two. Now Kyla feels that burden solely on her shoulders, and sometimes she rages at the weight of it, but sometimes it feels right. Or almost. Kyla only turns to look at him when she feels his fingers brush over her knuckles. He doesn't look upset with her. That's good at least.

"You spent a long time as Erin-and-Kyla. Duck and Goose. And now you have to figure out how to be Kyla Graves. Singular," Jason says.

Kyla shivers at the thought of deciphering who she is in her own right instead of in relation to. Figuring out the things she likes without having someone else to talk them through with. Quietly, she admits, "When you don't know the definition of a word, you ask for it in a sentence. I never thought about who I was without the context of her."

And then there's a hand on her wrist, and the bed shifts underneath her, bringing her back down. Jason properly settles at her side, his shoulder touching hers.

"I know who you are," he says firmly.

Kyla snorts. "No. You don't. You didn't even know who Erin was. You don't know anything." And that's the problem and the solution—no one knows and no one can know.

"I knew Erin just as well as you did," Jason says.

"No, you didn't," Kyla says immediately.

Jason snorts. "Yes, I did. I knew about your Test Kitchens, Kyla," he says. Kyla looks over at him. "I knew about Rowan.

About Peter. About the nasty things she would say about and to people. I knew about all of that and I just . . . well, maybe it makes me a bad person, the fact that I never told her to stop. But I knew who my sister was and why and I loved her for or in spite of it. I knew all her horrible little secrets and the good ones, and she knew mine."

"I never told her to stop either. I didn't want to. Sometimes, she was too much, but a lot of the time . . . it was fun. Maybe that makes me a bad person too," Kyla says. "A worse person than you."

"Maybe we can be bad people together," Jason says, conspiratorially.

"I think I'm on my own with this one, golden boy," Kyla says, voice dripping with mockery. Bad person, he calls himself, like he doesn't help old ladies cross the street.

"I've done bad things," Jason whispers, brow dipping into a frown. "I'm not perfect."

"Prove it," Kyla presses.

Jason swallows so hard, she watches his Adam's apple bob. "I'm a bit of a coward, sometimes."

"How?"

Jason's jaw saws back and forth, like he's gearing up to say something big. He looks like he has a secret, one that threatens to burst through the seam of his lips. Kyla sits up on her elbows, shifting back and forth.

Then the tension softens and Jason blows a raspberry, his eyes rolling up to the ceiling, his cheeks already pinkening.

"I had a crush on this girl for . . . a long time. Knew her since we were kids. And Erin would say, 'She likes you too, I swear.

She just pretends not to because it would be uncool, and cliché, because of who you are.' And I didn't believe her. Or maybe I did, but I was too chickenshit. Erin was gassing me up all summer. First, I was gonna ask her to the Fourth of July bonfire. Chickened out. Then I was gonna ask her to the back-to-school party in August. Couldn't do that. Then Erin made up this whole plan. She was like, 'Okay, so you're gonna win the very first game of the season, and it's gonna be good. You'll get the winning goal. Totally cinematic. And then you're just gonna mack her. Right there on the field.' And then I didn't, because my sister got fucking murdered. So. Yeah."

Kyla looks up at the ceiling again, folds her hands over her fluttering stomach. Kyla had read it wrong. Erin's disgust hadn't been real. It'd been a cover-up. Coward, he calls himself. Kyla has never felt that way about Jason Vaughn. He lives a life with his heart on his sleeve. If anything, Kyla finds him braver than most. So she decides to be brave too.

"She was right."

Jason chuckles. "About?"

"Everything."

"Good to know," he says.

"I can't kiss you in my dead best friend's bedroom."

"Well, I can't kiss you in my dead sister's bedroom," Jason says.

"Maybe in the morning. Somewhere not here," Kyla decides.

She doesn't have to look at Jason to know that he's smiling. "Maybe in the morning," he agrees. "Over breakfast at Fable Street? We'll get to school for second period."

She can picture it. Her picking at a short stack of pancakes, him diving into a Grand Slam. Tasting too-sweet coffee on his bottom lip. Kyla wants it. "Over breakfast," she whispers.

Kyla is lonely, and the only time she's not is when she's with this boy here. She reaches more firmly for his hand, linking their fingers, palms pressed together. This isn't a team yet, but maybe one day, when the secrets are behind them, it can be.

When Kyla wakes up in the weak light of the morning, she knows where she is almost immediately. It's the body at her side that feels foreign. Jason is curled away from her. She stares at the mole-marked small of his back. She reaches out to touch, but then her brain switches on and she rolls over and off the bed.

Everything always looks clearer in the morning. At least, that's what Kyla tells herself as she stretches her arms over her head. In the morning light the room's chaos is more orderly, more familiar. Kyla walks around to the place she avoided looking at last night, adjusting her borrowed sweatpants around her waist so that she doesn't trip over the hem. The one thing Erin had been meticulous about was her vanity. Each makeup product is organized by type and then by color. Her travel makeup bag sits next to her mason jar of Cook brushes, each fluffy and clean. It's the bag she used to bring to school, for touch-ups during the day. Kyla carries a matching one.

She brushes her palms over the brushes and sighs softly. She opens the bag, looking into it. She doesn't intend to steal, but she wants to hold something of Erin's.

Then she sees it.

A piece of paper, folded neatly. Slowly, she pulls it out. A receipt? No.

It's an email thread between two Cook Cosmetics accounts,

EVaughn and FCook, and at the very top, in Erin's perfunctory scrawl, are the words, "For Katy Too to review."

Erin never called Kyla by her finsta name. It was too risky. But Kyla recognizes Erin's swoopy handwriting on the note for Katy Too all the same. A note for someone who didn't exist, from someone who no longer exists. The sourness of bile starts to rise up from her stomach. She wants to read it, but she can't. Not here.

She's glad that Jason sleeps so deeply. She's glad that Mrs. Vaughn presumably drank herself into a stupor, and is hopefully still passed out. It's early enough that she won't have scraped herself together. The only person Kyla might have to worry about coming across is Mr. Vaughn, but if anything, he will just blink sleepily at her as he sips his coffee.

Kyla slides the note into her back pocket, and then like her friend, she is gone.

CHAPTER TWENTY-SIX

"Should I call the police?" Dad asks again, his head drooping into his hands as Mikky paces the length of the kitchen. Dad has abandoned his phone after so many calls have gone ignored.

"No. No police," Mikky says immediately. Nothing good will come of calling the police, even if Chief Hamish *would* bother to do anything about a missing teenage Black girl. He knows that much.

"It was a school night and she didn't come home. Your sister is *missing*," Dad insists.

"We don't know that," Mikky mumbles. "It's been one night. Maybe she slept over at Alicia's." He rubs the sleep from his eyes, attempting to chase away hours of exhaustion but not quite managing it. Mikky attempted to get some sleep after staying up until two in the morning waiting for the hearse's headlights to appear in the living room window, but every twist and turn in bed resulted in another thought about what might have happened to Kyla after she reversed out of the Cook driveway and whipped her way down the highway.

For all Mikky knows, she could've left town completely. He imagines her sitting on the side of the road, curled up in the back of the hearse, along the flat, covered by her puffer jacket. Mikky hates the image of that, feels his stomach turn at the very idea of Kyla all alone. He can't stop thinking about her words. "Why would I? You weren't *here*." Right and wrong all at once.

Mikky shouldn't feel selfish. His therapist has told him that focusing on his own mental health *isn't selfish*. And yet, he can't help but feel like it was. Like maybe none of this would have happened if he had been here.

"She would let me know if she was sleeping over. Those are the rules," Dad says. If only he knew how many rules Kyla revels in breaking now. "There is someone *out* there, killing little girls. I want to know where she is. Where did you last see her?"

"Don't say that, Dad. Don't even *think* it. I saw her by the lakeside," Mikky repeats, like he has for hours and hours, since Dad burst into his room at six, asking where Kyla was. It's not specific. Mikky's not telling *all* Kyla's secrets, not when he still doesn't know the full picture from her mouth, but as time passes and she doesn't reappear, he starts to feel like maybe he should. He swallows around the knot in his throat and scratches nervously at his wrist, welts rising where he'd been itching the entire night.

"We got into an argument," Mikky admits, under his breath.

Dad stills. "About what?" he asks, voice creaking.

"Erin," Mikky says simply.

Dad spreads his fingers on the tabletop, looking at Mikky like he doesn't understand him. "What did you say about Erin?"

"Why is it what *I* said?" Mikky demands.

"Because Kyla doesn't talk about Erin," Dad says like that's explanation enough.

Mikky laughs, long and hard. "Don't you think that's part of the problem, Dad?"

"Is there a problem?" Dad asks, shifting nervously in his seat.

Mikky's father isn't a bad father. He is trying, always. But he is soft, made of an eternal optimism that Mikky and Kyla both lack. In some ways—many ways—they are their mother's children. He has never known how to see the hurt in them, either.

"You know there is. I'm here because we both saw that there was a problem at the funeral. She was more than sad or grieving. She barely spoke. She was . . . barely there. You don't know what she said to me," Mikky whispers. He still remembers her talking about how lonely Erin would be, how she wished that she could bury herself next to her.

And she stopped talking like that, but Mikky sees that she's *still* lonely. Even surrounded by all those people, there's a gap that she keeps there, and it feels less like the catharsis of grief and more like punishment. Emotional isolation as self-harm.

"Because you two don't talk to me! Neither of you will ever talk to me. Mikky, you should've been *watching* her—"

Mikky shouts, "Why am I meant to keep constant track of her?"

"That's why you moved here!"

Mikky's eyes burn with unshed tears. "I . . . I'm just a *kid*."

Immediately, Dad melts and he reaches forward, folding Mikky into his body, smoothing his hand over Mikky's bonnet. "I'm sorry, I shouldn't have said that. You're right, you're right." He presses a kiss to Mikky's forehead. He's practically holding Mikky together as he trembles, fighting back sobs. "I know, Mikky, and it's not fair. It's not fair. You're not the parent. I'm the parent. I just . . . I just don't know what to do," Dad confesses.

Mikky's mom would never say that she doesn't know what to

do. Mom is so self-assured, like she was born onto the Earth to be a mother, even if she doesn't think so.

He still remembers her weeping in a moment of what he once thought of as weakness, but now knows was postpartum depression that grew into something more clinical, the night she left—"I wasn't meant to be a mother, I don't know—"

"I don't know how to help her," Dad says. And suddenly Dad's hands feel less like comfort and more like they are gripping Mikky to hold himself up.

Mikky tugs himself free of his father's hold.

"Put her in *therapy*," Mikky spits. "You *know* Mom's mental health shit. You know mine. It's genetic. This kind of thing doesn't really *skip* people. Maybe I'm not the only one who needs to be medicated."

"Thanks, I'll pass."

Mikky slowly turns to see Kyla in the doorway, looking well rested, a Dunkin' coffee cup in her hands. Instead of her clothes from the day before, she's wearing a soccer jersey and oversized sweatpants. She slides into the kitchen and drops the Styrofoam cup in the trash can, then goes to leave the kitchen again like nothing happened, but Mikky grabs her bicep.

Kyla makes to yank herself away, but Mikky is too fast for her. He folds her into a tight hug that she's too surprised to return.

"Oh my God, Kyla, I was so worried," he breathes, his knees soft like gelatin as he droops over her, his chin digging into the crown of her hard head. "I'm sorry, Kyla. I shouldn't have . . . ambushed you."

"I'm fine. I went to the Vaughns for the night. I was safe," Kyla says, her voice muffled by Mikky's shirt. She doesn't hug him back, but ever so slowly, Mikky feels her weight redistribute so that she's leaning into him.

"Why didn't you *call*?" Dad demands. "Or at least answer your phone. We almost called the police."

Kyla's nose wrinkles and finally she untangles herself from Mikky's arms. "The police? That would've been excessive. Now, if you'll excuse me, I need to take a shower before school."

"No," Dad insists. "No one's going to school. Not until we figure this out."

Kyla frowns. "What is there to figure out?"

Mikky can't tell if she's being willfully obtuse, or if she actually believes that there's not something deeply wrong with the circumstances of her disappearing and returning. He searches her expression for her usual obstinance, but it's not there.

"Kyla . . . ," Dad sputters. "You *disappeared* for hours. I couldn't reach you. Your brother and I called you about a hundred times each, and you didn't pick up, not one of those times. *That's* what needs to be figured out."

"I was fine," Kyla says flatly. "I'm always fine."

"You are *not* fine," Mikky retorts.

Kyla looks at him, unimpressed. "I'm not?"

"You think you can handle this on your own, but you can't."

Kyla sharpens. "You have no idea what I can handle."

But before Mikky can speak, the doorbell rings. Dad drags his hands over his face and looks at Kyla. "Did you leave anything at the Vaughns?"

"No," Kyla says softly. "And it's too early for Jason to drop anything over. He's asleep."

Mikky . . . *doesn't* ask how Kyla knows that. He looks down the hallway, lingering in the doorway to the kitchen as Dad goes to open the door. Mikky can't see who's there.

Then Dad says, "Chief Hamish, how can I help you?"

Mikky's stomach drops and he shifts from side to side, looking over at Kyla. She drags her toe over the lined linoleum, still acting unconcerned even with the cop at their door. He leans in and hisses, "What did you do? Were you *really* trespassing? Are you stupid, Kyla?"

Kyla snorts. "No. *She* gave me a key," she whispers.

Mikky can't tell if the "she" in question is Florence or Erin.

"I'm sorry to wake you, Derek, but we need to speak with Kyla," Hamish says. The ruddy-faced man doesn't look gleeful, exactly, but there's a feverish brightness in his eyes. "There's been a recent development in Erin's case and we want to have a discussion."

"About what, exactly?" Dad asks.

"Well, we want to know a little bit about her Test Kitchens."

Mikky hasn't seen Kyla rattled once, not since the funeral. But now, when she looks up, her eyes are round like cue balls, the whites showing. She's finally remembered that she's not invincible. Chief Hamish strains his neck to look past Dad, and Mikky shifts just so, making himself bigger in the doorframe. Without looking back at her, he gently shoves her just out of sight.

"Don't make us make a scene," Hamish warns.

Mikky pushes off the doorframe, stalking over as he says, "She's not here."

There's another cruiser behind the chief's, and he recognizes the same two officers that picked up Peter only three weeks ago. Mikky clears his throat and looks over at Dad with a raised eyebrow. A sense of vicious satisfaction wells in Mikky's chest as his father straightens his shoulders to prepare a mighty *fuck you* to the cop.

And then Kyla ruins it, saying, "I'm here."

It's hard not to whip around to look at her, to pretend that he's surprised by her being here. Sure enough, Hamish sends Mikky a reproachful look.

"I thought you said she wasn't here," he says.

"Maybe I can turn invisible," Kyla says coolly. She hip checks Mikky out of the way and meets Hamish's gaze with unrelenting steel. "I'm not riding in the back."

"That's just fine. You're not a criminal, Kyla," Hamish says.

For some reason Mikky doesn't believe him when he says it.

"Kyla, you don't have to do this," Dad cautions her.

"And if I don't, they're going to end up arresting me. So let me clear this up," she insists. Kyla doesn't look back as she walks down the driveway, arms folded over her chest, and wrenches open the passenger door of Hamish's cruiser.

"I'm coming with you. You don't get to question her without me present," Dad insists as he moves past Mikky, grabbing his car keys, not even bothering to change out of his sweats or his slippers. "Mikky, we'll be right back."

Mikky stands uselessly on the steps of his house, watching the uncomfortable procession of two cruisers and his father's car. He looks directly across the street and sees their longtime neighbor staring around the curtains. When she sees Mikky notice her, she shuts them quickly, but he knows that by noon everyone in Prophets Lake will have heard that Kyla Graves was escorted to the police department.

He turns on his heel, already sick to his stomach from being made a spectacle, and he fumbles with his phone, pressing call on the first person that he realizes he wants to speak to. He holds the phone to his ear, nervously listening to the ringing.

Nasim doesn't pick up. Mikky leaves a voicemail, saying, "I won't be coming in today. Don't tell anyone shit. I'll see you later."

Then he makes another call.

"Kyla?" a voice grumbles into the phone.

Once more Mikky *refuses* to think about the concept of Kyla-and-Jason, because it complicates things. If he does, all he'll be able to think about is how much Jason may know and the way Jason *didn't* tell Mikky any of it either. Instead, he says, "It's Mikky. I think Kyla might have been arrested."

CHAPTER TWENTY-SEVEN

Kyla has passed the Prophets Lake Police Station before, but she's never been inside. She's not impressed by the weak fluorescent lighting or the white and green linoleum, so old that the white is yellowing with age. Old coffee smell wafts through the air, and every eye is on Kyla as she's walked through what makes for a very sad, understaffed bullpen. The receptionist at the front is the only one who tries to pretend that she doesn't see Kyla. She looks young, looks freshly graduated. Kyla almost thinks she recognizes her, and wonders if she's the one who passed along that description of Rowan to Anthony.

"Right this way. Can I get you any water, Kyla?" Hamish asks, stopping by the watercooler.

"No, she won't be drinking anything. You won't be collecting her DNA that easily," Dad says furiously, and Kyla sighs, rubbing at her cheek.

"Dad, you watch too much television," she says, but she doesn't ask for water or anything else, just shifts from side to side, her jacket sliding off one shoulder. Kyla readjusts, but Erin's unread emails are a heavy weight in her pocket. She shoves one hand into it, feeling along the crease that Erin made. She'd wanted to be in the safe space of her bedroom when she found out what they said, but she'd never made it there.

"Right this way, Kyla. Would you be more comfortable with a female officer in there with us?" Hamish asks. He doesn't wait for Kyla to answer. He just assumes and beckons over a late-twenty-something-year-old woman with long, frizzy blond hair pulled into a severe bun at the nape of her neck. She looks . . . *so* familiar too. "I'm not sure if you ever met properly, but I think you might remember her from that unfortunate interruption of your dance practice. This is Officer Castellanos. Officer Castellanos, this is Kyla."

"I like your lip gloss," Kyla says, tone even. "Cook Cosmetics, right? The lip oil in Venetian Mask?"

Officer Castellanos stammers, "Yes, thanks—"

Kyla takes a step around her and follows Hamish into what is supposed to serve as an interrogation room. In the TV procedurals that Kyla catches on television when she's bored, they're big steel rooms with small, barred windows.

Instead, this room is a mess of warm wood tones that all clash, not quite the same color. A wide solid oak table, two cedar chairs on either side. Officer Castellanos sits down first, holding a notepad in hand. She's prepared, like Hamish warned her that she would be summoned to soothe Kyla with her womanly presence. It's just too bad that Kyla is never soothed.

"You and your dad can sit right there," Hamish says. He turns to Dad. "Derek, I want to be clear that this is about Kyla. You may sit there, but please don't interrupt."

"Unless I'd like to call for an attorney," Dad shoots back.

Hamish grimaces. "Again, I don't think that'll be necessary. We're just here for a conversation."

"Right, of course," Dad drawls with the air of someone who doesn't believe a bit of it.

Hamish sighs, used to the dismissiveness.

"Kyla, I just want you to know that you're not in trouble," he says.

It's cold in the interrogation room. She thinks it's meant to make criminals uncomfortable, but it honestly only reminds Kyla of the morgue. It doesn't smell like formaldehyde and decay, but it's enough to help Kyla feel more in her element than Hamish or Castellanos probably wants her to. Kyla folds her hands atop the table and meets the chief's eyes.

"I know that I'm not in trouble. I didn't do anything wrong," she says carefully.

"Right," he agrees. But he exchanges knowing stares with Castellanos, which rubs Kyla the wrong way, because what could they possibly know? Unless . . . "It's well established that Erin was a brand ambassador for Cook Cosmetics. When that happened, were you jealous?"

It's such a silly, gendered question. Kyla would laugh if she didn't think it would make things worse.

"No, of course not. I was happy for her," she says. "Now, who told you about the Test Kitchens?"

"You're not actually meant to ask questions back," Castellanos says.

Kyla snorts. "Oh, I'm sorry. I was under the impression that this was a conversation. Not an interrogation."

Dad taps her knuckles gently. "Come on, Kyla. Please, just . . . answer their questions so we can leave."

Stubbornly, Kyla looks away and Castellanos tries again. "I know this is very hard, Kyla. Everything about this is hard, but there's just some information we *need* to know. Can you help us?"

Kyla is exhausted by this tone that everyone seems to take with her nowadays. Everyone says her name with that pity-laden sigh attached to the end of it, as if she is ignorant of her own pain. She knows her pain and it is exhausting and all consuming. But she is also pragmatic, and she'll let that pain necrotize until it becomes something useful, like motivation. The motivation to make this conversation go exactly how she needs it to.

"What do you want to know?" Kyla asks.

"What are they?" Hamish asks. "The Test Kitchens."

Well, whoever snitched clearly wasn't stupid enough to spill anything real. She inspects her fingernails, picking at the nonexistent dirt underneath them.

"We're modern-day Avon ladies," Kyla says without elaborating. Very carefully, she schools her face. They know about the Test Kitchens. So what? Clearly, they don't know the details. Or, at least, not enough that they've called Cook in just yet. She can spin this.

"And you invite all the cool girls in your class?" Castellanos asks. "Keep it exclusive and secret?"

Kyla rolls her eyes. "Do you think only girls wear makeup, Officer? How reductive."

"Come on, Kyla," Dad warns again.

Castellanos doesn't rise to Kyla's rage bait. "Okay, that's fair."

"Did you have a Test Kitchen the night that Erin was murdered?" Hamish asks.

"Yes, we did," Kyla says.

"Could you tell us who was there?" Hamish asks.

Kyla thinks about her ledger in the glove compartment of the hearse, along with the money for the mortgage payment. "No, I can't."

"Why is that? Is it because one of them might have killed her?" Castellanos asks, voice hard.

"Whoever did *wasn't* there during the Test Kitchen," Kyla insists. She can still remember that night clearly in her mind. It was busy. They'd made a killing on the new palettes that weren't being shipped wholesale until November, right in time for the holidays and likely to sell out. Kyla and Erin had stayed behind and packed up the goods after everyone else had gone, even the drunk kid. It'd been tense. GloMo. It was always about GloMo. It did well with their customers, but Erin was always so *wary*, for some reason. She had held back and undersold how much inventory they had that night, and Kyla was *pissed* when she realized that they left money on the table. She was even more pissed when Erin blew her off.

But Kyla had been willing to be the bigger person. She'd asked if Erin needed a lift, and she said no. Like she always did.

"I'm trying to get laid. I'll see you later, Duck. Love you. I'll call you tomorrow. I need to talk to you about something."

Kyla glares down at the wood grain again.

"You are making this unnecessarily hard for us, Kyla. If you have any information about your best friend's *murder*, you need to tell us," Hamish says. He's done playing nice, voice dripping with disdain. "Because otherwise I can only think of one reason why you wouldn't."

"I don't know anything about her murder, okay? Don't you think I would've been the very *first* to tell you if I did? We finished up at nine thirty, everyone left, and she stayed behind like always," Kyla says. She doesn't realize she's raising her voice until she feels her throat burn. "I always leave first! And she does whatever she does and then she calls me in the morning! She always *calls*, but this time . . ."

Her voice breaks and Kyla shuts her eyes tight, forcing herself not to cry, even as she feels the tears burn. She has done so well not to cry this whole time. Crying isn't productive. It wastes energy and Kyla has no time or energy to waste. She takes a deep breath and through waterlogged eyes, Hamish and Castellanos blur in front of her. But through the blur, she can see pity and she grits her teeth, furious. This is why she doesn't talk about this with anyone but Jason.

"Kyla—" Castellanos starts.

A knock on the glass interrupts her, and Kyla rubs her face as she looks over her shoulder, through the slits in the blinds. They cut the man at the door horizontally in the strangest of ways, one right across his throat, one across his eyes. He's wearing a well-tailored suit in a dark, elegant charcoal, with a Cook Cosmetics soft-green tie. Kyla looks back at the two police officers, but their faces are back to being twisted in dumb confusion.

So, they don't know him either.

No one moves. And then the man knocks again, more firmly. This time he doesn't wait for a reply. Instead, he shoves the door open himself and with a smile that doesn't quite resemble a smile, he introduces himself.

"My name is Brandon Plum. My client will no longer be cooperating with the police." Brandon Plum fills the room with an aura of dismissiveness that the bumbling police of a small town can't hope to triumph over. Their authority crumples under the weight of his self-assuredness. When he gently touches Kyla's shoulder through her puffer jacket, she can feel it too, and she stops herself from questioning why he's here. "Kyla, you don't have to say another word."

"I'm sorry, who are you?" Castellanos blurts out. "Mr. Graves didn't call a lawyer, did he?"

Dad looks just as bewildered by Plum's presence. "No, I did not. Did my son . . . ," he begins, and then he cuts himself off. Mikky would never call a lawyer. With what money?

Their mother's? As if she even knows what either of them are up to, her precious son or the daughter that she doesn't bother to come see.

Plum tugs on his lapels and lifts his chin so that he can look down his Oxbridge-educated nose. "As a member of Cook Cosmetics' legal department, I am here to protect Cook's interests."

"Cook Cosmetics?" Castellanos sputters. "But we were asking about Test Kitchens—"

Hamish hushes her harshly, squirming in his seat.

"So, you're confirming that you were asking Kyla about one of our beta programs, the Test Kitchen?" Plum asks. He speaks with such casual confidence, like it's a real thing, not something that Erin and Kyla made up to make a few extra bucks. There's nothing in Kyla's stomach, but she feels it churn acid. They shouldn't *know*, but they do, and now everything will be for *nothing*. In a lawsuit with someone like Florence, the funeral home isn't *just* the Graves's livelihood, their history, everything that her grandfather had built. It's collateral. A way to flex the strength of their fucking dollar. Digging her nails into her borrowed pants, Kyla looks up at Plum and tries not to let anything show. "That's proprietary information. As Kyla Graves is operating as an ambassador and employee of said company, she won't be saying another word."

Dad's eyes are heavy on her ear. Kyla doesn't look at him. She's not sure what he'll read in the planes of her expression. Instead, she grabs control of herself and looks up at Plum with a half smile.

"You said nothing about being an employee," Hamish accuses.

Kyla shrugs.

Hamish forces himself up and storms from the room, his face thundery. Castellanos follows after her boss, casting nervous looks back at Plum.

Plum pulls out a small business card. "Mr. Graves, here's my card. If they pull Kyla again for a chat, you give me a ring, and I'll accompany her. Unless you'd rather her not speak to them at all, and that would be fair too."

"I'm actually sitting right here. You can talk to me. I can make decisions for who I want to talk to," Kyla says.

Dad frowns and shakes his head. "Actually, no. You can't. You're a child—"

"Not really," Kyla says. "And I want to talk to Mr. Plum. In private."

"Kyla, stop *hiding* things," Dad demands. "I want you to be honest right now and tell me what's been going on."

"You heard him. It's *private*. It's something that we can't tell anyone because Cook Cosmetics hasn't announced it. It's nothing illegal, I promise," she lies. She's pretty sure it's not legal *or* ethical of her and Erin to sell product that doesn't belong to them to random students at their school at an astronomically upcharged price.

"I'm afraid she's right in this aspect, Mr. Graves. Kyla does a lot of good work for Cook Cosmetics, much of it that you *can* see, but this part in particular is best discussed in private," Plum says with the same genial condescension.

"Please, Dad. *Please*," Kyla says. She doesn't beg. Ever. But she does now.

Kyla's never seen her father want to argue so much. He's not that kind of dad, always trusting Kyla to know how to handle herself, since she proved she could. And then he sags under the weight of it all and pushes himself up to his feet. He looks down at Kyla like he doesn't recognize her.

Then he says the worst thing he could say. "I'm going to call your mother."

It's worse than shouting. Kyla doesn't lower herself by begging him again not to, so he pulls out his phone as he exits the room and shuts the door behind him.

"You wished to speak with me?" Plum asks.

"You know about the Test Kitchens," she says. What Kyla means to say is: *Florence knows about the Test Kitchens*.

"We know about the Test Kitchens, yes," Plum says matter-of-factly. "We designed them, Kyla."

She sits up taller. "Oh."

"Yes. Oh," Plum says. "What we *didn't* know was how involved you are. What we didn't know is that you were benefiting financially from what is meant to be an extremely sensitive program."

He keeps saying "we," but Kyla can read between the lines. Florence Cook hadn't been displeased when she learned what Erin was doing with all that free product. It had been by her design. But what she *had* been upset about—what Kyla accidentally clued them in on—was that Kyla was far more in the know about the execution than Florence. They were upset about how clever they'd been too. But it's not Kyla's fault that they had the foresight and business sense to make some money too.

"For the time being, I've been instructed to let you know that you should cease all operations."

Kyla expected this. She goes to take a peek out the window. She can't see her father, but there's Mikky's recognizable head of hair. She jerks away as she recognizes the boy he's talking to. *Jason.* But then she's distracted by Plum continuing.

"... until you get the go-ahead from higher-ups," he finishes.

"She'll sanction this?" Kyla asks, disbelieving.

"She'll let you lead it," Plum decides. "The first official Test Kitchen from a brand-new ambassador. You'll do just as Erin did, take notes and give product feedback."

"I've been selling her product. And she's been making *nothing* from it. And you're telling me she's okay with that?" Kyla demands.

It's not in line with the typical behavior of a millionaire.

At first, Plum doesn't say anything as he stands too, joining Kyla by the window. He leans against the side, arms folded over his chest.

What does he see when he looks at her? Does he think that she's lacking in some way? Or does he see something more? It has to be more, if Kyla isn't to be arrested or hit with a cease and desist yet.

"Florence Cook takes care of her own, Kyla," Plum says.

"Am I one of her own?" *Was Erin?*

"You could be," Plum says. "She only asks that you follow instructions when she gives them to you. Hold off for now. Lie low. Make little noise, and I'll be here to protect you when you call."

"Oh?"

Plum's bloodless smile is corporate and sharky. "Part of the perks when you're one of us. You gave us a call yesterday. And we answered, Kyla. We'll always answer. Speaking of which, we'll address compensation once we send along your contract. I was even instructed to offer you a signing bonus."

It always comes back to money. Kyla fidgets with her jacket sleeve before she grabs her wrist to physically stop herself. "What kind of bonus?"

"I'm quite good at gathering information, Kyla," Plum drawls in his crisp accent. "I'm a learner. I enjoy finding things out. And I've found out quite a *lot* about you."

"Have you really?"

"Why, yes. I recently came into the knowledge that your family funeral home might be struggling with payments. How does Cook paying off the mortgage sound?"

It sounds pretty *fucking* good. Too good.

Kyla wonders if they gave these instructions to all their employees. Lie low. Don't ask questions. Follow directions. She can't imagine Erin taking well to any of that. It makes Kyla . . . doubt.

But she forces a smile and it feels like Erin's in her body, stretching the corners of her mouth into something toothy. "Fab. Do you want my direct deposit number now or later?"

CHAPTER TWENTY-EIGHT

Nasim is already in the parking lot when Mikky gets to the station. He's standing on the curb, staring down at his phone, his backpack abandoned by his foot, as his thumbs move furiously over the screen. When he senses Mikky staring through the windshield, Nasim looks up and nods over to the empty parking spots away from the police cruisers.

"I'm sorry I didn't pick up," he says before Mikky even turns the car off. "I was in the shower, and then I listened to your voicemail, so I had my mom drop me here before she went in for work."

His hair is still wet, curling against the nape of his neck. He's trying to remain calm, but his frenzied eyes say otherwise. Mikky swallows around the growing knot in his throat as he finally reaches the door, shoulders tense. Nasim doesn't maintain that same need for distance, wrapping his arms around Mikky's waist and pulling him in tight.

"What happened last night, after your sister ran?" he asks.

"She said she went to the Vaughns' last night," Mikky says.

"Do you believe her?"

"Nasim, they found out about the Test Kitchens," Mikky murmurs. *Somehow.* He tries not to stiffen under Nasim's arms as he asks, "Did you tell?"

In barely a whisper, Nasim says, "And what if I did?"

Mikky tears himself out of Nasim's embrace. "I would hope that you wouldn't do it without talking to me, Nasim!" he blurts out. "What the hell?"

Nasim frowns. "All I said was 'and what if I did.' I never confirmed. I'm just saying, we found evidence of your sister doing shady shit near the place that Erin died. Wouldn't you say that makes her a *little* suspicious?" he asks.

"My sister loved Erin," Mikky says firmly.

There are so many things he's not sure about anymore, but that's one thing that he is. He knows the depths of Erin's and Kyla's love for each other. He knows what he heard, what he saw. He knows that Kyla isn't okay without her.

"People kill the people they claim to love all the time," Nasim says stubbornly.

"You just need it to be her, because if it's not, the next best suspect is Rowan, and you can't stand that, can you?" Mikky demands.

"If you were being sensible, you'd know it can't be Rowan. They don't have a motive. The only thing that implicates them is that they saw her that night, but so did, clearly, a bunch of people. So did *Kyla*, who actually has a motive. The oldest one—money. And if anyone's acting suspicious and secretive, it's *her*. So, no, it's not about who I need it to be."

"Then I guess we're at an impasse, because I'm not going to let you accuse my sister of *murdering* Erin Vaughn. You're a scientist, aren't you? Don't make assumptions without proof!" He knows he's said it a touch too loud when he sees the receptionist's head pop up through the foggy glass.

Nasim glowers at him, and through gritted teeth, he forces out, "It's cold. Let's get inside."

Mikky shoves past him. The inside of the police station isn't all that much better. If anything, he felt more at ease outside. Nasim approaches the receptionist.

"Can I help you?" she squeaks out.

"We're just waiting for someone," Nasim says. "Anywhere we can sit?"

"Right there," she says, nodding to the cluster of blue plastic chairs bolted into the ground.

Mikky and Nasim sit in the most uncomfortable chairs known to man and gods alike, leaving one empty between them. The gap feels as wide as a chasm. Mikky cranes his head around and just barely sees the backs of Dad's and Kyla's heads through the glass window that looks into the interrogation room.

"Mikky . . . ," Nasim tries.

"I don't want to hear it," Mikky blurts out, and he hates how Nasim's expression just fixes into something more determined, like he's going to *make* Mikky hear it.

Gratefulness wells up in him when just at that moment the door swings open, and a tall, suited man with a head of thick dark hair and a pale-green tie swaggers in, holding a manila folder in hand, providing a welcome distraction.

He holds the door open for someone and Mikky jumps up. "Jason—"

"Where is she? Is she okay?" Jason asks, frantic. He still looks exhausted, lavender circles under his eyes, more wan than usual.

Mikky grabs Jason's arm, stopping him from following the suited man back toward the interrogation room. Jason jerks away immediately.

"Dude, they just picked her up to ask her some questions.

I . . . I don't know why I called." Except Mikky does know. The longer he looks at Jason, the more frustration beats in his chest again. "We got into an argument yesterday and I called her, like, a hundred times, only to find out she was at yours?"

Jason's expression hardens. "What did you fight about? She came to our house pretty fucked up," he bites out. "She wanted to see Erin's room."

Mikky can think of a billion terrible reasons that Kyla would want to be in Erin's room. To hide evidence. To find the money from the last Test Kitchen.

But he can think of one good reason too: they fought and Kyla went looking for the first person who ever came to mind when something hard happened to her—Erin.

"You must've known that she was supposed to come home. Why didn't you call me?" Mikky demands.

Nasim murmurs, "Maybe you guys should take this outside. You're drawing attention to yourselves." Neither Mikky or Jason heeds his words.

"We aren't exactly talking, Mikky. What did you argue about?" Jason asks again. He still looks defensive, guarded in a way that he never used to be with Mikky. They've almost never clashed about anything important until the past few weeks.

"Look. Come over here," Mikky says, trying to guide Jason to the side, but he stays rooted in the middle of the lobby, careful to keep his eyes on Kyla. Mikky groans and leans in. "Look, there's a lot going on that you don't know about. Things that Erin and Kyla were up to that . . . might not have been on the up-and-up. They had this thing going called the Test Kitchen."

Jason cuts him a side-eye but doesn't speak.

"Nasim and I found this ledger and we found out that they both had secret Instagram accounts, and we think they were hosting these things to sell Cook Cosmetics product at an upcharge. We just haven't figured out what they were doing with the money. But I think they had one the night that Erin was killed—" Mikky tries to explain in hushed whispers, but Jason fully turns toward him, fire in his eyes.

"What did I tell you, Mikky?" Jason demands. "What did I *tell* you?"

He's drawing attention again. The door to the interrogation room opens and Hamish and his officer file out. The chief blinks, looking between the two of them.

"Is there a problem?" he demands.

"No. No problem," Nasim says quickly.

Then Dad exits too, closing the door behind him, but Kyla isn't with him. Mikky looks back into the interrogation room at the back of that suited man still in there.

"Who is that?" Mikky asks his dad, then turns back to Jason. "Who did you bring with you?" He can't stop thinking about the soft green of the man's tie. It reminds Mikky of something.

"He's a lawyer. Cook Cosmetics' lawyer," Dad says.

Of course. The Cook Cosmetics packaging. Cook Cosmetics is here. Which means Florence Cook, in some form, is here. This is about the Test Kitchens more than Kyla. This all leads back to *her*.

Mikky takes a step closer. "Why did you bring a lawyer with you, Jason? What do you know?" he demands.

"Hey, don't change the subject," Jason barks.

"Lower your voice, Jason," Dad advises, even as he looks back, distracted by Kyla still in the room with that man.

"Stop playing detective!" Jason hisses. "Like I said, you need to stop worrying about what happened to my sister and start worrying about what's happening to yours, because look at what's going on now. You know she didn't kill Erin and yet she might be *arrested* because of you and your fucking friends."

Nasim rolls his eyes. "More like she got herself arrested for being an emotional terrorist. She's the one who called Rowan a liar. She's the one who told Peter about Rowan and Erin, making them look suspicious. Maybe her constantly talking about *other* people made them suspicious of *her*."

"She thinks Rowan reported Peter, so she told them to take it back since it wasn't true. And Rowan *was* hooking up with my sister. They *were* always sneaking around and that *does* look suspicious. Sorry to burst your fucking bubble," Jason says dismissively.

There's very little Mikky hates more than not understanding. The thing is, he agrees with Jason, but he can't stop trying and failing to understand why Jason is doing this. Why he is acting like he doesn't want to know what happened to his sister? And what that has to do with Kyla and what she and Erin were doing that night, whether it was before or after. All of it is about *that* night.

"For your information, I'm investigating *because* I'm worried about Kyla and I care about Erin. You don't *care* about what happened to your dead sister, Jason?" Mikky roars. "Do *none* of you care what happened to Erin as much as your own shit?"

Jason rears back like he's been punched, all his breath wheezing out of his chest. And then he lunges, swinging a fist that glances off Mikky's jaw. Mikky squares up immediately, elbowing

Jason hard, readying to knock him clear to the ground with his next swing.

"Boys, break it up!" Dad shouts.

Unfamiliar hands land on Mikky's shoulder, wrenching him back. "Not in my station," Hamish says as Nasim shouts, "Oh, so you're going to go after him first when Jason started it? Wonder why that is!"

"Hey!" And then Kyla's there, fighting her way between them. She glowers up at Mikky and shoves him hard, finger pointed viciously in his face. "Hey! What the hell is the matter with you?"

"He's the one who just swung on me!" Mikky shouts. He shrugs Hamish's hands off him, glowering. The air is thick with tension that makes Mikky vibrate with nerves.

"I *heard* you! I heard what you said!" Kyla shrieks right back. He's so rarely heard her raise her voice, and now it's the second time in two days. Her face changes to accommodate the extra sound that comes out, jaw almost unhinged like a snake's. "Don't ever, *ever* accuse him of not caring."

Mikky's hands flutter uselessly. "I wasn't—"

"You were. And you're wrong. He's the *only* one who loved her as much as I did," Kyla says, and her voice shakes with the grief she's finally, finally showing. "You don't know what this is like for us, Mikky. You can pretend all you want, but you don't understand. She was a part of me. I feel like half of me is *gone*. And you're accusing Jason of who knows what and letting your friend accuse me of *killing* my best friend when part of me died that day too. I am *dead* and none of you seems to realize it."

Except all of them have seen it. And he *has* said something, over and over again, even. And it seems that every bit of effort, all that Mikky has given up for her, didn't matter to her at all. Mikky drowns in the oil slick of his own rage, choking on his spit as he tries to find the words, but Kyla continues on instead.

"You know, I actually do have something to say to you," Kyla declares, turning to the police chief.

The suited man calls gently, "Kyla."

Kyla ignores it, staring wild-eyed and spiteful at Hamish, waiting for him to ask.

"What is it?" he asks, greedy.

Mikky knows what she'll say before she opens her mouth. He looks over at Nasim, who must too because he is ashen, and then Mikky reaches for his sister. "Kyla, please don't."

She jerks back out of his reach, bumping right up against Jason. She doesn't flinch away from *him*.

"Rowan Villareal and Erin were in a relationship. It was a secret one. Erin was embarrassed because Rowan is a loser. Rowan was embarrassed because they thought Erin was a vapid whore. They'd argue about it a lot but it was like foreplay for them. Rowan would come after every Test Kitchen to see her, and they used Florence's house to hook up all the time. The last time I saw Erin was after a Test Kitchen and Rowan showed up like always before I left. I saw them arrive. Do with that what you will."

It's circumstantial, not enough to convict. But it might be enough for a desperate man brought under the microscope by a viral moment that dragged cameras up and down the East Coast to his tiny town of 6,063.5.

Hamish looks over at the woman cop with frizzy blond hair.

"Put out an APB on Rowan Villareal."

CHAPTER TWENTY-NINE

Mikky is an army of one when he enters Prophets Lake High School the next day. It's just like the funeral, or the first day of school again, where all eyes are on him. Mikky anticipated this. Dr. Grosse did too, during an emergency session with her. She tried to give him the advice that the opinion of strangers had no bearing on his character. Mikky knows that's true.

But he's armored himself anyway.

Mikky doesn't feel *safe* from the eyes, per se. He's just a lot higher than their line of sight in towering platforms, with kohl lining his eyes, smothered in safety pins and dark denim. He's unapproachable. He's himself.

Mr. Reynolds passes him back his chemistry test as he enters the class. Mikky looks down at his eighty-four. Not bad. A solid B. He sits down next to Alicia and asks, "How'd you do?"

For a moment Mikky isn't sure if she'll speak to him or not. Then she does, and Mikky realizes that while everyone knows what went down at the police station, Kyla hasn't gone so far as to excommunicate Mikky socially. He would feel grateful if he didn't feel nauseous about it.

"I got an eighty-nine. You totally calmed me down and it was like I could remember *everything* after I just breathed," Alicia says.

"Sick," Mikky replies with a small smile, and earns one from her in return. He tries to keep that upbeat feeling when he looks to his right. "And you, Nasim?"

Nasim looks straight ahead like he hasn't heard Mikky speak at all. It's a chilly throwback to Mikky's cold shoulder just a few days ago. Gregory looks between them like a child caught in the middle of a horrible divorce—Mikky would know all about that—then leans forward, clearing his throat.

"I got an eighty-two," Gregory volunteers nervously.

Immediately, Nasim jerks forward to block Gregory, effectively cutting off the conversation. Mikky rolls his eyes at the move, seeing it exactly for what it is. Nasim giveth friends, and Nasim taketh too. As if he's fucking God.

"Real mature," he jeers. And then quieter, and under his breath, he mutters, "Asshole."

Mr. Reynolds starts going over the test, focusing specifically on the questions that the entire class struggled with. Mikky turns to Alicia and gets her to do what she does best—gossip.

"So . . . I'm sure you heard," he whispers.

For once, she keeps her voice low, looking over at Nasim with wide eyes. "About Rowan? Yeah," she says, with the same vicious satisfaction that Mikky saw on Kyla's face. It's clear that Alicia feels that she—and the other girls on the dance team—have won. "They were picked up from homeroom. I heard it was wild."

"Did the pigs . . . sorry, cops, put them in handcuffs?" Mikky asks.

Alicia shrugs. "Nope." She speaks like she's a reporter. No, like she's a spy, meant to gather all the available information and report back to her handler. Kyla. Mikky wonders if it was Erin before her. He wouldn't be surprised. Kyla playacts the dead girl she misses more than anything else in the world, all of Erin's worst attributes hooked around her like an albatross, like that alone will fill the gaping wound left by Erin's absence.

"What *are* people saying?" he asks, even if he's not sure he wants to hear.

Alicia purses her lips. "Well . . . Peter is thrilled. It was kinda embarrassing, right? Erin Vaughn cheating on you with Rowan Villareal of *all* people. And then Rowan lying to the cops about Peter, on top of cucking him? He felt totally played, but now that Rowan got arrested and their ex is saying stuff about how they cheated on her, how she always saw them texting someone else when they were together, how they made her look stupid, how they're finally getting what they deserved, I think he feels vindicated. So . . . it's not looking good for Rowan. And your boyfriend . . ."

Mikky purses his lips and has to dig his fingernails through the tears in his jeans, into his skin, to stop himself from looking over his shoulder at Nasim. "What did he say?"

"He got into it with Sabrina yesterday. He came to school late and was telling everyone to fuck off and that Erin was up to shit with Kyla, which . . ." Alicia trails off, biting her lip. "Never mind." She looks back down at her test and up at Mr. Reynolds again, and Mikky knows that he won't be getting anything else out of her, as they edge too close to the Test Kitchens.

He tries to dial into Mr. Reynolds's lecture, but he can't manage it. His thoughts keep spiraling outward. All the pieces are there in front of him, but he still can't see how the seams fit together. At the center, there is Erin, dead. And in her orbit—

Kyla, Rowan, Peter, Test Kitchens, Cook, Cook, Cook. There's something there, and he's not sure what or how. But he knows that Florence Cook is the key.

Mikky doesn't believe in coincidences, not recurring ones anyway. It's not a coincidence that Jason showed up to the police station with a Cook Cosmetics lawyer in tow, and suddenly, the police could no longer ask questions about the Test Kitchens. It's not a coincidence that Florence Cook came to the memorial and that it went viral. It's not a coincidence that it brought Prophets Lake under the great white eye of the American mainstream media, with Cook Cosmetics championing justice.

Mikky can find the answer. He has to.

The library is nearly deserted during lunch, but Mikky's not surprised. Everyone's too busy gossiping in the lunchroom today.

Mikky spots Nasim and it feels like a strange redo of their first lunch. But this time, Nasim looks up and sees him too. He doesn't break eye contact, doesn't pretend that he doesn't see Mikky. But when Mikky grabs the chair across from Nasim and tugs, it tips back but doesn't pull out. Mikky looks down, under the table, and sees Nasim's ankle hooked around one leg of the chair.

"I didn't say you could sit," Nasim says.

"I don't need an invitation." Mikky tugs harder and Nasim's foot slips, letting the chair screech out. Nasim isn't the only one who can be stubborn. Mikky sits down heavily, practically straddling the chair. He grabs at the edge of the seat. "What is your problem?"

"I don't have a problem. I just don't want to talk to you," Nasim says.

"I'm not the one who arrested Rowan."

"No, your sister took care of that, right?" Nasim retorts. "They were released early this morning at, like, three. Not enough evidence to hold them. If you cared."

Mikky can't really say that he does.

"Good for them," Mikky deadpans.

Nasim slams his hand on the table. "They're the prime suspect now. The police are pulling their phone records now, tracking their car, searching their *house*. Media got wind of it and they're camped on the Villareals' lawn now. Soon the truth won't matter. Everyone's going to assume they killed her or at least had something to do with it."

And that's . . . that's bad. Mikky knows that. Rowan is an asshole. Ignorant, sometimes. But a queer, nonbinary kid being accused of *murder*? That's fucked, especially if they didn't do it. But, then, what if they did? They were the last one to see Erin after the Test Kitchen *every* time. Mikky has to assume Kyla's telling the truth that they saw her after the last one too.

"So, it's better that the Black girl goes down for it, then?" Mikky retorts.

Nasim's hands clench into fists. "You *know* that's not why I think it's her."

"But that's what the world would think, right? At least, that's what you're saying matters most about Rowan's situation," Mikky retorts. He knows he's being mean about it, but Kyla is haunting him, just like Erin's ghost haunts her. "She didn't hurt Erin. I don't know who did . . . but it *wasn't* Kyla."

"And I know it wasn't Rowan," Nasim insists. "Meanwhile, Kyla has been acting guilty this whole time. Painting a target on Rowan's back to cast suspicion on them. Hiding the Test Kitchens.

The ledger. Withholding information from police. Breaking into Florence Cook's house. And the *money*. We still don't know what she's doing with the money that they were making. But you won't acknowledge that. You're still on her side."

Mikky knows all of this. He knows Kyla and all her gory mistakes. And yet—

"I'm always going to be on Kyla's side," Mikky says simply.

Nasim lets out a deep, heavy breath. "Then . . . we're done." It's so final.

"Are you . . . are you breaking up with me?" Mikky asks.

Nasim's mouth is downturned at the corners like he's holding words back. But there's no reason to hold them back anymore. "Maybe if you'd actually had the courage to make your feelings clear and ask me out, but you didn't, so . . . what is there to break up?"

He takes one final look at Nasim and thinks about the possibilities that have just evaporated. Mikky's fine. He'll *be* fine. He knows all about broken brains and broken self-esteem and broken relationships. He can solve a broken heart, too.

So he stands sharply, sending the chair clattering to the ground. The librarian hushes him, as if there are more than five people in the room, but Mikky just abandons the overturned chair and shoves through the front doors, narrowly avoiding Gregory, who clutches his lunch to his chest.

Mikky moves on autopilot, twisting down each hallway until he enters the cafeteria. He scans it, searching. He finds Jason first, sitting with his soccer team at one table. He looks up once, and pretends not to see Mikky. Well, fuck him too. Mikky doesn't *care*. He's not who Mikky's looking for anyway.

In one fell swoop, Mikky is a freshman again, lonely and alone, isolated. He wraps his arms around his middle and grinds his fingertips into his sides, like he can mush the peeling parts of himself together and become whole again. Mikky's breath speeds up. His heart rate begins to elevate too, a rabbiting thud, and then—

Then he sees her.

Kyla is in the middle of her lunch table, sipping a Diet Coke, unsmiling. Despite everything that happened yesterday and all the ensuing attention, she looks amazing as always. A perfect base, winged liner, her fingernails freshly painted with dark cherry. Unlike Mikky's nails, chipped and chewed, a few fragments of paint hanging on to his nail beds. Kyla doesn't look up as he stomps forward, not like her team. Sabrina stops midsentence, her mouth gently open. Alicia gawks from her perch next to Kyla.

"Ah, can we help you?" Sabrina finally asks when he arrives.

"Move over," Mikky growls out between clenched teeth, his breath whistling as he tries to get a hold on the way the world is sliding beneath him.

Mikky hears Alicia and the other girls move, shuffling farther down until there's an empty seat just big enough for Mikky to slip into. His thigh presses tight to Kyla's like a brand. He drops his backpack behind him and puts his hand on the table, palm facing upward.

"Hold my hand," Mikky wheezes. "Don't let go."

She doesn't owe him this. Mikky knows that, in some ways, he fucked up. He hasn't said sorry either. But he believes her. He's always going to believe her, even after the lying and the scheming and the intimidation campaign. Mikky doesn't always recognize

Kyla in her self-destruction, but he does know that he came back for *her*. He stayed in a town that he didn't want to be in, for *her*. His little sister. When he looks at her, he's always going to see *his baby*. Mikky's always going to stay for her.

There's a brief moment where his palm is cold. And then Kyla does as she's told. Squeezes hard.

And doesn't let go.

CHAPTER THIRTY

Kyla waits outside the school building for about thirty seconds before she starts tapping her foot out of impatience. Mikky doesn't normally take long to exit, but now that his friends—and notably Nasim—are ignoring him, he especially has no reason to be taking a thousand years.

Her fingers dip into the pockets of her puffer again. October is still a few days away, but fall is already making itself known with a biting chill. Her fingers graze over the edge of the note in her pocket, which she still hasn't found the mettle to open by herself.

The back of her neck itches as she considers leaving him. She doesn't owe him anything, Kyla tells herself. And then she thinks about the bewildered terror on his face at lunch as he tried so hard to catch his breath but hadn't been able to. His hand had trembled in hers, and even when she finally had to let go, she felt the echo of his panic on her palm. She hadn't caused it directly, but Kyla is self-aware enough to know that she's contributed. She can't silence the part of her that thinks maybe she does owe him a little bit of the truth.

And maybe after the last two days she wants a bit of his truth too.

Outside the haze of malice, Kyla has enough perspective to

see that Mikky's standing by her. Even when he doesn't know everything. Even when Kyla *knows* how suspicious and secretive she's been, Mikky has been on her side. In all Kyla's life, there's only been one other person who's always been on her side, believing her without question. Erin. She owes it to him, to give him that same grace.

Mikky is a wraith cloaked in sadness. It's only a little pathetic, the way he trudges out, neck hanging low. His stupid not-boyfriend is pretending not to watch him from across the parking lot. Fucking Nasim Talebi. He's probably the one who reported the Test Kitchens in the first place.

"Mikky," Kyla calls.

He stops and glares at her like he didn't sit down with her at lunch and hold her hand. Like it's all her fault.

Well, she'll give him that one.

"What? I'm trying to get home. Go to dance practice," Mikky says.

"I canceled dance practice." She's been doing that a lot. Everything Erin and Kyla built up is starting to disintegrate. Regionals are in early December, and an eleven-minute routine doesn't just come out of nowhere. Kyla and Erin had promised each other they would win again, and take it all the way to nationals. The girls' loyalty isn't wavering, per se, but Kyla knows some of them think that she's lost it. The others—the younger ones—attribute it all to Kyla's questioning and Rowan's detainment. Alicia and Sabrina are stepping up, trying to manage so not everything falls on her. They're good for that, but still. Kyla shakes away the thought and presses her fist into her hollow stomach. "I'm starving. I thought we could go get something to eat. On me."

"On you?" Mikky asks, nose wrinkling.

Kyla thinks of the envelope of money in her glove compartment. "Yeah, I'm good for it," she says. "And I know a place where not too many people go."

"Fine. I'll meet you—"

"Let me drive you," Kyla interrupts. She doesn't leave it up for discussion, just turns on her heel to go to the hearse.

She sits in it and watches him dillydally at the door, going back and forth in his decision, like he wants to run from her. But Kyla knows Mikky will come. He knows that she wants to talk, even though she hasn't said.

When Mikky gets into the passenger seat, Kyla waits only long enough for him to shut the door before she takes off. She doesn't turn on the radio, but she doesn't speak either, though she thought she would. It's odd, feeling so unsure of herself, and she shifts in her seat, her tongue swollen in her mouth.

"Where are we going?" Mikky asks.

"This place called Fable Street Pantry," Kyla says. "It's a diner at the edge of town. Cheap."

Mikky nods slowly. "I remember the place."

He probably does. Their mother had taken them there a few times when they were kids, when suddenly she decided she hated the walls of the house and their father was busy at the funeral home. He definitely doesn't think she remembers, but she does, even if she tries not to. It was for babies because fairy tales are for babies. They aren't real, and real life demands enough of Kyla's attention.

When they pull into the parking lot, the hearse is one of three cars.

"Can you go into my glove compartment and pass me the envelope in there?" Kyla asks.

Mikky does as he's told, holding out the hefty white envelope to her. He inhales sharply when she opens it and pulls out a wrinkled hundred-dollar bill from a stack of them.

"What the fuck?" he asks. "You make that much money selling lipsticks? Dude."

"I think this is a story better told over pancakes," Kyla says.

The owner, Meg, looks up with a relieved, tired smile. Her gentle confusion settles in the lines of her bare face.

"Your young man not with you this time?" she asks.

Kyla laughs. "Not today. I brought my brother."

"Well, well, welcome," Meg says. She tilts her head. "Here are the menus. Go on and seat yourself. I'll come by with some water."

Kyla chooses the farthest booth from the door, and opts to have her back against the wall. Mikky sits across from her, grim-faced like he's prepared to hear about a family member's death. And in a way, maybe he is.

He waits for Meg to set down the waters. Neither of them reaches for them.

"What can I get you two kids?" Meg asks.

Mikky and Kyla blink down at the menu.

"I'll get the Just-Right Corned Beef Hash." Kyla says the first thing that comes to mind.

Mikky flips open the menu and says immediately, "Uh, Bluebeard Hotcakes for me."

"Sounds about right," Meg says. "I'll get that over to you two real quick."

When they're alone again, Mikky leans over the table. "So, do you want to tell me about the money?" Mikky asks. "And where you got it from?"

Kyla sighs. "Come on, Mikky, you *know* where I got it from."

Mikky takes a beat, looks at her like he's only just seeing her. She's glad that he's finally looking her in the eye instead of looking at just her grief.

"From selling those Cook Cosmetics products. Whose idea was it?" Mikky asks.

Kyla has to force the answer from between her teeth: "I thought it was Erin's idea."

Erin's gone and it still feels like Kyla's breaking her trust, spilling her secrets.

"You *thought*?" Mikky says.

"I did. But . . . it wasn't. Not all of it," Kyla says. "The money part was. The Test Kitchens weren't."

"What do you mean? Who came up with it?" Mikky demands. "And why the money? Erin didn't need it."

"No, she didn't," Kyla decides, even though it's not necessarily true. Not always. Sometimes Erin would ask for a *small* cut of the money, but when that happened, she would work twice as hard to have enough for Kyla the next month, as if she needed to pay her back, even though they were selling product that was rightfully Erin's to begin with. "But I did. She did it for me. And Dad."

"What does Dad have to do with this?" Mikky asks.

"The funeral home," Kyla says. She looks for recognition in Mikky's expression but doesn't find it. He really has no idea. It must be nice, being so blissfully ignorant to what really matters.

"The funeral home isn't doing well, Mikky. Dad can't keep up with the mortgage payments."

"What mortgage? The funeral home is paid in full," Mikky insists.

And that's the thing. It *was* paid in full. A generational family-owned funeral home. It's Kyla's legacy, and one she'll hopefully inherit proudly. There's something calming about the preparation room. Something comforting about the smell of formaldehyde. It might be unsettling to other people, but for her, it's always been another home.

Kyla knows that her father feels the same way, which is why when the hospital system started booming two towns over with their fancy crematorium, he'd taken the dip in customers hard but had been determined to weather the storm without sacrificing his staff. He needed to find a way to make sure that the receptionist was still being paid because she was a single mom with two kids at home—he'd buried her wife himself. He kept the catering coordinator on too, because he was fresh out of culinary school and couldn't seem to find a job in Boston. The casket deliverer, the floral designer, the funeral attendant, Kyla. So many people to take care of, so little money to pay them.

That's how she explains it to Mikky, laying it out like a story. The bank had demanded collateral for a loan large enough to keep them afloat and all Dad had was the funeral home to remortgage.

"I keep the books for Dad. I'm good with math. I saw . . . I saw he was struggling with keeping up with the payments," Kyla says. "And I knew I needed to help out. I just didn't know how. Erin and I talked about it and she . . . figured out a way."

Mikky's brow has been furrowed and it doesn't unfurrow

when she says, "She was already doing the Cook influencer program at that point. At first I only helped her with the Instagram posts. One of them went viral and she gave me some of her payment for it. It was enough for the month. But then . . . Erin was the influencer. She was doing the real work. It didn't feel right taking the money she earned. So, one day, she told me she had an idea. Her Instagram following was getting so big so quick, and Cook saw that, so they were sending her more and more product, this time exclusive and early access stuff. She said that maybe we should start selling it instead of just posting about it."

"But you said—"

"I know what I said," Kyla interrupts, fiddling with the edge of the table. "It was easy. All I needed to do was find a circle of people who wanted to be part of something exclusive. That was easy because there were tons of people at school and around here that follow Erin, and they engaged more with her posts than others. They were *fans*. They'd pay for entry and we'd swear them to secrecy. We'd show them how to do their makeup and tell them they were getting a three-month head start on using the products. And then they'd bid on them. They'd get invited back to tell us how they'd liked the products at the beginning of the next one. Erin would hand out these comment cards she made and they'd write their opinions and reactions down. I didn't really think much of it? I figured it was so she'd have ideas for videos when she eventually had to post about them publicly. Or she was using their thoughts to determine the exact kind of stuff to request from Cook for us. I don't know. I never bothered to ask. The money was what mattered, and the funeral home really needed it."

"But sometimes . . . she was weird about certain products. Sometimes certain products would be gone," Kyla says. "I should've thought about it more then."

Some of their customers used to beg for certain products they missed out on at the first auction. But when Kyla asked, Erin would just shrug and say, "Couldn't get my hands on it. Too close to shelf," or, "I think they're going to reformulate it."

"So, the night she died, there was a Test Kitchen," Mikky says. "Was it . . . out of the ordinary?"

"No. It was the same as always," Kyla says.

She sees it so clearly. It was mostly the usual suspects. Some of the private school kids from the area. A few of the students from their school that were flush with cash. Indigo Glass. And Erin was still feeling generous and inviting Rowan's ex at their request. Months before, they decided they felt bad for dumping the girl so suddenly, and she was still fucked up over it, even months later. The Test Kitchens might have been helping, but Kyla didn't know her well enough to be definitive about that. Kyla still remembers having to wait an extra half hour to stop feeling buzzed from the one glass of white wine she had. Then an extra fifteen minutes for some of the group to come back to pick up a girl and her friend after he got wasted on the fizzy alcohol. She had taken his keys, refusing to let him drive home, even when Erin complained that Rowan would have to wait longer in the car before they could come inside. Kyla was quick to remind her that she'd been the one to insist on having drinks there. Erin hadn't appreciated that, just like she hadn't appreciated their earlier tiff over GloMo. Not an argument, because they didn't do that. A "tiff." That's what Erin's mother called it when they disagreed.

When Kyla was finally about to leave, Erin promised to finish counting the money after Rowan left. She asked Kyla to take home the product that night and said that she'd pass along the money after taking out Peter and Anthony's cut, because even though accounting was Kyla's job, Erin insisted on splitting labor always. It felt a little like she was making up for their tiff too. Then Erin pressed a kiss to her cheek. Promised that she'd call in the morning because she needed to talk to her about something, but it could wait.

Kyla never got that call.

"The night she died, she had the money. It had to be close to four grand. But the cops didn't *find* her with four grand. They would've asked about it if they found her with that kind of cash," Kyla explains, and she can't quite keep the panicked edge out of her voice when she thinks back to that missing money.

"So . . . whoever hurt her has that money," Mikky says thoughtfully. "The murderer."

"That's what I think," Kyla says, when she means, *That's what I know.* There's no other explanation.

"Why are you telling me all of this now?" Mikky asks.

Kyla reaches into her pocket, feeling for the note again. "Because I just found out Cook Cosmetics came up with the Test Kitchen, not Erin. That's why Erin was collecting everyone's reviews. Cook Cosmetics was using us, and I might have proof."

She places the note on the table, twisting it so he can see whom it's addressed to.

"'For Katy Too to review,'" he reads. "That's you, right? And she's Eleanor Rigby?"

"You and Nasim *were* good detectives, weren't you?"

"Yeah, we kinda had to be after you implied that an innocent person murdered your best friend," Mikky says flatly.

"So, you don't believe Rowan did it?" Kyla asks.

"I did. For a while. But I don't think they're a murderer. I think that they're cruel sometimes. And insecure. But that doesn't make someone a murderer," Mikky says.

Kyla glares down at the table. "Spite may or may not have factored in my decision to tell the cops that they were at the house."

"Yeah, I got that," Mikky deadpans as he smooths out the emails, leaning down to read them.

Kyla blurts out, "I haven't read them yet."

Startled, Mikky looks at her, baffled. "Why?"

"I found the paper in her touch-up bag the morning I woke up at the Vaughns', before Hamish came to the house looking for me. I was going to read it when I got into my room, and then . . . everything happened and the longer I had it, the more daunting it got," Kyla explains. "She'd only address it like that, though, if she didn't want *anyone* else to know who it was for."

"What do you think is in it?" Mikky asks.

Kyla has a creeping suspicion. "The lawyer that came was sent by Cook Cosmetics. He's the one who told me that they knew all along. That it was *their* idea. They knew about the funeral home. They offered me some big signing bonus to pay back the mortgage, Mikky, and it didn't feel like it was for all my hard work. It felt like *hush* money. So whatever is in these emails may be what they want silenced," she says. "I'm telling you all this because . . . I want to read them, but I can't do it alone."

Mikky reaches forward, grabbing her knuckles, and nods. "Then don't. I'll read them with you."

From: <u>Erin Vaughn</u>
Sent: Aug. 5
To: <u>Florence Cook</u>
flo,
i've attached the group feedback on glomo here. most people really love it, but noticed a few things that seem a little off. one of my girls has sensitive skin and is having a bad reaction. that's not very glomo, right? anyway, see you next week, i'm coming to work with mom!
love,
erin

From: <u>Florence Cook</u>
Sent: Aug. 10
To: <u>Erin Vaughn</u>
Dear Erin,
As always, it was an absolute pleasure to have lunch with you. I regret that your mother was too wrapped up in work to join us. Now, on our previous conversation, I've spoken to our product development team, and they insist that this is the correct formulation. This launch is important to the success of the brand, and it remains on the launch calendar, slated for a late November launch. Please recommend to your friend that she use in accordance with the product instructions.
Best,
Florence Cook
CEO & Founder of Cook Cosmetics

From: <u>Erin Vaughn</u>
Sent: Aug. 14
To: <u>Florence Cook</u>
hey flo,
just wanted to let you know that she IS using it according to the instructions. dm'ed some of the others to follow up and they're all reporting weird reactions. i attached screenshots of the texts. flo, i really think it's kinda early. you reformulated the lip kits when i told you that it dried out lips, and this seems worse. can we talk about this over lunch?
love,
erin

From: <u>Erin Vaughn</u>
Sent: Aug. 16
To: <u>Florence Cook</u>
flo,
i'm sorry, did i make you mad? i didn't mean to. you don't normally take so long to respond.
sorry, and love,
erin

From: <u>Florence Cook</u>
Sent: Aug. 18
To: <u>Erin Vaughn</u>
Dear Erin,
I'm sorry, my dear. I've been tight on time. I was in Boston for the past few days, reviewing the build

> progress of the new location. It's coming along nicely.
> I had a thought, and I discussed with your mother, she
> thinks it's a grand idea—what if you host the store
> opening? "A Night of Glamor with Erin Vaughn."
> What do you think?
>
> And please hold on further Test Kitchens. I think
> we need to put more thought into how helpful they
> are. We'll discuss over lunch. We should make a day of
> it, just before school starts. And maybe your mother
> will be able to join. I hope she won't be too tied up.
> Best,
> Florence Cook
> CEO & Founder of Cook Cosmetics

"What the *hell*?" Mikky breathes, reading it all over.

Kyla blinks slowly as she stares down at the words, trying to make sense of them. She knows Erin and Florence were close, at least according to Erin. But there's a certain coldness to Florence's emails, a chill that sits low in Kyla's stomach and rises in her esophagus like bile. It tastes a lot like fury.

"So, she was sending feedback *directly* to Florence, about GloMo, and was telling her to reformulate it, and she didn't want to," Mikky mumbles to himself. He lifts the sheet of emails up to his face, as if bringing it closer will tell him more. "I wish she'd included the feedback when she printed this out. What kind of reactions? *Who?*"

Kyla leans away as she looks at the back of the paper Mikky is holding up, because there are words on the top half of the paper in tiny font. Lots of them. And at the very bottom, in the right-hand corner, it's signed: "All my love, Your Eleanor Rigby"

"Mikky," Kyla breathes, "flip the paper."

Mikky does as he's told. "Is this . . . it's a list of albums. Why would she put a list of albums on here?"

Because Kyla loves music. Kyla *breathes* music. "This is a message. For me," she says. "Get out a pen."

Mikky practically ransacks his own backpack in an effort to find one. "There's albums here but no singer or band names. Okay what's . . . *Believe*?"

"Cher. Duh."

Mikky slowly writes out her name.

"*Stankonia*?"

"OutKast."

"*GUTS*?"

"Olivia Rodrigo."

"*DAMN.*?"

This is one of Kyla's favorites to spin. "Kendrick Lamar."

Mikky taps the end of his pen on each name over and over again, looking for something. Kyla shrugs, shaking her head and leaning back.

"It's just a playlist. It doesn't say anything," she says.

"No. They're not. Look." And then he carefully underlines the first letter of each artist.

C-O-O-K.

Kyla sits up. She's a lot more awake now. "Oh, shit."

She's more critical of the list now. The longer she stares at it the more she sees there's a rhyme and reason to this. There's a noticeable space between the first four albums and the next two. *Lights Out* and *Songs in the Key of Life*.

"The second one is easy. Stevie Wonder. *S*," Mikky says, and he sounds proud of himself for getting that one.

"*Lights Out*. Ingrid Michaelson," Kyla says. Erin spun that one during one of their sleepovers after a Test Kitchen last May. "C-O-O-K-I-S."

"Okay, okay," Mikky mumbles. "What is Cook, though?"

Sign o' the Times is another easy one. Prince. *(What's the Story) Morning Glory?* makes Kyla and Mikky exchange an eye roll, their shared disdain for Oasis's "Wonderwall" top of mind. Kyla is stumped by *This Old Heart of Mine* until Mikky Googles it, and once she hears the Isley Brothers, Kyla is hit with a memory of her father humming to this album, when he still had CDs, crooning in the car as he drove her to school. *The Globe Sessions* is easy for Mikky—apparently their mother loves Sheryl Crow.

"*Dock of the Bay* is Otis Redding. I love that album," Kyla says.

Mikky writes it down. "P-O-I-S-O . . ." He trails off, looking up at her.

Loose is a Nelly Furtado album. But even before that, it doesn't take a genius to know exactly what Erin meant to spell out for Kyla.

"'Cook is poison,'" Kyla reads softly.

"She was *poisoning* people?" Mikky demands.

Kyla looks up sharply. "Cook Cosmetics is supposed to be a clean, vegan, cruelty-free beauty brand. It's Florence's whole thing. She's making up for the sins of her father."

"Making up for the sins of your father isn't cheap, Kyla. And that woman is *rich,* but she wants to stay that way. So . . . you said that Erin hands out comment cards for the products? Do you remember anyone saying something *out loud*?"

Kyla has to close her eyes and think back. For a moment she wants to insist that it wasn't her job. She knew her job. To keep the books, to plan the details, but nothing with the products. After all, an adverse effect from a product happens sometimes. Once, Kyla's lips blew up from a drugstore lip balm. You find what works for you. But Erin had written a note, *just* for Kyla, because this is more than that. Finally, it dawns on her, because she's *seen* the adverse effects, day in and day out.

"I . . . yeah . . . yeah, actually. Alicia has really sensitive skin. She's had a derm since we were in eighth grade, so she's really careful. She's been using the new skin-care makeup line, GloMo, for a few months now. She's been breaking out really badly. That usually happens when she's stressed, and I thought . . . Erin's murder has been really stressful. But it looks cystic and at one point, her skin was peeling a little. But she asked for more," Kyla says.

She hasn't even gotten her corned beef hash yet, but her stomach turns over. She thinks again back to Erin's quiet comments. "They're reformulating." "I couldn't get it this time." There'd been leftover GloMo from the Test Kitchen the night Erin died, which had surprised her. Alicia had asked for it. Kyla had given it to her at a discount.

"I would've never given it to her if Erin *told* me. I would've never—"

"I know," Mikky says, gently tugging at her hand until it falls away from her mouth. "Of course you wouldn't. But Erin . . . ?"

Kyla immediately wants to defend Erin. She wants to tell Mikky that Erin would never put anyone in danger. But Kyla knows better now. The Test Kitchens were exactly that—tests. Unguided and unscientific human trials. And Erin had known it from the start. She'd known and even worse, turned a profit from it. Erin wouldn't have done that for anyone except one person. Kyla.

"Erin loved me," Kyla whispers. Erin had loved Kyla so much, she'd put herself and everyone else in danger.

Mikky nods. "I know."

Kyla looks down at the tabletop, scratching at it. "But why would Florence Cook use us to test product on? Doesn't she have a huge lab?"

"Why do millionaires do *anything*, Kyla? Why did *you* sell the product?" Mikky demands. "Money."

Kyla inhales sharply.

"Researching and creating clean beauty products that are *supposed* to be vegan and cruelty-free on the timeline that Cook Cosmetics works on has to be really hard and really expensive or every brand would try it. There are cheaper options and Florence isn't stupid. She knows that. I bet they've been doing weird shit with product for a while and reformulating based on Erin's feedback," Mikky explains.

Kyla inhales sharply. "This time she refused," she murmurs. Flipping the paper back to the emails, she points at the very last email. "She's opening a Boston location, and it's *right* around the time that GloMo is supposed to launch. Late November? *Right* before Christmas?"

"There's no way she would push either back. She might have even . . . silenced Erin to get away with it."

Kyla jerks. "You think so?"

Mikky looks at her with a grim expression that says enough.

"How do we figure out if there really are weird chemicals in there? It wouldn't be on the packaging," Kyla says.

"We need to run some tests to see what's in them," Mikky declares.

"With what lab?" Kyla retorts just as fast.

"I know someone who might have access to a lab," Mikky says grimly. "But you're not going to like it."

Kyla can't imagine she will. She doesn't like many things anymore. Before she can ask who, Meg is back with their food, setting it in front of them with a sly, "Bone apple teeth," purposely mispronounced.

Kyla digs into hers immediately, her stomach yearning for food as her thoughts churn.

There's one big reason not to pursue this—the money to save the funeral home.

And one big reason to do it—because if it is poison and Erin knew and Florence *knew* that Erin knew, then maybe . . . *maybe* . . .

Kyla notices Mikky pause, his piece of hotcake hovering right by his lips.

"What is it?" Kyla asks.

"Just . . . why?" Mikky asks. "Why couldn't you and Erin ask for help with the funeral home? Why didn't you tell *me*?"

There are so many answers to that: *Because I didn't trust you, because you wouldn't be able to help me, because I'm used to solving problems with Erin or on my own, because you left me and Mom doesn't want me, and Dad's busy handling the big problems so mine feel small.* But the real answer is a lot simpler.

"Erin and I used to say we didn't keep secrets from each other," Kyla says into her plate. "Everyone else . . . was just not us.

We were a unit. But I'm starting to realize that's not true. None of it is. She was she, and I am me, and she did keep secrets. Every day I've felt like if I just looked to my left, she'd be there, but she's not. She never will be again because if I hadn't *left* that night, maybe she wouldn't be dead. Now I'm alone. It's what I deserve."

"Kyla," Mikky starts.

She looks up at him. "But you wouldn't let me be alone, would you?"

"Never," Mikky swears.

Kyla can't say thank you just yet. She doesn't know if she *is* thankful. But if they manage to prove that Florence Cook, a woman that Erin looked up to and adored, killed her best friend, she will be.

CHAPTER THIRTY-ONE

Mikky's never been inside Nasim's house. That's the first thing that hits him when he's back in the passenger seat, still reeling from the wall of information that Kyla dropped on him like it was nothing. He'd been too annoyed when Nasim had overstepped by sneaking into Kyla's room to be curious about the inside. And now he's not even sure he'll be allowed in. He tells her as much and Kyla looks at him like he's stupid.

"Weren't you dating?" she asks.

"It didn't really get that far," Mikky says.

"Wow."

"It didn't help that my little sister was being evil to his friend," Mikky snaps, and he's glad when Kyla shrugs and says, "Fair."

He's not sure what he would've done if she denied her bullshit. Probably had an aneurysm. That seems the most likely.

"Well, I'm sure I can convince him," Kyla says. She sounds far too confident for someone *so* disliked by Nasim. "What's the address?"

Mikky gives it and Kyla doesn't need directions. They both could probably find their way on foot. Prophets Lake isn't big enough to not know every street. Kyla turns into a cute little neighborhood where the houses are just slightly newer than where they live. There's something clean about them, but they lack the charm of their old Colonial.

Kyla parks on the street and hops out of the hearse, abandoning Mikky to be a frozen statue in the passenger seat.

Nasim made it unequivocally clear that he was dumping Mikky. That he didn't want anything to do with Mikky. It sent him into an entire panic attack, and now he has to see him again. Talk to him. Beg him for help. Well—

Kyla knocks on the window.

"Get out of the car, Mikky," she says. She wrenches the door open and grabs his hand in hers, and it's *warm* like at lunch. She squeezes his and tugs on his seat belt.

Mikky fumbles with unhooking it and then winces when it pinches his skin. Finally, he unfolds himself and follows Kyla up to the front door. There's no car in the driveway, but that doesn't mean anything—Nasim can't drive. Or it's still early, he might not be home yet. He could be by the lake or at the library or anywhere. And Mikky can't decide which option he dreads more.

"Maybe we should go," he says.

"Absolutely not," Kyla says, and then she rings the doorbell and knocks on the door for good measure.

There's no reason for Mikky to be panicking. Logically, he knows the worst that Nasim can do is close the door in their faces. He won't, like, attack them. Except Mikky looks at who's accompanying him and realizes it's actually very likely that Nasim may overreact, and oops, look, there's Nasim opening his front door and then aborting just as fast, leaving only a sliver open.

"Uh, hey," Mikky says, lifting a hand in a half greeting.

"What are you two doing here?" Nasim demands.

"We need your help," Kyla says flatly.

Nasim widens the crack in the door enough to give them the finger then shuts it in their faces. Kyla sighs and looks over at Mikky.

"He's so dramatic. You really like *him*?" Kyla asks.

"You are such a fucking asshole," Mikky declares, "and also the reason he wants nothing to do with me!"

"That's only partly why. The other reason is because *you're* the one who jumped to conclusions too fast."

Mikky twists. Nasim has opened the door a crack again and looks as if he regrets his addition to the conversation. He's staring at Mikky's clavicle, refusing to meet his eyes. Mikky reaches out for the doorknob and Nasim makes to shut the door again, but Kyla's faster. She shoves her foot between the doorframe and the door and Nasim stumbles back at the sudden obstacle, appalled.

"I'm trying to make things right," Kyla says.

"Oh, is that so? Turning over a new leaf?" Nasim drawls.

Kyla purses her lips. "Not quite," she says, and leans in, tilting her head like she's trying to decide how to eviscerate Nasim. She looks over at Mikky for only half a second, and then she takes a deep breath. "To be clear, I hate Rowan Villareal. They're just as bad as me. Calling me, a Black girl, 'feral.' Comparing me to an animal. Saying slick shit about how intimidating me and my brother are? Yeah. That's fucked. Maybe talk to your friend about why they felt it was okay to say that shit about me but not about the mean blond girl they were fucking."

Nasim winces. "They . . . they didn't mean it that way."

"Sure," Kyla deadpans. Then she softens. Slightly. Ever so slightly. "But despite all of Rowan's . . . faults, Erin really did like them. A lot. That's why she started hooking up with Peter. She wanted to make them jealous. So, I've decided in her memory, I'm going to clear their name."

Nasim folds his arms over his chest. He looks as gorgeous as ever, even with his eyes narrowed in distrust. "You're so generous."

"Aren't I?" Kyla retorts. "Look, I'm sorry for all the shit I pulled with telling the cops about Rowan and Erin, but I really *did* think they reported Peter to the cops. I now have reason to believe otherwise."

"And how did that have anything to do with you?" Nasim retorts.

"I was trying to keep a dead girl's secrets. But that doesn't make sense anymore, it only protects who killed her. I'm going to make this right by finding out who actually did kill my best friend, and according to Mikky, you're the smartest guy he knows, so I need your help." She looks like each word torn out of her is under duress.

"*My* help? Your brother can't be your Watson?" Nasim asks. He still hasn't looked at Mikky, but with the reference, Mikky starts to feel the toll of that.

"He doesn't have the specific skills I'm looking for," Kyla says smoothly. Mikky can sense that she's losing Nasim's attention, and she seems to too. She blurts out, "We're never going to be friends, but I'd love to go back to ignoring you after we figure this out. So . . . truce?"

For a moment Mikky is afraid Nasim's stubbornness will win out over his need to prove Rowan's innocence and he'll shut the door again. But Nasim's loyalty triumphs.

"Fine, truce," he declares, holding out his hand. Kyla shakes it once before she lets go, shoving hers back in her pocket. Nasim looks back over at Mikky and Mikky straightens immediately, called to attention. "And what do *you* have to say?" Nasim asks.

Mikky wipes his clammy palms on his jeans, trying to tear the nerves away, but they stick. This isn't something Lexapro can solve, for once. This is homegrown lovesickness.

Nasim folds his arms over his chest.

There's so much that Mikky wants to say, but he doubts that Nasim will want to hear it. *I hate your friend, I like you, you're stubborn, I like you, you're self-righteous, I like you, you don't listen to anything you don't want to hear, I like you, I think you might be right about Rowan but it's hard to acknowledge it over the other shit you were wrong about, I fucking like you.*

"I'm . . . not going to apologize for being on my sister's side," he says, and he tries to pretend that he doesn't see Kyla's head whip around. "But I will apologize for not hearing you out."

"Fine. I accept your apology. But that doesn't change anything," he bites out. Then he turns on his heel. "Come inside, you're making my house cold."

The Talebi home is nice and clean. It smells warm, if warm was a smell—like hot apple cider and bergamot. Just like the outside, everything looks newish. This is the home of a world-class chemist and the son following in her footsteps. Nasim doesn't lead them any farther than the formal living room, with hard sofas that Mikky's sure no one ever sits on and a piano he bets no one plays. The walls, though, they're a collage of Nasim's academic achievements. Pictures of him winning science fairs and perfect attendance awards and growing into who he is now.

Kyla barely gives them a glance, but Mikky could stare at

them for hours if he was allowed. Clearly, he isn't; Nasim nods toward the hard sofa where Kyla sits and Mikky joins her. Nasim sits across from them with a coffee table in between. It feels more like an ocean.

"So, you don't think it was Rowan anymore?" Nasim asks coolly.

"No. It's Florence Cook," Kyla declares. "All of it."

Nasim's mask slips and he leans forward. "I'm . . . I'm sorry?" he stammers.

Kyla is far more succinct in how she explains everything now that she's practiced on Mikky. She's even courteous enough to leave space for Nasim to declare, "I knew it," and, "Oh, I'm sure," whenever one of his theories about the Test Kitchen is proven correct. He is a lot more sober, though, when Kyla presents the emails that Erin had left behind, along with the translated note.

"Poison? Okay, so the products weren't ready. But she thought it was *intentional*?" Nasim asks.

"Maybe not intentional, but I think Florence lied to her and didn't care," Kyla says. "At the police station, I found out the Test Kitchens were Florence's idea. She had a lawyer there to tell me that she would give the go-ahead to start it again eventually. I'm supposed to give the products to the girls and report back."

"She wants you to fall in line and be a good little sycophant, just like Erin," Nasim says. "And Erin never said anything? Did as she was told, and then *charged* people for it. Impossibly evil, but smart."

Mikky waits for Kyla to defend Erin, but she nods slowly.

"It's deeply messed up," she acknowledges. "I had no idea."

"But she clearly wanted it to stop," Nasim mumbles under his breath, begrudgingly. "She wouldn't have printed the emails to show you if she didn't," he says, still entranced by it.

Mikky looks up, surprised by the grace that Nasim extends.

"She had this note in her touch-up bag, the one she carried around with her almost everywhere. She didn't want to leave it lying around," Kyla blurts out. "And she said she had something to talk to me about the next day. Maybe it was this."

Nasim nods his agreement. "Likely conclusion."

"We want to bring you some of the product to test. See what's in it," Mikky says.

Nasim rubs at his chin, brow furrowed, then he pales. "My mom works for them," he says quietly, like the thought has only just occurred to him.

"Did she work on GloMo?" Kyla asks. "That's what Erin was emailing Florence about."

Nasim frowns. "No. She's on the perfume development project that's supposed to launch in Q4 of 2026."

"Then she's not part of this particular aspect of Florence Cook's evil plot to poison the teenage girls of America. Congratulations," Kyla deadpans.

Nasim rolls his eyes. "Fine. I'll take a look at the product and I'll report back once I get a chance to test for toxins. But it's going to take some time."

"No," Mikky insists. "We don't have time. Not now that Rowan has been implicated. We need to do this now."

"I can't rush finding the composition of multiple makeup products, Mikky. That takes time and resources and I'm still only a student. I only have what's in our high school laboratory. You're going to have to be patient," Nasim says, like he's speaking to a small child.

Mikky rolls his eyes and nods. "I know, but I mean, we need to find out who Erin's killer is. We have a motive, but we don't have the killer."

"It's Florence Cook. I thought we established that," Kyla says.

Mikky nods. "Maybe, but we all know even if she gave the order, she doesn't do her own dirty work. Someone else did. Maybe the same person who told her that you and Erin were monetizing the Test Kitchens in the first place. Right?"

Kyla sits up straighter. "So, we have a mole," she whispers.

"Exactly," Mikky agrees. "You have to have another Test Kitchen with the exact same people that came to the Test Kitchen the night that Erin died. Tonight. One of them must be the mole *and* the person who probably killed her."

"Tonight is too soon. It's not enough time for me to test," Nasim protests again.

"It'll look suspicious if I do it tonight," Kyla agrees. "The lawyer warned me to wait until she gave the go-ahead again. But you're right, soon. Talebi, how long do you think you'll need?"

"At least a week," Nasim says immediately.

"Okay, then. A week. Then Mikky and I will run a Test Kitchen that Friday."

"And find the killer," Mikky adds.

"Then what do you plan to do?" Nasim asks like he's afraid to know.

Kyla does a gritted-teeth smile. "Make them suffer."

CHAPTER THIRTY-TWO

"Was it not understood that you're grounded?" Dad asks when they traipse into the house, the sun already long set.

Kyla and Mikky freeze in the foyer, exchanging narrow-eyed warnings not to say anything.

"It wasn't," Kyla says, kicking off her shoes by the door. "I've never been grounded before."

Mikky snorts. "Really? You're no Goody Two-shoes."

"I've just never been caught," Kyla mumbles, but not quietly enough for Dad not to hear. He folds his arms over his chest, but Mikky knows that he's not even mad. The lines in his forehead tell enough of the story—he's worried, beyond belief.

"You stayed out all night. On a school night," Dad accuses.

"At the Vaughns'. It's not like I was out partying," Kyla defends.

"So, the Vaughns kidnapped you, took your phone, tied you up, and *made* you ignore our calls all night?" Dad asks. His voice drips with sarcasm. It's in these moments that Mikky sees that maybe Kyla and Mikky *have* inherited more from their dad than their penchant for the macabre and a funeral home.

"Maybe . . . Cut her some slack, Dad?" Mikky suggests.

Dad points a finger at him. "You . . . *you* . . . you're lucky I don't ground you, too."

"I didn't even do anything wrong," Mikky protests.

"*You* nearly had a fistfight with one of your best friends in the middle of a police station," Dad sighs. Mikky winces, because . . . *touché*. "Would it *kill* either of you to let me know if you're going to be home later than usual? I don't really have many rules and I don't ask for much."

"That's fair," Mikky acknowledges. "Kyla drove me home today. We stopped at Fable Street Pantry."

Kyla slides along the floor to the kitchen and tosses her hair over her shoulder. "Also, flagging now that Mikky and I have plans next Friday night with our friends. Is that cool?"

"You two were *just* arguing," Dad says suspiciously. "And you're *grounded*."

"Shouldn't you be encouraging us to mend fences?" Mikky asks, leaning back on the counter.

Dad shakes his head again. "I have given you two so much leeway . . ."

"I'm not even in trouble, Dad. I told the police what they needed to know. We're not up to anything sneaky," Kyla says. It's a lie, but she undercuts it with a bit of truth when she says, without looking at Mikky at all, "I know that I haven't been easy since Erin died. I know Mikky came here because he thought I needed someone to lean on. And I didn't want to accept that. Now I do. I am. So. Can we hang out?" All that vulnerability, and *still*, she can't look Mikky in the eye when she admits it.

Dad deliberates for only a few hesitant seconds. "As long as it's none of that funny business that you got in trouble with Hamish about."

"I'm making cookies. You want any?" Kyla asks.

"Just two," Mikky says instinctively. Kyla gives him a knowing look, because she knows that he'll ask for two, and then balk at the second once he finishes the first, complaining that it's too sweet. But he'll get mad if there's only one. It hits Mikky suddenly that Kyla does still *understand* him. She gets him, and now he's finally starting to get the new her, too, even the prickly parts.

"So the two of you . . . you're good?" Dad asks again. Mikky thinks about that question. There were no real apologies between them. But there's still so much unfinished business to be taken care of first. Soon, Kyla will stop with the Test Kitchens, and they'll tell Dad about where she was getting the money, and they'll find a way to solve the problem of the second mortgage on the funeral home together.

When they've caught Erin's murderer.

Kyla stares at Mikky, like she's waiting for him to answer before she does. Mikky gets that. She's bared her soul enough for the day. You can push Kyla only so far.

"I think we're on our way," Mikky says to her, meeting her eyes.

Kyla looks at the ground, but he sees the corner of her mouth twitch.

Dad kisses Mikky's temple, and for now it's all enough.

Everything slows to a crawl the following week, the closer they creep to Friday. Day in and day out is a monotony of Mikky waking up at the crack of dawn and going to school as if he's not plotting to unmask Florence Cook and her patsy for Erin's murder. Every day, Kyla pretends that she is not affected by it all, like Mikky doesn't know she's jittery with purpose.

It doesn't help that his friends won't talk to him. Jason is doing his best to avoid Mikky, which means, in turn, he's avoiding *Kyla* to her not-so-secret disgruntlement. Despite working together, Nasim won't give him the time of day. Rowan still isn't back in school; their parents are keeping them out with all the suspicion around them, and the media's lenses like giant all-seeing eyes peering into their lives.

Every day, Mikky and Kyla drive into the parking lot where the media vans linger. Sometimes there are two or three, sometimes there are more. None of the news crews try to stop them anymore, but there's always the feeling that if either of them makes eye contact, they'll pounce. Others *do* stop, spinning narratives about Rowan and Peter and all the drama between them. Mikky can't help but think that part is a monster of Kyla's making.

The night before it all goes down, Mikky asks Kyla about it while she pops a pimple in the mirror, the bathroom door wide open. Mikky cringes as she finally busts the red swell on her cheek, white pus oozing. She looks relieved.

"So . . . the media. The cameras, you don't mind it?"

"I do," Kyla says. "But I think you might've been right. This could be a good thing now."

"Why?"

"We're gonna need everyone to hear about the shit show once we have proof so Cook can't cover it up. Come to my room," Kyla says after she washes her hands and marches back there, leaving the door open behind her.

Mikky hesitates over the threshold. He's been in here the once without Kyla, and he still hasn't told her. But he doesn't think it would be helpful to say anything now.

He stands awkwardly in the middle of her room, looking around, pretending as though he's seeing everything for the first time. But then Kyla goes to her vinyl shelves and pulls down a familiar crate, flipping it open. She tugs out her ledger and holds it up.

"You've seen this before?" Kyla asks.

Mikky looks at the ceiling. "Maybe."

"You snuck in here?" She doesn't sound . . . angry. More like she finds it funny.

"Nasim did and I called him out for overstepping," Mikky says. "And then I took pictures of the ledger."

"I can't believe you have a crush on him. Can't you make it go away?" Kyla demands, her voice still laced with amusement.

Mikky glowers at her. "And what about you and Jason?"

Kyla stops laughing. "What about me and Jason?"

"You know."

"I know what?"

"You came home in his clothes. As if Erin didn't have a full closet."

"Yes, let me put on my dead best friend's clothes," Kyla retorts.

"Don't act like you didn't leave clothes over there," he says. "Look. I won't say anything about Jason, you don't say anything about Nasim."

"Fine."

"Fine." And then Mikky can't help himself: "He's, like, in love with you."

"Shut the fuck up," Kyla says as she puts a Metric vinyl on her record player and starts it up. "Help I'm Alive" is shockingly apt, and Mikky wonders at the skill it takes to curate the soundtrack of your life. "Feel free to sit."

Mikky gingerly sets himself on the edge of her bed and watches as she reaches underneath, dragging out a flat storage case. She pops it open, revealing her treasure trove of leftover product. "So, we need a plan," he says.

"We have a plan. Have a Test Kitchen. Find out who suddenly has a massive influx of cash. Identify the killer. Turn the killer in to the police," Kyla rattles off.

"Sure. But how are we going to stop Florence from finding out what we're up to? We have to expose Cook, too," Mikky says.

"She'll probably find out the Kitchen is happening. She just won't know why," Kyla says. She sits down in a squat, elbows perched atop her knees. "And we're going to keep it that way until we have all the evidence we need. So, let's focus on the first part of the plan. Finding Erin's killer."

Mikky can tell that's the part of the plan that Kyla needs most to go well.

"Okay, fine. So, this Test Kitchen, who are we inviting? Has your list changed any since that night?" he asks.

"We had one new girl. She goes to private school and she was mutuals with Erin. We'd just finished the vetting process, but she couldn't get out of some family obligations that night," Kyla says. "I can soft block her from my account. After that, the list will be the same as that night. We don't add people very often."

Mikky nods. "Great. And you invite people through . . ."

"I need to post. Will you take a picture of me?" Kyla asks.

And that's how Mikky finds himself as acting photographer. Kyla sits on top of the product, her long limbs tucked against her chest, her eyes big and baleful as she looks up into the camera. When he tries to squat to get on her level, she commands him to stay seated and put the lens on .5.

"Are you sure that's the one you want to go with?" Mikky asks as he lies backward on her bed, staring at her with his head hanging off the side.

Kyla purses her lips as she fiddles with her phone, staring down at it.

"I'm posting now," Kyla says.

"What's the caption?" Mikky asks.

Kyla doesn't answer out loud. She twists the phone around so that he can read it, and being upside down, Mikky has to squint to focus on the words.

> FINAL TEST KITCHEN OF THE SEASON.
> EVERYTHING MUST GO.

CHAPTER THIRTY-THREE

As they enter Florence Cook's lake house, Kyla warns Mikky once and only once: "Don't interfere. No one should know what we're really looking for."

This is Kyla's domain, and Mikky will play the supporting role. He follows her painstaking directions as they set up for his very first Test Kitchen. There isn't as much ceremony to it as he once thought. Kyla opens up her box of products and lays out an assortment, organized by function, atop a soft, crushed velvet tablecloth that she throws over the crystal coffee table. Eyeliner and eyeshadow palettes to the top left corner. Lip pencils, lip plumpers, and lip glosses at the top right. A wide range of Cook Cosmetics' iconic product—the Radiant AirTouch foundation. Highlighter. Concealer. Setting spray. All in that perfect, soft-powder-green packaging.

Mikky can't help but notice the products that *don't* go onto the table, that signature green is veined with a light blue and gold, like cracks of light filtering through. Some of the very product that they passed along to Nasim.

"I don't want to put the GloMo out, but I think they'll ask for it," Kyla mumbles.

"Then we'll look for the people who *don't* ask for it. If they don't ask for GloMo, it's suspicious. It means they know something's up with it. They might be who hurt Erin," Mikky insists.

"You're right," Kyla says, even if she doesn't sound nearly as sure as Mikky is for once.

The doorbell rings, cracking through the tension, and Kyla jumps up, sliding around on her socks.

"They're here already?" Mikky asks.

"No, of course not," Kyla says, opening the door, and the very last person that Mikky could have expected steps through the door.

"Here's your order," Peter Moore says, holding a large brown paper bag that clinks as he steps in, not bothering to take off his dusty shoes. "Now, where's my money?"

"*What* are you doing here?" Mikky blurts out.

Peter blinks slowly, taking Mikky in, and then says, "So, you know about this, then? Are you Kyla's new partner in crime?"

Mikky sputters, looking between Kyla and Peter in disbelief. He assumed that Peter knew about the Test Kitchens. Of course he did. But Mikky had not expected him to be *involved*.

Kyla rolls her eyes. "He's our alcohol supplier. I don't like having to work directly with Indigo's brother. He's a creep."

"I heard you did last time, though. Trying to cut me out now that I know everything?" Peter grumbles as he shoves the bag at Mikky. Mikky only just manages to grab it and pull the bottles to his chest. "I really was just some kind of joke to you two, huh?"

"Peter, don't be like that," Kyla sighs. "I'm only doing this one last time. I asked you so I can pay you for your services. So, we're even."

"We're *not* even, Kyla," Peter snaps as he closes the door behind him. He leans back against it, like he doesn't want to go any farther into the house. "Did she start up with me first? Or with them?"

Mikky understands now—this isn't about money, it's about Rowan and Erin.

"With them. You were already helping us out with the alcohol supply. You were the basketball captain. She wanted them to be jealous and you were good for her image," Kyla says. She doesn't say it to hurt Peter, but Mikky can see that it does, beneath the macho bravado that Peter pastes on his face.

His stiff upper lip trembles under the weight of how hard it is to keep his composure.

"And I bet neither of you felt bad about it, huh?" Peter says.

Kyla reaches into her back pocket and it's just like before—a sharp wind being knocked out of Mikky—when he watches her count out six hundred-dollar bills from her wad of cash and hold it out in front of her.

Peter scoffs as he looks at what's offered. "You . . . are you trying to *buy* my cooperation?"

"I'm trying to end our business relationship on a high. What happened between you and Erin isn't my business," Kyla says.

"Yes, it is! Was!" Peter shouts. "You *knew* that it was Rowan that reported me, and you knew why they had a beef with me, and you didn't tell me until it fit your agenda. I bet you would have let everyone believe what they wanted to believe about me if you weren't worried about me telling the cops about the Test Kitchen. You're a bitch, Kyla. Even now. She's dead and you're still Erin's girl through and through."

Kyla narrows her eyes. "What do you expect me to say, Peter? That I told her to ditch Rowan, that you were the better choice? Well, I did. Erin didn't listen."

He doesn't look like he believes Kyla. Mikky isn't sure if he would either. Peter reaches forward, takes his hush money, and stuffs it in his jeans pocket. "Erin and Rowan deserved each other. Two selfish *users*. I hope Rowan goes down for her murder like they tried to pin it on me. Have a nice life, Kyla." Peter sneers as he leaves. Mikky quickly turns the dead bolt after him, in case he comes back.

Kyla folds her arms over her chest and exhales slowly. Mikky frowns down at the smudge of dirt left over from Peter's sneakers.

"Did you really try to convince Erin to break up with Rowan?" Mikky asks.

"Yes. I didn't like them. But not because Peter was a better choice for her. He was a better business choice. A smarter one. Like I said, I don't like having to deal directly with Indigo's brother, and Peter already knew what we were up to. I didn't want him to feel a type of way if he found out," Kyla says.

"Well, evidently that didn't work in your favor," Mikky says.

Kyla nods. "Clearly not." She sighs, and says, "Come on. Help me set out the wine. Now our *actual* guests will be here any minute. Look alive."

When the Test Kitchen finally starts, the wine bottles sit next to crystal wineglasses that look like they cost too much to replace and the foyer is stuffed with twenty-two people toeing their shoes off, their roaring chatter setting Mikky on edge. He hits his vape once for courage.

Erin's killer is most likely one of these twenty-two people. Some of them Mikky knows—Sabrina, Indigo, and Alicia stick out to him most. Many of them he doesn't. Kyla told him little about the others, just that some of them go to Prophets Lake

High School but a lot of them are from neighboring towns and private schools, and quite a few of them have parents that actually *work* at Cook. Not at the research levels, but others.

According to Kyla, that had been Erin's idea—except now, it's more suspect. Maybe that had been Florence Cook's idea, to keep their little beta program as insular as possible.

The most important part was that whoever was invited had the necessary funds to do what they wanted them to do—to bid.

Mikky sits in the corner and watches Kyla work in her element. She's quick to auction off a few eye-shadow palettes and highlighters. Every sale comes with a free foundation. It seems to mean something to Kyla, for her to be able to do that.

As she goes through the motions, Mikky keeps watch and listens. Everyone's a suspect, but Kyla wants him to look for certain behaviors. Anyone who asks about the Test Kitchen logistics is to be analyzed. Anyone who has more money than usual is to be assessed. And *anyone* who *doesn't* ask about GloMo is to be investigated. Kyla has already directed his eye to a few early GloMo loyalists, seeing if they change their stripes.

Gwen Milton, the daughter of a Cook Cosmetics' executive. Eddie Keating, the champion debater with a cardiac surgeon for a mother. Riley and Reese Newhouse, twins who board at a nearby school. And Alicia. Mikky hates the look on Kyla's face when she forces her friend's name from between her teeth, but she does it, grim-faced.

"Remember this is an everything-must-go warehouse sale. We have some old favorites too. This is a discontinued lipstick line. Matte finish. Long-lasting. Must be used with the liner or it bleeds. You've all swatched the tester. I'm only interested in it going as a set. We'll start at a hundred dollars," Kyla says. She has her ledger open in front of her, pencil poised over the paper.

"A hundred is steep for something older, Kyla," Indigo Glass blurts out. She looks around nervously, like she's afraid she's about to be outbid.

"And I already told you, it's been discontinued, and I won't be doing this for a while," Kyla interrupts. "Anyone going for a hundred?"

"Why exactly won't you be doing this again?" someone asks.

A logistical question. Mikky narrows his eyes at the girl. The one who gets the lead in all the plays. She gives him a weirded-out look, but Mikky takes a mental note of her anyway.

Kyla glares. "We're having a restructure. Don't worry about it."

Taylor Witherspoon, another private schooler with a Cook Cosmetics parent, lifts up his hand. He has the best makeup look in the room, and he knows it. He smiles with bright blue lips. "Two hundred dollars."

That seems enough to stir up some competition. It's not so much different from a yard sale, Mikky tries to justify to himself. Sure, Kyla is price gouging a bunch of students, but most of them look like they have too much money for Mikky to care. He can even tell himself that it's redistribution of wealth. And then he remembers where they are. And what Kyla is selling. And even if she didn't know it before, how what she's selling could be *dangerous*. Erin's emails called out the GloMo, but who knows how far it all goes?

Mikky watches patiently as the bids creep up. Indigo Glass is always looking around nervously but never takes part. Some of the girls, including the Newhouse twins, lose interest halfway through. But Taylor is rapt with attention, even when his friend tugs on his sleeve and tells him to join her in the bathroom with a shifty sideways glance that Mikky doesn't want to ask about.

"Sold for four twenty-five. No credit," Kyla says.

"I have it in smaller bills," the boy says, pulling out a fattened wallet, waving it at her, the monogrammed LV all over the front and back of the black leather.

"Small bills? That's a change," Kyla says, raising an eyebrow. She doesn't look at Mikky, but he gets the vibe immediately. That's unusual, then.

Taylor rolls his eyes. "Don't tell me you're getting *picky* about money now."

Kyla sniffs, holding out her hand, not even bothering to count the money.

"What about the GloMo line?" Gwen Milton complains, too loudly, clearly miffed about losing out to Taylor in the bidding war.

Kyla frowns. "We're not pushing that today, Gwen."

"You promise exclusive products, and you're not even going to show us more of the line that's coming out next month?" Gwen presses. "I haven't even had a chance to try out the brow serum."

"I really wanted more of the foundation," Riley Newhouse sighs. "I'm purging from this retinol I'm using, and if I could *stop* using the retinol, that'd be great."

Taylor Witherspoon sits taller. "Wait, I didn't get any last time. I want to try it too."

"See," Gwen pushes, lips curling back over her teeth. "We want GloMo."

The declaration feels like a hammer to a dam. Suddenly, everyone is speaking over one another, each customer demanding their own favorites. Eddie Keating wants more of that defunct palate from last time. The theater girl needs a limited-edition winter lipstick that really popped on stage last year. The Newhouse sisters have seen rumors online about a new blush set and want to know if Kyla has that yet. Lydia needs the old formulation of a primer—the gym gets too hot and sweaty during games and the new formulation isn't as good. And Gwen sits in it all, thrilled that she's gotten her way.

Mikky doesn't need to look at Kyla to know that she's three seconds from eviscerating Gwen fucking Milton.

But Gwen must not be able to tell because she adds in: "You've really fallen off since Erin."

Kyla stills. "Excuse me?" she asks, tonelessly.

"When Erin was still in charge, we had a way wider range of product available. I've already heard that there are samples of Cook's fragrance. My dad said they're getting ready to show it off in the shareholders' meeting next month. Erin would've had that for us," Gwen insists. There's no rhyme or reason to the mundanity of her cruelty. It just is, which only sends frustration spiraling through Mikky.

"That's enough," he says quietly.

Gwen sniffs, casting a bored look over at Mikky, then addresses the room at large. "You can't think I'm wrong. Am I being crazy?"

Mikky needs only a cursory glance to see that some of them agree. Even Sabrina and Alicia are considering the girl's words.

"I didn't think so," Gwen says, satisfied. "This isn't what

we signed up for. This isn't charity work, Kyla. We signed up for exclusivity and early access and the best. And that includes GloMo. Erin got that. That's why she was a brand ambassador. Erin—"

"You don't know what Erin would have done. You. Didn't. Know. Her," Kyla snarls.

Startled, Gwen sniffs but sits up taller, folding her arms over her chest. Kyla stands suddenly, her fingers dancing at her sides, like she's not sure if she wants to clench them into fists or pick at her cuticles.

"I'm not Erin," Kyla declares. "The Test Kitchen is under new management. So, put up or shut the *fuck* up."

She throws down her notebook, like she's disgusted by it. Mikky jerks to follow her. "Kyla," he starts.

"We're taking a brief recess," Kyla says like she hasn't heard him. "I need a moment."

Mikky follows her out of the living room. The crowd barely waits before they're gossiping amongst themselves, side-eyeing Kyla. Mikky follows her into the hallway before she turns around and puts a hand against his chest, stopping him in his tracks.

"I need a moment from you, too," she says. She won't meet his eyes and her breathing comes slow and deliberate.

"Kyla, that was . . . you're not okay," Mikky murmurs.

Kyla frowns. "I really need you to give me a moment," she forces out. "Stick to the plan. *Please.*"

Mikky came to Prophets Lake to help Kyla. To help her grieve. To help her emotionally. This is the first time she's expressed exactly what she needs from him. Mikky gives a jerky nod and steps back.

"Thank you," she mumbles as she turns and disappears down the hall, off deeper into the lake house that she seems to know like the back of her hand.

Mikky sighs and turns back to the living room. Some of the Test Kitchen attendees have scattered, including Gwen. He scoops up Kyla's notebook and holds it tight under his arm. He doesn't want anyone seeing anything they shouldn't.

Mikky starts to wander himself, trying to match names to faces as he sees the pockets of friend groups. It's hard to keep track of them all, of who's important, and of who may have connections to Florence Cook *and* Erin. But Gwen's definitely off the list after that show. Loud and annoying about GloMo. Same with at least one of the Newhouse twins.

Mikky's head spins with the possibilities as he goes into the kitchen, searching for her, only to find Alicia already there.

Alicia, one of the only people who had kept silent as they'd all argued over GloMo.

"Hey . . . Alicia, are you okay?" Mikky asks.

She looks up, her eyes red rimmed, and downs her glass of red wine, staining her mouth and teeth pink. She smiles shakily, and then seems to realize the foundations of that smile aren't so sound. She overcorrects, and everything about her brightens too hard, too much, to the point that it all looks painful. Especially her skin.

"I'm fine," Alicia says. She grinds her teeth, looking down at the marble countertop of the island. "I just . . . thought that there would be more of the GloMo. I really need to clear my skin. And it hasn't been working."

Mikky swallows.

"It hasn't?" he asks, even though of course he *knows* it hasn't.

"I was having a flare-up before and Erin convinced me to buy it, so I did. And it was working at first, but then it wasn't, so I started using more and it got worse. I have really sensitive skin. And now I . . . don't know what to do. So I keep going back and forth, using it or not. Sometimes it helps, mostly it doesn't," Alicia admits. "But I don't want to go back on the steroids I was using. It's . . . it's embarrassing."

There's something so vulnerable about her. She may be desperate but she doesn't have the teeth to kill Erin. Or the stomach. And even though she hadn't participated in the demands for GloMo, she clearly doesn't know about it. This isn't fear of being found out or revenge. This is shame.

"You should tell your parents you need to go to the dermatologist again," he says gently. "You want to feel good in your skin, Alicia. That's not a crime."

"Yeah . . . ," Alicia mumbles.

Mikky takes a step back and disappears from the kitchen, wandering down the hallway. He imagined this home would be sterile. Rich people's homes are always sterile. Everything brand-new, which Mikky doesn't get. He doesn't know how people can manage to buy things that haven't had a life to them already, a story. But this house is different.

There are pictures on the walls, documenting a girl's life. On the lake shore. In the Tobacco Fields. Her high school graduation—not from Prophets Lake High School of course, but a respectable boarding school nearby. Her college graduation from UPenn. The launch party for her cosmetics line. These are all similar to the things that Dad has on the walls at home. But there's a key difference. There's something so much more profoundly lonely about these photos.

There's no one else in them.

Not until Florence Cook is an adult. When she's an adult, there are many people in the photos. Powerful people. Each one more than the last. The mayor. The governor. A junior senator. The president of the New York Stock Exchange.

But no one *personal*. There's no emotion in any of them.

Mikky slowly presses the first door open.

He blinks until his eyes adjust in the weak moonlight. Florence Cook's office. He slowly walks along the bookshelves, looking at the number of chemistry books, rounding to her massive, old light-wood desk. There's only one photo here.

There is Florence Cook in tweed, surrounded by men and women in white lab coats. Cook Cosmetics Laboratory, her pride and joy, her baby.

Mikky picks up the photo and looks down into Florence's expression. He tries to decide if this is a woman that would have a teenage girl killed for finding the secrets in her blank face.

Yes. Yes, she is.

His thoughts are interrupted by a sharp knock on the open door, and he fumbles the photo, juggling it from hand to hand to avoid dropping it.

"Oh my God, be *careful*."

Nasim looks annoyed by Mikky's clumsiness, plush mouth twisted and his eyes near rolling into the back of his head. Mikky gently replaces the photo, opening his mouth, and then closing it while he tries to figure out what to say.

The words he settles on: "You're here."

"I'm here," Nasim says.

Mikky can't say that he missed Nasim, even if it's true. It would be humiliating. So, he asks, as businesslike as possible, "Did you . . . did you find anything out?"

"I had to get permission from Mr. Reynolds to stay after school to work in the lab and had to forge a note from my mom saying that I'm doing an independent studies project for an internship at Cook," Nasim says slowly.

"Oh, that's . . . extensive," Mikky says. He hadn't really given it much thought how Nasim would get access to the chemistry laboratory.

"Yeah. And then I only had enough time to test a few products from the GloMo line because I had to do a few tests on each to isolate the ingredients, but . . . there are PFAS in the cosmetics," Nasim declares. He looks at Mikky like he's supposed to know what those are, but Mikky stares blankly, rocking from side to side.

"And that's . . . bad?" he asks, taking the bait.

Nasim huffs. "Fantastic."

Mikky's hackles rise. "What?"

"You didn't bother researching what shouldn't be in it?" Nasim asks. "You really left me to do all the work?"

"You're not doing all the work," Mikky spits. "I knew that you would know this stuff better than me. That this is your wheelhouse."

"You could've made the effort—"

"I don't have time for this, Nasim," Mikky says. "Just tell me what PFAS are so I can go tell Kyla."

Nasim crosses his arms. "They're used in a lot of products.

Like, a lot. Cosmetics is just a small section, but they're meant to improve product consistency and texture. Also give this airbrushed sheen when applied."

"Sounds like something someone would want in their product," Mikky says slowly.

"Yeah. And a lot of people use them. It's a cost and time cutter because they already know it works. Less research than trying to accomplish the same thing the healthier way. But PFAS are not good for you. They're man-made forever chemicals and linked to all kinds of health issues. Birth defects, thyroid issues, cancer," Nasim explains. "I tested for high fluorine levels, which indicate the presence of PFAS. I found it in the undereye gel serum, the tinted moisturizer sunscreen combo, and the moisturizer primer. All foundational products for the GloMo line."

"How do they think they could possibly get away with this without destroying their clean-beauty ethos?" Mikky asks.

"You don't have to technically get FDA approval before you put a product to market. They can put anything in it and lie about it until they get caught. And if only a few people have reactions to them? That's not enough to make real noise," Nasim says.

Mikky shakes his head. "That's why they developed the Test Kitchens, to see whether the reactions would be bad enough to get them in trouble. But testing this out on *kids*? That's so fucked."

"Oh, so you can use your brain?" Nasim says under his breath.

Mikky snaps, "Hey, lay off."

"Lay off?" Nasim demands. "You're impossible, do you get that?"

"Me?" Mikky balks. "I'm an open book. You're the one who likes to play games. Giving me the cold shoulder and shit. Look, thank you for doing me a solid, but if you could get me those test results on paper or something, you can be on your way. And feel free to tell Rowan that they can thank the Graveses for getting them out of trouble. Since that's all you care about."

Nasim stills, staring at Mikky for a long moment.

"You think I did this—lied to my mom, to my teacher, and did all these tests—for Rowan?" Nasim asks, his voice trembling. "After all of this, you still don't get it?"

"No, I get it. You've made it very clear that you don't give a fuck about my sister or me."

"You're right. I don't give a fuck about your sister," Nasim agrees, shaking out his hands. "But I definitely give a fuck about you."

And then Nasim crashes into him and presses his lips to Mikky's. The world goes sideways and silent. Mikky stands there, his nose pressed awkwardly up against Nasim's, his teeth catching in the plush of Nasim's bottom lip. He's not sure where to put his hands, especially since he wants to put them everywhere, and then he has to pull back because he has to *breathe*, but he only separates himself a little bit.

Bewildered, Nasim takes a step back in until his chest is pressed against Mikky's and he slides a hand over Mikky's shoulder, fingers gliding into the nape of Mikky's neck, burying deep into the curls. This time Mikky leans back down and kisses Nasim properly, their mouths moving together and catching a rhythm. Nasim's lips are slightly chapped, and his fingers are burning, but his bony hips feel right in Mikky's hands, and he tugs him closer, so close, as close as he can.

Nasim pulls back first this time. "You're infuriating," he says.

"You're arrogant," Mikky retorts.

"You're too trusting."

"You're self-righteous."

Then Nasim looks so fond, a profound warmth hits Mikky in the chest. A kiss with a fist. "I like you so much," he says. He doesn't sound vulnerable when he says it, not like he's ripping himself raw to do it. It's like the answer on a chemistry test. A fact with evidence surrounding it.

"I like you too," Mikky agrees, and then they're kissing again.

Distantly, he remembers that he didn't want to get into a relationship with anyone in his senior year. Clearly, past-Mikky had no idea what he was talking about. Past-Mikky is a liar.

Mikky isn't sure how long they kiss, hands roaming. At one point they stumble closer to the desk and Mikky ends up sitting on it with Nasim sliding between his legs, hands dragging up his thighs. Time doesn't matter, only the way their mouths move together. It's why he's so disoriented when they're interrupted by a door opening followed by a slightly too loud voice that says, "Oops! Sorry!"

Nasim pulls back, eyes glazed over, mouth kiss-swollen. Mikky feels a rush of satisfaction that he has done that to him. Then Nasim turns, still caught in the apex of Mikky's thighs.

"Oh, Lydia, hi," he says awkwardly.

"Nasim Talebi," Lydia singsongs.

Mikky looks over Nasim's shoulder and frowns at the girl. She looks ghostly in this light, like she has too much powder on and it's creating a flashback in real time. There's a faint dusting of something beneath her nose that Mikky doesn't want to give too much thought to.

"How's your friend?" Lydia drawls. "Ro-*wan*? Bet they regret breaking up with me now they're being accused of murdering their sidepiece."

"Uh, they're fine," Nasim falters.

"Fine?" Lydia blurts out. She gets closer and Mikky can see her blown pupils, only a sliver of hazel still visible. "I can't believe they get to be fine, while I am still . . . *fucked*."

She has a wineglass in her hand. It's empty. Well.

"I'm really sorry about . . . everything," Nasim says slowly, picking at the rips in Mikky's jeans. "You didn't deserve that."

"No. I *didn't*," Lydia barks. "I didn't deserve any of this. But Rowan *definitely* deserved Erin. The two of them can go rot in hell where they deserve to be. All of you can."

"We didn't do anything to you," Mikky defends. All the floaty feelings from kissing Nasim have been chased away now.

"No?" Lydia drawls. "Just people like you. The *popular* people."

Mikky has never been accused of being popular in his life. He snorts, rolling his eyes. "Come *on*—"

"No!" Lydia shouts. "You don't get to laugh. Your sister is the most popular girl in school and she's doing illegal shit and she talks to the cops any way she wants and doesn't get in trouble. Who turns what is a literal interrogation back on a cop?"

Mikky frowns. "What are you even talking about? The cops?" he asks. Because there's no way Lydia would know how things went down at the station. No way. Except . . .

Lydia's still ranting. "People like me are just a joke, huh? Collateral. You know I had sex with Rowan for the first time *right* before they broke up with me. Like two weeks before. And when I asked why they wanted to break up? I didn't even get a real answer. I was a good girlfriend. And they dumped me for *her*."

Nasim swallows hard. "Yeah, that . . . that really sucks. That's really bad," he says.

Lydia continues like she's barely heard his acknowledgment. "God, Erin was so nice when I joined. Her boyfriend sees that *my* partner dumped me and then suddenly I'm invited to her special little club to make me feel better. I've known Peter forever, I thought he was my friend. Clearly, he *wasn't*."

Mikky finally peels away from Nasim. "Lydia, of course he was your friend," he says, soft and urgent. "But what did you mean about the cops? Kyla sassing the cops?"

Lydia is barely listening to him. "Erin told me that Peter told her what happened and she felt *so* sorry, and that I deserved so much better. And the whole time she's *laughing* at me. They thought I was a huge joke, all three of them. But they got what they deserved. All of them. Erin's dead. Everyone knows the person I'm in love with is actually an asshole. And Peter . . . well, he found out why you shouldn't fuck with your friends."

Nasim creeps forward. "What did you mean by Peter got what he deserved?"

"And the cops. *What* do you know about how my sister speaks to the cops?" Mikky adds urgently, leaning over Nasim's shoulder.

Lydia's rage dissipates and she sags like a balloon with all the air gone out. She looks down at the ground and sniffles, absolutely miserable, but says nothing.

Suddenly, Nasim rears back. "*You* reported Peter. Because you thought he was setting you up to be humiliated."

It sounds like motive. It sounds like Lydia would be so *easy* for Florence Cook to convince.

"Yeah. I did. My sister is a police officer. Officer Castellanos.

She got married last year," Lydia says, rubbing her arm.

Mikky's brain zings. Lydia. *Lydia*. She'd been the one who reported Peter, and she'd been the one to tell her sister about the Test Kitchens too.

"Did you hurt Erin?" Mikky asks, stalking closer, towering over Lydia.

Her moon eyes are big and shiny now, pathetically sad as they cast down.

"Look at me, Lydia!" Mikky bites out. "Did Florence Cook put you up to this? Did you hurt Erin?"

Lydia frowns. "I don't know Florence Cook."

"I don't believe you," Mikky insists. "How did you know about Rowan and Erin then?"

Lydia shakes her head. "I *don't* know Florence! And I didn't hurt Erin! I found out that Rowan was hooking up with her in June, right before school ended last year. I saw their car once when I was leaving here so I stayed out of sight and I . . . watched them go up to the house. And I watched them kiss in the parking lot too, after they were done. I don't even know what they saw in her. She was *mean*. She'd basically avoid them anytime they were at school. Pretended that they were invisible. She never even let Rowan drive her home. She'd make them leave and then go back to the house to wait.

"At first I thought it was a one-time thing. But it kept happening, after every Test Kitchen. I watched them show up when everyone had left. Then that night I saw Erin texting Rowan about *me* when she thought I wasn't looking and I *knew* that they didn't just dump me for her. They cheated on me. And she was inviting me here to make fun of me. I couldn't take it anymore so I left early, went to my car and cried. Eventually, I saw Rowan show up to fuck her, I guess. I waited until I saw them leave. Erin walked them to their car, kissed them, and then she went back, and I was going to confront Rowan once they were alone, but I couldn't. I just went home and cried some more. I *didn't* hurt Erin."

Mikky's head spins faster and faster with the onslaught of new information, but one detail finally surfaces from the rest.

Wait. *Wait.*

"Lydia!" Mikky starts.

"What?"

"You said Rowan didn't drive Erin home?"

Her red-painted mouth turns down at the corners. "No, they never did. They always left alone."

"Then who usually took Erin home?" Mikky asks.

Mikky always assumed that Rowan would drive her home after they hooked up. Erin couldn't drive. She'd failed her test more than once. It's the reason he initially suspected them. But if what Lydia says is true, that means someone else could have seen Erin the night she died. Someone not at the Test Kitchen.

Lydia shrugs. "I don't know. Someone in a Wrangler. It was nice. Custom green rims." She swipes furiously at her tears, glowering at Nasim like he's a physical stand-in for Rowan, before she storms away.

A Wrangler.

Mikky knows someone who drives a Wrangler with custom hunter-green rims. One person.

"Okay, so the last person to see Erin drives a Wrangler," Nasim says brightly. "We just have to figure out who that is. We can go check the parking lot."

"I know who it is," Mikky says dully. He stares down at his hands. They've doubled. Tripled. No, his vision is blurring.

When he looks up, Nasim's smile has dimmed.

"You do?" Nasim asks.

Mikky s stumbles to the door, cracking his shoulder against the doorframe. It's jarring, but he reorients himself around the pain.

"Kyla!" he calls as he jogs downstairs, looking around. "Kyla!"

Alicia peeks her head out from the living room, looking at him with a raised eyebrow. She's struggling with a bottle of wine, not quite able to wedge the cork out of the neck.

"Mikky, she didn't tell you?" Alicia asks. "Kyla's gone."

CHAPTER THIRTY-FOUR

Kyla can't breathe. She wheezes as she grasps at her dignity like straws. Her pockets are heavy, like there are rocks in them, but it's only stacks of cash. She drags her hands over her chest, clutching at her shoulders, her breasts, her neck, attempting to reassure herself that she is here. That she still exists in her own skin, even when she wants to crawl out of it. Her own skin is smothering her. Kyla can't catch her breath. She can't *breathe.*

Every inhale stops before it starts, hitching in her throat, releasing with a loud keen, as she stumbles around the back deck. Her sweat-slick palms slide along the railing and she slowly sinks to her knees, pressing her forehead to the rungs in an attempt to ground herself. There is no salt air to cut through, not from their man-made lake. Just musty earth and algae. Kyla was raised on this air and now it's suffocating her, making her go light-headed.

This town is *suffocating* her. She needs more than the moment she asked Mikky for. Her lips are tingling and her heartbeat is rushing loud in her ears, so loud, she can't even hear the music from inside anymore. Kyla lets her legs dangle through the rungs her hands are clutching.

The feeling ends slowly. Crawling away like a beast and sinking beneath her skin again. This is the haunting of her dreams, but Kyla's not sleepy. Not anything like it.

Is this what Mikky feels every day? Is this what her *mother*—

Kyla shuts the thought down, reaching for her phone tucked away in her back pocket. She opens her messages with Erin. She hasn't forgotten, but it's muscle memory. After a haunting, Kyla is supposed to talk to Erin.

Erin's last message to her wasn't words.

It's a picture.

It's Kyla, not paying attention. She's laughing, spinning on the deck she sits on now, dressed in shorts and a borrowed T-shirt. She's staring at the sky, the sun catching on the champagne highlighter on her cheeks. This is how Erin saw Kyla. She looks ethereal. She looks loved. She looks a way she's sure she'll never feel again.

Kyla hasn't posted this picture. She doesn't think she ever will.

"I hate you," Kyla whispers.

She types out the words and presses send. It goes through.

No one has canceled her phone line.

I hate you. She sends it again.

"I *hate* you," Kyla says. Once more with feeling. "I *hate* you."

She hates that Erin kept secrets from her when she thought she never would. She hates that it's only after Erin is gone that Kyla learns how deep those secrets ran. And even more, Kyla hates how it makes her *doubt*, that despite what she said to Gwen, she might not have known Erin at all either. She hates how afraid that makes her. And she hates how she doesn't mean what she's writing.

The fury that pumps through her, sharing space with every

other function of her body, wells to the surface. It doesn't dissipate the love, a love so strong that Kyla tried to tuck every part of Erin inside her, even the worst parts, because she couldn't deal with a world without her. Kyla wishes that she could *stop* loving Erin because then maybe it would stop trying to eat her alive.

"If you're gone," Kyla whispers, "then why are you still right next to me?"

Erin is *always* there. Erin with all her snark and charm. Kyla is never alone but so *lonely*.

"I don't think I'll ever forgive you," she says, like Erin actually *is* right next to her. She doesn't mind if she seems crazy. Everyone thinks she's crazy already, whatever that word even means. She's okay with proving them right. "But I'll always want to."

Kyla lies down on her back and stares up into the sky. She's never had aspirations of living in the big city. Not like Mikky does. She would miss the stars too much.

She and Erin used to lie in the backyard and look at the stars. Jason would bring them inside when they fell asleep out there. He'd hoist Erin onto his back and take Kyla's hand. A good brother.

Jason said that he knew everything. Kyla hadn't believed him then, but she believes him now. He never had to rediscover Erin like Mikky has had to rediscover Kyla. He'd known her ugly parts and loved them all, because he was her *brother*. He was there, from dawn to dusk. At all hours. Even the late ones like this.

Kyla doesn't stop looking at the stars even as her mind seems to freeze.

Even the late ones.

Her hands shake.

"Like you *always* drove Erin home, even when it was late."

That's what Mrs. Vaughn said, the night she begged to stay over. And Kyla knows Erin wouldn't let Rowan drive her home.

Kyla thought they invited everyone who could have seen Erin that night. Except they didn't. Once Rowan left, Erin would have needed a ride home. The only people she would have asked were Kyla and . . . Jason.

Erin hadn't been found until the morning. If Rowan had killed her, Jason, so dutiful and so loving, would have showed up to drive her home like always, and he would've found her body.

But he *hadn't*.

Kyla goes to her text thread with Jason. The last thing she'd sent: Good luck at your meet or whatever. He'd responded: You think you're funny. And then a heart. A heart she didn't want to think about then and definitely doesn't now.

She calls him. It rings and rings and rings and rings. Then the voicemail prompts.

"We need to talk," is all Kyla says. And then she hangs up.

Kyla could wait. She should wait. He's probably at the afterparty. The soccer match should be over by now.

She doesn't wait. She calls the Vaughns' house phone. They're the only family she knows that still has a landline. It doesn't ring for nearly as long.

"Vaughn Residence."

"Mrs. Vaughn?" Kyla asks steadily.

"Kyla Graves," Mrs. Vaughn drawls. Kyla can't see her, but she hears the slur in her vowels. She's tipsy, on her way to drunk, for sure. "It's late. Late, late, late."

"I know. But . . . I wanted to know if Jason was home," Kyla says.

"Why?" the woman growls out. Her vocal cords have to grate to make that sound, vibrating together painfully.

"I need . . . I need to talk to him," Kyla says delicately. "Actually, Mrs. Vaughn, I need to talk to *you*. I need you." She has said this to her before. When she got her first foundation, when she had her first period, her first dance. "I need you."

For a long second Kyla thinks that the call has dropped. And then Mrs. Vaughn says, "Erin is dead, Kyla. What else is there for you to talk to any of us about?"

The phone clicks. And the call ends.

CHAPTER THIRTY-FIVE

Three missed calls from Mikky.

Kyla stares down at her phone screen, drumming her free fingers against the steering wheel. She tried to pick up the last time but Mikky ended the call first. She wonders what he could have possibly found out, but he doesn't leave a voicemail.

She prepares to text him that she's fine, when she gets a notification. This one isn't another call. It's a voice memo.

Kyla doesn't hesitate to press play.

Mikky's voice fills the hearse: "Kyla. Kyla, where are you? I found something out. Rowan's ex, Lydia, is the one who reported Peter to the police. *Lydia.* And she said that they deserved to be in hell. Rowan and Erin. She hates all of you. She . . . I'm all over the place. Fuck, I wish you'd answer your phone. Okay. So I thought she was who we were looking for but then Lydia said Rowan didn't drive Erin home after Test Kitchens. Someone in a Wrangler with *custom* hunter-green rims always picked her up. Always. Kyla, Jason . . . he might've . . ."

Kyla stops the voice memo before it can finish, her stomach sinking. So Mikky has realized in his own way too. It'd be funny, if it weren't so grim. There are no lights on upstairs in the Vaughn house. No lights downstairs, either.

Kyla sits in her hearse, staring at the door. She should've grabbed something to bring with her—a golf club, a bat, a knife. Just in case. But regret isn't productive, at least not in this moment. And after all, Kyla isn't afraid. She's angry. Kyla texts back, I'm already at the Vaughns'. Call the police and Dad. Then she reaches into her glove compartment for the Vaughns' house keys.

Kyla climbs out of the car and walks up the driveway, past Mrs. Vaughn's Mercedes. She uses the spare key for the first time since Erin died, and enters the dark. It takes a moment for her eyes to adjust, but she knows she's not alone.

"He's not here," Mrs. Vaughn says, her voice coming from the left.

Kyla squints as she shuffles farther in, turning toward the living room.

"That's okay. I can wait," Kyla says. She shifts from side to side, finally making out the shape of Mrs. Vaughn's bloodless face. "You should be here for this conversation too."

Mrs. Vaughn frowns like she finds Kyla lacking. It's a stark difference from the softness that she used to offer her.

Kyla can tell immediately that Mrs. Vaughn has been there for a while, sitting in the dark, only a few candles lighting her way. There's an empty wine bottle on the floor, the last vestiges of what could be a luxurious charcuterie board but is abysmal as a meal sits on the table.

"Do you remember?" Mrs. Vaughn asks.

"Do I remember what?"

Mrs. Vaughn lets her head loll back onto the top of the sofa. "Do you remember the day that I took you to get your first foundation? To Cook?"

Kyla creeps forward, leaning against the archway.

"Of course I do."

A girl's first bit of makeup is a formative experience. Getting it from Cook Cosmetics, even more so. She remembers entering that magical wonderland of a closet, Cook Cosmetics green bottles everywhere, each with magic liquid in it that could turn Kyla into anyone that she wanted to be. She believes that even now, uses it every day to make herself into someone who does not hurt. She wonders if the alcohol makes Mrs. Vaughn hurt less too.

"My husband didn't understand why I would take you, too. He didn't understand you and E-Erin yet. Didn't understand that you two were . . . conjoined," Mrs. Vaughn says. "But I knew. I know what it is to be obsessed. And you two were obsessed with each other."

"Obsession" is the right word. Kyla and Erin had never felt there was anything wrong with it. Now, without Erin, Kyla can see a little more clearly what it blinded her to.

"But I also took you because your mother wasn't there to do it," Mrs. Vaughn whispers.

Kyla flinches. "Oh."

"Do you like your mother, Kyla?" Mrs. Vaughn asks.

No one has ever asked Kyla that. But she has an immediate answer.

"No," she whispers back. "I don't like my mother."

"Why?" Mrs. Vaughn asks as Kyla creeps closer and sits on the couch, turning her entire body so that she can look at Mrs. Vaughn properly. She is wan. Her eyelids are dark like bruises not even Cook can cover.

Kyla smiles sadly. "For a rational reason and an irrational one too."

"Tell them both to me," Mrs. Vaughn commands, and Kyla complies because this woman is sad and she's about to make her even sadder, accusing her son of her daughter's murder.

"The rational one? She left me when I was little. She decided that she didn't want me," Kyla says. One day her mother had suddenly decided that she wasn't fit to be a mother. That she didn't *want* to be a mother. And so, her parents had gotten a divorce and she left. After that, every court-mandated visit felt forced. Every holiday, every birthday, felt wrong, even if their mother began looking happier each time Kyla visited. So eventually she'd declared that she didn't want her mother either. Didn't want to see her anymore. It hadn't made her feel as powerful as she'd wanted it to. And then: "The irrational one? Because she took my brother from me."

Mrs. Vaughn's laugh is heady and low, shaking her head. "Boys are so much easier. They never find you wanting. Not like you girls. Maybe that's why she wanted him."

It's the cruelest thing anyone has ever said out loud to Kyla. Her eyes sting as she looks away from Mrs. Vaughn's sly smile, a poison dart that reminds her ghoulishly of Erin's grin.

"Don't say that," Kyla blurts out. "No. He was sick. Mikky was *sick*."

"Mothers can never get it right, can they?" Mrs. Vaughn whispers. Then she answers herself: "Erin never thought so. Your mother was wrong. *I* was wrong. Your mother was weak. *I* was weak. 'Mothers don't change the world.'" She sounds like she's quoting someone. It's a terrible thing to say, but feels familiar. It feels like . . . Erin.

"No," Kyla says weakly. "You were always so good to me. I love you. Erin love—"

Mrs. Vaughn reaches forward, cupping Kyla's face in her spindly, trembling hands. They're like bones, skin hanging even more loosely than last time she was here, her wedding ring slipping coldly against Kyla's jawbone. She rubs her thumb over Kyla's cheek, smudging her blush.

"Yes," she hisses, all warmth gone. "You may hate her, but I envied your mother, Kyla Graves."

Kyla shakes, reaching up to grab Mrs. Vaughn's wrists. The woman's fingertips dig in harder.

"Why?"

"Because she got to have you," Mrs. Vaughn confesses cruelly. "I used to wish you were mine. We always got along so much better. Or maybe we wouldn't have, though, if we were blood. You're more like Erin than I thought. You see your mother as weak. You think she *failed*."

"I never thought *you* failed," Kyla says, the words fighting their way out of her mouth as Mrs. Vaughn squeezes tighter and tighter.

The woman jerks back like Kyla said the magic words, hands falling away, and Kyla gasps.

"No?" Mrs. Vaughn asks.

"No. Listen, I know you and Erin didn't get along—"

Mrs. Vaughn tuts. "No. No. We did not," she says. There's that sound again, the one that scrapes. "Erin resented me. I tried to give Erin everything. I tried. I really did. But it was never enough for her. It wouldn't be until there was nothing left of me."

"I know, Mrs. Vaughn, I know," Kyla whispers, voice growing smaller. She feels herself growing smaller and she can't afford that if she's going to confront Jason, so she tries to redirect. "Where's Jason?"

"I had to work so hard to love Erin. She had to work so hard to love me," Mrs. Vaughn says. "It's easier to love a son. He's generous with his love to me. But also to his sister. Always his sister. Erin wasn't generous, she always wanted *more*. Things that were mine," Mrs. Vaughn says, petty and jealous. The same kind of pettiness she taught Kyla, except it's edged with petulance now. Nothing powerful about it at all. "I didn't want her to join Cook Cosmetics. It was the only time of the day when I wasn't a mother, wasn't lacking. There, I was Corinne Vaughn, Director of Global Marketing. I was Florence's right hand. And then Erin found her way in anyway. She met Florence and she was enamored with her. Erin wanted to change the world just *like* her, and she told Florence that, and Florence was so delighted, she decided she wanted Erin to join her in doing that. Sometimes even more than me. And Erin was everywhere again. Like oxygen. Except she was sucking the life out of me."

More and more, she doesn't sound like the same woman. It's what Kyla used to think when Erin would complain about her and their fights. So maybe it's a step closer to the real her.

"Mrs. Vaughn, did you . . . did you know about *everything* Cook asked Erin to do?" Kyla asks. "Because I don't think she wanted to take Cook from you. I think she wanted to leave."

"Of course I knew," Mrs. Vaughn retorts. She's speaking faster and faster, her words slurring more. "But it's an honor to work with Cook. Do you understand that? And it's hard work. A women-led business. Women executives. And it was still so hard for me to achieve that rank. Florence loved Erin, but . . . it's not the kind of place where you break ranks. Erin didn't understand that. She was so used to things going her way. But Florence is

Cook so Florence is law. And Erin resented me for reminding her of that again and again. That this wasn't her show. She didn't know where the line was and she refused to learn it. What we were doing wasn't any different from any other brand under the sun. Erin didn't understand that if you want to change the world, you have to *fucking* commit." Kyla's never heard Mrs. Vaughn swear, but it emerges guttural and ugly. She never thought Mrs. Vaughn capable of *ugly*.

Suspicion crawls up Kyla's spine.

Kyla looks out the window at the Mercedes in the driveway. The Mercedes that wasn't here last time she was here, that hadn't been since late summer. Then she thinks of the Wrangler that's *not* there. And who else has been driving it lately.

"Mrs. Vaughn . . . where's Jason?" Kyla whispers, this time her tone is different.

As if on cue, she hears the click of the lock. Mrs. Vaughn looks up, excited and tired and smiling.

"Mom, I'm home!"

Jason doesn't sound like himself. There's something false in his voice. The hearse is impossible to miss but he's pretending that she's not here. Kyla sits up taller, shaking away her fear. She watches as Jason keeps his back to the living room, carefully kicking off his sneakers. He's still in his soccer uniform, grass stains marking the back of his shorts. Even when he's barefoot, he doesn't turn around.

Kyla slowly stands, walking past Mrs. Vaughn with her plastic smile, and breathes evenly to keep herself from running. Or screaming.

She stands within an arm's length of his back. This close, she can see he's shaking.

"Jason," she whispers.

He turns so suddenly, Kyla jumps. He's smiling too. That same plastic smile. For the first time, Kyla thinks that he looks like his sister. He looks like his mother. All-fucking-American family. A wife who drinks, an absent husband, a devoted son, and a daughter going nuclear. All playing pretend while they do it.

"We won the game. It went into overtime and everything," Jason says. He grabs her hands and pulls her close like nothing is wrong. "You would know that if you came! Where were you? Like half your squad was missing."

He doesn't let her answer; instead he presses his mouth to her hairline. "Please . . . Kyla, leave," he begs into it before he lets her go and steps around her, moving toward Mrs. Vaughn. "Are you okay, Mom? How was work?"

"Tiring, pumpkin," Mrs. Vaughn says. She almost sounds like herself. *Almost.*

But now Kyla can see the cracks.

"Did you want a snack? I can make you something," Jason asks, still like Kyla isn't there. Like he can't see her. Or doesn't want to.

"Jason, did you drive the Wrangler the night Erin died?" Kyla interrupts.

He looks over his shoulder and laughs, hollow. She knows what he sounds like when he's laughing for real and this isn't it. "Of course I did. It's my car. I'm the only one who drives it."

"That's not true," Kyla retorts. "And you know it."

Mrs. Vaughn frowns. "What are you saying?" she asks, her voice softening into something baby-like. It's grating. Kyla doesn't know how it didn't grate her before.

"Nothing, Mom. She's just going. It's fine. Hey, Kyla, I'll . . . see you at school? Or maybe we can get breakfast? You skipped out on me last time," Jason says, looking down at his hands. He twists them nervously in his jersey, then looks down at the ground next to his mother's foot, where the empty wine bottle is. "Mom . . . I told you. No more wine."

Kyla takes a step forward, looking at Jason. Jason, who won't meet her eyes. Jason, who has had soccer matches on Friday nights since preseason started in August. Friday nights like the night Erin died.

"Jason, the night Erin died . . . it was the first preseason scrimmage," she says softly.

Jason is shaking. "Yes."

"It went into overtime. Out of town."

"Kyla, please, don't do this," Jason insists, looking up at her with those beautiful green eyes. He looks like he's going to cry. Kyla has never wanted to make him cry.

"You won. You were celebrating. It should've been okay, but . . . it went into *overtime*. And you were too far away to pick her up on time like you usually would," Kyla decides as she looks at him. "And it didn't matter anyway. You didn't have your car. Because your mother's broke down a few days earlier. Right?"

Jason gasps out a ragged sob. "No, you're right. I got back in time. I killed her."

Kyla creeps closer. "I don't think you did, Jason," she whispers. Then she looks past him and smiles wider. Nastier. Plastic. Like a Vaughn. "I think *you* did."

Mrs. Vaughn's smile slides off her face.

"I think that Erin forgot about the game. I think she called the house looking for Jason when he didn't pick up his cell and got you instead. I think she demanded you come get her and when you did, you argued. She told you about the GloMo issues, but you already knew, because you and Florence tried to *pacify* her with that store-opening bait. And I bet she threatened to expose Florence and demanded that you stand with her, and you couldn't take it. Not one more demand.

"And I think you were probably *drunk* because apparently you're always drunk. You just used to hide it better. I think it got physical and that you were so sick of her 'sucking the life out of you' that you took hers. And I bet you called your son, the one who's always so *generous* with his love, and told him what happened. I think you begged him to get you from Florence's house and he did. He probably *ran*, because you are his mother and he loves you," Kyla says. Her hands tremble at her sides and she has to grab the hem of her shirt to stop her fury from manifesting into something physical, too.

Jason shakes his head, frantically reaching for Kyla. She dances out of his grip. "No, it's not true! Kyla, please don't say that! Please *don't*—" he insists, his knees knocking together as he begins to finally fall apart. For so long he has refused to because he couldn't, she realizes. For his parents. For *Kyla*. "It was an accident! Mom said it was an accident. She fell. Erin just *fell*."

For once, Kyla can't find it in herself to be angry. Not at him. Not for *this*.

Mrs. Vaughn stands up, faster than Kyla expects. Her hand reaches out and she grabs Kyla by the collar, dragging her close with an uncommon strength. Her breath stinks of rotting grapes as she whispers, "I really thought you were different. But you *want*, too. That's all you do. Answers, attention, *love*."

"She didn't fall, did she, Mrs. Vaughn?" Kyla snarls, grabbing at Mrs. Vaughn's wrist. "Did you push her? Hard enough that she fell off the deck? Did you even feel bad about it?"

"I asked so *little* of her. She was ruining everything. She kept asking questions and *pushing*. It was *my* place, my one place, and then she was going to take it from me," Mrs. Vaughn hisses, shaking her head, frazzled. "She was killing *me*. Slowly."

"And you killed her. All at once," Kyla accuses.

In the distance, she hears Jason insist again, "No, no, no, she didn't. I'll say I killed her. Kyla, please. I should have been there, so really *I* killed her. Not Mom. I mean, she didn't mean to . . ."

Mrs. Vaughn's eyes are wide. "I didn't mean to," she repeats, in her soft doll voice.

Kyla sees her clearly now. "Yes. You did." Maybe not in that moment. Maybe in that moment she told herself it was an accident. And yet. Kyla knows she *had* meant it. Because she wants too badly for Kyla to understand why.

The world slows and she feels Mrs. Vaughn's hands move from her collar to wrap around her neck. Kyla can't breathe again. Her eyes bulge as the woman's hands tighten, and Jason jerks forward, grabbing his mother by her shoulders. She can hear him through a long, watery tunnel as she claws at Mrs. Vaughn's wrists, at her jaw, trying to pull away.

Prophets Lake is choking her. The walls are closing in, and her skin is shrinking, and there is only the yawning gape of Erin left, and all the grief that comes with her—

The door slams open.

"Get off her!"

Kyla feels herself being torn away from the woman that was not her mother, a fact she was never thankful for until now. Mikky's hands are locked around Mrs. Vaughn's wrists, keeping her in place, as she thrashes—or a drunk approximation of it. Nasim is on the phone with someone, kneeling at Jason's side, one hand on his back.

In the distance, Kyla hears the police sirens.

And finally, she begins to weep.

CHAPTER THIRTY-SIX

When Kyla begins to cry, Mikky doesn't notice at first. It's so quiet underneath the sound of Hamish storming in with his officers, Jason's hiccupping sobs into Nasim's shoulders, and the screech of what he guesses are Dad's tires pulling in out front. Plus, Mrs. Vaughn is a madwoman, her flossy hair out of control as she leers up at Mikky like she intends to scratch his eyes out, and he holds her wrists even tighter. Officer Castellanos—and, God, that definitely is Lydia's sister, they look alike—rushes forward, grabbing on to Mrs. Vaughn so he can finally let go.

"Did you see that? She was attacking my sister! And Jason, he's the one—" Mikky shouts, enraged.

"Mikky," Nasim says quietly from where he's holding Jason up.

Mikky looks over and . . . Jason doesn't look like someone who killed his sister. He is a wreckage, green eyes burning red.

Then Nasim juts his chin forward, his gaze skipping over Mikky to land on Kyla, tucked behind him.

Only then does Mikky turn. There is Kyla, tears streaming down her face, her body shaking. She swipes away at the tears furiously, shaking her head, trying to conceal them from him.

"You don't have to hide from me," Mikky whispers. "You can cry now. You can."

In the background, they both hear, "Corinne Vaughn, you are under arrest for the assault of a minor. You have the right to remain silent—"

That's enough to make the dam break, and then Kyla begins to wail, falling into Mikky's side, clinging to him. It's the most horrible thing Mikky has ever heard, wounded and terrible, and it's enough to make Hamish stammer through reading the Miranda rights to Mrs. Vaughn.

It's also enough to summon Dad from his car, away from asking the officers what's going on. He comes running in and Mikky holds out one arm, letting him in to wrap his arms around them both. The minute they're anchored on either side of her, Kyla's knees buckle and Mikky nearly sinks with her, straining to hold her up.

"It's . . . it's . . . ," Mikky stammers. He wants to say *It's okay*, but it's not.

None of this is okay, and Mikky doesn't want to be a liar. Mikky looks to his dad, and for once he doesn't look lost, doesn't look away.

"It will *be* okay," Dad promises. He presses a hand onto Mikky's shoulder, squeezing hard. "I'm going to take care of everything, okay?"

And in that moment Mikky lets himself believe him. He clings to his sister, clings to Dad, as Hamish escorts Mrs. Vaughn out of her own home, down to the station to book her. Eventually, Kyla's wails soften back to weeping and she is nearly silent again when Officer Castellanos approaches.

"It was me," Jason blurts out, shaking. Mikky jolts, looking over at him wide-eyed. "I did it. I did."

Officer Castellanos inhales through her nose. "Did what, Jason?" she asks slowly.

Jason looks like he's going to vomit, shaking hard. "I killed—"

"No, he didn't," Kyla says, voice scraped raw. "He's going to say he killed Erin, but he didn't. Mrs. Vaughn did. She *told* me. And she was going to kill me, too."

Officer Castellanos jerks back. "She *what*—" Her head whips around, and Jason looks shattered, his whole life scattered on the floor around him. "Jason, is this true?" Jason opens his mouth. Shuts it again. Officer Castellanos grabs his shoulders. *"Jason Vaughn—"*

"It was an a-accident," Jason stammers, almost a question. "She didn't do it on purpose. It was an accident. I promise. She told me. She told me it was an *accident*."

Mikky's never heard him sound like that before either.

Officer Castellanos whispers, "Oh . . . oh my . . ." She shakes herself, firming up her resolve. "Tell me everything. *Right* now."

Kyla presses her lips into a grim line and does the heaviest lifting. It starts with the mortgage and spirals out from there. The Test Kitchens, the auctions, the money. Rowan. Peter. Even Lydia, whom the officer balks at with shame. She neatly weaves in what Mikky told her over the voice memo—that Rowan was never allowed to drive Erin home. That *Jason* was the one to always pick Erin up, but that night Jason had a soccer game that went into overtime and Mrs. Vaughn's car had broken down just the week before, so she'd been borrowing the Wrangler. And through it all, Jason's expression grows bleaker.

Mikky frowns when Kyla never mentions GloMo or Florence Cook at all.

"I need you to come down to the station for a firm timeline of all this," Officer Castellanos says, rubbing her hand over her eyes.

Mikky sighs, heavy, and he leans his head against Dad's shoulder, resigned to going back to the police department *again*.

"Don't you see they're in no shape to do that?" Dad snaps, firm.

"Mr. Graves, please—" Officer Castellanos starts.

"No. It's late. They'll be at the station bright and early in the morning. Come on, kids," Dad says. He holds Kyla under his arm and gently guides her toward the door.

Mikky looks over at Nasim and Jason. Jason won't look up at them, and Mikky is still too caught in the whiplash of it, the relief of it not being Jason after all, but the horror of it being his mother, to know what to say.

He hears his dad speak instead. "Jason, kiddo, come on. You need to sleep."

Jason's pale face is lit up with grief. He leans into Nasim, someone he barely knows, tilted into his warmth. Finally, he says, "I don't . . . my dad's at a conference, I don't know when he'll be back. And I . . . I don't want to be alone."

Dad's smile is tiny, but it's there. "Jason, you will never be alone. Come home with us."

In the dark everything is slightly better. Mikky's always felt that way. It's why he's always liked the funeral home. The morgue. The cemetery. And the darkness of their living room, right now. Nasim's been dropped off at home. Everyone's showered and changed. Finally, Mikky no longer feels as if a guillotine hovers over his neck.

He looks over at the couch, at the lump of blankets that is Kyla. He wants to reach out to touch her, to make sure she's okay. He sits up from his own nest of blankets on the ground and spies Jason's form, pressed up against the side of the couch, parallel to her.

When he focuses hard enough, he sees his friend's hand up on the couch, Kyla's fingers wrapped around his, even as he sleeps on.

"Are you awake?"

Mikky jumps and drags his gaze from Jason's and Kyla's hands to her eyes, huge and glossy in the dark.

"I am," Mikky confirms.

I'm awake. I'm alive. You're alive.

"It was Mrs. Vaughn," Kyla says. Mikky suspects that she needs to say it out loud, to make sure that it's true.

"It was," Mikky whispers. "I'm sorry that it was. I know you were close to her."

Mikky has so many questions, but it didn't feel right to ask them before. Not with Jason looking like an empty shell, especially when they couldn't get his dad on the phone right away. For a moment Mikky had feared the worst—another parent leaving Jason. Only for them to learn that Jason's dad's hotel was in a cell phone dead zone when they finally got through to the front desk's landline.

"He wanted so badly to protect her," Kyla confesses. She's looking down at Jason with so much fondness that Mikky has to look up at the ceiling. It's too personal. When he looks back at her, Kyla has shuttered the intimacy in her gaze again. "But the minute he said it, I knew he was lying."

"How?" Mikky doesn't think he would question it, if someone confessed to him that they killed their own sister.

"Because of what I said in the police station. No one knew

her like I did, except him. And no one loved her as much as I did. Except *him*," Kyla says. She turns onto her side, rubbing her thumb over Jason's loose knuckles. "And that should have made me realize there was something wrong. That Mrs. Vaughn didn't love her like that."

"And . . . what about the money? From the night Erin died?" he asks.

Kyla frowns. "When you were in the shower, Jason told me that he has it. He hid it in his room. And when I asked how he got it, he told me that after he calmed his mother down and put her in the car, he went down to the beach to look at Erin. And he couldn't touch her because they'd find his DNA on her, but he wanted to. He told her goodbye, and then he saw the envelope . . . it fell out of her pocket on the way down. He said my name was on the front, and he thought that it was . . . a secret of ours. He couldn't tell me but he wanted to protect that secret, even with her gone, because he thought it was the least he could do. Jason *always* wanted to protect Erin."

She pauses, and when she speaks again her voice is different. "I want her to pay. Mrs. Vaughn. For what she did to Erin. And what she did to *him*."

Mikky understands her thirst for revenge. He doesn't feel it as strongly as Kyla does, but he gets it. "You didn't say anything about GloMo."

"The word of a high school junior, her brother, and his boyfriend against one of the wealthiest women in the state, let alone the country? No one's gonna believe us based off our findings from a school laboratory," Kyla says bitterly. "It's not enough. But it'll come to light."

Mikky knows she's right, at least about no one believing them. He's less sure about GloMo coming to light. Now that Florence Cook wasn't involved with the murder. And then he pauses. "You think . . . you think Mrs. Vaughn knew about the toxins in the makeup?"

"It's why she did it. Erin was asking questions and pushing her to stop it. She's the director of global marketing. I bet she had to know, in case she needed to do damage control. What if she uses that information to get Florence to buy her way out?" Kyla asks. "Florence has a lot of money."

And money opens doors in America, even cell doors. Money saves you when nothing else will. And Erin had died for it. Erin had been a lot of things—lively but cruel, loyal but selfish—yet she had tried to do the right thing and she didn't deserve to die because of that. No one did.

"If she tries to help Mrs. Vaughn, then we'll take her on. We said we were going to expose Cook anyway. For Erin. Florence may not have had Erin killed herself, but she's not blameless here. You up for it?"

Kyla huffs out a small laugh. "Bring it on."

After seventy-two hours of arguments and groundings and the most memorable phone call to their mother of all time, in which Dad forced both Kyla and Mikky to explain what they'd been up to, Dad finally lets them go back to school. Still wincing from their mother's unwieldy fury, and her threats of coming back to Prophets Lake to give their father a piece of her mind—God forbid—Mikky feels ready.

When they go to leave, Dad presses a kiss to both their foreheads and says, "Have a good day at school. Straight home after dance team practice. It's Kyla's turn to drive today."

He holds out his hand for Mikky's car keys and Mikky sighs, dropping them into Dad's outstretched palm. Dad nods, his eyes bright with something that might be pride amidst the worry.

"It'll be a long practice. I've been canceling a lot lately, and regionals will be here before we know it," Kyla says.

"Heard. Keep your location on," Dad says.

Another new thing from their father—he is more than a little active on Find My now.

Kyla sighs. "All right, Dad." Then she says, "One more thing."

"Yeah?" Dad asks.

"I still have money from the Test Kitchen. This last one and the one I did just before," Kyla says. Mikky looks up sharply, looking between Kyla and Dad. "I thought maybe you could use it for the mortgage."

While the cops had taken possession of Kyla's ledger as evidence, she never *actually* logged any of her payments from those last two nights.

"Keep your Cook Cosmetics money, Kyla," Dad says, leaning back against the doorway. He purses his lips.

Kyla's teeth click shut, her eyes widening.

"Dad, it wasn't—"

"You have been . . . so brave. So strong, for a long time, Kyla. But this has been a wake-up call for me—I'm the adult. I'll figure it out. That's *my* job. Not yours. That goes for both of you, you hear me?" Dad asks. He looks like he means it. He's not asking for permission or advice. "Now, get to school."

Kyla nods, head bobbing up and down.

"Have a good day at work," she says, bounding out of the house, her keys bouncing on her carabiner. As usual, she barely gives Mikky time to climb into the passenger seat before she pulls out of the driveway. "God, I'm so glad to see something that's not my room or the police station."

"Definitely," he says, still settling in as he shoves his book bag into the footwell and tugs his seat belt into place.

"Jason will be in for the second half of the day."

"You spoke to him?" Mikky asks.

Kyla nods. "Yeah, I wanted . . . to go, but Dad said I had to go to school, where responsible adults are, so I called. He's already at the arraignment with *his* dad to meet with his mom's lawyer. Jason didn't want to go at all, but I told him that his dad needed him, yeah? We kinda agreed that he'd sit at the back since there's already a shit ton of media there. Maybe that means that *we'll* be okay," she says.

"That would be a relief," Mikky says. Since it all happened, he's started dreaming about that nightmarish assembly, the cameras rolling from the corner, zoomed into Kyla's face. In his dreams, the lenses are pressed right up against all their faces and they fall in, devoured by the beast.

"And if they are too much, I'll tell them to go choke on their own vomit and die," she says.

"You're funny."

"I like to think so." They drive in a comfortable silence for a beat until Kyla speaks again. "I think . . . I think Jason and I are going to visit Erin tomorrow. The two of us," she says, her voice hushed like she's telling a secret. "Do you think Dad would be okay with that? I don't really know how the grounding thing works. He's never done it before."

Mikky wants to tell her that grounding means she's not really allowed anywhere. And yet.

"I don't think he'd mind," Mikky says honestly. "*If* you tell him."

"Oh good."

"I *do* think he would mind if you got a speeding ticket, though. You really need to slow down, Kyla," he says.

Kyla rolls her eyes as she takes a turn too fast into the parking lot. "Yeah, all right," she says, and pulls into her parking spot. She doesn't get out right away, though. She stays gripping the steering wheel tightly, watching people walk past, casting unsubtle looks at her.

The girl across from them even gawks from inside her shiny Lexus.

"We can do this," Mikky says.

Kyla looks up from the steering wheel, right at him, and Mikky sees her hands relax. "Of course we can," she says, and then she opens her door. Her entire demeanor changes as she exits the car, becoming casually unaffected. But she pauses as she goes to grab her bag, looking up at someone. "Uh, do you need something?"

"Certainly not from you, Graves," a familiar and welcoming voice says. Well, familiar and welcoming to Mikky.

Mikky scrambles from his seat, nearly falling over in his not-yet-broken-in Docs. Nasim stands awkwardly at his car door, tugging on his sweatshirt sleeve.

"Good morning," Mikky says, grinning.

Nasim squares his shoulders suddenly, and then he stalks forward, causing Mikky to nearly fall back into the car.

"Hey, you," he says, standing on his toes, pressing a kiss to Mikky's mouth.

Mikky barely has time to return the kiss before Nasim falls back on his heels, grinning up at him with that smug expression that looks so annoyingly good on him.

"Oh, we . . . we do that now?" Mikky asks.

Nasim nods sagely. "Yeah, we do. We also do dates now. Can I take you out on one soon?"

Mikky tries to fight the grin that spreads across his face, but not even he's that strong. "Yeah, of course you can."

"You're going to give me cavities," Kyla deadpans.

"Then all your teeth will fall out and we'll point and laugh," Nasim says cheerfully as he loops his arm through Mikky's.

Kyla gives him the middle finger. But then her eyes dart around, lively and alert. "Look alive, Mik." She points and Mikky sees them.

The wolves—the media—smell the blood. They linger by the doorways, some already speaking into the camera, spinning the tale of Erin Vaughn and her wicked mother, flattening all the nuance into something entertaining. A pretty sound bite that doesn't go even a tenth into the poisonous rot at the center of it all. None of them knows how close Jason was to taking the blame. None of them knows how Mrs. Vaughn would have been okay with that. Most of all, none of them knows about Cook. Not yet. But Mikky and Kyla will make sure they do. One day.

Some spot Kyla and Mikky, identifying them by Kyla's hearse. Mikky pretends not to see the huge lenses pointed at them.

"Okay," he says. He feels the pressure of Nasim's arm against his, grounding him.

"Okay," Kyla agrees. She squares her shoulders, throwing her hair back over one, readying herself to step out into the middle of the parking lot, right in the open, and not balk under the glare of every eye turning to her. "You ready?"

Mikky considers it for a long moment. He looks at Prophets Lake High School, where everything has changed and nothing has at all. There are secrets everywhere in this town of his, he knows that for sure now.

He's certain there are more he doesn't know yet. But there are none left between Kyla and him. And he's got more than one person to stick around in Prophets Lake for now. It feels good to admit that to himself. Good to feel like this could be home again. Kyla rolls her eyes at what's probably the sappiest expression that his face could ever make.

"*God*, Mikky," she sighs, fighting her own smile.

"Yeah, I'm ready."

ACKNOWLEDGMENTS

I will make an attempt to keep this brief. Thank you to Quressa Robinson for getting the ball rolling on this project. I should also like to thank my agents, Stuti Telidevara and Peter Knapp, for their support.

To my editor, Alexa Pastor, thank you for sticking with me when all I could manage to say when pitching this project was, "Teens in Sephora, but Twin Peaks?" Your feedback was crucial to getting this story right. Thank you for allowing me to write the worst versions of a character and encouraging me to be the best version of an author that I can be. I am forever grateful to you.

To Laura Eckes and Cienna Smith for creating the incredible interior and art that bring my book to life. I feel as if my ideas have evolved, and you walk hand in hand with me, visually nailing it every time. To my team at large at S&S BFYR, to Alma Gomez Martinez, Justin Chanda, Antonella Colon, amongst others, my gratitude remains immense. From the bottom of my heart, I thank you.

To my family, thank you and I love you.

To my beloved friends, thank you for encouraging me to touch grass. You know who you are. To Susie and Connor, thank you for answering my incessant questions about the beauty industry and punk music (the playlist helped). To Camryn Garrett and Christina Li, thank you for listening to me rant about this book over and over again, even when it was simply too late to be texting you both. Thank you for texting me back. To my cult of clowns, I cannot begin to shape my love into words. To Sarah, Alexandra,

ACKNOWLEDGMENTS

and Selina, I have no words. You are so dear to me that you're nearly a part of me.

To Mom and Dad, thank you for your support. The book is very dark, again. Sorry about that. I fear that won't change. To Alyssa, I think you'd like this one.

To my grandfather, I grieve for you every day, so much so that I had to turn it into words.

To David Lynch, I finished my final draft of this book on the day that you passed, and I write it in honor of all that I learned from and enjoyed of your art.

I aimed for brevity. I do not think I found it. Thank you.

ABOUT THE AUTHOR

Joelle Wellington grew up in Brooklyn, New York, where her childhood was spent wandering the main branch of the Brooklyn Public Library. Her love of the written word led her to a BA in creative writing and international studies. When she isn't writing, she's reading, and when she's not doing that, she's attempting to bake bread with varying degrees of success or strengthening her encyclopedia-like pop culture knowledge. She's the author of *Their Vicious Games*, *The Blonde Dies First*, and *Girls Who Play Dead*.